CROWDS
OF ONE

Critical praise for
Djelloul Marbrook's fiction

Guest Boy (2018, Leaky Boot)

What Marbrook does so well in *Guest Boy* is the contradictory elegance he showed in *Saraceno*. He finds the tender and poetic heart of very tough men. In *Saraceno*, it was low-level mobsters; in *Guest Boy*, it's men of the sea. They're a horny-handed bunch, and Marbrook's familiarity with ships and the characters of mean-street ports is deep and exciting. But Marbrook knows that these guys have a lot more going on within, and are simultaneously deeply tender philosophers. It's a mesmerizing book... You'll find yourself thinking about it long after you've finished reading.

—Dan Baum, author of *Gun Guys* (2013), *Nine Lives* (2009), and others

Guest Boy is a complex work: deep, passionate, exciting and beautifully written with flashbacks and imagery merging real and surreal. By opening up routes to the culture and history of the Arab world, *Guest Boy* helps us understand that world and our own.

—Sanford Fraser, author of *Tourist* and *Among Strangers I've Known All My Life*

... it is in books like this that I seek answers and guidance as I travel my own path to enlightenment and contentment. This book opened a struggle in me...

—Isla McKetta, editor, *A Geography of Reading*

Artemisia's Wolf (title story, *A Warding Circle*, 2017, Leaky Boot)

... Djelloul Marbrook's impressive novella ... successfully blends humor and satire (and perhaps even a touch of magic realism) into its short length ... an engrossing story, but what might strike the reader most throughout the book is its infusion of breathtaking poetry ... a stunning rebuke to notoriously misogynist subcultures like the New York art scene, showing us just how hard it is for a young woman to be judged on her creative talent alone.

—Tommy Zurhellen, *Hudson River Valley Review*

... lets his powerful imagination run wild, leading the fiction into unexpected corners where weird performers hold court and produce endings that both astonish and are frequently magical.

—James Polk, *The Country and Abroad*, former contributing editor of *Art/World*.

Saraceno

Djelloul Marbrook writes dialogue that not only entertains with an intoxicating clickety-clack, but also packs a truth about low-life mob culture "The Sopranos" only hints at. You can practically smell the anisette and filling-station coffee.

—Dan Baum, author of *Gun Guys* (2013), *Nine Lives: Mystery, Magic, Death and Life in New Orleans* (2009), and others

...a good ear for crackling dialogue ... I love Marbrook's crude, raw music of the streets. The notes are authentic and on target ...

—Sam Coale, *The Providence (RI) Journal*

... an entirely new variety of gangster tale ... a Mafia story sculpted with the most refined of sensibilities from the clay of high art and philosophy . .. the kind of writer I take real pleasure in discovering ... a mature artist whose rich body of work is finally coming to light.

—Brent Robison, editor, *Prima Materia*

Alice Miller's Room
(title story, *Making Room*, 2017, Leaky Boot)

This enchanting novella is a delicately wrought homage to Jung's famous principle of meaningful coincidence...

—*Breakfast All Day*, UK

... the story draws us into that mysterious and terrifying realm where the heart will have its say and all who enter leave transformed...

—Dr. Patricia L. Divine, Head Start program lifetime service award winner

Mean Bastards Making Nice (2014, Leaky Boot)

I love it. I admire it. It is you at your best.

—Novelist Gail Godwin on "The Pain of Wearing Our Faces"

ඏ

Critical praise for
Djelloul Marbrook's poetry

Far from Algiers (2008, Kent State University Press)

... as succinct as most stanzas by Dickinson... an unusually mature, confidently composed first poetry collection.

—Susanna Roxman, *Prairie Schooner*
(author of *Crossing the North Sea*)

... brings together the energy of a young poet with the wisdom of long experience.

—Edward Hirsch, Guggenheim Foundation

... honors a lifetime of hidden achievement.

—Toi Derricotte, Wick Award judge

... wise and flinty poems outfox the Furies of exile, prejudice, and longing... a remarkable and distinctive debut.

—Cyrus Cassells, National Poetry Series winner

Brash Ice (2014, Leaky Boot Press, UK)

. . . resonates with wisdom and a keen eye for the beautiful things of this world . . .a poetry that would make brash ice melt again.

—George Drew, author of *The View From Jackass Hill*

. . . a precision that occasionally recalls Yeats . . .

—James Polk, *The Country and Abroad*

. . . aesthetically pleasing, thematically intriguing . . .

—Michael Young, *The Poetry*

Brushstrokes and glances (2010, Deerbrook Editions)

Whether it is commentary on state power, corporate greed, or the intensely personal death of a loved one, Djelloul Marbrook is clear sighted, eloquent, and precise. As the title of the collection suggests, he uses the lightest touch, a collection of fragments, brushstrokes and glances, to fashion poems that resonate with truth and honesty.

—Phil Constable, *New York Journal of Books*

. . . looks at art the way a drinker drinks—deeply, passionately, and desperately, as if his life depended on it . . . makes you want to run out to your favorite museum and look again, as you have never looked before, until the lights go out.

—Barbara Louise Ungar, author of *Thrift; Charlotte Bronte, You Ruined My Life; The Origin of the Milky Way*

. . . one of those colossal poets able to bridge worlds—poetry and art, heart and mind—with rare wit, grace, and sincerity; a soft-spoken artist with the courage to face the "fatal beckoning" of his muse . . . crisp intellect, seamlessly interwoven with loss and longing. . . . poetry at its best: at once both gritty and refined, private and political, tender and tough as iron . . . well worth reading."

—Michael Meyerhofer, author of *What to do if you're buried alive, Damnatio Memoriae, Blue Collar Eulogies*

. . .delicately wrought. . . highly recommended reading. . .because, ultimately, this witness so clearly loves his subject.

—Eileen Tabios, Editor, *Galatea Resurrects*

Riding Thermals to Winter Grounds (2017, Leaky Boot)

. . . some very powerful lines, such as: "And then, near the end of my life, I become the man I wanted to be without the fuss and bother of giving a damn."

—Sidney Grayling, Editor, Onager Editions

CROWDS OF ONE

Book 2 of the
Light Piercing Water Trilogy

Djelloul Marbrook

LEAKY BOOT PRESS

Crowds of One: Book 2 of the Light Piercing Water Trilogy
by Djelloul Marbrook

Hardcover: 978-1-909849-63-1
Softcover: ISBN: 978-1-909849-57-0

Acknowledgments

"Ootwaert's Hoe," an excerpt from *Crowds of One*, appeared in *A Warding Circle: New York Stories* (Leaky Boot Press, 2017), and in *Prima Materia Vol. 4, Speeding Through the Night*, 2005. A somewhat different version titled "Artists Hill", won the 2008 *Literal Latté* fiction prize and appeared in *Literal Latté*, Fall 2008.

A full CIP record for this book is available from the British Library in the UK and from the Library of Congress in the USA.

Every visible object that is not a direct light
source is a kind of mirror.

Ibn al-Haytham
966-1040 A.D.

Frightened and cruel like a guilty child,
She shouted all the roses from her garden,
And threw stones at the winds: without a word
The unicorn slipped off into the forest
Like an offended doll, and one by one
The sparrows flew back to her mother's home.

Kairos and Logos
W.H. Auden
1941

Author's Acknowledgments

Endless thanks are owed to my wife, Marilyn, who has in so many ways made all my work possible; to James Goddard, my publisher, whose steadfast faith in my work brought it to light and buoyed me in rough waters; to Sebastien Doubinsky, who published my work and introduced me to James Goddard; to Brent Robison, whose wizardly videos and deft hand with e-books still astonish me; to Kevin Swanwick, whose radiance as a reader and advisor unfailingly enlightens me, and to Emily Brooks, whose artistic taste, good cheer and resourcefulness seem fathomless.

For David C. Wayland
1940 - 2012

Characters

(in order of appearance)

Amir (Bo) Cavalieri—American merchant seaman, son of Ulrike Theiss.

David Llewellyn—the therapist Bo calls in desperation at the suggestion of the St. Thomas priest Will Hallam, who spends the day with Bo after finding him weeping in the back of the church.

Ulrike Theiss—Manhattan painter; Bo Cavalieri's mother.

Alessandro (Sandro) Cavalieri—Bo's Sicilian stepfather.

Uthman al-Biruni—Pearl diver, Marxist rebel, Bo's friend and diving partner in Oman.

Amos Perchuk—the young psychiatrist assigned to Bo at Bellevue.

Rose MacQuarrie—Wealthy Scot who nurses Ulrike back to health in Algeria and is repaid by Ulrike's liaison with Rose's lover, Ben Aissa.

Weybrandt (Gundy) Gundersen—Merchant seaman, Bo's closest friend and shipmate.

Ute-Britt Broghammer—Barmaid in Hamburg, the subject of many of Bo's drawings.

Lakhdar Ali Wahab—Moroccan busboy; guest worker in Hamburg bar, Ute-Britt's lover.

Peter Tomlinson—Wealthy British writer of "famous route" books, owner of the North Sea trawler *Morgaine*.

Moira Sayre—Peter's companion; marine photographer and diver.

Said bin Taimur—Sultan of Oman, owner of two priceless manuscripts, one on sailing and one on medieval alchemy.

Dacia Wynne Wadeleigh—Bo's childhood friend, mother of mathematician Margaret Wadeleigh.

Margaret Wadeleigh—Oxford mathematician, Dacia's daughter.

Jurgen Theiss—Ulrike's younger brother; Bo's despised uncle.

Adeline (Addie) Compton—English conservator of ancient musical instruments, aikido adept, Margaret's childhood friend and love.

Hettie Warshaw—Former assistant to Dr. Josef Mengele; lover of both Ulrike and Sandro.

Jolene Gundersen—Gundy's Icelandic wife.

Hart Clement—Ulrike's last husband, Bo's second stepfather.

Lottie Donovan—Irish teacher at Cairnhall, Bo's boarding school in West Islip, Long Island, who taught eight-year-old Bo how to swim and stand up for himself.

1

There were no cell phones. No thumb yak. No laptops. It wasn't long ago, but it was another time. You dropped a coin and listened to it clunk. It was like clearing your throat, getting out of your head. Phoning wasn't the exhibitionistic, put-it-on-my tab show it is today.

By the time he hears David Llewellyn pick up he's ready with a spiel: "Will Hallam gave me your name. I'm trying to stay sober. I'm sick. I'm scared. I need help. But if you're going to tell me it's all in my head, don't bother."

"Sounds like somebody's been messing with your head. We'll see who it is and cancel his hunting license. Come on over, I'll wait. What's your name?"

"That's a problem."

"I don't know about that. It's kinda refreshing."

The Rev. David C. Llewellyn lives and works in the first floor of a brownstone on East Sixty-Ninth Street. Bo taps the brass doorbell button and hears a nasty vibration inside. A Giacometti man appears in the foyer. He's haphazardly pulled together. His blond hair flops over his forehead. He's taller than Bo, six-five at least.

"I hope you haven't remembered who you are. We'll get to it later. I find a lot of people don't fit their names." He shakes Bo's hand and uses it to guide him back to his office, which overlooks a dumpy garden.

Llewellyn teeters his bony ass on the front end of his desk, grips the desk with both hands and studies Bo as he stands in the middle of the room on the creaky bleached floor and watches Llewellyn as he would a vessel that isn't signaling her intentions.

"I suspect you've been flying too low." The way Llewellyn interrupts their standoff doesn't do much for Bo. A man who is uncomfortable with silence may be full of guile.

"Look," Bo says wearily, "I don't mean to be rude or anything, but what are you, some kind of nut?"

"You're not rude, you're astute. I'm some kind of nut."

Bo looks at him as if he's a subject he's just decided not to draw. "Okay. I've just spent thirty days with nuts, can one more hurt?"

"Possibly."

"I've been flying too low?"

"Yeah, but before I give my certifiably wacko theory about that I want to point something out. You said you don't want to be rude or anything. Did you mean it?"

"Sure."

"You don't want to be anything?"

"I don't do crosswords or Scrabble. I try to say what I mean."

"That's my point. That's good. So you don't mean to be anything? I like that. I like it a lot. You should take a little vacation from yourself. It's a great idea. You're pretty smart. Coffee?"

Bo nods.

"I don't cure people of their illusions, I don't cure people, I don't fix heads. You could fix the wrong thing. How would I know what's illusion and what's not? You could be the very living god—I'm always in fear of that—or a vampire. I don't know. And if you turn out to be the Christ himself I certainly hope you'll recommend me if I manage to be of some help."

"To my father?"

"Exactly."

Llewellyn takes the cup back from Bo's shaking hands. His small rimless eyeglasses brim with blue. Bo decides to like him.

"First thing is, I don't take clients I don't like. It's ugly business. They're going to mess you up. You're going to mess them up. Second thing is, I don't take clients who push my crazy buttons. Third thing is, I don't care if you've been hauling stumps for a living, this is going to be the hardest damned job you ever did, and I don't want you to whine. You're not a whiner, I can tell."

"How much do you cost?"

"I like your question."

"Does that mean you're gonna sock it to me?"

"I don't know. Have you got a job? Where do you live? How much do you make? How much time can you spend?"

"I'm a merchant seaman."

He notices a smile quivering at the corner of Llewellyn's thin lips. He tries to get pissed as he answers Llewellyn; instead he recovers a bit of memory. "I've got some money in the bank. If I run out I'll ship out."

"Forty-five dollars an hour, three times a week. If you start running out, we'll talk, okay?"

"I spend forty a week on booze."

"Don't. I can't help drunks. Drunks don't feel pain. No pain, no gain. It's up to you."

"What about your crazy buttons?"

Llewellyn usually tells prospective clients what his crazy buttons are—abandoners who remind him of his father, locked-down misers like his mother—but he likes Bo enough that he says instead, "If you push 'em I'll let you know. Somehow I don't think it's your shtick. I like you. Maybe you'll help me be a little less crazy."

"Do I get a discount?"

"That's the stuff. You stay that confrontative, we'll get there."

Bo squints as if scanning a ship in front of the sun.

Llewellyn asks, "Should I keep my language simpler?"

"That always helps, but I'm not illiterate."

"You're an officer?"

"Sometimes."

"I see I'm gonna learn something about the merchant marine. You play basketball? You got the body. You're an ectomorph, like me."

"No. Played some baseball in high school, college."

"College?"

Bo grins. He gets up, walks to the window and studies the sooty garden. "Seems my name is Bo Cavalieri. College, yeah,

I went to Columbia for three years, dropped out, worked on a United Fruit ship, then joined the Navy. Before that I went to Dwight Prep on Park Avenue. I read a lot. Merchant seamen, some of them, are like educated southerners, bilingual. You can talk fancy to me, I'll understand."

Knows how to mime a lowlife, Llewellyn muses, and says, "A-l-l right, thanks for the clue. You can talk bilingually to me too. I grew up in the coal fields of West Virginia, went to UVA on a basketball scholarship, drank a whole lot down there in Charlottesville and graduated confused about everything."

"Could you tone it down a bit? I feel like I'm being handled."

"What does that feel like?"

"Taking a shower with a new crewman hanging around," Bo says.

Llewellyn has been listening to Bo, but he's done a poor job looking. You're going to have to earn your money here, David. Forget your stock in trade. This guy acts like he's already done a thousand hours of therapy. But if he has, he's not likely to forget his name and address. Question is, do I give a shit? I told him I like him. Second thoughts? Yes, I do give a shit. It's clear to me this guy's brave. A tribe that really has to think about its members would give this guy a wide berth. I'd like to know why. Why would a man on the edge of despair act fully in charge of himself? "Sometimes I act macho," Llewellyn hears himself say, "when I'm feeling vulnerable. I wish you'd forgive me."

Bo Cavalieri, trying to get used to his own name, stares into the therapist's eyes and says slowly, "I understand. You don't need to be afraid of me."

The two men sit as silence snows on their words. The odds are about fifty-fifty to start that some good can come of this—not bad odds in therapy.

"I'll explain this memory business to you before you go. Then we'll make an appointment for tomorrow and start fresh. What happens is your brain gets bummed out and starts shoving furniture around kind of like Irene Dunne in *I Remember Mama*. She starts scrubbing the floor whenever something bothers her. The brain chucks out furniture, just throws it out the window.

Only for some reason it doesn't say this chair is okay, I'll keep it, this ironing board sucks, I'll chuck it. No, it just dumps things indiscriminately, like things falling off a truck: your name, how to tie your shoes, or how to drive a car. It's random. Your brain is not your pal any more."

"Is it anybody's?"

"No. Not really."

"That's pretty scary. I'm steaming with a totally unreliable navigation system."

"Worse than that. A bum navigational system, I assume, wouldn't deliberately play tricks, but your brain would."

"Now I'm scared."

"Look," he says, "you don't have to be scared if you can learn how to take your despair and fly."

Bo gives him the sort of look a girl gives a guy when his line doesn't hook her.

"On the wings of despair. That's what you do, you soar high over everything on the wings of despair. You don't put down on this and that, you don't peck at particularities or possibilities or eventualities, you don't give a damn about all that, you just soar high on the wings of despair."

"What about the hedges and the huckleberries? Don't I stop to eat them? Don't I stoop to catch a mouse? And where the hell am I going?"

"South. That's for sure. But as for everything else, don't worry. See, you're not this bird, you're riding him. You just leave it up to him. You're about to discover the pleasure, the many and manifold comforts of despair. You'll like it. It's freedom like you've never known. Just fly on the wings of despair, Bo Cavalieri."

Llewellyn stupefies himself. Where he got this poetic palaver he has no idea. It's unlike him. He loves it. He glances at Bo— he's been facing the bleak garden when he says all this—and he sees that Bo likes it too. Because despair is at the heart of the man's sickness. Bo gets up and goes to the hallway that leads to the front door. He turns, smiles, and undulates his arms and shoulders like a cormorant.

On the street he hails a cab and gives the cabbie his address. He sits back picturing the address. Okay, he's recovered some memory, but how much and for how long?

★

To keep out of bars and liquor stores Bo takes to backpacking around Manhattan, sketching whatever catches his fancy. He bolsters this regimen by buying a wallet-sized architectural handbook to identify periods, styles and features. After a few weeks he buys running shoes and starts jogging from site to site. He begins making breakfast and dinner for himself instead of eating among drinkers. He stops at pushcarts for lunch. He can't plan meals, so he buys what he needs each evening in Little Italy, deriving unexpected pleasure from the ritual. At night he labors through *Waite's Alchemy* until he falls asleep. It's just a funky old book he picked off a table on Hudson Street for fifty cents. As it turns out, it opens the door to the work ahead of him, this and a hunch Llewellyn plays in their third month together.

★

"You're a man who carries the vastness of the universe in his head," Llewellyn says one day apropos of nothing. "I should think this gives you a sense of proportion."

"The universe inside us is far more vast," Bo says. He says it so spontaneously that Llewellyn is startled. "I stole that from Ibn Arabi," Bo says.

"I doubt it," is the reply. What clicks then is what Will Hallam called Llewellyn's druidic inclination. He's a mystic in a profession given to debunking. Like Thomas Cranmer he believes in the real presence at Mass; unlike Cranmer he's capable of loving the disbeliever. He guesses that a man who takes fixes on stars understands the mystery of the correct placement of things, as the Druids did.

Had Bo given him an answer? He hadn't agreed that he had a sense of proportion. Or had he? Could this navigator be seduced into charting vastnesses within?

"I'd like a coffa cuppy, Dave."

"It'll probably taste better than my usual cup of coffee."

They grin at each other. Bo has become a gifted spoonerist but remains only occasionally aware of it. He speaks of the reader-meters handing out parking tickets like the kisses of Typhoid Mary. And once, when Dave casually asks him his ethnic background, he says, "Half Arab, half malapropist." He has trouble undoing his granny-knotted words, referring to plaid plates instead of sad traits, for example. When Dave points this out, calling it a kind of aphasia, Bo blows up. "What're you, trying to drive me nuts?"

"Somebody is," Dave says evenly, "and it's a shorter drive than you think. It always is."

"I knot words up sometimes, okay? I didn't used to. I don't know why."

"Why is just pocket pool while you wait for the bartender to get back to you and play Nazi doctor."

"Sounds good, Dave, but where's it going?"

"You're the navigator. I'd like you to lay out a course for me, Bo."

"Only I pay you for the privilege?"

"Right. That's the way it always is. We always pay somebody to drive us nuts. With misplaced love and fealty. We're convinced that without these Nazi doctors life isn't worth living. Trust me, if the doctors of Dachau hadn't existed we would have had to invent them. The people who fondle our nut buttons are extortionists. We pay them for the privilege of being abused."

Their session starts at two-fifty-five. At three-fifteen Bo gets up, stares bleakly at Dave Llewellyn and walks out.

Llewellyn takes the rest of the session for a little walk in his soot garden. He made a mistake saying trust me. Don't trust anybody who says that. He muses that Bo has decamped like an Arab, like a seaman, as he probably has many times from many places. Perhaps he won't come back. But therapy needs crisis. Crisis is the linchpin of progress. It's Wednesday. He'll wait till Friday to see.

★

21

When he returns Friday Bo brings the yellowed scrap of pulp paper Ulrike left him on his eighteenth birthday and hands it to Llewellyn:

Get out by 8:15 a.m.—and have your head examined.

"Why eight-fifteen?" Llewellyn asks.

Bo laughs. "Why Ulrike Theiss?"

"And she is?"

"My mother."

"You look like you just brushed your teeth with Bon Ami. Ulrike, huh? A Valkyrie. How old were you?"

"Eighteen years, three weeks. It was summer."

"She wasted no time. What did you do?"

"I was staying out late, getting drunk, which is what pissed her off, so I left everything except one suitcase full, rented a room in the Milner on Broadway, stayed there a few nights, then found a room on 70th just off West End Avenue."

"You had money?"

"Yeah, I was working in the Ziegfeld Theater watering down orangeade and checking coats. On weekends I was a bagman for a sack of shit named Jack Kaplow. He ran a slew of hatcheck concessions in clubs and I collected his take from the girls who were hooking on the side. That's where the real money was."

"And you were still going to Columbia?"

"Yeah, when I wasn't too hung over."

"Who paid?"

"Sandro the first year. After that me."

"And Sandro is . . . ?"

"Alessandro Cavalieri, my stepfather."

"So why didn't you talk to him?"

"Well, maybe I figured Ulrike had a righteous beef."

"Maybe? I don't think so."

"Sandro was sick. He'd had a couple of heart attacks. I figured he needed Ulrike more than he needed an eighteen-year-old fuck-up. I think I was wrong."

"I think you were very cooperative. Are you always so cooperative?"

"I'm a hard-ass."

"Except where Valkyries are concerned."

"Is anybody a hard-ass where Valkyries are concerned?"

"Maybe not. How'd you latch up with the sleaze?"

"An ex-con I used to drink with, Billy Salviati. I didn't know it at first, but he was Jack's insurance man."

"An ex-con sold him insurance?"

"Yeah, the trick was to convince him he needed it. Billy was convincing."

"What was wrong with college?"

"I was an ace at Dwight. Did my homework, walked the dog, jerked off and slept. Columbia scared me. I was a day student and I didn't have the sense to move in where maybe I could have made some friends. Besides, it would have interfered with my drinking. I liked a lot of things about college, the library, the faces. There was this handsome humanities assistant, a very nice man, who freaked out all the Catholic kids by suggesting that maybe Bernini's *Saint Catherine* was having herself an orgasm. But I felt like Charlie Chaplin caught in the machinery. I was always ducking a flywheel. It seemed to me—I wonder if I was wrong—you had to do an awful lot of sucking up to guys with obscene egos. I wasn't above that, but I didn't know how. I'd been reading Baudelaire and Rimbaud in French and the whole truth-in-degradation idea hooked me. I figured I was on the right track. I had only one real friend at Columbia. He'd been ahead of me at Dwight, but I had to spend a lot of time figuring out how not to hurt him—he was gay and after a while he started to be kind of voyeuristic about the life on the dark side that I seemed to be leading, and that hurt me. I got good marks when I didn't take an incomplete, but early in my junior year I decided to confide in the college dean. I guess he didn't like me because he listened cordially and then suggested I join the Foreign Legion to find myself. I took it for what it was, callousness, but I was heartbroken because it cost me so much to go to him. I needed help, but I didn't know how to ask."

"You asked. And this pissant didn't have the decency to respond like a fellow human being."

Llewellyn's outburst stuns Bo. He lets the clock tick noisily as he stares at Llewellyn. Then he swallows hard, blinks his eyes, nods and continues.

"I was sort of . . . I guess I had painted myself into a corner. Billy would've said, Why dincha kick his ass? My friend, Geraint O'Faolain, he would've said, But perhaps you didn't explain yourself to the dean . . . What're you shaking your head for?"

"I'm thinking what the odds were of your finding the one kind of caring soul we all need once in a while. Did this encounter with the dean make you cry?"

"I stopped crying when I was nine."

"You remember the year?"

"Yeah, because it felt like a couple of years before my first wet dream."

"What happens now? You walk out of the dean's office trying to be brave . . ."

"I dunno. Must've jerked off or something."

"This is not casual. You don't get points for sloughing off pain, you get more pain. I want a serious answer, otherwise I'm throwing you out. I'm serious. I care about you. I want you to care."

"Well, about jerking off, I don't remember getting the itch from the time Ulrike threw me out to the time I got married four years later."

Llewellyn doesn't know whether to shit or go blind. Bo has tossed two vital facts at him as if they were medicine balls and he doesn't know which one to put into play first. So he takes them as they came. "That's a pretty important piece of information you lost. A teen-ager—that's what you were, Bo—crammed to the eyeballs with testosterone—loses the itch for four years. I'd call that serious depression. Did you get laid during those years?"

"Three times. Cherokee, Estrellita and Helen. Jack's hookers. We skimmed his take and fucked each other to celebrate fucking him."

"What turned you on about these women?"

"They wanted to."

"Just that?"

"Cherokee had legs'd raise a dying priest. Estrellita had boobs Rubens would've killed for. Helen was sad, horny and getting old, and I liked her a helluva lot."

"Why weren't there others?"

"I was shy. I needed to be dragged by the handle."

"We'll see."

"What does that mean? This is not a papal encyclical I just issued here, Dave."

David Llewellyn is suddenly foolishly grateful that he has not underestimated his client.

"It's dogma, Bo. *I was shy, I needed to be dragged by the handle*—it sounds like somebody instructed you to recite that for somebody else. It's like some old fart of a priest prepared you for an interview with the bishop. What're you defending? Who are you defending it for? What's all this pat rationalizing about? All this flip dismissiveness—I take you seriously, I'd like you to take you seriously, because if you don't, you're fucked."

Bo thinks of long green Cohibas dipped in cognac. Something loosens, like slacking off a clove hitch. Something breaks up and floats free.

He has to get back to the marriage, he knows that, but Llewellyn too senses something breaking up. "Ever do any diving?"

"Yeah, I had UDT training in the Navy, I was a frogman."

It feels a little eerie to Llewellyn to flush this out. "I want you to do some diving. I want you to make a list of where you were up to the point your mind started blotting things out. You can chart it, like a navigator."

"What are we doing?"

"You don't take much on trust, do you? Guess I wouldn't if I were you. Hunting for treasure. Diving on wrecks . . ."

Bo has never told the priest he's dived on wrecks or found a famous caravel off the Omani coast. The eeriness of the moment makes his skin crawl.

"We can elaborate," Llewellyn says, "you can elaborate this metaphor. You can be a Spanish grandee whose lax crew loses your future for you. You can be a navigator whose foolish captain ignores you. You can be a pirate. That's how you can remember the events, but what you are right now is a salvor. It's a maritime salvage operation. What is a sighting called?"

"A datum."

"Okay. Your data are psychic—they're the memories that rise to the surface of your mind like the Flying Dutchman surfacing in the mist. X marks the spot: you write your sightings down, you fix them as best you can on your charts and you dive on them."

Bo examines the environs like an osprey, looking for clues to Llewellyn's inspiration. He hadn't told Llewellyn he was a diver, though perhaps it isn't too big a leap to assume a man arrested for swimming the East River and put in Bellevue for thirty days might be a diver.

"A navigator uses stars."

"That's good, Bo. Elaborate the metaphor. What are your psychic stars? What's your Polaris?"

"They can be people?"

"Yes. And ideas, ideals, dreams, goals, events, memories."

Bo stretches his skin with his bones to make sure he's still its inhabitant. Llewellyn's metaphor catches him up. His mind races around its parameters trying to meet Llewellyn's ingenious challenge. "It feels like launching a rescue in a high sea."

"I love it! The thing is, this is New York, this is where a lot of your wrecks, are. Go to them. Dive."

Llewellyn jumps up, grabs a basketball from the floor by his desk and starts to dribble. Bo, amused, gets up and tries to wrest the ball from the hillbilly. They feint, pass the ball a few times, knock over a table, dribble some more, then sit down with the ball in Bo's possession, as it has to be.

"Make things talk to you. They will. Okay. Time out. You've got your work cut out for you."

★

Land mines and booby traps. Spotty amnesia. You stand at a checkout counter trying to unload some change and there it is: you can count the pennies and nickels and quarters, but you're damned if you can compute the dimes. Land mines and booby traps: he tries to defuse his fears by remembering the types of booby traps he's disarmed. It's like steering by a compass that needs correcting. He calls up steam from a flooded boiler room. All systems are not go, they're fucked. He can jury-rig things better than most seamen, but what David Llewellyn doesn't understand is that divers depend on exquisite maintenance and planning, on equipment tested and re-tested days on end. And yet he remembers his friend Uthman al-Biruni and the other Arabs who dived with nothing but their magnificent lungs and half-starved bodies, wary of sea snakes but undaunted. And hadn't he himself, sick and tired and drunk, swum a fetid river? Four times he clamped limpet mines to the hulls of North Korean ships, swam away, turned and watched bodies and debris burning in the bloody air. I can do it. I can dive again. I can search the deep for caravels and legendary cockatrices and God knows what.

★

Fifth Avenue on occasion still looks as it did to Childe Hassam when he painted it in strawberry regalia, and Bo walks down it this evening musing how bold it was of Hassam to forgo the hard heraldic colors for something frothy and fey. He doesn't know it, but this musing too is part of something breaking up inside him, because he almost never thinks colorists' thoughts or entertains colorists' feelings. Not that he sees paintings as a dog sees them, in black and white and gray, no, he idolizes Titian's greens and Renoir's pinks and blues and Corot's silver shivers and even maligned old Bouguereau's sinister uses of darkness. Nor can he say that he himself forgoes colors out of humility so as not to trespass against such masters, no, he simply can't dredge color up. Yet walking down Childe Hassam's avenue, he has for the first time in his life a full-blown discourse in himself about the use of color. What colors would he use if he could use them? How would he use them? He'd rather try to take a hill from Turks than go to Grumbacher's, buy pastels and tubes of paint, go home and use them. But he feels fully committed to this discourse. Hassam looked up, at least four stories, but Bo Cavalieri, comfortable among the stars, wouldn't have looked up. He would have engaged the faces, the glances, the disappearances into archways, the halos of lamps, the mannequins posturing, the tantalizing preoccupations; he would have . . . something stirs down below the outraged pancreas, not a satyr or manticore, but . . .

He crosses Twenty-Third. He's been walking a long time when it comes to him: a sexual angel, an appallingly innocent angel emerging from him. His body is a chrysalis. He's always been viewed as a responsible seaman, bosun and officer, but he's never felt any responsibility toward himself. Now he feels a fledgling sense of responsibility for this angel with whom he's pregnant.

★

Some days he's like a diesel, pounding indefatigably. Other days it's like breaking bones just to get up, to shave, to care enough to brush his teeth and shower, to eat. Lack of interest in drink comes upon him like a benediction, bearing out Llewellyn's notion that he uses drink to slake the thirst of dragons. Which leaves me face to face with dragons, the dragon-keeper thinks as he approaches Fourteenth Street. Don't try to kill them, Llewellyn said. Learn their language. They're old, wise and irascible. They have a lot to tell you. Yeah, if they don't eat me first, he thinks. Then he hears Llewellyn say they won't eat the person who frees them.

So in the morning, Bo wakes and says, Good morning, dragons, I'm listening. And when he goes to bed, after sitting for hours in the window sketching in fingerless gloves, he says, Where to, dragons?

★

"The humorous mind is more susceptible of remedy than others," Llewellyn says on his next visit. "I speak the language of dragons, know why?"

"You're gonna tell me."

"They hate dirty tricks."

"They tell you that?"

"It's a quality I assign them, that's all."

They smile.

Bo maneuvers the session over to accounts of his daily routine. Llewellyn lets him run on in the manner of a man forced to listen to pap. "Is this the way you want to spend your money?"

Bo wheels out from behind a couch in back of Llewellyn and confronts him. He clenches his fists at his side. "I'd rather talk about my grocery list than admit I'm the kind of person dirty tricks are played on!" he shouts.

They listen to the words fall like shrapnel. Llewellyn sitting, his patient shivering in front of him. Then Bo turns and walks out fifteen minutes before the end of his session.

He runs west on Sixty-Ninth, blubbering like a sucker-punched boy. A west wind splatters his tears across his face. He remembers Charlie Stanton, that spoiled son of a Grumman executive, punching him in his solar plexus behind the school while he was taking his jacket off, and how he'd been too outraged and shocked to fight. He recalls his stint as an elevator operator in the Beacon Hotel on Broadway. The lonely wife of a Tulsa executive who used to send out for booze and whores when his wife was away tousled his hair as she left the elevator one night and he'd burst into a fit of uncontrollable weeping as he took the elevator down to the sub-basement where the whores were let in. Why? Tousling a young man's hair isn't a dirty trick, is it?

He stops just past Madison and listens, surprised that this boyhood habit of speaking with Bo as if he were somebody else has reentered his life.

Why would a street-smart eighteen-year-old crank that singing sarcophagus up and down a dank shaft in the Beacon, ignoring its lit hieroglyphics, struggling to catch his breath, stop his tears? He remembers the old hand control—back then an elevator really needed an operator. Over all these years he's forgotten those tearful ups and downs. He tries to remember what caused him to ignore people waiting for the elevator as he expressed the sarcophagus up and down in a squall of tears. A Dutch diplomat's young daughter who touched his arm when she boarded or left the elevator, the Texan who sent out for cigars and booze and tipped him lavishly, the resident Holocaust survivor in a wheelchair who used to pat his elbow and say, Such a nice boy. The memories splatter his face.

His discourse continues down Fifth Avenue, the sun spilling on the West Side. A warm calm embraces him as the afternoon wind drops.

He isn't thinking of the priest Will Hallam who sent him to Llewellyn, or of praying, when he finds himself climbing the steps of Saint Thomas Church. He isn't thinking of anything, but the word surcease comes to mind. As he seats himself by the baptismal font he asks himself again who spoke with Bo at Cairnhall. Who spoke to Bo, dodging Sunday school and spending the morning with the great plow horses Dolly and Daisy? Who spoke with Bo sitting on Dolly or Daisy eating Concord grapes on their vines? Who spoke with Bo digging a pit and roasting freshly dug potatoes?

As he continues down Fifth Avenue he thinks again of the sad Tulsa wife in the Beacon Hotel. She had the air of a sacred dancer leaving her bracelets pulsing in the air. He thinks after all these years that she must not have been a smoker because smokers soak themselves in perfume. He's guilty of something concerning her. Why, the prosecutor asks, had he not had the compassion to consider what he might do for the lady? What did you want him to do? asks the defense, carry her off from her husband's money to a furnished room rattling with empty beer cans, engage in a cheap dalliance? He was a boy, a troubled alcoholic boy. Also, the defense puts in reflectively, there must have been a comfortable decency about the boy for her to have teased him. And was it a tease, after all, or a self-steadying gesture, reassuring herself that there was still some goodness, some innocence in the world? Way to go, defense! Now comes the sentence. You could have made some small gesture had you not been so taken with yourself. Yes, goddammit, and Jesus could have hit the sack with Mary Magdalene and told Peter to pay her. There he is on still-swank Fifth Avenue between Saint Thomas and Saint Patrick, straining blasphemies through his teeth like a baleen whale, and in high old New York style not a blessed head turns. Bo laughs.

His mind turns to sea winds and starry nights. At sea Bo is the repository of ships' oral histories and folklore, a one-man bomb squad by virtue of a steady gaze and a palpable quietude. Ask the navigator, the men tell each other. And when, as in recent years, he ships on his Z-card rather than his officer's licenses, his know-how and demeanor give him license, and Malay and Singaporean mates feel free to ask him to solve a problem in their domains. He thinks of the times when foreign deck officers, perplexed by some crisis, turn to him after one of their number chucks a thumb at him as if to say, Ask the Yank. Of course their willingness to consult with him is partly rooted in knowing that very few Americans choose to ship for such low wages with Asians, Africans and South Americans. Many times, in the midst of babel, a captain asks Bo to use one of his licenses to stand in for an officer hurt or fallen sick.

At Forty-Second Street he veers westward into the weave of pimps and pickpockets, heading for the Hudson docks to watch the ships. He doesn't need to see their flags at the stern, he knows them by their stack insignias: Hapag-Lloyd, Maersk, Lykes, Lukens, Evergreen, Sea-Land, he knows them all. He smells the diesel oil, the xylene, paint, bad food, hot metal, tarred line, scorched cable, detergents, carcinogens everywhere. He's had so many homes he can't count them. Make your passages, mothers, he tells the ships, I've got a few to make here where I started.

Think I'll walk down to Little Italy, chew some calamari, talk a little bad Sicilian. He scrubs the sob in his chest. He passes under the Westside Highway on the cobblestones and abandoned tracks. Chelsea 2-0336, Aunt Erika's number. The synapses are reconnecting, as Dr. Amos Perchuk at Bellevue said they would: Remember, Bo, the brain has more cells than it uses. What's dead is dead, but as you sober up the synapses hook up around the dead cells.

★

Llewellyn's office is in the back of an unimproved brownstone at the end of a gloomy shotgun hall. You walk into an office and find its occupant sitting behind a desk looking up at you, you say hello., he says have a seat. But Bo stands in the doorframe, thinking he'd rather kill North Koreans or Chinese or Arabs than sit down in David Llewellyn's office.

"You're a navigator, Bo, so I have a proposition for you, but I need a little help with the lingo."

The words feel like rotgut. Bo shudders as they go down.

"When you want to go from one place to another on a chart what are the places called, Bo?"

"Each course goes to a datum. You go from one datum to another. You mark the datum with an X, because any other mark is inaccurate."

"Okay, I think the way you're going to get through this mess is by plotting a course. Start from here. So where to next?"

"That's up to the owner, it's his money."

"It's your ship and it's your money now. Point a forty-five and shut your eyes. Who do you see? That's where you need to go. Or you can go to wherever you get the willies just thinking about it."

"You mind if I sit down?"

"Well, see, that's a problem, Bo. The purpose of being here is to go somewhere. And if you don't wanna go anywhere, there's no point being here either."

"I don't like games."

"There's a reason you don't like games, Bo. A good reason. Tell me where you've had the willies."

"West Islip, Long Island. Edinburgh. Hamburg. Oman."

"You've been to lots of other places. Korea, for example. Probably been in a lot of scrapes. What's special about these data? Is that the word, data?"

Bo goes to the window behind Llewellyn. He studies the desolate garden. Then he walks over to the door and studies his escape route. I don't have to do this. There's a bar on every block. I don't have to play with this smartass on my dime.

"You don't have to play this game, Bo. You don't have to play anybody's game. You've lived your whole life trying not to. But what if you lost something back there? Something that would make everything taste better? Something better than booze? Sit at my desk. Please. Take a pencil, make a chart. Go to the willies."

Llewellyn gets up and sits down in a far corner of the room by a cabinet filled with his collection of antique vials. Bo walks over to his desk and sits down. He picks up a yellow notepad, turns it horizontally and starts sketching. It takes him ten minutes. Then he gets up and brings the pad to Llewellyn. He gets down on one knee beside Llewellyn's chair.

"See, this is West Islip. It's my boarding school, Cairnhall. It was during the war. It was an Anglican school for British kids who escaped the bombing. I was there from age five to fifteen. I don't wanna talk about it."

"This is Edinburgh. I had just left Oman. I was looking for an elderly Scotswoman who knew my mother in Algeria. I found her. My mother went there in the thirties to paint. She got malaria in this oasis called el-Kantara. Rose MacQuarrie, the Scotswoman, was rich—she was studying Sufism. She brought my mother to her villa and nursed her. My mother repaid her kindness by having an affair with her husband. He was nineteen, Rose was, I dunno, older. She thought maybe he was my father, or maybe some teen-age gofer named Amir was, she didn't know. My name is Amir. She hated my mother, so naturally we made love. Forget I said that, it wasn't like that. I really liked her. She didn't know how to waffle, she didn't know how to lie."

Llewellyn fought off his own questions. He didn't want to knock Bo off course with professional asides.

"In Hamburg I used to go to this rathskeller run by an SS veteran. There was this Arab kid, a dishwasher. He was in love with the barmaid, and I couldn't figure out how she felt. So I kept sketching them until I got it. She did love him, but she wasn't sure she should, you know, him being a wog. Then one night my good buddy, Brandt Gundersen, he was the chief mate of our ship, gave her two hundred dollars for a fuck. She took it thinking it'd pay for a falafel cart for Lakhdar, the boy. He found out and hung himself. Ute-Britt, that's the girl, and I spent a whole night in his attic room with his body. We cried and held

33

each other, and then I took him back to Morocco because I didn't want him buried where that flathead Gundersen did this to him. The cops were glad to get rid of his body. I left the ship and never saw Gundy again."

Llewellyn writhed with questions, but there was this one shot at getting Bo to go somewhere useful, so he sat like a man full of piss.

"In Ceuta, after I buried Lakhdar, I met this Englishman and his, well, I thought she was his companion, but turns out she's his sister. They had this great research ship—they were doing a pretty good job screwing it up. He writes books about famous trade routes, and she's a photographer and diver. Peter Tomlinson, that's his name, asked me to take them to a repair yard. They'd fired their captain for stealing. So I took them to La Spezia in Italy. Then they asked me to take them to Oman. He wanted to write about the pearl route from Oman to the Mughal court. I took them. First time I ever skippered a ship. I have master's papers, but I like navigating. In Oman I met this Arab rebel. He had a price on his head. He liked me and showed me a sunken Portuguese ship. Turns out she was a caravel. Nobody ever saw a caravel wreck, so this was pretty important. Things were getting dicey by then between me and Moira Sayre, Peter's companion. We started to make love one night and I noticed her hair roots were as blond as Peter's. I put two and two together and got my ass outta there. Don't get me wrong, I didn't have any feelings about incest, it was just, it was a working relationship and there wasn't any place for me in it.

"Anyway, the old sultan in Oman took a liking to me. And a couple of years later when I got back to New York and started swimming the East River and drinking more than usual and forgetting who the hell I am—like I ever knew, right?—some guy finds me and tells me the old sultan's dead and he left me a book. Some book. It's a medieval Arab manuscript called *The Book of the Disclosure of Secrets.* He tells me the old man left me one of the fourteen rutters of Achmed ibn Madjid. Madjid was a famous navigator. Made Vasco da Gama look like an amateur. When I met the old man we had some fun talking about Madjid."

Llewellyn studies Bo's chart. He draws his breath at the accuracy of the coastlines from Long Island to the British Isles to Europe and North Africa and the Middle East. While speaking Bo had decorated the chart with Roman galleys, Viking longships, Arab zarooks, sea monsters between Sicily and Tunisia.

"May I have it, Bo?"

Bo nods.

"Okay, you're a diver, right? An underwater demolition expert. I want you to hoist the diving flag, go to Cairnhall and dive. Dive deep. There's treasure there. You think it's your death, I know, but it isn't. This is very dangerous work. Korea was a piece of cake. Bo, I know because of the life you've lived that you're going to understand me when I say you have to go where you fear. Please don't answer me. Anything you say is going to be fucked. Just think about it. You have to dive on Cairnhall."

Bo walks out. Llewellyn slumps in his chair, holding Bo's chart. It could've gone worse.

★

There is a next time and in the meantime Llewellyn decides Bo's silences are navigational aids. The man will discover why he drinks, why his mind jettisons motor skills and archives. Cavalieri is a cat in motion. Even drunk he doesn't drown.

"I wanna know about Geraint O'Faolain and your wife," he tells Bo.

"I'd rather eat shit and die."

Bo slumps in a chair and stares at Llewellyn. The clock sounds like a hammer. "I met Carol in a Dairy Queen when I was in UDT training. She was a kid. All the guys were in love with her, she was fresh-faced and blithe. When I brought her to New York Ulrike stood in her doorway and screamed. You can imagine how a seventeen-year-old kid felt. Carol hated the Navy. She ran away in a couple of weeks. I shipped to Korea. End of story.

"Geraint, he didn't have a nickname, you couldn't imagine him having one. He loved Yeats. We used to sit in his attic bedroom in Brooklyn Heights and recite Yeats. We were nuts about poetry. He died in an airplane crash over La Guardia, same year Carol took off."

"End of story?"

"Yeah."

Llewellyn snaps his bones one at a time out of his chair and takes up a post behind Bo's chair. He puts his big basketball hands on Bo's shoulders and begins to knead them. "You can't junk such people, Bo, such dear people, like old Buicks. They have to be grieved, and when you're a drunk you can't grieve anybody, especially the loss of yourself. So now you have to. They deserve it. You deserve it."

Sobs convulse Bo, but no tears. He hiccups and then the tears come, and the two men sit and listen to the clock.

2

An hour and a lifetime away Woofy sits in Cairnhall's rotting attic, antic among lacrosse sticks, her rouge too red, eyes too blue, heart mildewed.

How should a girl care when he finally comes?

He knows her name. He knows who left her there. Worse, Woofy-Poofy remembers him.

Amir Cavalieri—they called him Mouse till he beat them up—Dacia Wynne's boon companion. He and Dacia left Woofy here to guard their memories.

It's what they had to do to live, leave their memories with someone fond. Now, if he's back, has he changed his mind? She would like to know what happened to Dacia. He knows. He looks like he knows. Only Dacia would bring him back to Cairnhall.

"Woofy-Poofy, that you?"

She plays rag-doll dead to see what he's become.

He takes her over to one of the dormers and examines her. No one has touched her in more than twenty-five years. She fears she will crumble. He sits with his back to Montauk Highway and the wail of the Long Island Rail Road. She sits grumpy on his knees and they return each other's gaze. He takes a little sailor's ditty bag from his jacket and threads a needle in a beam of late afternoon sun.

Guess he knew I'd be in disrepair, she thinks. It's like him to fix unimportant things. He was always doing that. But what kind of man would carry around a sewing kit?

They sit in the light of one of the huge attic dormers. He'd easily breached the huge old grange-style building. Some doors hang loosely on one hinge and it looks as if nobody has tended it for more than twenty years. Only the land is worth anything.

★

On his second visit another intruder finds him there, propped against a truss beside a steamer trunk, a big green and yellow English railroad car in his lap, talking to a rag doll on his knee. He wouldn't have noticed her except for her indrawn breath.

"Sorry to startle you," she says. "Well, I would have startled you, I'm sure, if you weren't busy."

He stares up into her blue appraisal. She's tall, only an inch or two shorter than he. Her vivid complexion, even her bangs, argue that she's someone he knows. Never one to respond before he has to, Bo keeps looking at this interloper's face. Before he does answer, he looks inquiringly at Woofy, which moves the grave young woman to smile.

"Yes, it's amazing, isn't it? I mean, this is Woofy-Poofy. I was hoping she'd talk to me, tell me where I buried things, but she belongs to someone else, a friend of mine. She keeps someone else's secrets."

Margaret doesn't know which unnerves her more, his queer equanimity, or Woofy-Poofy, who stirs as much in her as she has stirred in the man. Maybe he knew Dacia. But it was wartime. The children came and went. English from the cities, Jews from the Continent, Americans whose mothers riveted tanks.

She tells him why she's come but not her mother's name. Bo Cavalieri, he says. But she remains merely Margaret. Maybe if he asked her surname she wouldn't have trusted him.

"Well, I know this place pretty well, what's left. I'll show you around if you like."

She likes. She likes better that Bo Cavalieri doesn't chafe while she talks, waiting his turn. He seems willing to listen forever. He seems to taste her words. It quickens her pulse.

They walk through divers rooms. "Alan and Jerry lived here, Jewish brothers from Vichy France, they had nightmares. They were my friends, especially Alan. Maddy Britten lived here. She liked to kiss, but she had fetid breath. I liked her older sister, Alice."

38

He answers her questions when he can. He doesn't ask about her mother. That's odd, isn't it? She is thinking about it when they come to a long second floor room on the west side of the clapboard mountain. A porch overlooks Great South Bay. He looks through the ruined French doors to the bay, then turns to her. "This is where Norman Hanks raped me. Put something around my neck and told me it would feel good. Afterwards he said he'd kill me if I opened my mouth. When I got back to my bed from the bathroom there was blood in my bed. I was eight or nine. End of childhood."

He says it hoarsely. His green eyes don't falter or blink. He looks at her as if they know each other. Body patience pervades him. His blood stops groaning. He walks over to the exact place where his bed had been and then he walks out towards the porch like a sentry who has been relieved. He doesn't know where the memory of the rape had been, all he knows is that he's never spoken it.

Her body's vigilance lets go.

She sits on the rim of an old iron-clawed bathtub, the space of a small room between her and Bo. She looks out to the bay of shiny mud for a long time. Then she comes out on to the porch and stands next to him.

"Let me tell you why I'm really here. It was something my mother wrote to a friend, Louis-Baptiste. I don't know who he is. She never sent it. I found it in her papers after she died." She takes a twice-folded letter from the pocket of her denim vest and reads it to him, their shoulders touching:

"I loved only once. Too soon. Before I knew how. We were comrades in arms. We'd sling our arms over our shoulders, line up our feet and fall into step. We holed up in the cord grass listening to the sea oats, and when it was hot and still we blew on the golden hairs of our arms and legs and studied each other's irises. No one else's breath ever smelled sweet enough to me, no other body friendly. We stuck our fingers in each other's secrets and put them in each other's mouths. We cut the turbid air with our own ammonia. Every other lover smells old and rancid. I resent their intrusion."

He cradles Woofy-Poofy in his arms, rocking her. When he turns to face her there are tears in his eyes.

"Dacia," he whispers. "Let me show you where *Ludilon* was. She's talking about *Ludilon*."

She nods and picks up her mother's story as they walk down creaking staircases and out to the ruined gardens. She knows about *Ludilon*. She wants to know what he knows. She stares at him. They come to Luckett's Pier at the end of Wycoff Lane, fallen like a drunk's belly into silted water. She's lost his attention and he's polite enough to let her know.

He hears the angels sing. In Korea they did not stay him when, like Norman Hanks, he too used a garrote.

"I'd like to dive on her. She's here, I'm sure. She was holed—they wouldn't have bothered to move her."

"*Ludilon?*"

"Yes." He takes off his shoes and socks and wades into the eelgrass. Then he turns to her. "I'm sorry. I shouldn't have expected to find her. Please go on, I would like to hear." He sits in the wet sand.

When Margaret reads again her voice is low. He has to lean toward her.

"It wasn't Zoe, my mother, who ended it, pulling me out of Cairnhall and taking me back to Felixstowe when I was hoisting my quim with my panties. It happened before. We'd begun to taste different, you see, but that's not what really ended it either. It was just before we decided what to do about that. We were getting pungent, rather punched up."

★

"Zoe?" He shakes his shoulders as if he's gulped a shot of whiskey.

"Yes, my grandmother."

"Punched up? That's an English expression isn't it?"

She continues Dacia's story without answering him.

"Everything was so urgent. It was frightening. But we trusted each other so much it would have been all right. After all, we tasted rather fishy and, growing up by Luckett's Pier, that was familiar. God knows what would have happened. What did happen is he copped out. Yes,

that's what my lovely pal Scat did. He was called Scat because Elspeth Carwithen, who ran Cairnhall with her husband Cary, loved jazz even more than she loved the Anglican hymnal and used to spot him boogying to gibberish, which I believe is called scat. So how was I ever to forgive him for changing? I haven't, you see. Forgiven him. No, I don't. There's a hymn where men make strange. Well, that's what he did. Scat made strange and I grew afraid of him. He was twelve by then, or thirteen, I can't remember. I lie. Yes, I can see that I lie. It's God I don't forgive. He shall have to give me back my friend another time for that. Will he, do you think?

"I suppose he was interfered with. It happens in these schools. I escaped because . . . well, I think you would instinctively know that if you interfered with me something would happen to you, wouldn't you? You might think it odd I should say that, but in future if you remember I did say it, it will help you understand the person who made Margaret, the person, that is, who would much rather have made her with somebody else. A specific somebody. Yes, well, that's enough of that. I imagine he's dead and now I'm dying. You just wouldn't intrude on that Dacia, you see, and I rather think my daughter Margaret is like that."

"I hated her then," Margaret tells him. "What right had she, with all her sang-froid, to leave me to read how she'd tasted in a boy's mouth when she was young and vinegary? What right had she to send me off to Saint Agnes in Berne and then to Cambridge and treat me as if it were her crown duty and then leave behind this testament to what I'd already missed and could never have? I'm sure some writer could make it sound like mother love, but it was another cold day in hell to me. She hid all that until she didn't need it anymore, then saddled me with it so that nothing I would ever have would be as pure or good."

Bo's green eyes turn gray. He looks away. He pulls a handkerchief from his back pocket and wipes his face. He looks up to the sky before he turns back to her. He looks down. She hopes her daring will be rewarded with a story. But what she feels is danger. He takes her skirt in both hands and pulls it up.

"You have your mother's legs. She loved to run. She was a great baseball player, did she ever tell you that? I'm Scat."

Margaret Wadeleigh, mathematician, stands in the blood-loud salt air running computations to keep calm. Does she blush? With her complexion, how not? Is she angry? Humiliated? No. She looks down gravely at her long legs, her skirt hiked in his hands, and when she hauls her gaze up again she notices her nipples, and he notices them. She's bemused. She thinks it's time to compose her face, but by the time she does he's up to his shins in eelgrass looking over to Fire Island and she stands holding her skirt. She toys with feeling foolish. What she feels is vengeful, and it feels tangy, clean and good.

As if his back were a mirror ringed in Saint Elmo's fire, she sees herself naked in it, the dark line parting her almost invisible pubis. He's naked. Her nipples etch glyphs on his back. I am not for crucifixion, they signal, not to be nailed. She grinds his buttock until her thighs run wet, and her hands come around to his groin. Then the mirror is before them. They burn in green fire watching themselves gravely. Not the ghoulish green of Saint Elmo's fire but the green flash that for a few seconds turns the horizon and the sea emerald when the sun drops on cloudless evenings. The green flash of Scat's eyes in the sun.

She doesn't think he'd understand her smile. But she's wrong.

★

They ride home together, the three of them, Margaret, Bo and Woofy, on the train. Or is it the four of them? As they stand on the platform at Babylon, Margaret says, "My name is Wadeleigh."

"Your father's name?"

"Mmm. He was an intelligence officer. I look like her, don't I?"

She has had sex with the man in a manner of speaking, but nothing can have prepared her for his starved, broken-hearted gaze. She's naked again.

"You do, Miss Wadeleigh, but your mother's eyes—Dacia's— were rather Asian for all their green."

She hasn't given him leave to call her Margaret, although she expects Americans to snitch familiarities, and she finds herself sorry he has not called her Margaret. "It's Margaret, Bo—Scat." She touches his arm, as her mother touched the arms of people she liked, unaware that he too emulates Dacia in this.

"There's a certain tone, kind of mannered, that suits romance novels," Margaret tells him on the train. She has taken Woofy from him and is holding her. "I know this tone so well that I can reproduce it at will, but my mother said only a few meaningful things to me, so that's why I read that letter to you. Well, that's not really true. I did it because I resent her writing it. Bitterly. But perhaps if I can see that it helps you somehow, then I won't be so bitter. Does it help, Scat?"

"I'm thrilled to see her again, but it upsets me that someone who looks like her is so angry at her."

"Because you loved her."

"Because I love her."

Then you'll just have to love me, she thinks, and is astonished at the thought. She watches him studying her. I will have something that is yours and only yours, she tells Dacia, something from the place where you lived, something your fingers knew, something you tasted. Like all young women of her breeding and education, she tries to speak properly, she tries to say something that tasted you, Dacia, but it forces her to say someone who tasted you. I will have the boy who bestirred your little crotch and kept it wet forever. She's heartily embarrassed by her thoughts and alarmed when he speaks.

"Your mother's cheeks turned red when she was excited."

I am not excited, she tells herself, but her privy parts belie it.

In Penn Station they exchange addresses and telephone numbers and agree to go out to Cairnhall again in a few days. They have nothing to do that evening, but she for her part is dazed and needs to regroup and he finds himself afraid of Dacia's corporeal ghost. They walk away, then turn to catch each other watching. His blood pounds. "Dacia," he says, and even at ten yards she hears it and refuses to let herself be offended because it's her key to him.

*

Woofy reminds him of Dacia more than her daughter does. Woofy's blond pigtails, tied with little blue bows at four places, recall Dacia's pigtails flying as she outran everybody, running,

43

always running. Her huge blue eyes, now faded, recall Dacia serving him air tea in a little tin play set in a gazebo. Had they ever talked? They had both been taciturn.

He buys a bag of remnants on Mulberry Street, blue and red and yellow, denim and satin and velvet, and when he gets these home he sets about cutting and sewing, repairing Woofy. But no matter what he does or says, she won't speak, and he begins to wonder if she wished to stay at Cairnhall. She won't even tell him that.

That night the phone rings twice, then rests.

★

He pulls Woofy from his backpack when he meets Margaret at Penn Station. It disconcerts her. As she is her mother's simulacrum, so is Woofy. As before, she takes the rag doll from him and inspects her. Has she ever known anyone who would meticulously restore an old doll for himself? None of the avuncular and lecherous dons who taught her, none of her upper-class colleagues at Cambridge.

Here is a dangerous man, Margaret. If I make him love me, if I can, to spite Dacia, will I not also make him love me for Dacia? Will I not requite what never was requited in her? And where will I be then? Who will I be? My clothes hurt my skin. My skin obeys my sexual parts and emits signals for a studious man: its dew point, a sinistral tic of my upper lip, and primordial fragrances of which none of us are any longer aware. My usual severe stare has become sidelong. My nipples are insolent. I am struggling against his gravity and losing, squirming like a schoolgirl being felt up, and yet he is the very model of a proper older gentleman, far more proper than I am accustomed to. I wish I could feel as comfortable with him as Dacia was, and yet her last testament is that she became uncomfortable with him. Damn! I am Margaret, not Dacia. I own what I feel, I own what I am. She is dust. I will not do anything in her behalf.

"Anything."

"Anything?"

"I'm sorry. I was thinking and a word escaped."

He grins. Her sentence reforms itself on his lips and she is pulled towards explaining it.

She draws herself up, tucks in her chin, emphasizing the way her lower teeth jut truculently. "I was telling myself, instructing myself, that I will not do anything in Dacia's behalf. My relationship with her was not good."

"I think it's brave of you."

Damn you, Bo Cavalieri, damn you to hell. She knows in herself a grand compulsion to find him wrong, to fault him, to be offended by him. She has never felt so contrary towards anybody, except of course Dacia, and he's clearly determined not to behave as if he were Dacia's surrogate. That thought, too, vexes her, because it's possible he simply isn't like Dacia and can't imagine being her surrogate.

"I should tell you . . . I want to say, that is . . . well, I can't imagine a man sewing an old rag doll back together again and . . . it moves me."

He'd now demur, say it wasn't a very good job, say he did it out of respect for Dacia. She waits.

"I understand."

"You understand?"

"Yes."

"Well, that makes one of us." She clings to Woofy, feeling less foolish for having gotten off a wisecrack. But Bo looks at her fixedly, and she knows that if the boy he'd been looked at Dacia like that, Dacia would understandably have taken every other man less seriously.

On the train they sit across from each other. The south shore villages flash by—Wantagh, Massapequa, Merrick, Lindenhurst—and as they do she becomes aware that her companion, the key to her mother's sexuality, her rootedness, is too much the gentleman to catch her in the act of studying him. True, he might well have been her father. So?

"I imagine we share something in common besides Dacia," she says. "You have to know something about mathematics to navigate, am I right? Perhaps we even came to it for the same reasons. And being half-Arab you would feel quite at home among the stars. More than half of them have Arab names."

"And do you, being English, feel quite at home among the certainties of mathematics?"

"I deserve that, don't I? It was a racist remark. The English are awful about that."

"No more awful than the Arabs. They always rather pitied the English that they never could be Arabs, so the two got along rather well, pitying each other."

"Actually I became a mathematician precisely because of those certainties, and it was only later, when I got into absolute math, that I had to wrestle with uncertainties. You see, whatever Dacia's protestations about loving me, they could not be quantified or proven out, and I wanted some fixed and reliable things in my life."

His failure to answer tries her. "I could as well have made some tasteless remark about your German heritage, couldn't I? The Germans have never been slouches in the field of mathematics, have they?" But she misunderstands. He's not sulking about her tastelessness.

"I know what you're talking about. I joined the Navy and then the merchant marine for the same reason—I understood the rules of the game. When you grow up in the hands of a mother who refuses to tell you the name of the game, you gravitate towards things that are fixed in their courses, like the stars."

So here she is, taking part in the most meaningful conversation of her life, the kind she's always craved to have, and resenting it because her responses are sexual. She leans forward to veil her nipples.

"Did you encounter racism at Cairnhall? It was a rather English school, wasn't it? Didn't the Carwithens' daughters also teach there?"

"I didn't and they did. The racism I encountered was in Ulrike, my mother, and her brother, my uncle Jurgen. I used to wish my father would find me and kill Jurgen. I was a little African souvenir of her messing around, and not knowing my father and not being told made it hard to feel an identity. I grew up, the first five years, speaking German and I picked up more German in the merchant marine."

His thoughts stray to Ute-Britt Broghammer, whose son, Tariq, has been well educated at his expense. When Ute-Britt's letters and photographs caught up with him at a union hall in Naples he realized that her son was Lakhdar's—probably she hadn't known she was pregnant that night they spent together in his attic grieving Lakhdar.

His thoughts have so many places to wander, Margaret thinks, so many experiences to fondle. And yet she knows that they're two of a kind in their austerity, neither of them accessible to comfort. They're too formidable, too discouraging. Born of formidable mothers, they have not been thawed in the womb or by the friction of birth. They move like ice in the ocean, attractive, dangerous and remote. We are changelings, she thinks. Our eyes are direct to others, but to us they are sly. Because of damnable Dacia I have found this frightening man, this all too familiar and compatible man, and it is all wrong and anomalous, just as my heritage is. And his. Worse, my useful body, so honed and pampered, is in open rebellion. Not only does it disobey me, it mocks me. It's doing somebody else's bidding.

He is watching. His turn. But unlike him, she's rude and catches him out. His lip quivers and she knows her answer. He has a rebellion of his own to put down. She smiles, but he manages only a nod.

★

Did you consult me, Bo, about this return trip to Cairnhall? Oh no, just as neither you nor Dacia consulted me when you left me there. Well, Dacia did hug me and command me to take care of her friend, I'll give her that. Maybe Dacia's dead, Bo on the way, but I'm angry. They ought not to have left me so meanly. One of them should have taken me.

Woofy is grumpy sitting beside him in the train, grumpier in Margaret's lap, and downright pissed on the walk from the station to Cairnhall. She is in her way much older than he. Why tell a betrayer squat? His surgery moved her, but not much, unauthorized as it was. It was his calling her Kouf that struck her. How does she know it was Kouf and not Koof? She knows because long ago, when she and Dacia lived downstairs and its paint still held Cairnhall up, he told her. Dacia named her. She was certain the boy never told Dacia his name for her. So, yes, she'll speak to him, angry though she is, because—because Dacia asked her to care for him.

"Dacia lived in this room," he says when they're back at Cairnhall, "at the head of the stairs from the pantry. She never moved around. But I did. I lived in four or five different rooms. She had only one roommate, Dolores Selfridge. Sometimes I had four or five other roommates. When I arrived I was small. Dacia and Dolores were taller. Hayden, the Carwithens' granddaughter, took an evil liking to me. She was a big girl and used to waylay me. She'd jump on me from behind or trip me, and then she'd pin me down. After a while, not knowing what to do next after tackling me, she'd pee on me."

"Oh, that must have been fun."

"It would have if she'd been Dacia."

They look at each other and sputter with laughter. She can positively see Dacia doing it.

"This horticultural practice stopped at some point, I suppose?"

"My friendship with your mother made Hayden sullen."

They climb the servants' stairs to the third floor and turn into the bedroom that leads to the attic.

"This is where Peter Butler and I made model airplanes, the kind you built with tissue and balsa. The room always smelled of dope. My favorites were the Stuka and Messerschmitt 109. This is a bad room."

He turns away and goes to the double window.

"A bad room, Bo?" She touches his sleeve, amazed at her body's friendliness toward him. She has been carrying Woofy and now she speaks to her.

"We need to know what happened here. We think maybe if you help we can remember other things too." She turns Woofy towards Bo. Woofy stares at him a long time. He's tired. The sun begins to sink. Cairnhall cracks and creaks. Owls stir. Rats scratch.

He considers the priestess's use of *we* and *other things*. Then he hears Woofy.

Other things? Like being born?

I don't know, Bo, I imagine it was rather like gutshot, Woofy says in Dacia's East Anglia accent. What I can tell you is Ulrike the Ice Queen had a habit of getting out of a cab and shaking your face by the chin and then hauling you up here for a beating for your own good.

I was bad then?

Oh no, Bo, they were bad. The adults were bad. Your mother was bad. I had the good fortune of living among angels. But it never occurred to me angels would abandon me.

They grew up, Woofy.

Really? In that case, why are you here?

Point taken, Kouf.

Well, they always had complaints, the teachers. And the Ice Queen encouraged them. It was all so penny-dreadful. But then you did go mad, Bo. I remember it well. Quite mad. D'you want me to go on?

Margaret sits on the floor in the shadows of a corner. She thinks she hears them speak, or perhaps it's only the memory of Dacia's voice.

It was after the rape and the hanging. Yes, after them you were quite mad. Not right away, mind, but in a year or so you were thrashing everybody, even bigger boys. You laid siege to Cairnhall. We were thrilled. We talked about it, the Dresden dolls, myself, the bears and bunnies and clowns, the little train conductor. We all talked. Dacia was afraid. She shivered. We were so close then, Dacia and me. I think I still smell of her. Do I?

Oh yes, Koufie, you do.

The rape comes back easily. He's ready to hear. Bunny told her about the rape. Bunny was there. Bunny's gone now, dust. Dacia told her about the hanging, how the bullies, the Stanton cousins, Tory Gilpin and Hayden of the ruling family had strung a rope to the ridge beam of the barn, tied a slipknot around his neck and pushed him out of the hayloft. He was so strong he'd opened the knot and dropped into a pile of horse manure.

Why's he grinning?

Well, Kouf, that explains it, I guess. See, in my more manic moments, shaving usually, I call myself Happy Harrison Horseshit.

He shudders in her blue reproof. Yeah, I know. Can't tell you how not funny it is. I became a sailor, Kouf. A frogman actually. I know knots. Being hung must've hooked me on knots. I was doing okay till I met this kid in Hamburg. Reminded me of myself. Hung himself for love.

I should think your childhood would have taught you not to stick your neck out for anybody.

You'd think that, yeah, but thing is I was trying to be someone nobody would want to hang. You know, a good boy.

Are you?

"Yeah, a good hanged boy," he says out loud.

The words startle Margaret from her reverie, which, she feels, is becoming clairaudience. She springs out of her corner. "A good hanged boy?"

"Tell you about it on the way home."

If she doesn't signal any interest in hearing it it's because she feels she already has. That's foolish, of course, but she's come upon so large a piece of Dacia Wadeleigh that she can't revert to any comfortable part of herself. Her inheritance from Dacia, which she'd thought bankable and forgettable, is turning out to be encrypted. No mathematician can spurn this challenge. She's not so much voyeur as seen. She passes over into that surreality that mocks our certainties. And she has, rolled in a rubber band, a gift she knows will accompany her the rest of her life and be there when she dies: Bo has drawn her sitting where *Ludilon* had been, one knee raised, her arm draped over her knee and her chin resting on the arm. She never likes photographs of herself, perhaps because she's too fair and vanishes into the light, but she's mad for this sketch. It justifies everything.

3

Addie Compton's mud-colored building in Murray Hill is seedy enough to discourage speculation. One can imagine behind its rotted sashes and muntins an old woman nibbling dried fruit and nuts, farming worms and leeches and cackling to nine cats, but not an athletic changeling who occasionally somersaults from workbench to workbench as she restores musical instruments while listening to Bach, Tallis and Telemann. Addie, for five years Margaret's roommate at Saint Agnes School for Young Women, is a conservator and historian of musical instruments. Her zany impulse to invent—concoct might be a better word— instruments that only she can play has earned her a coterie of writers and artists (but not musicians) who have soirees in her second-floor walk-up.

Where Margaret is apparent, Addie is fey. Her silky brown hair, cut like Lancelot's, conspires with her lithe body and facile fingers to writhe in and out of reality, so that only those who watch her closely believe they've seen her face. That face, plain at a glance, is upon capture intelligent and sensual, and most people have trouble remembering it.

In their last year as roommates they formed a casual, almost abstract sexual bond. Margaret admired Addie's fingers, agile and competent. One evening as they sat on Margaret's outsized bed reading, Addie rested her hand on Margaret's thigh. Because Margaret had hiked her nightie up over her knees, she was unable to decide later who had initiated the encounter, but after a while Addie strummed her silky pube and she opened like an evening primrose. Soon Addie was calling it her favorite instrument and her whatnot. Once, when she reached for her whatnot, Margaret slapped Addie's hand and pushed it away. It was a tease and a come-on, and soon Margaret was calling it her wantnot. Nowadays, in Addie's absence, she thinks it her whatnot without a thought for implication.

When Addie wrote to say she would be returning to England to undertake some research at Oxford, Margaret replied that she planned to come to New York to lecture, and that's how they swapped homes, Addie to Lechlade at the headwaters of the Thames and Margaret to Murray Hill.

★

Winter closes in after the second sortie to Cairnhall. Margaret and Bo find they're both cold-air enthusiasts. She mentions something about ice-skating at Rockefeller Plaza. He says how about a frostbite sail out of City Island? At the rink she finds he's a speed skater and played hockey at Cairnhall. With Dacia. On Long Island Sound he teaches her the rudiments of sailing in a twenty-four-foot sloop. He's as gingerly as a long-lost father. But there is about him—she catches it when she glances at him sidelong—a wry elfishness Dacia must have known.

She has his attention, she wants it, but what to do with it? Does he presume it would be beyond the pale to make love to her? Are there any middle-aged men like that? If she invites him, will she lose him? Surely a man who had been so curious about her mother's body is curious about hers. She spends a great deal of time in Addie's mirrors trying to see herself as he does. She's bigger than her mother, but not as athletic. Where her mother's eyes were South Atlantic green, hers are Baltic blue. What about her mother hooked Bo and never let him go?

She's coming from one of these seances before the mirror—coddling her briny cooch, thinking of Addie, then Bo—when she decides to write to Addie. She wonders if her presence in Lechlade is as strong to Addie as Addie's is to her here. She and Addie have hung around words all their lives. She writes painstakingly, recalling the most elegant writings of mathematicians she admires:

"There is a moment before an equation comes together—not for nothing the Arabs call algebra al-jabara, the joining—when you feel it coming. I don't know, don't care really, what it says about me as a woman, but that moment has always been more exciting, more desirable than orgasm. Alone with the abstract beauty of number and autoeroticism I've always been content, complete. My real sexual curiosity runs not to men but to what women imagine alone with their momentous sexuality. I rarely imagine men when touching myself, women sometimes, but usually I'm ordering the cosmos, playing God, and then God and I come together—al-jabara—and it's perfectly okay with me, proper, that God is not an anthropomorph."

She pauses to consider if she's making love in this way to Addie, in Addie's workshop where everything depends on one person's touch.

"I love the zero more than I've ever loved a person—and look how it resembles a woman's orifice (I want to say oracle). Am I an androgyne, a tribade? It interests me not a whit. I was too absorbed to care that my instructors called me brilliant; it remained to be seen. Their praise diminished them. But when I began to solve problems that needed to be solved I defined for myself my second obsession—the first of course was number—how had Dacia instilled in me this awe, this passion? That I inherited some directive chromosome I had no doubt. Dacia could add, subtract, multiply and divide faster than anyone I knew. But these are dumb numbers, darling, she would tell me, like stick figures scratched in stone, like cumbersome Roman numerals. She meant not the numbers, but the rote equations and calculations. Look to the Arabs, my darling, she would say, with their heads full of stars. Numbers will take us to them, the stars, she said. How had she seen in me this gift? It seemed to me she hardly ever talked to me, but what she did say carved itself in granite. Even when I said I supposed I would teach mathematics, she said, Oh no, my darling, that's pedestrian, you must do much more.

"And now there's Bo, half Arab, half German, his head abuzz with Deneb and Arcturus, searching his memory, diving down to the wreckage. Oh Addie, please don't think I was just leading up to him. I wasn't. I needed to say all I've said, really. His name is Bo Cavalieri.

53

I'll tell you about that, too. I found him, stumbled upon him really, in the attic at Cairnhall. He was talking to a rag doll he'd just stitched up. Can you imagine a man walking around with needle and thread?"

Margaret, the bone instrument, remembers Addie's fingers. She studies the instruments and pieces of instruments hung on brick walls, the books about the violin-makers Carlo Bergonzi, G.B. Guadagnini and Nicolaus Amati, hoping for some help, the right chord, a chord other than that plangent one Addie found in her. Where she finds the musicians, Addie in Lechlade will find Leibnitz, the Bernoullis, Descartes and al-Khwarizmi's *Al-Jabarawa'l muqabalah,* the keystone of trigonometry. She continues her narrative aware that its gems are being purled into its embroidery, hidden in plain sight.

"Addie—he, this Bo Cavalieri, is Dacia's—the only person she ever loved, a childhood love so powerful it haunted her all her life. The one person to whom her little strings were ever attuned. The rag doll was hers. He was sitting there on the dusty floor and it was all coming back to him, and who should appear, rise up before his very eyes, but Dacia's daughter?"

She walks around the shop, touching Addie's tools. Why has she so much trouble telling Addie Compton this? It's a good story, isn't it? She hurries back to the table to write more.

"I know the moment just before I decided to love him as well as I know all those other mathematical moments. He was standing barefoot in eelgrass in a tidal gut showing me where there had been a little foundered boat he and Dacia loved. I became . . . I was engorged with anger at her, and I decided that I, a grown woman, would have him, and not her, and that would be sweet revenge. Addie, you know how you used to love to watch me chalk up equations and then rub them out with my sleeve or cross them out? Well, cross out engorged with anger, because I'm not sure that's what I was engorged with. After all, I'm more or less permanently angry at Dacia. Every man who has ever been interested in me has tried to fill me with himself until there's no space in which to turn, nowhere to go, and I resent it. But this man carries in himself a sense of vastness. There seems to be no one, nothing he is compelled to

54

fill. Is this what you tried to tell me about Bach when I was enamored of some tumultuous Russian? Being with Bo Cavalieri is like listening to a Bach concerto. But it was the shopgirls who made me realize it, the effect he had on them. We were Christmas shopping. I don't suppose you'd like to Christmas shop with me, I'd said. I hate shopping, I said. I expected a yes or no, but instead the man asked me to talk about the people I'd be shopping for. And I did. We sat in a Schrafft's and I babbled on about my friends. He had wonderful ideas, exquisite taste.

"But I found myself watching the shopgirls, or, more exactly, watching them watch him. There was this pinched lovely at FAO Schwarz who could not take her eyes off him and who eventually seized an opportunity to ice him. Gratuitously. Anomalously. I was startled. But if he noticed, he didn't show it. I don't think it registered on his scale at all.

"Then there was this black Irish beauty who kept fumbling at the cash register, so absorbed she was in his movements. When she finally caught his attention she blushed so brilliantly I felt her heat. There was a buxom blonde who kept stroking his arm at Bloomingdale's as she showed him anoraks. Were they all abused children, sexualized at an early age by an older man? Were they all unconsciously seeking a better father? There were shopgirls who held his gaze and others who winced and averted their eyes. It was marvelous, but where did it leave me?

"Well, he was his usual cordial self and I was my usual frozen self. It was like one's sense of certain numbers responding to an order one had yet to apprehend. That is, you get the order right but you don't as yet see the principle. That's as far as I got trying to figure out this phenomenon, and then I knew what was lifting me to some recognition: the more this man saw the more he felt responsible to what he saw. He took it on himself to respect the responses of these shopgirls, to, as it were, salute their needs, their daft foibles. What I was seeing in the grave recognitions of his face was respect for humankind. I don't know how it came to me standing there in a corner of a store called Cacique, watching girls watch this middle-aged man searching through the racks for gifts for my friends, but it lodged in my head only a short time before I felt that great Arabic numeral open under my navel to await my calculations. I was disconcerted but not embarrassed. I hunched my shoulders over to give my nipples respite from my bra. Bo looked up at me quizzically

from behind a rack and I laughed and walked straight to him and passed my hand from his temple to his chin, realizing that I had never before touched a man fondly, for the fun of it. Calculatedly, yes—shoved and joshed, punched an arm playfully, tousled hair maybe, but never carefully, slowly, fondly touched. He gave it no recognition, so as not, I think, to spoil it. But I saw his eyes lose their focus and shudder in orbit.

"As we left Cacique I took his arm firmly, pulling him sideways, and said with a gaiety I never felt before, I feel as if I've discovered the Rosetta Stone. He said, I am Hatshepsut, lord of lands I have never seen, queen of night and day. I said, You? No, you, he said. Did you know that Hatshepsut, not Ramses, may have ruled Egypt during the Exodus and that she referred to the Israelites as unreliable workers whom she kicked out in exasperation? I said, I see you don't spend all your time at sea reading Playboy. *Seamen don't read* Playboy, *he said. Hatshepsut, I mused, I'm Hatshepsut? I tugged his arm. He smiled and I felt wildly complimented. I think he knew I'd perceived in him something that pleased me inordinately, and I knew in that moment that this man would never come on to me, I had never to be guarded with him, because he was content as I was to nurture whatever flowered between us until we could see it unfold. I was crazily happy, I felt I could walk this way with him, observing faces, forever.*

"We stopped in one of those white tile and brass trattorias where they make pasta in the window and Bo engaged the host in Italian. When we finished and had our espresso I said, You and my mother were really too young to have sexual feelings for each other. He looked pained. I was sorry I had disadvantaged him by not casting it as a question. My need to say it baffled me. It was as if I were warding off danger. I'm sorry, I've trespassed, I said.

"He seemed relieved by my apology. No, he began, we became friends when we were eight and we were in the throes of puberty when your grandmother took her away. I felt all wrong in my skin for putting him through this, but it was important to me, and he knew it. Now I think of it, it was important to him. It was terrible. He said he felt responsible somehow, as if it were his fault she was taken away. Some awful things had happened which he couldn't tell her and now can never tell her, and he needed to tell her because she was the only one he trusted, the only one he cared about.

56

"I said, My God! She told me the same thing, that she felt it was her fault she was being taken away. I believe she was molested in that damned place. She denied it without my asking, that's suggestive, isn't it?

"He looked at me hard and I could see he was grinding his teeth. That damned, dear place, he said. Molested. My friend. My only friend. He closed his eyes. I felt I couldn't breathe. I didn't know what I wanted him to tell me, but I felt it coming, urgent as sex. Then he spoke again. She had green eyes, he said, deep green eyes like the southern oceans. We had our secret homes—a nest in the bullbriars, an abandoned ice house, Ludilon. We used to feast on Ludilon's foredeck, which was still up out of the water, on potatoes we dug up, and quince and Concord grapes. We'd dig a hole in the sand and bake the potatoes on driftwood fires. We were going to rebuild Ludilon and escape together. We used to rip maps out of books and hide them in Ludilon's doghouse. We'd sit there munching hot potatoes and making our plans. The fact that there was still flatware aboard her seemed providential and reassuring. Something happened there alongside Ludilon in the sea oats when we were ten or eleven . . .

"He was going to go on, to tell me, but he started sobbing, and it took me weeks to get it out of him. Something happened that forever linked sea grass and wheat with womankind. As the two of them lay in the fecund lap of the tide he smelled not the Dacia of a giggler's pee, dirt and naughtiness, but the Dacia coming to be, tangy, electric. As he stared at the golden hairs of her thighs touched by the light breeze, something in him wound tight that would never loosen. He saw the bright black pupils dilate in her green eyes and the corners of her mouth rise and tic in a way he would search for the rest of his life: Dacia than whom there would never be a like, in a moment none would ever equal. It was damned hard work to get that little scene out of him and when I did I despaired, not just of what our friendship might become, but of me. I despaired of me. I would never be what Dacia had been for anyone. I hated her, not as a child, but with an adult rage. And some of that hate slopped over on him.

"I loved some mentors—you knew some of them, Addie—or what was in their heads—and then was dismayed how they mistook my innocent covetousness. Now this solemn man has in his head something I would lay down my life for—a moment nobody would ever feel for me.

"I didn't mine it up out of him in mercy, but my mind immediately made a vivid picture of what happened as the two of them lay in the grass alongside Ludilon. Bo was looking at me as if he'd seen his own mortality for the first time. We were leaning shoulder to shoulder against a big oak in Central Park. Spring had come early. He turned towards me and said, Hatshepsut. My reserve and resolve and anger broke down together. No one had ever given me a gift as generous as this picture of my problematic, taciturn mother. I ransacked my mind to return it as handsomely, but it wasn't my mind that came up with an answer. I did what I imagined Dacia did, I straddled him, and stroked myself against his thighs and then ground myself against his rib cage, frightened and commanding, until the current passed. He held my arms and stroked my hair, and wiped away the spittle from my mouth with his thumb. I leaned forward against the tree over his head, his face between my breasts, and waited and feared he would say, Dacia. But when I looked into his face he just nodded as if he understood much more than I did.

"He said, We used to scamper out on the roof between the gables and count the stars. Deneb, Dacia, that's what I often said taking a fix at sea. Did he call me Dacia then or was he quoting himself at sea, before he knew me? He laughed and said, Once when I was going off watch I wrote down Dacia for a star fix in the log and the next day my relief said to me, Hey, is this one I don't know?

"I said, I like that story, Bo, did it cause a problem? Can you imagine me, Addie, straightening my skirt, squirming in my gooey panties, and trying to act perfectly natural?

"God, how strange to like the man as much as my mother liked the boy. Is it the ultimate retardation? There's no cheap talk in him. I soil my panties on him and he talks about the stars because he's not sure I've made up my mind, he doesn't want to put our friendship at risk. You would ask, Addie, wouldn't you, whether I excite him. I do, I do excite him, I know, but I don't know how I know. Dealing with him is like playing with numbers—he has no intent, nor do they. And yet how could this be? The abused are deceitful, lost in games, untrustworthy, bent. Unless they have risked the recognitions of the damned. And that is what he's about, isn't it?

"When I got up off him, he politely averting his eyes, I knelt by his side, grinning. He looked quizzically at me and I kissed two fingers and put them to his lips and said, *Suffer.* He knew what I meant. It was a tease. But he said, *Suffer the little children and forbid them not to come unto me.* I was taken aback. Jesus Christ is not the retort a tease wants. But I knew he was remembering their Sunday school, his and Dacia's. Yes, I said, she told me, the big banner over the door said that, didn't it? God, how I wish he had suffered us to come unto him. I was willing. I kept wondering how. I felt moved, literally, from one place to another. I have to pee, I said. He laughed. Wholeheartedly, as if he knew exactly what I meant. I think he did. I got up and started off. Then I spun around and said, Don't go away. He said, Are you flirting?

"No, I thought, I'm playing. I've found my toys, the ones they put away, and I'm playing with my mother's playmate, her friend, her lover. As I walked over to the rest stations I passed from puberty to womanhood: I wasn't looking in the mirror any more.

"Attracted persons thrum. After that day in the park I felt that if you put your finger on our bones you could feel it. I am, after all, his hope of consummating a terrible longing, and he has begun to grope towards an opening, a way for us to deal frankly as sexual persons. I'm not making it easy. I've never flirted and I'm enjoying it immensely. He has told me about an older woman who aroused him when he was fifteen and had come to live with his mother and stepfather in Manhattan. She was a refugee. He's told me a lot about this woman, more than I want to hear, and I was grasping for a way to evict her when a very odd thing popped out of his mouth: 'I think the lesson Hettie Warshaw taught me is that it's not beauty that turns us on, it's something we've experienced connecting with someone.'

"Well, of course, I had to know who this Hettie Warshaw is, and he didn't want to tell me. When I was in the Navy, he said, my buddies dreamed about making it with Marilyn Monroe, but she didn't do a damned thing for me. Ha, I thought, I'm about to discover his type, which was absurd because I am his type. But so, of course, would be the women who remind him of Hettie Warshaw. I can't say this turned out to be a fruitful game, Addie, because he promptly told me that as a young moviegoer he pined terribly for Danielle Darrieux and Vivien Leigh. While I thought he had good taste, I had to wonder how the memory of fair athletic Dacia had let him out of its thrall long enough to savor such exquisite brunettes. I was still trying to dispose of Hettie Warshaw, so I said, So you're quite comfortable lusting democratically after prototypical blondes and brunettes. Then he said something that drove me straight around the bend. He looked at me as if I'd farted and said, I have the comfort of the eunuch.

"Addie, you're the only person in the world, for reasons you'll readily remember, I can tell this to. I felt incredible relief when he said this. And I felt exhilaration, like a hound given the scent. Notions whorled in my brain. I could live with the man as two women might live with each other. I could perhaps abrade that sad comfort and arouse him. He was wounded. I could lick his wound and heal him. I . . . I could live with him as I could with you, Addie. He was a man I needn't fear. But what would spare him from my contempt?"

4

The way we edit our lives enslaves us. We become creatures of our editing.

Bo speaks of the comfort of the eunuch as a man who navigates sob to sob.

In the morning Margaret edits the eunuch out of her report to Addie Compton. Their relationship flourishes more in silence than speech. After Scat's example, she too dives on ruined societies to discover her contempt. She sits at Addie's bench remembering what she hadn't written into her letter: *If he and I ever got into it, there would be blood on the floor.* Get into what? What in God's name does she mean? It seemed clear last night. She has walked through a dark wood and acquired a tic, an obsession. His admission of impotence has caught in her mind like an unfinished equation. The idea arouses her through the day. Next night she wrestles with her panties, her bath towel, her sheets in the salacious pleasure of discovering his most grievous hurt. By morning she has convinced herself they're meant for each other. He's become a manageable man in his confession of powerlessness. She accepts her mother's gift. She stands in the bathroom mirror brushing her teeth fanatically. Thank you, Dacia.

But she finds she can't let it go at that. She has to know about Hettie Warshaw. She finds Hettie in the phone book on West Forty-Sixth in Hell's Kitchen.

She shouldn't do this. But her training and experience, if not her morals, require it. Dacia and most of Margaret's professors had been proprietary about what they knew. She had to wrest knowledge from them. She learned early at Cambridge that a handsome young woman calculating equations faster than her

Plumian and Lucasian mentors would encounter resentment and so she became, to a certain extent, devious. If she takes this man to her bed, if they wander in each other's sexual hauntings, if she's going to exult in trumping her mother, she needs to pick up the clue he's dropped, and that means Hettie.

It tells her something right away about Hettie that Hettie does not ask if Bo knows she is calling. Hettie, too, likes conspiracy. Perhaps Margaret has information she'll enjoy. Margaret is exhilarated less by seducing Dacia's lover and more by the evidence that sexual bonds, even when left in limbo, flourish past hope of consummation.

★

"I'd like to know what a boy becomes with such a memory of paint, women's sex, turpentine and linseed oil in his nose. And I forgot the most important thing: rejection. I don't know what it smells like, but I'm sure it smells bad. Can you tell me, Miss Margaret Wadeleigh, what is the smell of rejection?"

"Eau de toilette."

"Hah!"

"Your hah feels manipulative. What perfume were you wearing that summer when Bo became aware you were a woman?"

"It was a long time ago."

"It will be yesterday until the two of you die. I'm surprised to see you dissemble. Your needle is stuck."

"I never liked the English."

"We'll survive it."

"You don't like Hettie Warshaw, do you?"

"On principle I dislike people who refer to themselves in the third person. About you, I don't know. I need something from you, and now I know you need even more from me."

"Hah! What do I need from a stuck-up shikseh, tell me?"

Margaret enjoys Hettie's flagrant patois. She's heard its like once or twice in movies but has never bumped into it. Incited, this vaudevillian would be outrageously funny, and it's clear that plummy English hauteur is just the thing to incite her.

"That wouldn't be cricket, as we disliked English would say. You know how to play the game, Hettie Warshaw—I think you'll play this one too."

"You gotta lotta chutspeh, girlie."

"I wouldn't call it that."

"You would call it love maybe?"

"Maybe."

"I don't know about love. When I had it I felt sick, not myself, and since I didn't wanna be anybody else, love didn't seem to me such a good thing to have. Hah! The ice lady smiles. You gotta pretty smile, Missy, you should indulge it."

Margaret's groin relents, something Hettie would have appreciated, signalling the birth of a certain pleasure in the old woman's company. About her smile, she wouldn't call it pretty, but it's wolfish and attracts some people, like her. Hettie too relaxes, seeing she's met a woman as guarded and pensive about the sexes as she is. She could like this willowy inquirer who does not smile easily.

There aren't many of her mother's characteristics that Margaret is pleased to have, although she's well enough satisfied with her physical attributes and thinks she has rather outdone her mother in this department thanks to her profligately handsome father. But she has inherited more than her share of one of her mother's characteristics she does like—her mother's total lack of impulse to fill up a silence. Here too she improves on Dacia. Dacia had been wont to simply stare if she didn't feel moved to speak. In fact she's puzzled why Bo doesn't remember this about her. Perhaps it came later, a hollowness dug out of her by the loss of her childhood confidant. But Margaret has a frank if not inviting gaze, and few feel shut out or daunted by it. She treats Hettie to it now.

"There's something in us," Hettie says at last, "that does not want to give what is innocently wanted, and after a while the innocents do not ask us, and then they're not innocent anymore. What does he ask?"

"Bo?"

Hettie looks through this diversion.

"He asks about Dacia. I remind him of Dacia."

"So what does Dacia ask?"

"When she was alive she never asked anything of me. My mother was intolerant of idle questions. She thought we all know a great deal more than we pretend and she was impatient with the pretense."

"She was right. Since she didn't like idle questions, you better not make her mad."

"You believe the dead are among us?"

"I believe we are the dead and many among us are undead."

"I'm not sure I understand that, but it's unsettling."

"When you are old you may believe it, but if you can believe it now you will live to see a miracle or two. Would you like that?"

"I wonder if I'm brave enough."

"Brave does not count. I know. Will is what counts."

"Will in the service of what? It seems to me bravery is an opportunity that's offered you. Will is something else again. I have nothing to push it toward. I'm content."

"What Hettie Warshaw has to say a person who is content does not hear."

"One might say the same of Christ."

"One might. But then one might miss the point."

"Which is?"

"You are not here, lady, to do a magazine article, you are here because you met a man. You want something from him. Something good, I have hope. You need to do something to him, I have fear."

"I was going to say I want nothing from him, but you make it impossible to say anything at all."

"It is not a good one, your answer. Your mother was a poker player maybe?"

"I doubt it." The thought of Dacia playing poker amuses her. She doesn't doubt it at all.

"I doubt it too. Y'know why? Because he loved her, so I think she did not have the makings of a poker player."

"I see. And I do?"

"Perhaps because you were born with such a face."

"Closed, you mean?" She remembers that Addie once called her a red rose locked in a block of ice.

"Unassailably beautiful."

"That's"—Margaret sputters—"bull!" But she no sooner says it than her brow wrinkles in puzzlement that she's said it. Addie's word, whatnot, comes to mind, unwelcome. She fails to notice Hettie's language has become more refined. "You amaze me," she tells Hettie.

"What can amaze a mathematician? Oh, that I am not always a slangy yid maybe? My girl, you would pee your pants to know what I have read, most of which one way or another I remember. You should make such a face to remind an old lady she started to talk about your face. The wrong men will always love you for it."

Margaret, who can't abide poorly written numerals, sees in Hettie much that she admires about the zero. Their meeting is not going well. But Margaret sees that Hettie likes women, likes to flirt, probably has done it for a living in a certain sense, and so she decides to pose for Hettie, to bathe Hettie in her gaze, to stretch her legs out for her, let her silk blouse commend her nipples. Even at her age—Hettie is now in her early sixties—there's not a plain or straight line about her. She's the Slavic odalisque she had been, blue eyes shrewd in Tatar bones, Circassian complexion vivid enough to keep the most enervated sultan edgy. The two women stare at each other, their lips slightly parted, holding smiles at bay.

"Why are you beating around the bush?" Margaret asks.

"Whose bush am I beating around? There were plenty beating around mine."

In spite of the acuity of Hettie's word-switch, which amuses Margaret, she purses her lips and taps her fingers on the arm of her chair.

"All right, Margaret Wadeleigh, just so you should know, I'm not so proud what I did to that boy."

"You led him on?"

"Easy for you to ask at this remove."

Margaret sits up. The use of such a formal construction alerts her to be wary how Hettie Warshaw uses patois to massage listeners. This woman lives in a flat chock-a-block with books, rolled maps, replicate statuary and stacks of clippings.

"I understand, Hettie. I've never been in that position, so it is easy for me to say."

Hettie leans over sideways to examine Margaret from another angle. "Would you know if you had been in that position, Margaret Wadeleigh?"

Margaret remembers herself at this moment standing naked in Addie's mirror. "I wouldn't, Hettie, no."

"Tea and sympathy it was not. Hettie Warshaw's tush was not made by Fabergé, so I'll tell you what I think—I've had a long time to think—I liked so much how bad he wanted it, I said to myself, better he should not find out it's just another tush. He made me feel like a girl, so I acted like a girl. Me, the halfling of raping goyim, acted like a silly little girl who learns nothing."

Now all the empathy women might feel for women and act upon, if not for the distracting hurly-burly of their commerce with men, rises in Margaret's chest and chokes her.

"I thought that only the blue eyes of Jews wept," Hettie says.

"Did you really think that, Hettie?"

"I try to."

"He was my mother Dacia's first love, her great childhood chum. She always spoke of him wistfully. They were children, but they formed a magical bond. She's dead."

"Did she have a happy life?"

"I don't know. She was responsible and cold. I met him in the ruins of the boarding school they attended. I knew right off it was him, but I didn't say so. The mathematical probability of meeting him like that is almost nil. As we walked around the place I found myself asking, What is it, Dacia? She inhabited me. I'm a mathematician, you see, so . . ."

"In the eye of the zero anything is possible. Omar Khayyam."

"Perhaps. Yes. He would say that. He was a mathematician and mystic turned into a romantic sap by an Englishman. The more you know, the more mysterious everything is, and you oppose that because it frightens you. Mathematics leads you to it, but as a practitioner you resist."

"Only a Muslim with his belief in predestination could have put the zero to use. Anybody else it would have frozen."

"You've studied the history of mathematics."

"I've studied a little about a lot. So he told you about me?"

"That you were his friend."

"I wish I had been. From me I am sure he learned he would be disappointed in life. If you reject pure love you better have a damned good reason, something besides a stingy twat."

"Pure love or pure want?"

"You're still a girl to ask such a question. But I tell you, that boy was not capable of pure want. It was like drinking at the fountain of youth to torture that boy."

"Torture?"

"Torture. Take my word for it, I'm an expert. Don't be a torturer. Are you a torturer?"

Margaret, certain that Hettie will find in her reserve the telltale marks of a torturer, stands and joins a dwarf clique of Sumerians, Cycladians and Egyptians at a window.

"Yes," Hettie says to her back, "a good person struggles for composure, an evil person is composed."

Margaret turns to stare at her.

"If I wasn't evil I'd be dead, Margaret Wadeleigh."

"You give yourself airs."

"I'm okay, you're okay? Oh no, life is not Tchaikovsky and ice cream sundaes, lady. Life is what you can bear to look at and not flinch. Well, you can flinch a little, but after a while you don't because it's so interesting."

"Dear God, you are more than I bargained for!"

"Maybe you don't bargain hard enough."

Margaret barks out a laugh. Then she tells Hettie what she knows of Bo, not her feelings but the facts. When she finishes she asks for a drink.

"Over there behind the Shekineh."

Her eyes follow Hettie's finger to a semi-abstract drawing of a veiled feminine form in colored chalk on black paper.

"The Shekineh?"

"Yahweh had a consort. The priests got rid of her. Shekineh, Kali, Nut, Gaia, the Black Virgin, Magdalen, the White Goddess—is all the same—the priests would have no work if not to kill her. That's their job. You didn't know that? The liquor is behind the Shekineh."

Margaret pours two snifters of cognac. "I know about Kali. Are you Kali?"

"You picked a good one."

"Are you?"

"Kali is a good dancer, makes Salome look like a hootchy-kootchy girl."

"You're evading."

"Well, I wouldn't walk out of Auschwitz on my own two feet and dance the Blue Danube, which I doubt is blue any more."

Hettie studies Margaret with a medical eye. Margaret enfolds herself as a naked girl in a doctor's office might. She feels anger toward this specular probe.

"Yes is the answer to your question. I am Kali the destroyer. I danced at Auschwitz." While she has given Margaret the satisfaction of an answer, she has not lifted the siege of her eye. It feels like somebody else's eye. It is. "There's a word in English could have been invented for you. Comely. How do you use it?"

"I suppose it's rather a quaint word now."

"Not the word, girl! How do you use your comeliness?"

"With clinical discretion," Margaret says.

Hettie's smile is like the sagging of jack-o-lanterns. "Good, that's good," she says, "I think I am able to like you. As for me, comely I was not, but sexy I was."

"Are!" Margaret says, puzzling herself by stretching the little word into a whine.

"It is very nice God gave you looks to conceal the fire in your brain. But when you want something you have to pay for it, and I don't think you got anything I want."

"You've already been paid, Hettie."

"Yeah? You did a lot of multiplying to come up with that conclusion, my girl."

"I don't think so. I don't usually stand for evil old ladies stripping me naked with their eyes unless I want something."

"How about evil young ladies?"

Hettie's pleasure moves Margaret's lips to twitch. She is visited by a long-ago summer that belonged to Dacia. She senses what she'd always assumed a woman could not sense: the fright of a boy growing up among hair-raising titillators, and while she's not ready to rejoice at being a woman, it feels comfortable for a change. She's inclined to show this pesky woman the Sheffield steel of her reserve, but Hettie's courage, her fearless introspection, deserves better, and Margaret is nothing if not fair. Besides, has she not encountered the quintessential New Yorker, batty and foxy, peering straight out of her craziness at yours? I'll show you mine, you show me yours—that's worth something to a donnish English lady wooed from Cambridge to Oxford.

"You got my number, Margaret Wadeleigh?"

"Yes, I think so, Hettie Warshaw."

"Herr Doktor Josef Mengele thought so too."

"Mengele? The ...?"

"Yeah. Himself. I'm gonna tell you about him, and Ulrike Theiss and Bo Cavalieri and Alessandro Cavalieri and Greta Garbo."

Margaret settles into a faux-Noguchi chair, breathing the bouquet of her cognac and hiding behind her glass. This is more like it. But she has to endure a bit more persiflage.

"Who would think I would live so long to sit here with a Margaret Wadeleigh and spit up my secrets? What's a Margaret Wadeleigh I should care?"

"At present it's being patient with a Hettie Warshaw."

"Oi, with such a pisk you shouldn't eat."

"English English always sounds a bit acerbic to an American."

This is too glib for Hettie. "Hey, you sell that to the heinies. A Hungarian yid you cannot sell it to. Your mommy and daddy gave you your English. Mine I had to pay for with what you wouldn't want to know."

"I do want to know, Hettie. If I were the remorseless bitch you seem to think me, I wouldn't be here."

"I see you English are hanging onto the language."

"It's bloody well all you Americans have left us."

"You Americans? Yes, I'm American. I'm so American I think God, when he allows himself to hope, does it here."

"Oh, I don't know. No mathematician would posit so provincial a god."

Hettie rises. "You would like to sit in my garden?"

"You have a garden?"

"I'm too old for it now. My friend, Mr. Billy Salviati, takes care of it. I gave it to him."

Margaret imagines a squat, stooped goombah yakking with Hettie over vino. When Hettie shows her a picture of a tall, preternaturally handsome man in early middle age Margaret stifles a gasp. "Is this recent?"

"Last year in our garden."

Salviati reminds her of Bo, both of them severe, their faces made of planes and shadows. The name Billy seems as improbable as Bo and Scat. The real difference between the two men is Billy's focus. It permeates his photo. "I would be hard put to imagine what he does for a living," Margaret says.

"You would be even harder put if you knew."

"I see."

"Maybe you do."

"I would like to see Mr. Salviati's garden. Would he mind? Gardens are so private."

"Billy, he would not mind. We have to see if the roses mind. We don't do anything without their permission."

5

When Hettie pushes up the roof hatch a half flight above her fourth floor walk-up Margaret finds herself entering an intimate bower of white climbing roses illuminated by hundreds of faerie lights. The bower is inhabited. In its shades she sees Pallas Athena and the moonstruck face of Alexander the Great. There are others, too. The night air is redolent of the gardens at Sissinghurst. Margaret's spirit lifts like a sloop scuttling on a freshening wind.

"Roses make commitments to you that other flowers won't," Hettie remarks. "They're not stingy."

"Where did you learn to garden, Hettie?"

"In that cesspool, Auschwitz. Everything grew well there."

"Dear God."

An easterly breeze, aerating the city's inverted thermal helmet, flutters thousands of leaves.

"She exists, no doubt," Hettie says.

"Who?"

"God." Hettie grins.

"Because we need her?"

"Because she needs us to feel, to love, to hate, to betray."

"And to be loyal and compassionate?"

"That too."

"It's a chess game."

"No. She is evolving, always coming to be. We are co-operators, we have an equal role—it's a partnership."

"You believe that after Auschwitz?"

"I can't not believe it."

"I don't understand."

"I think you do. That's why you're here. Love is a thing to do, otherwise it's like shooting cocaine. When you see it's something you have to do, you co-operate with the circumstances, you and God. If not, you're just a greedy little shlockenheimer collecting sensations."

"And that's why you feel guilty about Bo?"

"Guilt I do not feel. I missed an opportunity, that's all. God is very cautious about the doors she opens. Most of us are so busy listening to doors close we don't hear them open. We are so busy listening to ourselves think, we don't hear her think. You have to hear God think. That's religion. The rest is priest shit."

Margaret swirls her cognac, remembering that that is the exact sensation one has when numbers come together.

"So sit," Hettie says. "What is he like, our friend?"

"Observant. He's suffered."

"What else."

"It has made him honorable."

"He was honorable. His life is a kiln. No fire, no steel. So he didn't crack?"

"Oh, I think he did, many times probably. Yes, I know he did. But in the dark he finds ways to be reborn."

"I asked you did he crack," Hettie says, "and you said he finds ways to be reborn." Hettie comes up close and peers into Margaret's face. "That's quite a leap, my girl. Our friend is a revenant, yes, a walking dead boy."

Margaret wants to keep Hettie's attention, so she weighs her words carefully. "Why a revenant boy?"

"Because he was a boy when he became one of the walking dead. A boy he stays. It's not like a vampire. He doesn't do evil to return."

"A golem then?"

"You know about golems? No, a golem is made, like Dr. Frankenstein's monster. Amir Cavalieri is a revenant boy."

"Is Mr. Salviati? Is that why you like him?"

"Yes. You can never breathe enough life or warmth into such people."

Margaret shivers, but not from the cold. The idea of opening to a revenant boy sets up a current between her navel and clitoris and rocks her with expectation. Something in her own nature closes on this idea and owns it. She imagines at the far outposts of her imagination an existence in which she and Scat and Billy and Addie prowl together in some other dark and shifting dimension. She's breathing hard when Hettie, having decided that Margaret has a metaphysical side, picks up her story.

"In the summer the boy came home for a month or two. Sandro had a little place in Echo Tarn in the Catskills. That's where they stayed. It was a very nice arrangement for us all, except the boy. I went back and forth on the bus all summer. Usually it was two hours, but it could be late. In those days there was no throughway. The Coharie Bus Company was doing you a big favor, picking you up, and you had to cool your heels while the driver flirted with all the waitresses along the way. But the boy was always there waiting for me. Wherever I went I had lovers waiting. But to the boy I was God. He was burning with a fire you could see through because there was nothing rotten in it. For him I sang Magyar songs. No kidding. I would get out of the stinking bus and our faces would be like Winesaps we were so glad to see each other. I would take his hand and we would swing our arms together and I would sing those Magyar songs. After what those Magyars done to me I cannot tell you how strange it was for me to sing their songs.

"Then when we would be down in New York in bed, Sandro and me, he would say, Tomorrow I go see the boy. And you know what, I see the same thing in Sandro's face. Why do you love this boy so much? I say to him, and Sandro—you never know what he's gonna do he loves life so much—he kisses my titties and he says, I had a dream when I met the boy. He was eight then. The whole crew, you know, all the people in my life, even Charlie Lucana, we died and woke up in heaven, and here was this boy, and we all started up again. You know, Charlie organizing everything, me fooling around again with Nellie from San Francisco, my goddamn relatives and the fools they married whining around me for money with their phony stories, the same old shit, and God is nowhere in sight, not even priests, and the boy pulls me by the arm over to a fountain and he gives me the most wonderful drink I ever tasted. I ask him, What is it? and he says, It's different here—and all of a sudden I understand everything and everywhere I look it's different. So when I woke up everything was the same and I felt lonely. But I had the boy. You understand, Hettie? C'mere, I'm gonna fuck you till you can't stop laughing.

"That's what I always did, laugh. Sandro, an old man, he brought me back from the dead. But I always remembered Sandro's dream and my question about why he loved the boy. There are certain faces when you see them you see God and your whole body flashes hot and cold. And if you have that kind of face you gonna have a hard life because whatever is crazy in people they gonna pile it on you. Sandro knew this, but he could not say it, and the saddest thing to him was he could not live long enough to protect this boy. He tried, believe me, but Sandro betrayed the boy, which later on I'm gonna tell you about. You can be born to be betrayed.

"His mother was always saying, What're you looking at? Why are you looking like that? One day when Sandro heard her he said, He's looking at you, you crazy bitch. She said, it's like, uh, I don't know, the evil eye. Now Sicilians know the evil eye, so Sandro says, You ought to know, you live in the mirror. Sandro said what he thought straight out. I always have to pee when such things happen, but Ulrike turns to me and says, Hettie!—Oi, she sounded like an SS bitch—What is he talking about? But Hettie knows with such a person a little sexy is a good defense, so I say, Hettie's gonna do a little pee-pee. You know, to remind her if she wants to see my wee-wee again she better not involve me in that rigmarole."

Margaret shifts on the wrought-iron bench and wonders if her face shows its heat. Hettie puts a cool hand on her cheek, smiles wantonly and said, "Better to leave the three of them thinking about Hettie peeing than what they were up to before, eh?"

"You were sexualizing the boy!" Margaret blurts.

"It was fun, yes. I told you God arranges to be tormented."

"That's nonsense. You titillated that child in front of your lovers, his parents. You, not God."

74

"Maybe you're a good mathematician, but you don't know arithmetic. Like Einstein. To add things up takes courage. I had the courage not to be a stick. What I did not have the courage to do is what we're talking about."

"What you're talking about."

"Same difference. I see you listening."

"I need information."

"For a hoity-toity girl you got a mouth a lot like mine, only it shouldn't stop up your mind so much." Hettie purses her lips and nods. "You know," she says, "you're like a little girl wiggling because she has to pee—you don't know if you wanna hear this story because you're jealous. Oh yeah, don't put on airs. Jealous. Maybe only a little bit jealous of me. What you are really jealous of is that innocence. So listen carefully, Margaret Wadeleigh, and this old lady you are a little jealous of maybe is gonna give you something big, something you need, because I like women.

"Innocence is what we got to have from these angels that pop out of us. It scares you more than death. Ulrike and maybe even Sandro too would have put me in jail for corrupting the boy, stealing his innocence, but all I did is show him his love is worth something in this terrible place. You see God in the street, in a park, at a party, and you close your nooky like an oyster on its pearl, like Judas if you wannabe a Christian. You don't say, I see you, God, because you know what she wants you don't wanna give—and don't worry, you're not saving it for your lovers or your kids either. You know what I'm talking about? Not sex. Sex is overrated, it's what we do instead of acting like human beings. Sex is what we rub off on each other. You think for a minute if I gave this boy my holy grail, I thought he would go squealing wee-wee-wee all the way home and Hettie would be on her way to another Auschwitz? Don't think it for a minute."

"He told me you were kind to him."

"Kind is what I was not. To grow up he has to see that. In love I was. With a boy. Sue me."

As Margaret rises she sees the SS numbers on the underside of Hettie's forearm. She patrols the garden, touching rose petals.

Then she returns to where Hettie sits and says, "I can see he would love you."

"He was in his little Auschwitz," Hettie begins again, "and he knew that I knew. You know, that boy taught me how to swim. In a little hole in the pines in Echo Tarn where a dozen girlchiks are making moony with him he has eyes only for me because I talked to him, I listened, I made him laugh, which was not easy. Why should I not listen to an angel? I listened to the devil.

"One day we are walking home. The heat is so hot you can hear the wires sing, and he is telling me every katydid has a katydidn't, and we sit down in a little meadow to rest, and I put his head on my selfish little lap and I tell him, Someday you will have a beautiful wife to love you, and he says, I don't want a beautiful wife, I want you, Hettie. I'm not beautiful, I say. And he sits up and says—you have to get this to know where he spends his time—you're more beautiful than Primavera, Hettie. Primavera, I say, I should be so lucky or maybe so cursed. You like redheads? You see, I could not simply take the gift. This boy, he looked and found my innocence for me, but I did not reward his. So you, you don't play with my old friend who I never saw again after Sandro died—or I'll haunt you till you forget your name."

"I won't. I promise you, Hettie Warshaw, I won't."

"Here's an Alba rose for your hair. See, I break the thorns for you. I believe you."

Margaret tries to plant the rose in her fine hair, but it falls and Hettie reaches over and fixes it with a bobby pin. She closes her bright eyes, a gesture in which the younger woman finds respite, and after a while she says, "I see you with a wreath of wildflowers on your head in a dark green Druid glade. You know why your country is so green? Limestone. You are not happy, not sad in this glade. You are serious, like a priestess. You have the same aura as my companion, Mr. Billy Salviati, lavender. Amir's was always white with gold specks. Is it still?"

"I don't know. I can't see auras."

"You will see his someday. I am sure your mother did."

"If they exist, I'm sure she did."

"Dacia was a mystic?"

"How did you know?"

"She respected her child."

"She was a Theosophist. She told me mathematics is the key to religion. She encouraged me. She did always talk to me, when she chose to talk at all, as an equal, a better even."

"That is why you're here, nothing else."

No one has ever pinned a rose in her hair—she's too austere—or called her a Druid priestess. She would have felt rewarded if she had come for only this.

"This is for you, Margaret, not Amir. This, what I tell you. We don't know how certain coordinates cross, but we have to be there when they do. New York is holy. I felt it on the boat before I got off. A thousand, a million coordinates cross here. That is why great books and paintings are made here. The engine of God this city is. You can feel it hum. I know a girl, a little like you, not as strong, a friend of Mr. Salviati, and she sat here too, asking about him, like you're asking about Amir."

"Is he like Bo?"

"I'm thinking. Nobody would say yes but me. Billy you think should scare you, he scares a lot of people, but if your heart is pure Amir would scare you more."

Margaret closes her eyes and listens to herself breathing, and she hears Hettie think she is beautiful.

"They call you Peggy, Meg, Maggie?"

"No."

"That's good. It's just a way you let them tie your hands, it's not as innocent as it seems."

"Hettie, I'm really just his friend."

"Was your mother more?"

"Much more, if she knew how."

"Do you know how?"

"It's a friendship, Hettie. We are both trying to find something. We like each other. It's not a romance."

"That's nice. It would be nice if we liked each other more and loved each other less. Love is egotism."

"You said Ulrike painted you?"

"Yes. I'm a whole race of women in her paintings. My

head's too small. My tits are a tinsmith's work. My tattooed thighs could grind up Cossack regiments. Everything around me is incidental—a stuffed fox, a broken mandolin, balloons, a book opened for effect. This Prussian golem made a world of me. Let me show you. I bought a couple of lithographs."

They abandon the roof garden and climb backwards down a spiral staircase into Hettie's library by way of another roof hatch. From a galvanized bucket full of maps Hettie draws out a rolled print and holds it in front of Margaret. Two torpid women strike a pose in a painted Egypt. Their hips are geological, but their heads are frighteningly small, the faces vapid. Each has undergone a radical mastectomy, but the remaining tit juts warlike. Either the women wear skin tights or they're painted. A fox on a leash prowls behind them. An unstrung mandolin lies at one of the women's feet. Through the window an annular sun, Ulrike's trademark, stalls in the sky. It's a world in which men do not belong. But in this case, Margaret wonders, why the enormous hips?

"They're rather frightening," she says. She looks to Hettie for meaning, but Hettie too is baffled.

"I don't think these women have clitties," she says.

"You are going to try to distract me, aren't you, Hettie?"

"Yes. I have to see how I'm going to make a connection. Maybe it won't be such a good connection. Who would have thought when the Russian army got to Auschwitz and those lovely boys ran around the place puking and letting us out that my little button would ever itch again?

"Three years working with Mengele I was ready for a Prussian. So why did I come to America to pose naked for another kraut, to help her make a world without men which I wouldn't live in for a million dead Mengeles? She was beautiful. Men I had seen enough of. Mengele, you know, couldn't raise it from the dead. It's the only thing about him I liked. It was the only thing I recognized as human. I think it saved my life. My brains did not, my looks did not, it was not even my pity. It was . . . I understood his humiliation, his desperation, and I had the good sense to show him nothing except that I smelled so good.

Is that a laugh or what? I helped him with his little problem, so he would think twice before he drowned me in ice water. I think it's possible I'm the only person in the world who had a laugh at the angel of death's expense. And why? Because under his desperate tongue—he's licking me like a dog—I found out who I was. So I must have had a notion I was posing for Ulrike Mengele. She certainly loved me like a Mengele. For her I did not maybe smell so good. Fear is very erotic. You wanna know what damned is? It's not a Hungarian yid who knows what Josef Mengele tastes like. No, damned is what Ulrike Theiss shitted and chose to call her son. A son of Ulrike's would be confused. I can persuade you to believe me because this boy—who would believe a half-Prussian, half-Arab called Amir Cavalieri?—I wanted him for a lover as much as I wanted him for a son.

"He burned," Hettie says, "he burned with such a fever for me I will remember it ten lives from now. Many men have burned for me. I'm an expert on how men burn, but they don't shed any light. And this boy, this little boy, when he was fifteen, when he was sixteen, he did. He healed me of wounds not even Christ suffered.

"An old priest told me in Auschwitz, This is Golgotha, Hettie, the Jews are dying for our sins and it is my great privilege to die with them. If he had been a young priest would he have said that? I dunno. Christians know Christ was a Jew, but they don't feel it.

"You know what naked is? First, I'm going to tell you what naked is not. It is not standing naked staring across a ditch at a machine gun. No. Also it's not poor tootsies showing their coochies to a camera. Naked, for a woman, is letting a woman study you till something else enters her mind."

Margaret's moistest hairs tingle.

"And if she studies you to distraction you never get dressed again. After this, rape is better. A camera is blind. But a woman sees, and if she can paint, you are naked for the rest of your life. Ulrike could never paint me enough. For Ulrike God is what stands in front of her naked. Mengele, you know, he thought he could surgically remove their superiority from the Jews. He did, he thought they were superior. I told him so. It just popped out of my mouth. Hettie, I thought, you have talked yourself to death. But he laughed so hard I had to go get him water. You could say for twelve years the Joimans had the Jews on their minds and we would still be numbers in that ocean of filth. Yes, we commanded them as much as they commanded us, and now we always will, and vice versa. You wouldn't say I was on Ulrike's mind, you would have to say I was her mind. I knew exactly what belonged to me she wanted—fine sweat that shimmers on my lip, on the damp curls and rose hue in back of my ears, the way my upper lip pulled together when I was concentrating, my nipples so small and bright and my tits so happy. She couldn't paint them! She had the skill, but her vanity shlimazeled her. After all, I was not what you would call an androgynous girl. I was at least three thousand years old. As a lover I preferred Mengele. I posed for her many years. I needed the money. For fun I took Sandro, but him I didn't need. Mengele made me pregnant once, which for him I assure you was a major accomplishment—I practically had to stand on my head. So he says, Hettie, you know, we cannot have another Jewish god. Then I really make that hyena laugh. I say, I agree with you, Herr Doktor, one has been quite enough. It made him so happy he held my face in his beautiful hands just like he was a real human being. But he butchered me. What came to Auschwitz was a beautiful young woman made of Hagar's tears and Ivan's sperm, what came out was a golem.

"Now Sandro Cavalieri, he was thirty-five years older than this Ulrike when I met her."

Margaret notes that the depersonalizing usage, "this Ulrike," has not been used with regard to Dr. Josef Mengele. She muses long enough that Hettie stops and watches her. Hettie must have been some piece of work to keep the Angel of Death seduced.

"Hello? The mathematician is home?"

"I was thinking what a vamp you must have been."

"What was I telling you?"

"About this Ulrike."

"I was modeling for the Art Students League. This is how

I met her. She asked me to model in her studio. This is how I met Sandro. He had the face of a Roman general. His hair felt like silk and looked like steel and he had all of it all his life. He walked like a standing bear. I made his golden eyes shine. He sang like Caruso. Caruso was his hero. A man whose hero is Caruso is somebody to think about. So I thought about him. And one day he says, Hettie, I don't want you to take her money. Her money? It's his money, which tells you something about this man. So I say whose money am I gonna take? He says he's gonna give me some of my own. I say, yeah, and what am I gonna give you, Mr. Cavalieri? You think I lived in hell to be a prostitute? I think you lived in hell to be a mensch, he says. How do you know such a word, you a big Mafia type? Besides, a lady cannot be a mensch, for that you must strain your borscht with your beard. Two things, Hettie, he says, first, there is no such thing as the Mafia. That cripple Roosevelt made the word up. Second, you are not a lady, you are . . . you are Primavera. Primavera— Oi veh, now I have the only real man I ever met and his angel stepson in love with me. Mengele, you Lucifer, you should see me now, your favorite kike is acting like one, she's an operator. So if Mr. Roosevelt made this word up, what were you and your old buddy Mr. Lucana doing all those years, singing in the choir maybe? I like you, Hettie, I like you a lot, you got . . . Chutspeh? I say. You got balls! he says. I ask him, You wanna lay a lady who got balls? He held my titty like an angel in one of those Italian pictures milking the Madonna. For the first time since the Nazis came to Budapest my little flower opened all by itself. I didn't even need to help it with a thought.

"Sandro, he was what you call a legitimate businessman, you know, like dry cleaning in Hoboken or delivering bread in Lodi. He made fur rugs. That was a laugh. What he made was money. And me. Now I am the Cavalieri family's lover. I keep their circulation going. Sandro is true to his word. I have a lot of money, which I spend to help my boss, Mr. Isaac Herman, pay his taxes and his wife's doctors, because with him I also have a relationship, which makes a very busy Hettie, but all the time I'm thinking about the boy on whose brain I am a fever.

Il Saraceno Sandro calls him, my little consiglieri. His real son, Isadore, died at twenty-five of the TB. He was a musician, a composer. Sandro sent him to Juilliard. Sandro's brother, Joe, said the boy should be a lawyer, but Sandro says, You stupido, any lying bastard can be a lawyer, only God makes a musician. Sandro must have educated a dozen nephews and nieces and grandchildren. He had two daughters, a doctor and a lawyer. Mechanics he called them. Anybody can do that, he says, but a musician, an artist, they are sent by God so we don't have to be so sad. You still believe in God, Hettie? he asks me. Yeah, I say, but he needs a good psychiatrist. He says, You make me laugh, Hettie. You make my kishkehs sore, I say. We roll around in bed, we pour wine on each other and lick it up. That old man had more life in him than Hitler's army. The more I am coming to life the more I am wanting the boy. You would think with Sandro, Ulrike and Mr. Herman I would have my hands full, not to mention my husband because he didn't count more or less. But after Auschwitz this is a picnic and besides why shouldn't I be God for a change? The green-eyed boy with the face of David I wanted. This is what you would call puhvoise—excuse me, to say the word right does not do it justice. But I did not survive so much to think it perverse. I knew better than to make what I felt so cheap."

"If you mean Michelangelo's *David*, he doesn't look like that any more. But he is handsome in a rather hawkish way."

"Sue me, we're talking baby fat here. Also, I knew better than to think if I pulled down my drawers for this boy it would spoil everything, because this boy was a zaddiq and zaddiqs don't talk because they know we don't have anything to talk about. So what is my excuse that I let him burn in hell where boys that age live? Would you believe it—such a cheap idea I had in my head I myself can't believe it—I wanted to be an American? Americans don't do such things, right? I wanted this boy more than I have wanted anyone. I felt it was my right to have him. God owed me this boy. So I should say I have enough problems already? After Herr Doktor Josef Mengele how can you have a problem? I often think, wherever that voimin is, Hey, you should

82

see Hettie Warshaw now. She grows roses on the roof, she lived to forget more than you ever knew. Would I kill him? No. He's too evil to die. I hope he lives forever. Death is too good for him. But I know he remembers Hettie, because I amused him more than any goy and he has to think for the rest of his life why. Nobody appreciated the Jews like the Joimens is why they killed us so well. And just in case you think what I say about the boy is not serious, you should know it was me, Hettie Warshaw, kept the records of what that devil did. Stick that in your hat. You think the Joimens were tough? I kept the records about hypothermia. I ran the clinic. They killed my husband, my first husband who was not even a Jew. He was a Magyar, but he would not throw out the Jewish patients in our hospital in Buda, he would not tell them which members of the staff were Jews, so they shot him in front of my eyes. Oi, such brave soldiers! Me they were so interested in raping they did not think I could tell them. Would I? A person who knows such a thing is one in a million. I laughed to myself when I heard those heroes invaded Russia. That's gonna be some snowball fight, I say to myself."

"One night we're all having dinner at Sandro's. Sandro's cooking veal marsala, so he's pounding the veal with a mallet. Amir's cutting up vegetables, which have to be introduced— Sandro bows when he explains this—at just the right moment. There are maybe eight or nine people. Sandro is always inviting people off the street, even bums. It's one big happy family. We sit down to eat. Ulrike's baby brother, Jurgen, is there, like I haven't had enough Jurgens already? Amir is sitting next to his mother, his eyes are following Sandro like Sandro is Jesus Christ.

"Sandro sings, he gets up and feeds people morsels like a Jewish mamela, also he's drunk, which in Sandro's case you never know what is going to come out of his mouth. He asks the boy to recite a poem, one of his own. But Jurgen keeps talking—this, you have to understand, is a schlemiel's schlemiel. He says, I think . . . and Sandro butts in, That's good, you should do more of that, but now my boy is going to give us a poem. The boy recites. Everybody claps. But the boy is looking with those steady green eyes at his uncle Jurgen.

"Whatsa matter, Amir? Sandro says. I don't think Uncle Jurgen likes me, the boy says. Ulrike says, Your uncle loves you, what a rotten stinking thing to say! I still remember the way she measured out those words—rot-ten, stink-ing. She knocks him out of his chair with the back of her hand. He hits his head on the refrigerator. Sandro says get up, boy, come over here to me. The boy starts to move and we see blood on the refrigerator.

"Ulrike says oh for God's sake, clean yourself up, stop blubbering and apologize to your Uncle Jurgen. Then she adds, Every time I do something nice for you, you reward me by ruining my life.

"Apologize? Sandro yells. Ruin your life? You crazy bitch, I'm gonna ruin your life! He jumps up and grabs her. I jump on his back. The boy jumps on him. It was a wonderful evening, all the guests enjoyed themselves, and the boy and I go for a walk with his dog Fritzy, another Joiman. The dog was born black with a little white vest, so Amir, who had a sense of humor—I wonder if he still does—thought he looked like an SS officer and named him Fritz. SS dogs I seen, they did not look this Fritz. He was a nice dog. What an evening, but you see how Sandro and Bo loved each other. He listened to the boy like he had something to say.

"Something's funny. You smell it burning? This crazy woman, she comes over here and for twenty years, if you were not so lucky as to see her arm, you would not know where she had been. Then she starts thinking about Amir Cavalieri and also she is thinking about Joimens again. Maybe I gave that boy a bigger piece of me than I thought. Maybe I gave him the will to survive. We did have a little affair. We did and we didn't, which most of the time is better than we did. I'm gonna tell you about it, but I have to explain how I got here instead of back to Buda, which was not exactly in the first place Miami.

"The Russky boys when they got done with vomiting and shooting the Jurgens and the Fritzes and the Heinrichs, they noticed all those blonde tootsies, including me. I was a strawberry blonde, now I'm a henna redhead. So now I get raped, I think, by the whole Red Army. I mean, would it be asking too much to just shoot us? We are crouching in a corner of Herr Doktor's laboratory—he was on a business trip, is what he told me—me and the heinies, and me I'm more blonde than most of them, so I figure if I'm a little lucky I can get myself shot. You wouldn't believe it, but the heinie ladies—they were guards and nurses, Einsatzgruppen and so forth—they are looking at me like I'm supposed to do something. They think maybe I speak Russian? German, yes, it was the language of hospital administrators. Hungarian, of course. Yiddish too. There's this officer. I can tell because he doesn't look like a kulak. The heinies start with their Our Fathers and their Hail Marys and me with the kaddish, which I hardly remembered. I did notice the heinie tootsies did not seem to think Mein Kampf would do them much good.

"You! he shouts in German, Are you a Jew or are you just smart? I said, I'm a smart Jew, what're you, a language student or maybe a Cossack who rapes Jews?

"He looks at me over these little wire glasses. Oi veh, he says, my name is Pavel Blumenthal, captain, Red Army.

"I ask him how could you have such a name?

"How could you survive with such a mouth? he says. Does the mouth have a name?

"My name is Hettie Warshaw.

"Come with me, Hettie Warshaw.

"What happened to the heinies I think I know. Should I care? They could have told Pavel Blumenthal I helped Doktor Mengele, which is why I think I know. Pavel Blumenthal, who was a very nice man with a Russian wife he loved, arranged a passage to the American lines. So go be an American, Hettie, he says, and shakes my hand as if I were a real person.

"The rest is not so interesting, but it was a very good thing God in the person of Doktor Mengele spared my good looks because Americans, although they are not devils, are not angels either, which I expected. After Auschwitz what's not to expect?

"Probably when I'm growing the doctor's rutabaga in nineteen-forty-three Sandro buys a little place in the middle of some trees upstate in Echo Tarn where the artists infiltrated the anti-Semites and started to contaminate the place with happiness. This is the worst thing Sandro ever did, except to get sick and die. You think that sounds funny? Let me tell you, there are people in this world who make you very angry when they die because they filled you up with their life. I wanted to kill him when he died. Who could imagine such a man would die? What a betrayal!

"So. In Echo Tarn and also in other places I am thirty-seven years old, I am in love with a boy, and I am sleeping, you should excuse the expression, with his stepfather and his mother. Doktor Mengele would have been proud of me.

"Now if you're wearing your skin only because Josef Mengele happened to like it on you, you have a lot to think about. One thing I thought about on the boat was that I would be good to the Pavel Blumenthals of the world, men like Isaac Herman. One way or another—which is what murderers and rapists teach Jews—I would be a decent woman, not so I could stand up and say, I am decent, but so that somebody should not be so frightened or cold or sad in this terrible place.

"Anyway, my time with Sandro is when Ulrike and the boy are in Echo Tarn, but Ulrike is always calling and asking me up there because she needs a model, among other things. Sandro, he goes on weekends on the bus, because he can't see to drive any more. Ulrike, she can't drive period, except drive a person crazy. So there she is three miles from the town and she can't drive. This is a vacation? It is an exile. This is a vacation for Sandro and me. Everything depends on the boy and his bike. I bet you he got legs like a Roman soldier.

"One summer it never rains. Seven weeks, no rain. We are in a garage, which Sandro made into a studio for Ulrike with a big skylight, Ulrike and me, naked in heat you wouldn't believe. The cicadas are roaring. She is standing in front of a big easel. I can see sweat running down her thighs. I am sitting in my own stew. After a while we go to wash in a big tub and the boy wheels his bike into the studio, right through the door. I think he thought we were in the house because Ulrike left another easel on the patio outside the front door. Think about this. Even we could smell ourselves in that room, so all his life that boy is going to smell that room, us, turpentine, oils, a torture the Nazis were too dumb to think of. The boy looks like a red apple. He spins his bike around and gets out. As I lean over the tub to sponge my nooky, I see him stop in the turnaround, turn his bike upside down, take off the drive chain and examine it. Ulrike is behind me, touching my nipples and rubbing herself against my buttocks.

"After a while we take a nap on the couch. I wake up hearing Ulrike shouting outside. I run over to the window. She is barefoot in a frock, her tits swinging around like she was in a trance. At first I didn't see, then I see she's whipping the boy with his bicycle chain. He is down on one knee, holding his arms up over his head, but she gets past one arm and wraps the chain around his head. Then she starts pulling him around with the chain.

"I cannot tell you how calm I was, yes, calm, because it's exactly like a thousand scenes I saw at Auschwitz. She wraps that chain around his beautiful little head. It's tearing the flesh off his skull and he has to follow her. You stupid, rotten little bastard, she's screaming. One of those words may have been true. But I see he is not crying. His eyes are as calm as mine. I run out with a jug of water and throw it in her face. Look what the little jerk has done, she says.

"What? What has he done? I ask. Everything he gets he destroys, she says, meaning the bike. Actually he was rather mechanical. He was fond of taking his bike apart, cleaning and oiling its parts and putting it back together. I saw him do it.

"The sun was going down and it was like blue from Ulrike's eyes had splashed all around, on a dogwood tree, on bushes, on the gravel, on us. Ulrike walks away, just like that. So I carefully pull off the greasy chain, take him inside and dress his poor little head. I don't think Christ's head looked so bad. I am worrying about what Sandro will do. Ulrike sticks her face in the doorway.

"See if you can put some brains in his head while you're at it, she says. He is really too big already, but I am standing and he is sitting on a stool and I don't want he should see me cry, so I put my arms around his head and tuck him under my breasts.

How he can tell the wet of my tears from the wet of his own blood I don't know, but when he looks up we both start to bawl, and I think it feels so good we keep on bawling until maybe I got a little worried about what's going on or is going to go on if we keep on bawling in each other's arms. I still smell his blood, the heat and grease and me. I hug him again, fast, so maybe the day should not be a total loss, and I think of Mengele. Thank you, Doktor Mengele, I always think of you.

"You know what the kraut beat him for? Taking his nice bicycle apart? It was not a nice bike, it was junk. She beat him for ruining her life. This was an episode, an episode in the life of Camille. Have I got a word for you: retainer, you know from retainer? One of Camille's retainers might fail to bring her flowers or food or medicine uphill from the town on his bike so she doesn't have to get it herself. This kid is more Jew than I am, I say to myself, because whatever he does or doesn't, it pisses off the kraut.

"But what could I do? What would make a difference? I am married to Mr. Robert Hawkins who is half Mohawk and half unconscious. I have to give him a blood transfusion every morning to get him up. I am sleeping with Mr. Isaac Herman Thursday nights so he should not die of grief for his wife, who treats him like he is a schlemazel instead of the saint he is. I am playing David and Bathsheba with Sandro, who is wearing me out and getting younger by the minute, and Ulrike is making a race of Amazons out of me while dripping the purest Aryan shvais and whatnot all over me. She is my Mengele, because once you find a Mengele you need a Mengele. Believe me, Freud would have paid me to lie on his couch. Hettie needed three other Hetties to live such a life.

"Robert, he was a research chemist. My chemicals he would not research. Hopeless he called me. Me, hopeless? He thought that was funny, but when he said that I asked myself if a blind man can be a chemist. He thinks a hopeless lady walked out of Auschwitz on her own two feet? I have fonder memories of Mengele than I have for that remark. Which is why my name is Warshaw, not Hawkins.

"A Hawkins would not live to see Red Army Captain Pavel Blumenthal. A Hawkins did not live to see me that long. When he found out it was not hats I was making Thursday nights he wrote a note, went up to the roof where we lived on Morton Street and jumped headfirst. The note he left me he also sent to Mrs. Hawkins, his mother. I cannot live in this whore's stink, he said. What did he know of stink?

"That was a few years after Amir disappeared, so I'm a little ahead of my story. You want to know what happened? It's not so interesting. I am coming home six-thirty on Friday and I see the police and a truck and a little crowd, like all the suicides in Budapest before the Nazis sent us to health spas. So I stand and look, like a gentile, and somebody says, That's the wife. Then I know it's Robert. This nice policeman comes over and he says, What's your name? Hettie, I say. You don't want to look, Hettie. You don't wanna look at what I seen, Mister Policeman, I say. Robert looks like a pile of rags. They had a cloth over his head and it was red. I would have picked it up, but there were children, so I went upstairs and made coffee, read Robert's note, and then I sat in a chair by the window all night with the lights out. I did not cry, but for a year or two I had this knot in my chest, which Sandro used to rub with a hand as big as my face.

"Mrs. Hawkins spit in my face at Robert's funeral. Stinking Viennese whore, she said. Why did she say that? Do I know Vienna from Gehenna? For a Jew it's all the same. Robert thought he made me an American. What can a person make you? I was not a bad wife, but I could not be anything he would like. What a thing to say—stinking whore!

"Once he bought me a book for my birthday. *Les Fleurs du Mal*, and he puts this note in it, To my very own flower of evil. Dumb I am not, but I thought he meant I was like a rose, a brave little rose growing in a pile of empty Zyklon B cans. I cried. Now I know better. He was one of those men who thought what the Nazis did was like a dirty magazine. I excited him because of what he thought they did to me. From Robert I inherited bills, from Josef Mengele I inherited a love of roses.

He loved roses, he taught me all about them. If you think they were evil because he grew them, you would beat the child for the sins of the father.

"So I stayed on Morton Street and that is where poor Mr. Herman died one night in my arms. Such a kind man. He had two passions in his old age, me and baseball. Baseball, he told me, is like countries playing. I wrinkled my nose when he said that. Hettie, you don't believe me? No, Isaac, baseball goes by rules, countries go by breaking them. Hettie, my dear Hettie, he says, hugging me, Forgive me, he says, you are so right. See what kind of man he was. He left me his business, which I was running anyway. He had a daughter, Rosalie. You know what Rosalie told me when he died? She was her father's daughter. She told me, You were the only pleasure he ever had, Hettie. For this I cried, for Isaac I cried.

"Sandro had a problem only I could see. To keep the boy he had to keep the mother, because the boy could not see what I saw. Sandro also wanted to keep me. We have no secrets, Hettie, he told me. I had lots of secrets. One of them would have killed him—that I did not love the boy like a maiden aunt.

"A question I keep asking myself, Why was Pavel Blumenthal standing there and not some Cossack? But that is not the question, the question is why didn't the boy come to me when he left Sandro's house? Because of Robert? Because he knew about Sandro and me? Because in my direction was pain. More pain. Where did he go?

"Find the boy, Hettie, Sandro says to me. I should have known he was sick or he would find the boy himself. Sandro was not blind. Probably, he thought, Hettie will put my house together again and I won't ask her how. Only Ulrike, she is the only one who gets what she wants. It seems she has a very dutiful son. My feet were not so happy to walk to Sandro's house without the boy. I asked at Columbia. He quit. I asked the cigar store where he used to work. He quit. I go to the Ziegfeld where he used to water the orangeade. They don't know from nothing. I ask the hatcheck girls because he collects money from them for some shyster. They also don't know from nothing.

"This is when I notice I am not so young anymore. It is also when I notice Sandro is packing up to go home. That's what he called it. The zaddiq, the holy man, holds a special place in the world, he holds things in suspension. If I could find the boy I could put the Cavalieri house together my way, and now that I am ready to do this, it's too late. So every afternoon I am walking off my tootsies looking for Amir, but Il Saraceno is gone. No zaddiq? Sandro says. No consiglieri, I say. And we sit and schlumpf. Then Sandro says, Hettie, it's a funny thing, there are roses in Ulrike's cheeks, she's a new woman.

"I seen it already, I said. He says, Whuddyou mean you seen it already? The heinie girls in the camp, the more you could smell death the prettier they looked, like they been making love or was pregnant. Sandro goes to the cabinet over the kitchen sink—I always remember, this big guy in nothing but an undershirt with his balls swinging back and forth—and he pours himself a whole water glass full of Kinsey Silver Label—a rich man and he won't even drink Gold Label, but he would give you that shirt off his back—and I help him drink it and we make love like two dead ducks. I know the boy does not mean to take anything with him, but the only favor he did was for his mother, as usual. I keep on looking. I find out that first he goes to this cheap dump on Broadway, then he takes a room on the West Side. The landlord tells me the last time he saw him his face was beaten to a pulp, but he didn't know what happened. I couldn't tell Sandro that, so I swallowed it like bad fish and got sick. And that was it, I never heard another thing."

★

Margaret caresses the open eyes of Anubis, Egypt's jackal-headed god of judgment. "*Get out by 8:15 a.m. and have your head examined*—that's what Ulrike wrote the night before his eighteenth birthday. He told me. He kept the note. That's what happened."

Hettie puts her hand on Margaret's. Together they blindfold Anubis. "When I ask you what provoked it I know it could have been one thing or another, anything."

"He'd been drinking heavily for several weeks, staying out late."

"He had good examples."

"By the time I met him," Margaret says, "you could say he'd had his head examined."

"What was wrong was not his head. So that's the story. Sandro would have killed her."

"Exactly. Bo believed Sandro needed her more than he needed him, so he must not have known about you and Sandro."

"He chose not to know."

"I think so, yes."

"He didn't even have a Pavel Blumenthal. I could have fixed it. They all needed me."

"Who did you need, Hettie?"

"The one I didn't take."

"I don't think so."

"You don't think so?"

"I think you all got what you wanted, even Bo."

When Hettie studies her visitor she sees the bloom of rage on her cheeks like too much rouge, she sees her lucent eyes glitter, and Hettie's heart slows in fellow-feeling.

Margaret paces the room agitatedly. She kicks a galvanized bucket of crystals. The girl, Hettie thinks, is caught in a maelstrom and maybe nobody will ever like her enough to yank her out. She goes to her liquor cabinet, a secretary really, and pours half a tall glass of cognac. "It's not Silver Label, but maybe we should share it anyway." She takes a big swig and hands it to Margaret. Margaret's hand trembles. She sips the cognac staring at Hettie, who asks, "You got a man somewhere?"

Margaret thrusts the inside of her lower lip against her upper teeth, and the gesture strikes the older woman as desperately poignant; it recalls her own lifelong habit of pursing her lips in tight spots.

"Would it make a difference?"

"I like your question even if you don't like mine," Hettie says.

"If I had a man somewhere, you are the last person I would share him with."

"Easy to say to an old lady," Hettie says painfully.

"I am sure you were more than Ulrike's match."

"You don't listen too good for a person with such a brain. Ulrike wanted me more than anyone. Out of me she got paintings like a man making a tribe, out of Hettie she got all her begats. Why do they always say the artist and his muse? Women got no muses? Didn't you listen to me, Blondie?"

"I hear your anger."

"Anger! What you hear, what you see, what you think is bupkis. What makes your little flower open and fill the garden with the shortness of your days? What makes your little bubbies tiptoe and dance when your ass is dragging? Follow your feet. What does your head know? Ask your friend about lighthouses. You know what they tell you? The dark is better. You wanna know something? I could make you a very rich lady, but you I think gonna walk outta here poorer than you came because you are worse than Yahweh with his judging this and judging that. Judgment Day is in your crotch, my girl, but how you gonna know if you keep your panties on?"

Margaret shakes her body like a dog shaking off water. She's ready to go, needs to go, but this last remark captures her. She has given this crone a fine gift, a kind of closure, and she is being abused for it. She recognizes that Hettie uses abuse to egg herself on, but Margaret can't overthrow a lifetime above the hoi polloi to enjoy Hettie's abuse. Still, she knows what Hettie has just said is the key to the lock on her entire view of mathematics. To enter that mysterium has been for her always a secret sexual thing, otherwise her work would be arid and she would have walked away from it long since. When she works, sometimes in a fever, her little flower does open. And so she finds herself staring into the amber glass in Hettie's lap. She has gone to the oracle to be ambushed by dismay. This woman talks with a cunning dirtiness to make one give up thinking what to say next and how to react, and that is a kind of generosity Margaret has never encountered.

★

Hettie has bowls and buckets of crystal, but Margaret is leaving with no holohedral crystal—nothing she acquires here has as many planes as are required for a complete symmetry—and Dacia's daughter requires symmetry, her true lust, over against the chaos to which her mother beckons even from her grave.

Hettie collapses in a big chair by the window, tears in her eyes, overcome by compassion for this austere, decent Englishwoman. She knows Margaret is encaged by her armor, and the very propriety of her mind checks her at all the crucial points where she might give in to adventurism.

Margaret goes over to Hettie, kisses her forehead and says, "Thank you, Hettie Warshaw." Then she leaves.

★

She's exhausted. She totters down the crumbling steps. Her eyes don't want to focus. She walks straight into a man in an expensive Navy blue cashmere coat. "I'm so sorry, I didn't see you," she says. He's carrying a bag of groceries—a stick of French bread juts from celery tops. He's very tall, taller than Bo, and looks down at her with a chiseled smile. She knows she's bumped into Mr. Billy Salviati. "I've been to see Hettie." He nods. She can't stop herself. "I'm a friend of Amir Cavalieri, d'you know him?" Again he nods. He seems to her a Tuscan prince exiled to B movies, saddened but not diminished by it. "When I said I didn't see you, well, of course, one's not supposed to see you." She can hardly believe she's said such a thing, but she's never before encountered a stranger from whom she instantly demands something. Billy takes his right forefinger—he's a southpaw—crosses her lips with a smile and vanishes inside.

Margaret turns eastward towards Eighth Avenue on Forty-Sixth, her feet catching on the pavement. At the outskirts of her mind three, then four inchoate figures toil in sexual congress. They mount each other and part and mount again, gray, mindless and driven, and she longs to be there, and yet recoils. She remembers that once, leaving the Prado, some of Bosch's creatures followed her.

She tells herself she hankers for her library and her bee skeps, augers, dibbles, cold frames, blackboards, the cedar butterfly house, her bird and bat houses—and the singing harp on the door to her cottage outside Lechlade. Her fingers feel soiled with touching Dacia's things and she wants to plunge them into familiar soil, her soil.

She doesn't think she'll miss Bo Cavalieri, forever her mother's, but she wishes with foolish resentment that he had let her keep Woofy-Poofy. She thinks she will not miss him: she plans to make a pilgrimage to Greenwich, to walk along the prime meridian, to feel time and space stop, and east meet west, to get off gravity's whirligig and so to win herself back. She has thought of walking this glass-covered and illumined line at night with Bo, but now it would be something to keep from him, in the Wadeleigh tradition, one might say, and that would shove the man off into the vast and anonymous sea where he belongs. She likes her resolve so much she puts off realizing she hasn't asked Bo for Woofy. She has always liked her resolve and never reckons what it carries in its wake.

Even as she picks up the phone in Addie's apartment to call the BOAC for a ticket the knowledge shudders through her that she will some day, like Dacia, grieve for Scat, but she isn't ready to do it. Besides, she's grieving for Billy Salviati and being galled that he's not exactly an experience she could pin on Dacia or Bo, is he?

"I am simply too filled up," she says as she takes her drying undies off their hangers in the shower. She looks into the mirror to see the woman who has said it, but the mirror cannot hold her eyes. They go straight to her loins, which give the lie to what she's said. I shall call him and tell him. Tell him what? I shall write to him, give him my address, say we might meet again. He knows she lives in Lechlade, she'd said so. But he won't come looking. Not him. No more than Billy Salviati would. They're past caring. What she really shares in common with them, she decides among Addie Compton's instruments, is the knowledge that what people do is their story.

★

Dacia's green-lit eyes illumine his thoughts. Whatever, whomever is ill-complected in this light he abandons. Concerned for this light, lest it finally flicker out in him, he goes to sea.

The gifts we seek from one another, even those we're not above stealing, are not the ones we come away with, but most of us stubbornly resist the lesson. Whatever Margaret wanted from Hettie Warshaw, whatever Hettie chose to give her, it's not this—the certain knowledge that Bo Cavalieri is unlikely to find anyone else in the entire universe who can replenish the light he craves. She's never felt such power. She's never been as scared or angry.

At Kennedy Airport she is sick of her adamancy and haunted by her mother's belligerent lower lip. She's gone more quickly from his life than Dacia and has no mother to blame. Out over the Atlantic past Montauk she throws up, stewing in her behavior. She calls dozens of times but leaves no message, writes no letter. At Heathrow she stands on the tarmac staring westward until her sense of place ebbs away. She doesn't feel at home in England or her skin, and she wonders if she ever will again. A southerly wind blows her hair across her face and when it falls she remembers a recurrent dream: she's naked on a silken bed surrounded by men in tuxedos studying her.

Bo calls seven or eight times, leaving a message on Addie's machine three times.

How could it have been different? He knows the question has possessed him all his life, when Dacia left and before that when he began to know that pleasing Ulrike would be a trial.

Could it have been different if he'd told Margaret that twice he'd seen her mother lit in violet and then gold? She hates her mother. Perhaps this report, if she believed it, would cause her to hate Dacia more. Or perhaps she needs to know and never will.

6

"Do you think you're predisposed towards Jonesy women, being a Jonesy man?"

Bo looks blank, leaving Llewellyn to wonder whether he's trying to get Llewellyn to work for his money or has never heard the slang. "You're stonewalling me, Bo?"

"Maybe I just don't like your question. Questions are how you cop a plea, right?"

"Right."

The wall clock hammers away at the silence.

"I'll take a risk. Pulling Joneses is what some women do, but Jones needs a witness and you caught on very early in life to the beauty of not being one. Am I right?"

Margaret has forced him to relive the pain of losing Dacia. Bo sees that now.

"Ever notice certain girls can't resist a window?" he says.

"The Jones girls. I know 'em well, I treat 'em for virulent narcissism. They think if they look fast enough they won't be there, confirming their worst fear. Funny thing is, they're not there. So to act out, they take a powder on somebody they're damned sure will be hurt, just like they were. Mostly they're abused children. You can have two parents and a family and be abandoned, you know."

"Simple as that?"

"It must be—you figured it out."

"So there's not a dime's worth of difference between me and the Jones girls."

"A good shrink would pat himself on the back hearing a client say that. Good, he's pricking his own grandiosity, the shrink might think. Good. But to me the differences between people are as vast as the cosmos. I always feel awed and privileged to visit those worlds."

"This witness thing—bad behavior is no good if there's no one to witness it, right? So you have to pick your victim carefully. It should be someone you can watch suffering. And I'm both these people, right, Dave?"

"I've never encountered a man who had the faintest notion what those girls were up to in all those windows. Most men think they're fixing to spend money, and maybe they are, but mostly they fear, like the vampire, that they won't be there, and they're trying to buck themselves up. No, I kind of think you're like Baron von Frankenstein's monster thrashing about alone in the woods."

"I'll get a crew cut," Bo says.

To his next visit he brings a chart of the southern skies. "I thought, if you're going to visit worlds, you ought to have some charts, Dave. It seems we're both navigators. This is the Southern Cross, see?"

The gift delights Llewellyn. He says he'll frame it and hang it.

"Have you ever wanted to make a map, Bo?"

"A chart? No. I revise 'em, you know, jot down new data, stuff like that. I lay in course lines based on time, fuel, cargo, weather, et cetera. I'm always looking for better charts and filling them in with local knowledge."

"You're making charts now, Bo."

"Scary shit. Hell, I became a navigator to have charts."

"How long have you known that?"

Bo puffs up his cheeks and blows. "I didn't know I knew it."

"Tell me about charts."

"On my dime?"

"Yes."

"Charts, you want me to talk about charts? Well, Americans make big wallpaper charts. Gotta roll 'em into tubes. The Admiralty makes tidy little sketchbook-size charts, easy to handle. I use the Brits' charts and update them with our data, but when you have a lot of local knowledge you need the big Americans to put it on. I keep the wallpaper current for the Coast Guard. They know the game. Things change—spits, sandbars, wrecks, races, buoys, bells, channels—everything wobbles, changes, even earth's axis. Thousands of years from now Vega, not Polaris, will be the north star."

"What doesn't change?"

"Sea lanes, trade routes, seasonal winds."

"Loneliness."

"Days are shit-lonely, radio chatter, scorched coffee, dumb jokes, girlie magazines. Clear nights I live for, lots of company up there, plenty of action. Some nights the sky crackles and moans or sings. I can see Orion and Pegasus and the others."

Suddenly he can't remember Llewellyn's explanation for his memory loss, so he asks him.

"Guess the last few things we said stopped your clock," Llewellyn says. "Give that some thought. I'll give the explanation another try. It works like this. The booze doesn't work anymore, so the mind takes time out. It says, 'I won't tie your shoes or plot your course or remember telephone numbers, I may even erase your name and address to clean up your act. Have some respect for me for a change. I've been trying to send you messages and you've been scrubbing them. Love me or leave me.'"

"Thanks, Dave. I'm gonna sign out early. Gotta lot to think about."

"No rebates," says Llewellyn, "and while you're thinking, try to do some feeling. You're deficient in that department."

★

Bo is a qualified cargo officer and that's what he remembers as he walks west on Sixty-Ninth. Some government cargoes are sealed, can't be cracked, but it's always better to know what you've got in the holds. You've got to balance the tonnage so the ship doesn't list, and you've got to know what to do if she does. You've got to know if the cargo is volatile. What the hell is in the hold? What am I lugging? What's its dead weight? What's the destination? I've been hauling ass under junk flags. Gotta clean up my act. He spraddles his stride as sailors do in rough seas.

He needs a few more years to complete his twenty years of steaming under an American flag, required for a union pension. He has much more sea time than that, but often under foreign flags of convenience. By shipping under such flags American owners avoid American safety standards and wages. By now the people he'd known in the union halls would be gone. He might as well be a foreigner. His Coast Guard licenses are still in order, and he has licenses from half a dozen other countries, but his union tickets have long since expired. He doesn't want to ship with big oil's toothless company-union tanker fleets. They're mostly coastwise anyway. He's stayed ashore long enough to run down but not deplete his savings. He needs to go back to sea.

He spends a week walking around Manhattan, sketching and trying to figure out what he should do about getting a ship. Foreign ships are easy to get. They like experienced officers like him. But he's no longer young and needs a pension. He foresees a time when he might like to live somewhere, instead of shipping somewhere. Sicily, maybe. Or the Scilly Islands of England, where the weather is balmy. Or maybe Morocco. His master's ticket makes him look good to the shipping companies though he doesn't like to ship as chief mate or master.

Confront and clarify, Llewellyn said. So Bo begins to draw Margaret from memory and to ask his drawings what he wants from her. He thinks at first he wants nothing. That's fair—he has nothing to offer. But he sees in his drawings that he wanted her to stay. And, if he wanted her to stay, would he offer only the comfort of the eunuch, as he'd put it? Still, she seemed content with a sexual companionability not unlike his with Dacia.

Then the drawings of Margaret give way, imperceptibly at first, to Dacia, until finally here Dacia is, her squarish face with its bangs and tiger eyes and bold eager mouth. He hasn't seen her in all these years, has no photos of her, and yet here she is as if it were only yesterday that Zoe took her away. Better yet, he begins to draw the whole Dacia, with her surprisingly long legs and fallen socks, one foot locked behind the other bashfully, although Dacia was not bashful. He muses about that. She did lock one foot behind the other and he was always afraid that when she broke into one of her frequent dashes she'd fall on her face. Perhaps it was only for him that she locked one foot behind the other. Soon he's drawing her in her summer frocks. All these years his mind has kept Dacia better by far than any archive would have kept snapshots. Surely such a mind deserves his respect and care.

★

By the time he visits Cairnhall again he's eavesdropping on a conversation between Bo Cavalieri and Boffsider 90. At Cairnhall Amir used to talk to Amir, raising the question of who was talking to Amir. Now Boffsider 90 is talking. Bo meets him in the mirror one morning, likes him, and after a few polite exchanges, begins thinking of himself as Boffsider 90. Bo and Amir are the other guys. Boffsider wants to continue sketching Dacia in spots where they conspired—their gazebo, their bullbriar hutches, the icehouse, the tidal guts, *Ludilon*. And sitting in a world of thorns, it comes to him that he'd not asked Margaret for photos of her mother, nor had she offered them. She's had enough of Dacia, she's competed enough, sulked enough, fumed enough, regretted enough. When Boffsider 90 crawls out of the bullbriar he walks east towards the bay and the old Concord grape arbors. They're still there, choked with poison ivy. He remembers they'd ridden Daisy and Dolly, the tufty old Belgian plowhorses, into these arbors to reach the grapes. Then he remembers the early morning they spotted the most luscious, dewy cluster of grapes they'd ever seen, and Dacia had stood up on Daisy and started to climb for the cluster. He looked up her long slightly bowed legs as the white sun played under her frock and laughed in her hair. She looked down just before picking the grapes and smiled a berserkingly carnal smile he'll never forget.

That night in his loft he thrashes and turns—first remembering Margaret's grave and businesslike rubbing against his chest, then her mother's smile—until he realizes that the long comfort of the eunuch is deserting him.

This is what he tells Llewellyn next and is appalled at the priest's response.

"Are you going to be a stupid bastard all your life or what?"

Bo grins but doesn't like it and wrenches his jaw with his hand as if to shake the grin off.

"I mean," says Llewellyn, "this is all pandowdy, you know? You've had an indigestible life. There's no way on God's green earth for you to swallow what's happened to you. But you just go on pouring molasses all over it and slopping it down like pandowdy. Whose ass are you covering? It certainly isn't yours. Who are you pimping for? Where do you think stiff upper lips and sugar coating and making light come from, do you know? They come from the victim covering up his abuser. Abused children have stiff upper lips. They cover other people's asses. They make pandowdy out of shit with molasses. Get it?"

"So I should eat shit and die?"

"I like your question."

7

"My name is Weybrandt Gundersen. I'm a merchant seaman and a drunk, and I'm sick to death of scaring my friend and my wife Jolene. I need help."

When he sees what he's done to strange faces he says, "I'm sorry, I'm truly sorry, and I'm scared."

A skeletal old man in a shabby, shiny black suit next to him pats his fearsome cropped gray head. Gundy wipes his eyes and blows his nose in the wiper's red bandana he uses for a handkerchief.

Brandt, as Jolene calls him, has been wrestling the anaconda, the one that drops out of trees on tropic afternoons and flattens you just when you've convinced yourself you might get through the day without a shot.

The thunderous man has so much crawl space in the Norse holds of his body and such a big pump of a heart to clear his bilges that the notion he might be a drunk was about as interesting to him as the notion his father was a Maori. A sober Viking is a profane idea, like a rabbi's reluctance to speak God's name. He's had his funniest times and his most intelligent conversations filling his hollows with Hatuey, Kirin, Cutty, Metaxa, Hennessey, and any other piss o' the nymphs, as he calls his nemesis.

Then one night as he takes his six-foot-seven scar-faced old chump for a walk he sees an open door to a parish hall, walks into a Wednesday meeting of the AA at Saint Alban's Church, sits down and listens to six or seven testaments, stands up and says it.

★

Jolene doesn't have to know what he said about her to the AA. So he dresses up the story when he tells her.

"Well, I think that's good, Brandt, but maybe not as good as you think."

God, she pisses him off. Jolene never nags him. It's beneath her dignity, but it's always clear to him she wants him to do something about his drinking.

"I don't suppose it'd be too much to ask what the hell that means!"

Jolene settles her arctic gray eyes on him, inviting him to find a corpse frozen solid in them. He knows who the corpse is.

"Goddammit, Jolene, I told you I don't give a rat's ass where he is. Probably dead. J'ever think of that?"

"Not a chance, lunkhead. He's right up there in that flat head, and I don't think AA's gonna do you any good till you talk about it."

"Fat chance."

Having made that clear, he takes the chump for another walk. And the chump takes Poodle with him. That's what he calls her, Poodle. Thing is, she isn't a poodle, she's a little Chinese crested gargoyle and acts as if she and Brandt are related.

Best to nail shut the coffins of chimerical friendships endangered by sobriety. They're hospitable to ghouls.

Jolene Gundersen can't imagine how Brandt, a man who'd gone to sea as a cabin boy, can sail sober in a sea of drinking lepers. He knows no other life and, much as he loves her and their slapdoodle saltbox slumping down Weehawken's Library Hill, death always takes the seabag off his shoulder the day he comes thudding down the gangway.

She knows Bo Cavalieri had been his boon friend and drinking buddy. She knows he'd been something more, a brother. Something terrible had happened—probably Brandt's fault.

She'd given it a shot. It was all she could do. She'd never had to live with a man grieving for another woman, but their table is always set for Bo and they're hurt and hollow in his absence. She's sick of it.

Her business card says, *We don't need the United Nations, we need a massage.* To put her money where her mouth is, she tirelessly gives twenty-dollar massages to keep people out of trouble.

They met at a party at the King Olav V's Seamen's Kirke on East Fifty-Second Street. As morose a party as he'd ever seen, except perhaps one Scots New Year's wake in Providence, Rhode Island, where the dead bodies sat waiting to sing *Auld Lang Syne* before trundling back to their graves. Jolene was sitting across the hall when he first laid eyes on her. She had one of those astonishing faces that makes you catch your breath. He knew he shouldn't fly too close to that girl or she'd singe his wings, but he felt like a hapless moth. This big Icelandic girl, with her florid looks and spring-loaded exuberance, generated heat. He broke into a ferocious grin that turned up the lights. When she saw him struggling in her magnetic field she got up, walked right across the hall and held out her hands to invite him into the dance. His goose was cooked.

He thought for a long time afterward that he wanted to fuck Jolene violently, but when he did he did it slowly, thoroughly, instilling in him a wondrous gratitude that he looked forward to more than his comings and goings in her. Like big ball bearings they were soon rolling their urgent gravities against each other and falling in love then and there and only later among their sibling likenesses.

He was twenty-two, already a mate on a Hapag-Lloyd freighter. She was nineteen and, until Brandt, never dreamed she would find anything like reverence in a man. Like many Norwegians, he'd sailed under other flags, convenient to owners, not crews, spoke fair English, and figured he'd retire some day when he was a little less immortal, but not until that night in Manhattan did he think of having a home.

Jolene Karlsdottir de Ciantis lived in Weehawken across the Hudson. Everything about her made him smile. Her name, for example. Jolene wasn't a Danish name. Danes in English-speaking countries didn't usually follow Danish surname practices. As for Karlsdottir de Ciantis, well, what the hell did he know? He'd never really wanted to know much about anybody. He wanted to know everything about Jolene.

But he got a little drunk. He got a lot drunk. Jolene had filled a leg too, or what he did next probably would have ruined him with her. They were on the ferry. She knew a little hole in Hoboken she thought he'd like. He'd have liked hell if she were there. That's when he did it.

"Your bun as blonde as the rest of you?"

He flushed like a starboard running light. She turned her back to him. He knew she was crying. But when she turned back to him she had her dress hiked up with her right hand and her panties pulled down with her left hand, and damned if he hadn't seen towheads duller than that bun.

So, not to be outdone, Gundy surprised them too. He cried. Just burst out crying, big squarehead like him, couldn't stop blubbering. And because Jolene Karlsdottir de Ciantis knew why Weybrandt Gundersen cried they got married. In Weehawken. She knew he cried because nobody ever did anything for him so uncalculating, trusting, kind.

Whenever later things got tense, Brandt would say, Show me your bun.

That's how he became an American.

Jolene, named for her father's American girlfriend, had been mailed to her aunt and uncle in New Jersey from Iceland when she was nine. Her mother and father preferred dank melodrama and booze to her bright face. They couldn't look at Jolene's face. It hurt their eyes. They'd squint like drunks hauled out of the tank into daylight. That's mostly what she remembered of them, that squint. They needed to star in their own bad soap opera. When her austere grandmother, Margrethe, had enough of it she shipped the child off to her childless younger daughter in America and stared down the mock-indignant parents.

Her Aunt Lise and Lise's husband, Vincenzo de Ciantis, a Sicilian-American from over on Elizabeth Street in Manhattan, loved her from the moment she got off the plane. Lise taught fourth grade. Vince—nobody would call a man so somber Vinny—was a welder and a sculptor. From them she'd had nothing but love, approval and help. They were her parents and friends, and if their girl loved this yeti from Oppdal he must be okay.

Jolene and Vince had a secret. It made her life with Lise and Vince work. It made her life a pleasure. Right from the start he'd show her his work in the garage. But he'd never say anything. Before long she saw he was trying to get something about her right, something in the work. She'd go straight there from school, before Vince came home, to see what he'd done. The human figure acquired new possibilities after Giacometti and Lehmbruck, so Jolene gave herself quite an education studying Vince's figures. After a while—when she spun on her heel to look real quick or sidelong—she'd see things manic and comic that would remind her of her own nature. Then she saw that Vince was trying to portray her irrepressibility. She couldn't have called it that, but she knew.

The infertile Lise, who thanked God for this unbidden daughter, had been drawn to the grave, pock-marked Vince by his wordlessness when he was a sailor in Reykjavik. The way he looked at her, head cocked, smiling shyly, said she could trust him. Her own relationship with Jolene started off garrulous. They'd giggle and cackle and nudge for hours while sparks flew in the garage. But as the years passed Vince's wordlessness rubbed off on the child. Lise had the sense and generosity to let it.

The women were in good and safe hands. They knew it. In Weybrandt Gundersen Jolene had not chosen less. Until Vince keeled over in his garage one night he and Brandt were fast friends. They even wrote to each other when Brandt was at sea. When Vince was gone his two Danish muses went right on tickling their palms on Brandt's flattop as they flitted by him doing chores around the house.

He hardly ever thought of Norway again.

★

His father had nearly crippled him with his belt buckle by the time he ran off to sea. All he remembered was his mother's stone eyes and his father making a man of him. He wouldn't do it if he didn't love you, his mother said. That's when he canceled her mother ticket. Then the north seas, gray and severe and true, were his mother, the southern seas a warm and friendly aunt, like

Lise. Fathers you could do without. And if there was any man he wouldn't stomach, that man was a bully, captain or oiler, it didn't matter. Don't mess with Gundersen. He ain't mean but he ain't meek—the word got out while he was still an able seaman.

So, by the time his mother, the sea, introduced him to Bo Cavalieri he was prepared to see a kindred spirit in the quiet, lank frogman with the ingrained Navy habit of doing a thing right.

I'm giving you a brother, Brandt, his mother said.

I'll look after him, Brandt thought.

Not that Bo needed looking after, being himself a man willing to look after the world's most alienated men, all but the fuck-ups. Fuck-ups too numerous to count amused Gundy—he collected and prized their misdoings—but they left Bo cold. He'd teach a willing hand anything he knew and be more patient about it than any seaman Gundy knew, but bad asses and fuck-ups he'd send back to union halls without even asking the skipper by your leave. Bad asses were part of a mate's fate and sometimes part of his nature as well. Gundy was resigned. Ships had to crew up and get up steam on time, and more than once he said to Bo, "Will you cut us some slack for Chrissake? This ain't your tight-ass Navy, y'know. We're in the business of making money, not spending it."

And Bo would look at his watch, shake his head and say, "If we don't get a pierhead jump I'll do the sonofabitch's job myself."

Few skippers, having seen Bo chip and slop zinc chromate and sludge rigging fifty feet aloft with his men, were willing to make a case over this peccadillo. So more than once they sailed one or two assholes short.

★

It's hard to say, maybe not worth it, what makes a person a drunk. Jolene lives in her body. It doesn't have a lot of empty storage in it. So she doesn't look to what made Brandt drink too much. All she knows is that after his last job on the *Vestris* he had a whole lot more stowage inside him for booze. It was like somebody skipped rent and he never could bring himself to rent the place out again.

Now she has that feeling some sailors get about ice. You can feel it out there. You don't need radar. Maybe it was Brandt standing up at the AA. Or maybe standing up at the AA is part of that feeling. After a while she can hear it, the ice moving, creaking. If a good seaman tells a good captain he feels it, the captain sets an ice watch, maybe even changes course.

She can tell Brandt's listening too.

He gets down on the floor on all fours one night and starts growling at Poodle. Poodle growls back. The two of them crawl around the house growling at each other. Poodle gets tired first. She gets up into his face and gives him one of those when-are-you-going-to-grow-up looks and he goes out onto the second floor back porch, pulls out his pipe and has himself a long, thoughtful smoke.

In fewer than three creosote-laden Weehawken days he's sitting in their kitchen talking about Bo Cavalieri. This time she gets out his pipe and fills it for him.

"On every good ship"—he starts—"when I say good I don't mean how she's made—there's a loner nobody's got a beef with. He's the ship's luck. You can have a perfect ship, but if you don't have this guy you're out of luck. If you got any brains at all you don't fuck with him. I'm talking deck. Engine I don't know—they have their own beliefs.

"Bo was a special kind of loner. He made you forget he was one.

"First time we shipped together was on the SS *Atlantic Whitemarsh*, an old break-bulk freighter. I gave him a third mate's job. Made some union muckymuck named Conway madder'n hell. That's how Bo came up the hawse from the deck, all by himself with a little help from me. The *Whitemarsh* was one of those tramps looked like a roach gone belly up, kingposts everywhere, the kind of ship most people think of when they think about merchant ships. It was before containers and ro-ro's when ships still looked like ships, not goddamned wedding cakes.

"I was chief mate, so he reported to me. He'd been a Navy

boatswain's mate as well as a merchant bosun, so I reckoned to keep a sharp eye on him to make sure he didn't act like we had a hundred deck apes to do the job of one ordinary, even though I liked the looks of the man.

"First thing I noticed he was a goddamned cat. He was everywhere so fast I couldn't keep an eye on him. Second thing I noticed was his knowledge of marlinspike. He could tie more knots than any of us ever heard of and splice a cable like it was manila. Third thing I noticed was his way with the others. We had one of those second mates could navigate but was Joe Klutz out on deck. Cavalieri right away saved him from screwing up without embarrassing him. The ordinaries and ABs liked to work for him, followed him around like old dogs telling him their troubles.

"How many knots you know?" I asked him one day.

"More'n anybody needs," he said.

"Usually you need a bowline once in a while, a clove hitch, a square knot and a good technique for faking down and paying out line, but this guy had a whole marlinspike book in his head. He made boatswain's lace for the guys' foc's'ls and showed 'em how to make up a tugboat bowline, a fast kind of flashy way to make up a bowline. He'd chip paint and sludge with the best of them. Most bosuns just supervise and shit the mates. Hell, I'd never seen a mate on his hands and knees before. That's how he gave orders mostly—he'd just hunker down and start working.

"We had a kraut captain, a good old fart which is why I knew I could hire Cavalieri, name of Gus Altdorfer. He used to stand on the bridge and nudge me whenever he'd see Bo down on his knees working. Gus purely damn loved it. He'd'a been amazed to hear Bo speak German, but with a name like Bo Cavalieri it never occurred to the old boy.

"Docking or undocking—deep-sea sailors are hardly ever as good as lake or tug men at it—I hardly needed the bosun or the second mate with Bo around. The man talked so damned little, I often saw him give an order by just pointing at something with his eyes or signaling with his hand, usually with a little grin like it was a joke he shared with the men.

"Later I heard that sometimes in union halls guys who'd sailed with him'd ask is Cavalieri the bosun before they signed on to a ship. They were looking for him. Bosun is usually the union steward. Some bosuns suck up to the captain or mate, others turn a beef into a brouhaha, but Cavalieri'd just wait for the right moment, come out with a solution and more often as not the skipper'd say, Okay, thanks Bo, and that was that.

"Most captains'd pay a chunk of their own salary for such a bosun. A bad bosun is like sailing with a short crew, you're in for it and you sleep bad. Good bosun's next best thing to being home for Christmas. For some of us anyway. Probably not him.

"If a port had a museum or some art galleries, that's where he'd go, usually with a little backpack. It took me a few cruises to find out what he had in the pack—sketchbooks, pencils, charcoal, chalk, stuff like that. But he'd always find the crew toward sundown and put in some wet time with us. He wasn't a big drinker, not then. Oh he'd get messed up every once in a while, but it wasn't religious. In the Navy you never see the officers drinking with the enlisted and in the merchant marine you didn't see the licensed and unlicensed mixing too much either, so he'd wait till the unlicensed invited him over and they most always did because they figured he was one of them. Pissed off some officers to see him so content with the deck apes and black gangs, but them kind ain't worth diddly anyhow.

"He had a habit if he'd been on a ship awhile of making these drawings—people working, faces, machinery, tackle. If he saw you liked something he'd give it to you. Of course after a while damned near everybody wanted a picture. I'm not an artist, but I knew damned well that had to be unusual, so one time, maybe it was our third ship together, I said, So you don't think much of your talent. I mean I see you just give the stuff away. And he said, Of course not, if I did I'd be an artist. Well, hell, you couldn't touch that with a boat hook, not unless you knew something.

"We shipped together on and off oh maybe thirteen years. I helped him study for his second mate's ticket. I'll never forget it because he didn't take a single damn course, he just cracked the books and hung out in chartrooms. Only navigator I ever knew had all fifty or so navstars in his head. I used to imagine the inside of his skull was like a planetarium. I don't know if he had a photographic memory or what, but he had Bowditch & Knowles in his head chapter and verse and he knew most harbors better than the pilots. When he took the second mate's test down on the Battery he passed that three-day sucker first try. So he started shipping as second mate, but even then he'd sign on as a bosun or even an AB if he felt like it, depending on who was aboard and where they were going.

"Then he just disappeared. We were in Hamburg on this Greek clunker, the *Vestris*, and he got mixed up with some German girl and I never saw him again. Course he spoke German, so maybe he's still there. Hell, for all I know he's shipping for Hapag. I asked them at the Masters, Mates and Pilots Association and any other union I knew and they said damn if they knew. I put a notice, the kind you always see some crazed wife or girlfriend writing, in the *Seafarers International Log* and a couple of other trade papers, but nothing happened. He didn't own anything I could tell, so he had no address except his last one and my letters kept coming back saying return to sender, no forwarding address. He usually rented down in the village somewhere, liked to be around artists. I visited two apartments he lived in different times. There'd be a bedroll behind a Japanese screen, a couple of white chests with cushions on them, and that was it, except for paintings on the wall and star charts.

"It's funny, I was so sad about missing him, all I could think of was where in hell're the paintings? You could say we were brothers. Better'n that really. I could date it back to when we got slopped sitting on a dock in Alexandria and passing a bottle of Courvoisier back and forth and he told me about the Vikings, that'd be my ancestors . . ."

"Not mine?" Jolene says.

"Yeah, Jo, yours too. And the Arabs, that'd be his, how they used to run into each other at sea and they'd both think they'd met the devil's own. Jesus, it was funny the way he told it. Course, when you're snockered you always think you're having a great conversation. The Vikings would say, These goddamned wiry demons can sail fifteen points off the wind, so they gotta be devils. And the Arabs would say, We met a race of—what'd he say, genies maybe?—with big blue holes in their heads and muscles like horses, so they gotta be devils. Then he explained the lateen rigs the Arabs used that let them sail close to the wind and maneuver real tight, and the Vikings, they used square sails and needed a following wind, so the Arab ships scared the crap outta them. Jesus, I remember that night better than all the hurricanes I ever rode out. There we were sniffing the crotch of the sexiest damn city I ever knew, chucking that good stuff down and smoking big cigars, me too damned mean-looking for my own peace of mind and him sorta like a long shadow, two fuck-you-all sailormen without a care in the world.

"Well, that's what I thought then. Oh yeah, we had something else in common, scars. I have this big white one from the corner of my right eye down to my mouth. Guess it's kinda ruddy now. You'd think I was some kind of brawler, but it was just a souvenir from my foolish youth . . ."

Jolene had heard the story, but she thought it best to let him ramble. He told it like she'd never heard it before, like she never noticed the scar.

"When I was a third mate I tried to break up a fight between two Rican BR's and got a face full of steel for my trouble. Scares the shit outta guys who don't know me, makes me feel like a jerk. His was different. Every time he got a haircut you'd see this ugly mess of ridges in the back of his head and the few times I saw him without a shirt you'd see the same thing across his left shoulder. He got caught in a MiG strafing run in Korea, trying to haul a dead pilot through the canopy of his plane. Shrapnel tore him all to hell. Every once in a while you'd see him picking little glass slivers out of the scars on his head. I asked him about it once and he said shit happens. Then what? I says. If you could make him smile you could make him talk. So he told me about it. His name was Les Richardson, he says. I went to Columbia with him, he says. He graduated, I didn't. Now he's dead. You liked him? I ask. Yeah, he said, yeah, he was a big football hero from Utah. They used to give you tickets to go into this big Quonset hut and take exams. The proctors didn't know who you were. Fuck, that was okay, I didn't know who I was either. I took Les's ticket and went in and faked his English exam. He was a fuck-off but a nice guy. I guess he was in the NROTC because I caught up with him on a carrier in Korea. He was flying Banshees and I was a coxswain and a UDT man. We went out and tried to rescue them when they went down. I got caught in a crossfire from the beach and then this MiG came in low and chopped us up like dog chow. There were three of us. Two guys bought it and I hauled Les's dead ass back to the ship.

"I don't know why, but something about Bo's story pissed me off good. You're a professional loser, y'know that? I says. God, I wish I never said that. I mean, you know, I loved this guy. Anyway, he thought about it a while and all the time I'm kicking my ass, then he smiles this crooked little smile and says, Yeah, so how come the hero's dead and I ain't? And the funny thing is, you wanna talk about heroes, that's how he got a Silver Star, which the Navy don't hand out like Purple Hearts. Course he got them too, coupla times. Christ, if there was any words I'd liked to never've said it was them, cause he must've lost it, like I put a curse on him or something, which maybe is what he figured out by the time we got to Hamburg and that's why I never saw him again."

★

Who the hell's he talking to, Jolene wonders, explaining about his scar as if he were on a telephone and his listener can't see it. Her bones want to walk out on her skin. It's spooky, this doctored prayer of his. It sounds like something you'd tell a phone-sex line on your dime. Sure, she knows he whored around after he met her, but he wouldn't do it under her nose and everything else about their marriage was fine. She doesn't believe that crap about the half-German Bo latching up with some fraulein and staying there. She knows damned well Bo Cavalieri is far more married to the sea than her husband.

What's this about? They'd heard the ice move, both of them, and this phony story is what he comes up with. Here's a Weybrandt Gundersen she hardly knows.

Now, sitting in the kitchen four nights in a row, like it's a Maundy vigil, hearing about his life at sea, she recognizes fully that she has married a rare man. She knew he was good. Vince saw that right away, and she trusts Vince's judgment even now.

But this kitchen talk, him puffing slowly, while she darns socks and sweaters, sets her to marveling.

For example, there was the time the Wonder Bread across the street, Bill Conley, whose specialty is to weird you out and then cut you off, said to Brandt, Hey, pal, how're you? It was the first time she realized the emphasis was always on the *you* with Conley. Brandt had spread his feet and stared at the guy. Now, she thought, where did he get the antenna to pick up on that? The guy's invalidating your ticket, right? She didn't get it, but he got it as naturally as a pitcher popping bubble gum.

Jolene, rapt Swedenborgian, can't get Brandt to come with her to the Church of the New Jerusalem. He never says a word against religion, hers or anyone's. He just won't go. He must have encountered enough piety in Oppdal.

And yet he comes home three years ago with an appallingly papist tattoo he got down in Pernambuco's Olinda. She examines this Twelfth Station Christ on his arboreal left forearm over and again. Nowhere has she seen such a profoundly crucified Jesus. When she traces it with her fingertips sobs rise in her chest. But he won't talk about it except to say, "Some bozo needed the money."

He dislikes tattoos. Being big, he's never had to prove anything by getting one. He's never been a longhaired, earringed, bearded, bare-chested, necklaced or mustachioed man. Never had to be. But he doesn't disdain such men. You just do what you have to do to get by. Jolene figures the tattoo is something he needs to get by.

But as he sits for four nights talking about Bo Cavalieri she sees that the tattoo is like Vince de Ciantis's sculptures after he got to know Jolene Karlsdottir. It incarnates how he feels. She knows more than that: the tattoo isn't Cavalieri or Brandt, it's their sacramental friendship. Still more, it's their love. And it's characteristic of Jolene to understand that the love between her and Brandt will be whole again only if Brandt goes back to Hamburg and brings home the horrified child he left shanghaied there. She knows, really, that her husband must do what long ago Bo Cavalieri had instinctively done: take the child home.

★

That was three nights before the phone rings and Bo Cavalieri is on the other end after seven years. She picks the phone up in the middle of another story. Maybe he says some more, maybe not, she doesn't hear. She stares through her kitchen window down onto the entrance to Lincoln Tunnel until tears blind her. She just stands there. She can't find words. Then she turns around and says, "It's Bo."

She grabs Poodle's leash. She won't stay and listen. She can't, like the Israelites, complain that all she has to eat is this manna.

Gundy jumps up and knocks over their coffee pot. He's not one to play anything cool. "Where the hell you been, you sonofabitch?"

"You said it," Bo says.

"I'm fuckin' pissed at you, droppin' off the face of the earth like that."

"I need your help, Gundy."

"You got it. Where are you?"

"Cross the river."

"Get over here."

"What's your address? I'll see you tomorrow."

"You kiddin'? Get your ass over here now."

Bo takes two hours to get over to Weehawken. He's forgotten how. He unfolds himself out of a cab and starts up Jolene's gardened walk. He's wearing his old pea coat and a lopsided grin. To Gundy he looks like a camp survivor. When he gets to the top step the two men look into each other's face, their jaws jutting. Gundy looks up and down Leyden Street as if he doesn't want to be overheard. "Jeez, I missed you, you skinny bastid." He

116

clamps Bo's shoulders and starts to shake him, making sure he's there. Then he falls on him and holds him till he starts to get embarrassed by his sobs. He shoves Bo inside and back to the kitchen where he makes a fresh pot of coffee.

Jolene and Poodle are down at the corner of Leyden and Hasbrouck. When she sees them go inside she starts home.

When he sits down across the table from Bo Gundy pours them coffee. "So?"

"So I've been shipping. Junk flags. Liberian. Panamanian. Singaporean. I forget 'em all. Booze, shit pay, no questions. Then I got sick. Face turned red. Liver wouldn't kick over. I felt like dunnage. One night I'm lying on my ass watching this parade of shitbirds—big turds with tin wings—march across the ceiling. I couldn't stand up, so I started crawling around the room examining the grain in the wood on the floor."

★

Maybe there are no better moments, if you reach an age to savor it, than two people genuinely happy to see each other. After all, it's always before the trouble starts. Jolene Gundersen reached such an age early in her childhood, so it's all of a piece with her nature to clasp her hands in delight to see her husband Weybrandt and his friend, Bo Cavalieri, hug each other after years of separation. But she's braced for the trouble.

Gundy has heard the anaconda drop out of the trees, and he's listening now.

Bo is clueless. He has no idea he and Gundy are holding onto the same boat, trying to stay sober. He never thought a sober Weybrandt Gundersen would have acted differently that night in Hamburg. He isn't forgiving Gundy because he wants something. He isn't forgiving Gundy. He's simply changed. Gundy suspects he can grant Bo a favor and still not get back his old friend. Bo himself is somebody who'd do a favor not expecting it to have an afterlife. Gundy looks to Jolene, busying herself about the edges of the kitchen, for help. She gives him the best advice she can—zip your lip, she signals. He tries that, but he was never as comfortable with silence as Bo, so he plunges into conversation.

"J'ever notice the different tones of bell buoys? I hear some—mostly up by the Scapa Flow—they make me think of God. I hear others—chintzy little ones—drive me to drink."

Bo figures he has two choices, sit there and savor the notion of a chintzy bell buoy and how it might sound or jump down Gundy's throat. He likes the second choice better because he says, "You don't need a chauffeur to go that route, you drive yourself."

"Remember the *Transmontana* over to Palermo," Gundy says. "Cap'n Joyce, crazy ole man liked nothing better'n a storm, calls you up to the bridge and says, Bo, some of the Eye-talian friends here tell Naval Intelligence we liketa pick up some fireworks, musta glommed some onta the hull 'cause we sure'n hell didn't let no foreigners on board, did we?"

Bo doesn't remember.

"See where I'm headin', old son? You say, Yessir. You knew that crazy old bastard wanted you to take a dive. Without tanks I can't stay down long enough, you says."

It begins to come back to Bo.

"You remember what that whacko said? He said, Well, we can't wait for the Navy to come outta Naples and we can't ask the Eye-talians 'cause this here cargo's classified. So you, bein' an ole frogman, Bo, and believe me, I hate to ask, but I was wonderin' if you would take a little look-see, you know, for God and country and all that happy shit. It ain't a order, Bo, I mean that, he said. Damn, that's what that sumbitch said and me shittin' my pants 'cause I figure we must be carrying an atomic bomb. You remember what you said?"

Bo looks at Jolene like he knows Gundy is going to tell him. She winks. But she has no idea where this is going.

"Been a while, Cap'n, you says. Lotsa new technology, but it won't blow our asses off to look. Then you looked at me like maybe you knew it could. So, when you leave to get suited up, Joyce says to me, Best goddam bosun in the Muriken merchant marine. And I says, I sure'n hell hope he ain't gonna be the best goddam dead bosun, Cap'n. Well, considerin' what we're hauling, Gundy, if that happens we won't be around to mourn him, Joycie says. I looked at that ole coot hard as I could tryin' to figure out how many pages in the SOP he skipped and then I says, I'll order the crew off, Cap'n. Joycie, he looks kinda confused and sad. He says, Yeah, you do that, Gundy. Means you too, Cap'n, I says. Hell no, what can you be thinking, Chief? he says. I forgot, see, the sumbitch likes trouble so much. But I needed to press the point, so I says, I'm thinkin' we ain't underway, Cap'n. If she blows, that's all she wrote. Eye-talians cross the way, they already got up steam. No call for two to go up with her. Bo knows that. Hell, he ain't even gonna look back is how his brain works. I said that, Bo."

"Well, that's very nice, Brandt," Jolene says, "but I'm sure Bo doesn't understand it any more than I do, do you, Bo?"

One of the things that binds drunks to each other and makes them think there's no better friendship in the world is that they think they're talking in a marvelous code that shortcuts all the usual flapdoodle and gets them straight to the mysteries of life. A bit of this magic thinking comes back to Bo when he thinks he knows what Gundy's talking about and takes a stab at it.

Still looking at Jolene, his Adam's apple bobbles and he says, "Drunks always think they've got a few lives to throw away. Only interesting thing I remember about Captain Joyce was he wasn't a drunk and still liked to put his neck on the block, to say nothing of everybody else's. You and me, Gundy, we weren't that interesting, just a coupla goddamned falling-down drunks."

Jolene looks away from Bo to her husband. He hadn't been very brave beating around the bush like that, but he was afraid that whatever set Bo off in Hamburg would bite him again. She figures that, as usual, her husband needs a little help. The difference is she isn't going to give him any.

"I can't tell a story like you can, Bo, you know, like the Arabs and the Vikings. Can you still tell a story, Bo?"

"I don't know, Gundy. Without the booze they don't come out right, I don't think. Whudda you think?"

"They don't come out too good. Hell, maybe they never did. Truth is I'm not as full of shit as I used to be." He sits there grinning like an orangutan, liking what he said.

For two bozos who'd brawled and staggered their way around the world more times than they could remember they sure are having a helluva time telling each other they're off the sauce, Jolene thinks.

"Truth is, Bo, I don't drink anymore. I mean, I gave it up. Truth is, well, it started to taste bad after . . . you know, after . . ."

"I'm off it, too, Gundy. You go to AA?"

"Yeah. You?"

"No, I dried out in Bellevue."

"You wanna come? With me, I mean."

Most boozy friendships don't survive sobriety. They're not between people anyway, they're between poseurs and their props. Sobriety ties the tongue and kicks out the props. If one friend is still drinking he's apt to feel ditched and judged by the other, but he won't fess up. He's more likely to judge. Old so-and-so can't hold his booze, huh?

Watch a few old black-and-white movies from the thirties and forties. The characters can't navigate a room without pouring themselves a drink. They can't take good or bad news without drinking to it. They can't converse or say anything witty or fortify themselves against adversity or recover from ordeals or rise to ideals. You can hardly imagine a room in one of those movies without a bottle or two in it. The bottle is even more common than the bad music. Would a teetotaler write such scripts? They sure don't show much faith in the human psyche.

If you eat the star-shaped San Pedro cactus in Peru you feel like you're flying. Maybe you will fly over the Nazca Lines in the desert and see the big starship airfield and the condors that are drawn for miles in the desert. Nazcan pottery shows falcons flying with the San Pedro in its talons. But without San Pedro you must have more imagination and be braver.

Bo hasn't been sober long enough to see friendships slip away, to grieve and then finally feel well rid of them. He doesn't have any to forfeit, and in any case he's never run short of reasons to be rid of anybody. But he must have had a premonition that he and Gundy are going to have to do without foley artists and special effects because he fetched a box of Cohibas out of his fridge before setting out for Weehawken.

We don't get many chances to make a thing come out right. Most of the time we settle for half right because we're not up to the challenge. But something in a seaman wants a thing right and maybe that something pipes up louder in a sober seaman.

"About the girl . . ." Gundy says.

Jolene holds her breath. She sits in her chair in their kitchen like a finch about to take wing.

"Her name is Ute-Britt Broghammer. The boy's name was Lakhdar Ali Wahab. I buried him in a town called Oued Zem in Morocco."

Bo says it slowly, carefully.

Jolene gets it all. She hears the old anger. She even thinks she can spell the names. The girl is alive, the boy not—she gets that too—and most especially she gets that Bo is not about to cut her husband any slack.

But Gundy isn't looking for any. He pulls his ubiquitous ballpoint out of his shirt pocket, grabs a paper napkin and shoves them at Bo. "You better write them down for me." This is better than any movie Jolene has ever seen—she likes Garbo's savage teeth—she watches Bo not as a rival for her husband's love but as a doctor who can heal him or a saint who can give him grace.

Bo writes, hanging the umlaut on Ute's name, following Lakhdar's name with the Arabic. "I don't know much Arabic, but this is the way his name looks. He hung himself in his attic when he saw Ute-Britt go off with you."

Christ Jesus, Jolene thinks, he's not giving an inch. Bo stares at Gundy, his face stony. He has taken the whole thing as an attack on himself, she sees, on his Arab self. As if he'd read her mind, Bo turns to her and says, "It's not just he was an Arab kid, it was like Gundy and Ute-Britt were my mother and her whole goddam family."

There are a lot of ways to go from here. Gundy could be pissed that after years of sulking Bo has brought this mess to his home in Weehawken and dumped it on their kitchen table, in the lap of their marriage. That's one way to go. And

121

if you go that way you have to feel that Bo's more or less permanently half-cocked and never will be a pal again. Then, on the other hand, you can say he's clearing the air to resume their friendship, putting everything on the table so there'll be no misunderstanding, nothing to brood about. If you go that way, you have to ask yourself where he gets off dumping this on Jolene. Then there's the possibility that he doesn't give a shit. Jolene doesn't seem upset at either man. She wears the glow she has coming back from church meetings.

Bo collapses backwards on his chair, slumping. Gundy leans over the table and scratches his flattop with both hands. Then he looks up at Bo. "It was the worst thing I ever done. I didn't get it about the boy. It was about you. I wanted to find out what turned you on."

There, Jolene thinks, that's it, you can't strain the sex out of friendships, but you can have an eye for the precariousness of things, and one night in Hamburg it all broke down. Her gigantic husband just got too damned curious and got someone killed.

Bo grips the table and looks into his friend's face, slack-jawed. "Me? You dumb fuck!"

Gundy lets out a kind of gulp that would have been a yelp if he'd gotten his mouth open. The flesh around his eyes bunches up and the dunked crescent of his mouth starts to quiver. He looks over to his wife and finds her grinning. He looks back at Bo and sees his lips trying to stitch up a smile. Then the three of them explode into laughter. Gundy hammers the table and stomps his feet. Jolene dips her hand into a bowl of cold oatmeal and glops her husband's face. When Bo looks at her she throws a dollop at him too.

They let honesty save the day. They thought they had anyway, but Bo isn't about to say how complicated his feelings about Ute-Britt have become. He isn't about to say what Lakhdar's drawings revealed or what he knows about Ute-Britt's feelings. But he does say, "I send her money."

That sets Jolene to wiping her hands and thinking. He sends her money because my husband boffed her? He sends her money because of the boy? He sends her money because he boffed her? Maybe left her pregnant. He sends her money because my husband left her pregnant?

It stings Gundy. Gundy can't claw truth out of his head but he tries. He works on his jaw too. I boff the girl, the kid kills himself, and Bo sends her money. The girl was pregnant when I boffed her. Who made her pregnant? I get three choices. I only like one of them. Actually I don't like any of them.

"You send her money?"

Jolene's ready for them to drop it. There is a time to let well enough alone. She aims a kick at Gundy under the table, but one of Bo's long legs gets in the way. He looks at her with a crazy grin. "All right," she says, "I give up, whose baby did she have?"

Bo takes a dog-eared snapshot of mother and child out of his wallet and hands it to her. "It's not mine," he says. Not Gundy's either, she sees. Gundy and that girl would have had the blondest, bluest-eyed child in the top of the world. "Like me," Bo says, "half Arab, half German."

"What's the boy's name?" Gundy asks.

"Tariq." But Bo knows that whenever Ute-Britt says it his own name is never far off.

★

In the old days by this time of day Jolene would be fortifying their coffee. Now she has to face that they'd run out of sailor's gas. Well, she doesn't have to, they do.

Gundy, never one to wait to be waited on, gets up and starts messing with a fresh pot of coffee. "Used to like this stuff, now I hate the hell outta it. Smells like benzene."

Bo grins at Jolene and reaches for the Cohibas in the brown paper bag. "Give these up too?"

Gundy falls on the box, holding it up and sniffing at it. Then he pulls out his rigging knife and cuts the seal.

"Hell, I might just have one myself," Jolene says. She feels a small hope that their friendship might not dry up.

Bo says, "Gets pretty old grunting Tagalog on junk ships months on end. Course that wasn't the reason I got to be a dumb-ass drunk. Couldn't keep the dragons happy any more. So I had to go down to the cellar and see if maybe I could kill 'em. I was swimming the East River at night, maybe a dozen times, drunk out of my skull, and they picked me up and parked me in Bellevue."

Jolene has gotten up and is standing behind Bo massaging his head.

They're silent. Jolene likes this silence. She thinks it bodes well. She picks out two cigars, unwraps them, cuts their heads off with Gundy's knife, hands one to Bo and keeps one herself. The men think of Calvados, of dipping their cigars in it, but they say nothing. They just look at each other forlornly. Then the three of them light up and start to fill Jolene's immaculate kitchen, where she never lets anybody smoke, with blue smoke.

"The way I figure it," she says, "you can't load up with grain where you've been carrying light sweet crude unless you strip the sludge in those tanks."

She knows right off what Gundy's look means. It means, Jeez, Jolene, that's like one of those sayings you bring home from church, sounds great but what in hell does it mean? Bo looks more encouraging. She takes another stab. "You gotta give up some things for new things, better things."

"Like what?" Gundy says.

"Like thinking straight for starters. Like cutting out the bullshit. Like . . ."

"Thinking before you boff"—he grabs the napkin to see who he boffed—"Ute-Britt Broghammer."

"Something like that," Jolene says. She says it laconically, but she is unspeakably proud that he understands he has to speak the girl's name.

Puffing away in her kitchen with her men, as she's always thought of them, Jolene remembers the pot roast marinating in her fridge. She has one of those wicked inspirations for which she is notorious among the brethren of The Church of the New Jerusalem. Sauerbraten, she announces when she serves it after midnight.

"You think maybe the Norwegians're thick," Gundy says to Bo, "she thinks anything she makes is Danish."

"The Norwegians are thick," Jolene says. "So are the Germans. Right, Bo? I'm serving sauerbraten in honor of Bo—he is a kraut, you know—and Ute-Britt Broghammer."

Poor Gundy swallows hard and wonders how often Jo is going to bring it up. Then he gamely lifts his glass of mineral water. "To Ute-Britt and her friend, this half-ass Arab here—yeah, and to Scandinavian diplomacy. Can ya spell it, Jolene?"

The Gundersens trade their hallmark wait-till-I-get-you-in-the-bedroom look when they see Bo is going to need the Heimlich maneuver if he can't get his choked-down laughter out. Jolene runs around to the other side of the table and slams his back. Neither of them had ever seen Bo laugh freely. "Oh Christ," he says when he stops shaking, "only diplomatic Scandinavians I ever met were Swedes."

"Hell, those Nazi-suckers ain't Scandinavians," Gundy thunders, laughing along with Bo.

Late that night Poodle takes the men for a walk along the Edgewater waterfront. "It's not just I'm tired of grunting Malay, Swahili and Baroombian, it's my pension. I gotta put in a few more years under Old Gory. You think you can get me back in good with the union, Gundy?"

"What's Baroombian?"

"I made it up to see how much damage Johnny Walker did to you."

"I'll pound a few heads, Bo, but you gotta promise me something."

"This is gonna be good."

"I want you to ship chief mate."

"Well, hell, Gundy, I'll ship chief if you ship master."

Gundy cuts Poodle loose and stares at his old friend. They squint and cock their ears as if to get past the drunk laughter from a restaurant barge.

"This is serious shit, Bo, y'know that? I mean we pretty near boozed our way 'round the world five or six times thinkin' we were pretty smart shippin' out less than we could be. I don't know what the name of that game is, but I know it's a drunk-ass game. Something like fuck'n run, maybe."

"Maybe."

"I'm not sayin' maybe, asshole, I'm saying you ship chief or I don't help you."

"Okay, captain, if that's the way you feel about it."

"That's my buddy." Gundy crunches Bo's shoulders together with one arm. "We might could get over this thing, y'know. Being sober, I mean."

★

When he returns from Weehawken late the next morning and looks into his ashen loft from the freight elevator he sees the red eye of his answering machine winking. Few people outside of David Llewellyn know where he is or have reason to call him. He goes into the kitchen area near the elevator and makes himself a mug of coffee. Unless he needs light he usually walks around among the shapes and shadows chiseled by the light from outside. He rewinds the answering machine and waits. He finishes his coffee by the time the tape stops. Something must have screwed it up. He switches to play and listens. He hears crackling. He knows it's a good tape, so perhaps it's a long-distance call. Then he hears the caller hang up. The next call crackles, then offers some background noise—a door shutting, some classical music—then another hang-up. The next caller breathes, but it isn't what cops would call a breather. Each call is somewhat different and yet similar, the same background noise. He's dismayed at their number. He rewinds the tape to count the calls—twenty-two, twenty-two hang-ups in twelve hours.

Time-shares in Carolina? Swampland in Florida? Grape stock in California? He's never good at being flippant even in the privacy of his head. As usual, he knows more than he cares to cop to. These calls are from Margaret Wadeleigh pacing in her bone cage, flirting with her feelings, encoding autoerotic dispatches, dramatizing her ambivalences. But none of these reverberations describe the truth of the massed calls, which is that Margaret hurts. He understands this better than he's ever understood anything. These calls are not whimpers but long, eerie wails. Her calls achieve the one result that would disquiet her most, they awaken his longing for her mother. He sits on a black canvas footstool in the shadows watching the sun probe his loft, inhaling the attars of the neighborhood.

He thinks of Margaret in Lechlade, on her knees in her garden, attacking her blackboard, crossing out and going at it again. He tries hard to portray her as she herself would approve, he tries as hard as any masturbator would try to see her reaching down, sufficing herself. But all he can see is Margaret demented by the huge presence of her telephone. He doesn't want to be the sort of man who inspires such calls, but what sort of man is that? He doesn't want to feel their misery. He doesn't wish for the sake of his early love that her daughter should suffer, nor does he wish for Dacia's sake that her daughter should wish anyone to suffer. As the light lumbers into his dark space he sees that Margaret Wadeleigh and Ulrike Theiss act in the manner of a European countess who has a little tussle with an Arab boy one hot afternoon in a Moroccan alley and now studies him distastefully as she straightens her panties.

8

After his second mug of coffee he plops the answering machine in a bag, bears it to the Hudson and gives it up. Instead of relief he feels the panic of losing an irreplaceable instrument over the side. He goes home and sits in the shadows. His one gift to himself, his reminder to himself that it might be possible to live after being found so distasteful, is to unwrap a Cohiba and smoke it. He smokes it slowly, listening to the street, to the cables slap in his elevator shaft, to the fridge cycling, to a fluorescent buzzing. Then he walks over to the counter where he's laid out his Coast Guard papers and licenses from eight foreign nations. He's looking them over dourly when the phone rings. He doesn't think she will speak. He wonders if he will say her name. Unaccustomed to announcing his name or even answering telephones, he picks it up on the fourth ring and says hello.

"Bo? Is this Bo?"

"Yes."

"It's Ulrike, Bo. Your mother."

My mother. Myyy—mother.

"Bo, it's you, isn't it?"

Yes, he decides, it might be, yes, it would be all right to be him. "Yes, it's Bo." Ulrike always prompts him to question everything, even his name.

She's exhilarated, as if she has marvelous news. He remembers the sound. It foreshadows something bad. Countess Hot Pants returns to her hotel and perhaps her husband after being naughty.

"It's Hart, Bo, he's quite sick. I don't know what to do."

"Hart?"

128

"Your stepfather, Bo."

He pulls another cigar out of his pocket, unwraps it and lights up. Mother Hubbard, yeah, the guy Sandro called Mother Hubbard. Owned the building next to Sandro. So he not only gets to play the Arab boy, he gets to play the goddamn hotel and the concierge and the husband too. He looks out the window and grins. This husband is clearly a fucking wimp. All things being equal, he'd rather be the countess's panties.

"Where are you?" Would Kuala Lampur be too much to ask? He pulls the grinning mask off his face—Ulrike's usual theatricality, not Hart's illness, amuses him.

"Cape May. We were driving up from Sanibel and we stopped to see friends. When we left we stopped for coffee. He went to the men's room and he just keeled over. Somebody found him sitting between urinals. How soon can you come?"

"Not more than four hours. What hospital are you in?"

"I—wait a minute—I don't know."

"Let me speak to a nurse. You go on back to . . . Hart. I'll be there soon."

"Uh, thank you, thank you, a million thanks."

When he puts down the phone he walks the depth of his loft to a big star chart between his two big east-facing factory windows. He traces the Southern Cross with his middle finger as if he needs it to get to Cape May. His life is as it always has been. No one to call, no arrangements to make, except to rent a car. He has without knowing it achieved a state of grace rare among abandoned men or women—the habit of letting it alone when someone in whom he dared to hope re-enacts the familiar scene, the habit of not spilling himself over into a bad scene. Where Margaret is gone, or why, doesn't matter. She's as surely gone as her mother, without ado or adieu. But Dacia hasn't chosen to go and it seems likely and even comfortable that he will recall her tears when he dies. Someone had wanted him once and he had returned the gift. Now it finally comes to him that their custodians never gave it a thought.

As he passes the counter that divides the kitchen from the rest of the loft he does something he saw the holy man do in

Oued Zem. He picks up a cracker crumb and puts it in his pocket for future use. It is, the Maghrebi Arabs would say, baraka. The closest English word is grace. He picks up a little grace. Maybe he'll feed it to a bird.

Using the pearl-handled Solingen straight razor Armin Steegemueller gave him, he nicks his jawbone, applies styptic and continues shaving, but he finds himself refusing his eyes the pleasure of his company. Someone's waiting up there above his nose, someone he dreads. A darker, feral being whose gaze is so intent it will gut his eyes if he looks. So of course he looks. He sees the jackal-headed messenger god, Anubis, the god who guides the dead wherever they're going.

"Hey babe, lookin' good."

This part of his craziness he was accustomed to long before the DTs. His mirrored familiars are Set, Kali, Lord Krishna, a long row of Sufi ruminants and now Anubis.

"How's tricks? Where's your pal Charon? Pickin' up Styx? Gotta message for me?"

This badinage staves off discourse. Usually it erases the interlocutor, but Anubis hangs on, fading in perfumed steam, reappearing.

"What's that they say about getting long of tooth? Hey, I don't expect you to declaim like Laurence Olivier, but you got the staff, make a gesture or something. All right, fuck you then."

You too.

He can't be sure he heard that, used as he is to answering himself, but he likes the idea of it.

He packs a shoulder bag, stuffs in a sketch pad and pencils and chalks, leaves a spotlight on the Southern Cross, leaves a message for Llewellyn, and sets out for Cape May.

★

How desolate Ulrike's life must be to call him. How like the artist to describe Hart slumped between urinals. He heard the humor in her voice even in her extremity.

Mother Hubbard down between urinals. Hart would be out in the street complaining about people setting out trash in front of his building when Bo came home from school. Once he told Bo to tell his father to get his pavement fixed. Bo told Sandro and Sandro jumped out of his chair shouting, "Where is he, where's the son-of-a-bitch?" Hart, always cordial, amusing, sardonic, his pale blue eyes filled with misgivings, had given him a speech about how proud he'd be of his father if he could persuade him to do his civic duty. Bo preferred Sandro's response. He recognized smarm even better than Sandro. Ulrike's family almost drowned him in it.

The only mean experience he ever had with Hart was when he wrote to Ulrike that he would like Sandro's E.W. Lane version of *The Thousand and One Nights* because it was frescoed with marginal annotations in Sandro's hand. "Of course you may have the book, if I can locate it," Hart wrote, "but I feel constrained to remind you that your mother has no fiduciary responsibility to you whatsoever." What made the man feel so constrained? Protectiveness towards Ulrike against the importuning of an undeserving son? That's what he believed until the weight of it anchored him in his drunken abyss of hurt and shame. If he'd been fairer, less hawkish, less foreign, more gracious, more loving, more acceptable, perhaps Sandro's *Alf Layla wa-Layla* would not have been so great a gift to ask nor such a chore to give. If he'd looked like those English choirboys at Cairnhall perhaps Ulrike herself might have written. Of course, dear, you may have Sandro's book. How are you? When shall I see you?—things his classmates' English parents might have written. Given the exaggerated effect Hart's reply had on him, too bad he couldn't have known that Hart, the lethargic antiquarian book trader, had already sold Sandro's book.

Bo loves English drawing-room movies because of the civility with which the characters treat each other, because a prodigal son's rights are coped with, because certain things are beyond the pale, because people incur obligations to each other. Once out of Cairnhall he lived with the barbarians, however much he had been savaged in Cairnhall, and he knew that some of them were fair and acceptable, and he was not.

Why in God's name is he driving like your average son

to Cape May? Once more to prove he's not so different after all from the fair children of Cairnhall, from Dacia whom he loved? To prove, despite his Saracen blood, that he's decent and honorable? Sandro wished him to be proud of his Saracen blood. The Sicilians inherited much from their Saracen overlords, their favorite overlords, including the blood feud and memories of slights that wait generations for satisfaction. But it was too late for Sandro to detoxify him. Sandro didn't know what happened at Cairnhall. Bo buried it too deep. Sandro never understood that Bo didn't feel like Ulrike's child, that he was merely coping with the hand dealt him and would prefer any number of Sicilian mothers.

To look like Ulrike is to have your papers in order in this country. Germans know all about not having your papers in order. Isn't it a movie cliché? To look like Bo is to be in trouble, something like trying to stay calm in a Paris bus while being studied by a Gestapo officer. Maybe the Sicilians understand this. God knows they had their problems with the somewhat more acceptable Irish in this country. But the Sicilians had each other, in great numbers, and better yet they had the Black Hand, their little thing from the Arabs. Bo, until he encountered Sandro, had nothing like that, and so he spent his early life either charming or ducking Gestapo officers and their stooges and quislings. He traveled in mufti, civilian clothes, knowing that looking too much the Saracen is asking for it.

Fiduciary responsibility? God. A Sandro still on his feet would have shaken the teeth out of the man. I've got to go see Sandro's grave at Woodlawn. Then I'll grab a bulk carrier and get the fuck outta here. Here? he hears Llewellyn ask. You mean inside where you live? Belay that, I'll ship where Gundy tells me. He'll get my union papers reinstated. They owe me the fucking pension. But, as always, he likes the thought of getting out. He likes it too much. He hates the new container ships. They don't even look like ships. They go back and forth to the same damn places. Elizabeth, Rotterdam, Felixstowe. Their crews mostly try to make a living by shipping as little as they can and working as little they can when they do. If he ships one more month than he must to get his pension, instead of studying at Cooper Union, instead of taking himself seriously, he may as well pack it in. He puts his musing down to entertainment. In the end he'll do what he always does, follow his feet. But he notes that when Ulrike calls he puts on his watch cap and pea coat—to have an identity in the face of her stranger's stare. He's the stranger. He knows that. And his father before him knew it. But at least his father got something for his trouble. Whatever else he could be, he's a seaman. That belongs to him.

The overwrought Victorian houses of Cape May bemuse him. What fun those carpenters must have had, like bosuns with their Turk's-heads and monkey fists and gig lace. He wishes he could stop and draw the gingerbread, the cupolas, widow's walks and madness of roof valleys.

Once inside Edison Memorial Hospital he thinks about Llewellyn's title for a play about Ulrike's life, *Entrances and Denials.* Curtain going up. He wonders if he's prepared to applaud. He finds her on the second floor, two nurses comforting her. "Don't cry, dear," one of them is saying, "you'll spoil your pretty eyes." That earns Ulrike's attention. She stares gratefully at her latest benefactor. Now there's a cunning nurse. Ulrike must be 75 by now. C'mon, ole buddy, he tells himself, don't be a spoilsport, get with the mood. "She's terribly upset," the other nurse tells him, "are you the son?" There's a question. He grins lopsidedly. Then he nods courteously. It isn't her fault for asking a foolish question. Who would steal a scene from Ulrike? God knows he's tried. Now it's a luxury not to. She looks up at him with eyes that set him reeling among movie stars: Barbara Stanwyck, Ida Lupino, Loretta Young. No, not quite right. He has the right one: Maria Schell. Yeah. He smiles comfortingly, rubs her back and asks, "How is he?"

"They don't know."

"We've just finished the tests," the artful nurse tells him. "Doctor Chandrivar will talk to you in the morning. Mr. Clement should sleep now."

He can't remember how long it's been since he's seen Ulrike, and he can't remember if he ever knew Hart's last name.

133

"Doctor Ranieri has given him a sedative," the nurse says. "There's nothing more we can do tonight."

"Ask them what's wrong with him," Ulrike says. The nurse shakes her head at Bo.

"Have you eaten, Ulrike?"

"Of course not—how could I eat when Hart is so sick?"

He remembers that this is the kind of invitation he's always RSVPed to make sure the one with the suspicious teeth gets a good look at his throat. "Well, you have to eat to keep up your health so you can help him, Ulrike. C'mon, we'll get a bite to eat and find a place to stay."

The reenactment of the family scene unfolds well. He's still the revenant coldly going about things while the human beings live and breathe the drama.

Ulrike knows he's competent. It's competence born of indifference in her book, but reliable just the same. A son of hers would care and show it, but you could rely on this bird of a different feather to make the right arrangements, to act as if he's a devoted kinsman. But a keen observer such as herself senses the chill in his demeanor. It never occurred to Ulrike and doesn't now that these deplorably useful traits in Bo are classically German.

That the two Quaker country nurses seem unbothered by Bo's chilliness doesn't escape Ulrike's notice as cleanly as it once escaped her that Hettie Warshaw admired and loved him. In the din of conveying her emotions she doesn't trouble to apprehend what she might be feeling about him now. But she does know it's bitter to her when one of the nurses, patting her ropy hand, says, "Your son is here now—everything will be all right." He thinks of a black funeral he'd attended, the chief mourner arriving on the arms of nurses.

The remark prompts her to go for her compact. Bo manages not to smile. He tries instead to focus on the suffering and fear of a man he hardly knows. That seems safer, higher ground. He does after all know something about fear and pain. About motherhood he knows nothing, and it may be that alone that enables him to respect Ulrike Theiss. Empathic as he is, he knows where his empathy can't go as surely as he knows where not to send a laden ship.

A man from whom others vanish or abscond, he's learned that as with snakebite the antidote is the venom: he too vanishes. As a young man he put his hand down his throat until he felt his crotch and pulled himself inside out every time it happened. By the time he was seventeen he was undergoing the transmogrifications of Doctor Booze, the wax museum director. Now here he is cajoling the only person present at the creation to eat. As he watches her order an extra-dry Rob Roy in the lounge of a Ramada Inn, he thinks of Llewellyn's other title for Bo's biography, *Pimping for Mom*. He'd have brained Llewellyn with a belaying pin if he'd had one, but he was just so damned desperate he burst out laughing. A literalist wouldn't know what Llewellyn meant, but a literalist doesn't know what anybody means, or pretends not to. Llewellyn thought it was a breakthrough, him laughing, but Bo was laughing because he'd been sailing all his life and had never even seen a belaying pin, although he knew bosuns used to impose discipline with one. He listens to Ulrike ask the waitress where she put the Scotch in her drink.

He goes to the men's room and as he stands in front of the urinal he hears Sandro say, Ask him if he's still worried about Ulrike's fiduciary responsibility. He stitches a few rebel hairs into his fly as he hears Llewellyn say, And tell him to relax, Ulrike's gonna take good care of him. He looks down at the septic cake and thinks, With role models like you guys I should roll drunks for a living.

In this wicked frame of mind he rocks out of the men's room on his sea legs in time to catch a pitying grin from the waitress. He winks. "Hey, what can I say, I got lucky and drew her for a mother." The woman, who looks like she's had plenty of similar luck, tries dumbly to figure out how to giggle and flirt at the same time.

When Ulrike finishes her veal scaloppine (something you should never order in a motel restaurant), broccoli, salad, strawberry ice cream and a third Rob Roy, and he his sole almondine (not a good idea either) and salad, she theatrically produces her purse and shells out thirty-four dollars. When she heads for the rest room he checks the bill. It's for thirty-two dollars. He puts down another five and flags the waitress. "I don't believe she's your mother," the waitress says. He taps her arm with his fist a bit sadly. "Hold on to that thought, hon."

There he is, comfortable with riffraff, as always, Ulrike thinks as she comes back to their table in time to see him laughing with the waitress.

In the lobby he stops to study a vulvar Erté copy. "Great stuff, huh?" She laughs. He does know art. "Does Hart like art?" he asks.

"Books, he likes books, not to read, just to collect dust. His idea of art is Rockwell Kent."

"Oh, representational art," Bo says gamely.

"He's very sick, you know, Bo."

Well, that'd explain it.

"Let's see what Doctor Chandrivar says in the morning."

"Couldn't you ask for an American doctor like the one we spoke to?"

"He was Italian."

She looks at him with one of those you-don't-want-to-piss-off-the-queen looks.

"Well, with a name like Cavalieri, what would I know?"

"That's not your name, you know."

"Yeah, but Bo Theiss doesn't have that certain *je ne c'est quoi.*"

They both laugh and chant in unison, "Bo Theiss isn't your name either." Ulrike has two moods he likes. This is one of them. The other, long dead and mummified in the paranoia of the arriviste, is Red Ulrike, the egg-throwing commie artist taunting cops. That's his fondest memory of her, even though she risked being carted off in the paddy wagon, abandoning him in Union Square park.

"You don't drink any more," she says in the car.

"Only at Bar Mitzvahs."

"You still work on boats?"

"Ships."

"Do you?"

"I retired," he lies.

"So what do you do?"

"Think about working on ships."

"Sounds boring."

"Yeah, I've had an uneventful life."

"I've never understood you, you know."

"Count your blessings. You were born to paint. You been painting, you know, with Hart?"

She understands his question. "He takes up a lot of space. He's the kind of person when he's in the room everybody sort of gets plastered to the wall."

"Only an artist would say that." It isn't what he thinks. What he thinks is, I sure hope you've been living in big houses.

Doctor Rajendra Chandrivar, wrapt and defended as he is in his own good will, can't outweigh his Tamil darkness in Ulrike's eyes, so she consigns Hart to Third World ministrations with a disgust that not even the doctor in his courtliness and concern can miss.

"Your father," he tells Bo, "suffers from the long-term effects of leukemia and he has congestive heart failure. We should take a few days to stabilize him. Then you can put him under the care of his own physician. Shall I have another doctor see to your mother, sir?"

Bo looks with rueful inquiry into the young doctor's eyes.

"I see she doesn't like me."

"The people she doesn't like, Doctor, are legion. She's a bigot. I'm sorry. Also, he's not my father."

"It's good to meet you, Sir." Chandrivar offers his hand. Bo takes it and clasps the man's arm as well. The two third worlders smile complicitously.

"What do they say?" Ulrike asks him in the lounge.

"We can move him in two or three days."

"What do they say?"

"He has heart trouble. We should take him to his doctor in New York and get a second opinion. Then we'll know what to do."

She searches his face and accordingly he's careful not to lower his eyes, which might signal hopelessness.

9

Towards the end of the second day Hart awakens. "Where's my hat?" he asks Bo. Ulrike had gone back to the Ramada to nap.

"I'll look around."

"You're Bo?"

He nods.

"You've grown up."

The fatuousness of his remark dawns on Hart immediately. They laugh.

Bo makes arrangements. He calls Hart's Park Avenue doctor, Marvin Crane, for an appointment and asks Chandrivar to forward Hart's medical transcripts.

"The prognosis must be guarded, you know," Chandrivar tells him.

"Further hospitalization?"

"Soon enough, I'm afraid."

Bo has called the nearest rental-car place to arrange to leave off his rental. He drives there and he takes a taxi back to Hart's car.

Once they're in Hart's car some of Hart's natural garrulousness returns. He acts as if he's made a new best friend. Sick as he is, it doesn't escape his notice that Bo insists he sit up front to hold motion sickness at bay, and it endears him to this man he's rather feared. Bo is not a chip off old Sandro's block by blood or inclination either, he decides. Hart never experienced violence, although the whiff of it titillates him, hence he mistakes the mask for the real thing.

"What do merchant seamen read, Bo?"

"Louis L'Amour, Mickey Spillane."

"What do you read?"

"Charts."

"Seriously?"

"Seriously."

Hart manages an engaging smile.

Bo relents. "I buy through the mail. I think my last book was Nabokov's *Pale Fire*."

"Then you bring them home?"

"No, I leave them in the Seamen's Church Institute, places like that."

Hart is silent for twenty miles. The idea appeals to him, and yet he feels reproached, for he has kept every book, every handbill, every poster he ever acquired. He owns the complete leatherbound Bulwer-Lytton in twelve volumes and has not the faintest notion what's in them. He has Maya Deren film posters and John Barrymore handbills.

"Why do you do that? Leave books in different places."

"If I figure it out I'll tell you."

"I hope I live long enough to hear it," he says brightly.

"Try," Bo says.

"Uff," Ulrike whooshes in distaste.

"Your mother, being immortal herself, regards death as an uncouth gaffe."

Bo smiles. Hart is pleased to be found amusing.

It's becoming clear to Bo that Hart too likes English drawing-room discourse, but for a different reason. He likes archness, the smug satisfaction of getting off a good one. He must have studied the actor Claude Raines in particular.

What drew Ulrike to a man with a dowager's hump? What drew Hart to a humorless Prussian?

"Oh, I suspect she's well acquainted with death," he says. "Artists always are. They experience it as they paint."

He looks in the rearview mirror and finds Ulrike's eyes wide and fixed, seeing rather than hearing the thought. He notices a small sardonic smile, the kind one might begrudge in a truth coming from the wrong person. He's never become used to being the wrong person.

"Your mother believes in the power of positive thought. Do you?"

He does, but he loathes the question in its context. He wonders if Hart is probing for his embitterment.

Hart releases him from the question with a smile.

★

Worse news in New York. Marvin Crane—his sanitized Savile Row name ill fits his used-condom look—dispenses stingy and suspicious assurance with digoxin. It's clear to Bo this Park Avenue pouf hasn't studied Chandrivar's report, probably hasn't even studied the many reports from Hart's lab tests.

"Excuse me, doctor, but what is it exactly you recommend?"

Hart looks at his advocate gratefully. Ulrike looks as if she has urgent business elsewhere and shoos Crane's poor old secretary bird out into the lascivious wink of a New York autumn.

"Your father knows, I've talked to him many times."

"In that case it will be easy for you to review what you've told him for me. Do you know he's taking twelve different prescriptions? How can he keep all that down?"

"Are you a doctor, sir?"

"No, are you?"

The receptionist gasps with glee and Marvin Crane exits, a shaken gel of smarm.

When Bo rejoins them outside Ulrike asks, "What did Doctor Crane say?"

"A complete check at Albany Medical Center is the next step."

Hart had told him he thought New York hospitals dispensed bad blood, so Bo improvises.

"There, Hart, that's a wonderful idea," Ulrike exclaims.

★

The bluestone once lugged down the Hudson by barges to pave an earlier Manhattan blunts the murderous sunlight, but now the fields of glittering cement and sheets of granite and glass hone the mind to thousands of dangerous points. Bo knows nothing about their living arrangements. They own properties

140

in Manhattan and in Echo Tarn, some hundred and ten miles straight up the Hudson gorge. He knows Hart wants to spend his sickness in Echo Tarn. That's why Bo thought of a hospital in Albany. After so many years not bothering to tell him anything, they're acting as if he knows what to do, where to go, how to help. Under the circumstances one thing is as good as another.

"We should get some things," he says.

"We have everything we need at home," Ulrike says. Does this mean her terraced apartment overlooking Roosevelt Island in a neighborhood whose sport is Garbo sighting? Or Echo Tarn? He decides she doesn't give a damn and neither does he. He drives them straight up the Henry Hudson Parkway and over the Tappan Zee Bridge to Echo Tarn.

A lifelong collector of Hudsoniana, Hart regales Bo with stories of iceboat races, sturgeon fishing, shad runs, bluestone quarries and the Esopus Wars, and when he exhausts himself he asks, "Have you ever sailed up the Hudson, Bo?"

"Sailed no, steamed yes. I've been on tankers that pumped their bilges at Peekskill and came back down to the Kull acting like environmentalists."

"What does that mean?" Ulrike asks.

"It means they're killing the lordly Hudson," Hart offers. Sometimes it's hard for him to face that he's stayed with Ulrike so he can go on impressing somebody. "Did it upset you, Bo?"

"I hate tankers. Dipping brass sticks into fuel holds all night long in mosquito-infested pump-outs is not my idea of seamanship."

"What's that you do?"

"It's called ullage. You have to both pump out and fill the tanks to balance the ship. You don't want her to list, because it costs big bucks to right her."

Once they cross the bridge he feels Echo Tarn, still sixty miles away, open like a moray's maw. He feels the little town as a flush on his westward cheek, redolent of turpentine, linseed and varnish, Hans Hofmann palettes thick and dizzyingly whorled, Gauguin palettes tropic and contagious, Hettie and Sandro and the Ulrike he was born to offend.

But another sensation flits like a moth on the hot circumference of his awareness—in Echo Tarn color became proscribed, too hot to handle, too likely to traitorously conjure odor and, with odor, humiliation. Color was Hettie's cheeks, Ulrike's tits warlike under her shirt—the heraldry of their temperaments, enemy and berserking. Color could not be used. It could not be settled with, you had to surrender to it.

"Why didn't you become a captain, Bo?" Hart asks.

"They leave the navigator alone, like the radio officer."

"Yes, you would like to be alone," Ulrike says.

Their eyes meet in the mirror, hers belligerent, defying him. But it's Hart who responds. "Isn't it really quite amazing," he says, "that at the same time she's asking you to help she's baiting you?"

What's quite amazing is Hart Clement's saying it, or anything of the kind. Bo takes his eyes off the approaching Red Apple Rest to study Hart's frightened face.

"I'm not asking for a damned thing, I never have, you are!" She sounds as triumphal as an organ trumpet fanfare. Hart smiles appreciatively at Bo. This is a conundrum Bo likes. Has Hart tried to forestall an incident? Or does he smile because he enjoys one? He had been her paladin tilting against the trepidations of a dark son. Is he playing let's you and him fight? Bo decides that Hart Clement is simply unable to resist pointing out that he understands an abiding characteristic of Ulrike's nature. Perhaps, if he had not shared his death warrant with her son, he would have kept silent, but now he prefers to deepen his relationship with this stranger whose severity fascinates him. In the silence of men more than willing to let Ulrike have the last word, Bo speculates that Hart has probably been ill for a long time. Maybe his curiosity kept him alive. His questions aren't pro forma.

"Which school did you go to become an officer, Bo?"

"I didn't. I came up by the hawsepipe, as they say. I just read books and watched. There's usually some old Scandinavian out there to teach you if you really want to know."

"Why Scandinavian?"

"They often go to sea as boys and come up the pipe, so they're sympathetic, if they like you."

He said two things he knew would scratch Ulrike's craw: he watches and somebody liked him. His watchfulness she knows firsthand, the other thing sticks its tongue out in her face. His body jerks involuntarily in its contempt of the thought.

"Must be hard to live with such tough guys," Hart says.

"They're not so much tough as sane enough to know they're too crazy to live on the beach."

"Why can't they live in the mountains, why do they have to live on the beach?" Ulrike says.

"The beach is their word for land, any land."

The three of them chuckle more or less amicably.

"How many years have you been at sea?" Hart asks.

"I dunno. More than twenty or I couldn't retire. More including my five years in the Navy."

"Does that count?"

"It used to. I dunno now. They used to like Navy guys, now they think they're job competitors. They figure, if you're unlicensed, you're too used to working, and if you're an officer, you're too used to having a hundred guys do the same job."

"Is that true?"

"Not exactly. The merchant fleet's full of grasshoppers, on at Boston, off at Norfolk. That costs the companies, that and safety regs, so they either register their ships under a foreign flag or they try to cut back their crews until the only thing that's good is the overtime."

"Have you ever sailed under a foreign flag?"

"Yeah. Panama, Greece, Oman, Singapore, Liberia, Bahrein, Kuwaiti, you name it. Bad pay, good crews, better'n they deserve, really."

"What was it like?"

"I'll tell you, Hart, I'm a little tired, but we'll talk later."

"I'm sorry, I know this has been a strain for you."

Bo is moved to a disclaimer, but he thinks better of it. It's nice of the man, he thinks. He wonders if the death haunting his marrow might be making Hart something of the boy he'd been. As he drives vagrant thoughts of Margaret look in on him and, like a wide-awake and mischievous boy, he thinks of his answering machine full of her hang-ups sinking in the Hudson.

★

Echo Tarn is commanded by the pristine spire of the Dutch Reformed Church, which seems to pray like Christ in Gethsemane for deliverance from dirty girls with tambourines, bogus veterans, scam artists and some of the most self-important shopkeepers north of Madison Avenue. The air is charred and thick. Standing on Hart's moonless driveway, Bo senses still water. The decadent scent of honeysuckle stands in the air like perspiration on a lip.

"The timer lights are off, Bo—be careful," Hart says.

"Let me have your keys. Tell me where the breakers are. Is there a flashlight in the car?"

"Ooooph." Valkyrie down. When Bo gets to the passenger side to help Hart he finds Ulrike in a swale leading down to the street. "I've twisted my ankle," she says. Hart has fished a flashlight out from under his seat and hands it to Bo along with a set of keys. Bo picks Ulrike up. He expects her to resist, but her body seems strangely grateful. She is much lighter than he expected. He tells Hart he'll be back to help him and brings Ulrike inside.

Now that Hart has an ally against the dark, he's exhilarated. All this—since Bo's arrival in Cape May—is more real to Hart than his sickness. Sitting with his feet hanging out of his car, he reckons that he's not as afraid of death as much as dying under Ulrike's tutelage. He realizes that ever since he inherited this hotel and the house next to it twenty years ago he's been afraid. His mother and father, accomplished musicians and hoteliers, ran The Granada with style and panache. When they died it fell into disrepair and, in spite of his notorious schemes to restore it, schemes in which he enlisted every flimflam man in the county, Hart never reopened it. It sulked for decades a block from the village green, the town's biggest building, a rebuke to the tax assessor, a thorn in the fire chief's side, a magnet for vandals and bums and the whiskey talk of Ulrike's and Hart's coterie of dirtbags.

Hart trudges into his house through the kitchen door in the back, leaning heavily on Bo's arm. "Call the police," Ulrike barks. Bo remembers something about the timer lights.

"Bo will take care of it," Hart says confidently. The words feel like cobwebs on Bo's face. He wonders if Hart even knows where the breakers are. He searches the walls with the flashlight and spots a gray panel next to the fridge. He finds the breakers off and unmarked so that he can't tell if one of them governs the fridge. The house explodes with light. Ulrike shields her eyes. "Not that much!" she screams. Hart starts to laugh. Pretty soon he's laughing so hard his guts hurt. He loses his balance and falls against the fridge. "You goddamned freak, what're you laughing at?" she says. Now Bo is about to laugh. Nothing makes any sense. He figures he better get some ice for Ulrike's ankle. This impulse nearly asphyxiates him. How stupid of him to think there would still be ice. When he opens the fridge door he's assailed with the stench of rotten eggs, brisket and what seems to be dozens of doggie bags and styrofoam crates from restaurants. Hart pukes on the spot.

"What's he doing that for?" Ulrike asks.

"The refrigerator," Bo says, trying not to puke himself. "It stinks."

"I don't smell anything."

Bo looks at Hart. The poor man has plopped into a chair that seems to be used to hold the broom closet shut. "She doesn't," Hart says. Sick as Hart is, nauseated as Bo is, the two men shake with silent laughter.

Bo ties a handkerchief over his nose and starts disgorging the fridge with abandon. He fills two leaf bags and throws them out into the backyard. Then he opens all the windows to the chill autumn night.

"The raccoons will bless you, my boy," Hart says.

"I'll put it all in cans as soon as I get the fridge going."

Two of the twelve breakers are soft, so he figures one of them must belong to the fridge.

"There's a primary box in the basement," Hart says.

He helps Hart into the front room away from the kitchen. Ulrike rummages through drawers and closets, claiming the place has been looted.

"She always does that," Hart whispers.

Bo searches the Clement fen, so architecturally inviting on the outside, for the basement stairs. He realizes they must be outside. When he probes the dark with his flashlight out back he finds bluestone steps. Black water laps over the top of the third step from the top. Judging by the height of the overhead, it's a full basement. Given Echo Tarn's notoriously high water table and carnival springs, the basement must have a disabled or burned-out sump pump. He'll have to wade around until he finds the fuse and breaker boxes. The more serious issue is the furnace and hot water heater. Have they been drowned or are they elevated enough to elude the water? And what about hot wires in the water? He realizes he shouldn't have thrown the secondary breakers. He goes inside and tells Ulrike and Hart he'll have to find some candles and then turn off the power for a while.

"That's ridiculous," Ulrike says.

"It's a personal affront, you see," Hart explains. Bo appreciates having an interpreter. He'd forgotten the nuances of her perversity.

"Hart, do you have any hip boots around?"

"My father was a trout fisherman. There are some wading boots in the closet next to the china in the dining room."

"Oh for Christ's sake, let's go to my house," Ulrike says.

"I would like to die in my own house," Hart says.

The boots turn out to be moldy black rubber coveralls.

"Stop it, I can't stand it anymore," Ulrike screams. She's screaming like a banshee when Bo turns to go back out to the basement, but not before he notices Hart smiling pleasantly in the candlelight. Bo mourns the ocean. He'd rather electrocute himself than see Ulrike's house, Sandro's house, Hettie's house— they're all one to him at that moment, one meteor screaming through black, soulless space.

He gets into the rubber fishing gear and slogs down into the flood. It's a small space, probably dug out before the kitchen was built over it. He shudders to see two long black snakes winding over the surface of the water at the level of his crotch. He remembers the addled copperhead that bit his calf at the Big Deep when he was thirteen and how sick he'd been. Ulrike insisted it was all in his head since there could be no snakes in such a populous place. In fact the region is known for its copperheads and rattlesnakes. He'd puked and sweated and shivered himself free of the venom, and now he can't remember how he felt about Ulrike's reaction. He spots the switch and fuse boxes screwed high on the wall between floor beams. He spots smudges on some of the glass fuses and replaces them from a box of spares stored on top of the breaker box. Then, as he cycles the breakers, the sump begins humming and a bare overhead bulb lights up. The gas furnace and water heater are suspended from the floor overhead by steel braces, well out of the water's way. The sump has to be in a well somewhere. He finds it by its hum and tug on the water. It's mucked with debris. He cleans it and it starts slurping water.

Back upstairs he cycles the secondary breakers and the fridge bolts to life. He opens the upstairs windows.

"Let's have a nice fire and a good stiff drink," Ulrike exclaims.

Hart struggles in the front room couch but can't get up. Bo carries him over to a recliner by the fireplace and finds a blanket for him while Ulrike pours three killer Jim Beams.

"Here's to your swift recovery and a wonderful future," she says.

Bo salutes with his glass and sets it down obscurely. Hart sips and gags. Ulrike slugs her drink down like a Cockney sailor. The night breeze tumbles down the mountain. In an hour or so the hoary conspirators and elderly newlyweds settle down and doze. Bo ties the lids of the garbage cans, wondering if the dextrous raccoons can slip a carrick bend, such trivial thoughts having often kept him from rounding his own bend.

He washes up in the filthy bathroom off the kitchen and sleeps in the car with its windows down. His last thought before sleeping is of Hettie's perfume cajoling the secrets of her pores.

★

The next day Bo makes some emergency appointments and they set out to the Albany Medical Center. Hart walks to the car, a feat Ulrike praises theatrically. The hospital admits him for tests.

He has been at the hospital four days when the physician in charge, a gray fox to Ulrike's liking, says to Bo, "I'd like to test her too. Some of his symptoms are problematical and she may have caught something from him. It may be a sexually transmitted disease. I'd like to examine her too."

"She doesn't like to undress."

"She wouldn't have to. For a blood test. But I would like to examine her. Can you persuade her?"

"No."

"Well, let me take another tack. He's dying. They're both old. She says she's sixty-four, but that's preposterous. She must be at least ten years older than that, am I right?"

Bo nods.

"It's not unthinkable to let nature take its course. It will anyway."

"You said the disease may be transmitted sexually?"

"Yes, as far as we know. I mean, you're safe, as far as we know. Assuming I'm right, of course."

"And assuming I avoid any exchange of fluids."

"Yes."

"What about any others?"

"I know what you mean, of course. But consider their age. You don't think they've been sleeping around?"

If the fox were Chandrivar Bo might pursue this conversation, but this guy is palpably full of himself, so Bo shakes his head and says, "What can I do?"

"Ensure. He can probably drink Ensure. It's full of vitamins. You can buy it over the counter by the case. I'm changing his medication to help him get it down. He's not going to improve, but sometimes miracles happen. As for your mother, well, we don't know, do we?"

"Good news!" he announces when he returns to Hart's room. "Tomorrow you go home. New medicine, much easier to take. Prognosis good, but you need plenty of rest."

"See, Hart, I told you, there's nothing to worry about!" Ulrike says.

Hart gives Bo a pale fish eye. Neither he nor Ulrike press for details.

★

Back in Echo Tarn, Ulrike, a catastrophic cook whose tactic is to make a mess of things with brio until someone rescues the meal, immediately sets about cooking the brisket Bo neglected to throw out. She plops it in an oversized pot and boils it until Hart's house fills with vomitous fumes. Her victim, a near-professional chef, calls Bo to him in the sun room. "What in the name of God is she doing? I have to throw up."

"Seriously?"

And with that Hart throws up and looks utterly humiliated.

"What's he doing?" Ulrike calls.

Bo claps his hand over his mouth and runs out. When he returns Hart has managed to clean himself up. Ulrike is changing his bedding.

"For God's sake, he's not even sick, and he threw up!" Hart says, mimicking Ulrike. The two men smile at each other.

Bo opens the front door, takes a few deep breaths and goes to set the nauseating pot out in the backyard. He returns to Hart with a glass of Ensure and medicine, now reduced to three pills.

"Now that's revolting," Ulrike pronounces after sipping Hart's Ensure. "The man needs to eat."

"The man needs rest," Hart says.

"Bo, there's a laundry in the hotel," she says, "could you?" She points to the bedding and clothing on the floor. Hart rolls his eyes. He doesn't envy Bo. The Granada is always ready to spring a nasty surprise. The power is out. The immense basement, which had been a cafeteria before the water table and a sea of health codes arose, is flooded some three feet. Bo fetches Hart's fisherman's gear from the cottage and wades into the hotel basement to search for the breaker panels. He finds an entire wall covered with them under the lobby. He also finds a big sump pit. Something must have kicked the breakers out. When

149

he finally replaces a few fuses, an enormous pump at the bottom of the sump pit bellows into action and Bo laughs. He laughs too hard to stop.

He's remembering the pump-man on the *Holyoke* who went mad and started pumping sea water into the crude oil holds. The captain had sent Bo with the ship's pistol to lock the pump-man in his fo'c'sl and shut down the pumps. The captain should have sent the chief mate or the bosun, but they were blubbering drunks. He wipes his eyes and remembers how he listened to the pump-man's life story before locking him up. Then he returned to the bridge and told the captain, "His fucking wife's been giving his paychecks to some Jimmy Bob preacher in Morgan City, Louisiana."

"He didn't just piss in the crude, d'you know what he cost the company?"

"Who the hell'll know, Skipper? This goddam life's enough to drive Jesus crazy."

"Yeah, well, tell ya what, Bo, if he's got a grip, let him go back to work in the morning."

"Got a little hootch, skipper?"

"Thought you were off the sauce."

"It's for him."

"He's a fucking Jehovah's Witness!"

"It'll calm him down."

"Or make him crazier'n he already is. Jesus, you're a bleeding heart, Bo. Here, give him a swallow."

The pump-man, who listened to heavy metal music with a black light lit in his fo'c'sl, wore him out with grateful puppy-dog looks the rest of the trip.

Bo laughs again to think how much machinery that load of crude ruined. Just call me a crazy pump-man, he mutters.

The news seamen get is rarely good. What they discover is worse. But the pump-man's wife made him the most sympathetic man on the *Holyoke*.

"He works his ass off for shit pay and what does his fuckin' wife do, she stuffs a turkey with his paycheck," the bosun said.

"Shit pay? He makes more'n you," Bo said.

"Jeez, you got a way with words, y'know that, Bo?"

Standing in the scummy bilges of The Granada, he misses that profane, humorous life. No departures, just arrivals. No Christmases, no birthdays, no graduations, no home. Just the sea. No letters—he could remember only one letter, from the Navy Reserve Association asking if he wanted to join. It had been forwarded by the Seamen's Church Institute. Oh yeah, there had been that notice in the union paper: *Bo, I miss you, your friend Darlene in New Orleans.* Darlene, the half-Cherokee hat-check hooker in the Club Nauti.

"Hey Bo, 'scuse me, hon, somebody misses you," the AB who spotted the notice shouted to him in the Brooklyn union hall. "You miss her, Bo?"

"Like the clap," he said. But he didn't mean it. He remembered Darlene fondly, how he'd helped her in the hat-check concession on New Year's Eve and they'd skimmed the tips and gone off on a weekend toot.

Next door his second stepfather is dying and he's laughing, true to form, the bad son. He climbs up out of the basement, sits down outside on the bluestone steps of the ghostly hotel and takes out a long green cigar. An old woman comes by and starts dead-heading petunias in the dilapidated barrels on the front terrace. "Do you live here, sir?"

He looks back at the facade, then he shakes his head.

"The police don't allow loiterers, sir."

"It's all right, I'm a friend of the owner."

"Oh I don't think so, sir. He's dead."

"Well, don't tell him, it'll just upset him."

"Oh, for heaven's sake, what's the world coming to?"

She might have said more but for Bo's steady gaze. He goes on smoking his Cohiba, wondering what next. He hears the pump throwing up into the municipal storm drain, he hears ships signaling in Rotterdam harbor, children playing in Livorno, foghorns and gulls contesting, cognac corks singing in bottlenecks on balmy Cuban nights. He closes his eyes and slips the place like a submarine easing out of Groton on a Sunday night. How lonely to be sober, bereft of demons, fully in possession of memories. If I'm to finish it well, sooner or later I've got to call somewhere home. But tonight he can't imagine one.

★

Ulrike waits out old age expecting to recover from it. She considers death an elective procedure. Mounting evidence to the contrary, such as Hart's obvious mortality, convinces her she's surrounded by conspirators. She doesn't go to the doctor because she doesn't want to hear bad news. Hart's explanation, as Bo learns in the morning, is more penetrating: she doesn't go because she doesn't want anybody sticking his finger up her ass.

Ulrike suspects people fake old age so as not to live up to their responsibilities as her playmates. "What the man needs," she announces in the morning, "is good food."

"Everybody has a walk-on part in her life," Hart whispers to Bo. "Don't let her poison me, Bo. I want to go without help." Speaking her name seems too much of an effort. Bo pats his shoulder and starts to leave when Hart clutches his sleeve. "And we had better not try to attract any attention," he continues. "She's left a lot of dead ingenues in her tracks." A collector of Broadway ephemera, but never a theatergoer, he warms to his musings while Ulrike mans the kitchen percussion section. "There have never been any understudies, Bo, can you imagine it? When she stops the theater goes dark. The electricians better believe it."

"It will be interesting to see if it does," Bo says.

"Perhaps you'll find a way to let me know."

Bo should appreciate Hart's bravado. He thinks he should, but his immediate problem is that this man of evident perceptivity has drawn his life into a knot with Ulrike's and yet can say at the end that he chose a walk-on part. You couldn't say Bo is incredulous, but his mind sends to the void to know how a man can die so foolishly. How would Anubis weigh such a life? The man has not taken himself seriously. In spite of our trumped-up and suspect admiration for such people, they're entirely untrustworthy. Has he taken anyone seriously? Should Bo take him seriously? The luxury of choice is past. You have to take a man seriously who's puking all over himself. Stink leaves no room for rumination. Bo is accustomed to luring perceptivity out of strangers like cobras out of trees. He's done nothing to draw Hart's, not being interested enough, and yet Hart voices for him a central fact of his life, a fact he can't himself even imagine, that the light Ulrike begrudges him gutters in her presence and yet might not survive her. Hart might as well have said, My life is forfeit, but yours is at stake. In proximity to Ulrike Bo can never be sure he'll again see the stars. He can't even be sure they still shine. Always a sucker for insights, he does not like Hart for this one, and he knows it because he has no urge to draw the man.

He goes outside, drags two trash cans filled with stinking leftovers to the road, and then enters The Granada to check on its pump. The grand pile was finished in nineteen-twenty-nine. Its style, a mixture of mission and bricolage, draws a lot of attention but offends the bony Dutch and English architecture that distinguishes the Hudson Valley. He decides its builder must have harbored a good bit of contempt. Across the driveway Hart's cottage with its distinctive eight-sided cupola was built in the 1880s. A bay window in front and many colliding planes give it a Victorian whimsy. The muse of both buildings was clearly Boob McNutt. The kitchen ceiling fan snuffs the stove's gas burners. The sump pump in the basement throws torrents of ground water against the foundations of the cottage. The sumps of the hotel are cleverer. The front pump drains the basement into the town's ruinously expensive sewer system, while the back pump empties into a topped-up and illegal septic tank. The water from the rear pump then proceeds to flow back and erode the hotel's foundation, while various junctions of its waste-water system overflow into the basement. The roof gutters of both buildings are canted away from the downspouts, assuring their contents will loosen mortar and seams. The crowned macadam driveway hunches rainwater off into the hotel's basement window wells. The list of pretentious errors goes on and assaults Bo's sailorly mind, which demands Bristol conditions but appreciates a good joke.

★

He makes a withdrawal from his account with Llewellyn when he recognizes that afternoon that Hart, like all bunco men, has a knack for discerning what you want and dangling it in front of you. In Bo's case it's insight. He's an insight junkie. Cynical people fondling their worst traits in the dark of their purposes— that would do for a description of this situation, except that Hart and Ulrike have no purposes. They're utterly content in their troublemaking.

When he comes back into the house, Hart has his head in a fungal toilet. The place stinks of piss, shit, puke and bad brisket. He gets to the bathroom in time to see Ulrike attempt to flush Hart's head down the toilet. Hart doesn't seem to object, but when he gets up, Ulrike commands him, "Stand up straight, you look like an old man." Hart leans back against a wall. It's the last time he'll stand alone. "I am an old man, and I would like to entertain a few decent thoughts in peace before they carry me up the hill, so would you please get this woman out of here? For the love of God?"

Bo nods and drapes Hart's arm around his shoulder. He drags him back to his bed. When he turns Ulrike is staring at him with that who-the-hell-are-you look he knows so well. He picks up the phone and calls the motel in Bluestone to which she has summoned some of her Manhattan retinue. "Claire," he says, "this is Bo Cavalieri, Ulrike's son. She has to leave for New York now and I thought you might like to go with her."

"She knows who you are," Ulrike says.

"I couldn't take any chances," he says with a smile. He turns to look at Hart. The old devil looks as if it's dawned on him dying might be fun without Ulrike.

Ulrike doesn't fight to hold her ground like the Hitler Jugend. Claire and three other tipsy pals arrive within the hour. Bo walks them all to the bus stop on the village green and leaves them there. "You'll keep in touch?" she asks Bo for their benefit. He nods. "You never have, you know." He nods agreeably.

If ever there was a time to have a slug of something it's now. He shudders as if he'd had one and walks a Manhattan block back to Hart's cottage. There he begins to straighten things. Hart used to walk around Echo Tarn with two front teeth missing. Ulrike at some point insisted on dentures. There's as much denture effervescent in the house as there is ampicillin for nausea, but nowhere can he find Hart's teeth.

★

Now he begins what will become nightly patrols of the familiar village, collecting himself, shaking off the excretions of the bars and the cottage, ransacking memories. He remembers the town well. The pietistic spire of the Old Dutch Reformed Church (seventeen-ninety) still prays for deliverance from the follies below. The essential street pattern of the village is as he had biked it as a boy. But the buildings have been so monkeyed with as to obscure the esthetic of the original in the name of commercial improvement. It's now chock-a-block with skewed contours and antic angles. There's nothing left of its aquiline Dutch and English lines. What he doesn't know but will soon learn is that Echo Tarn had become maddened by codes whose more proper locations are swank developments in Darien and Old Lyme. Echo Tarn's fey self is everywhere dogged by feckless political correctness. It's left to announce its former nature by an embarrassment of faerie lights killing every forlorn sycamore in sight.

He wonders if the cops are still the high school bullies, if the volunteer firemen are still a bit picky.

He remembers the faces of the nineteen-forties, absorbed in work, often work in the Gurdjieffian sense, and although he likes the young people of the sixties and seventies, admires them even, it doesn't seem to him they have the hard-won individuality of the earlier faces.

He peers into the gallery windows and sees that adventurous painting has been succeeded by adventitious schlock.

Plastered over a yield sign at the western end of the green is a manifesto denouncing a "liberal town board for suffocating shoestring entrepreneurs with red tape, enacting one grandiose code after another like a bunch of tight-assed arrivistes in Connecticut WASP nests." He loves it. He remembers when the town was indeed run by fascists. They would gladly have

155

suffocated everyone who didn't look like the first cousins with whom they'd had entirely too much to do.

He sits by the troutful Bearkill at the county bridge. Downside on the hill in front of him his Columbia Flyer's brakes had failed when he was ten and he'd careened down to the bridge knowing there was a two-foot gap between the guard rail and the stonewalled walk over the bridge. Through this slot he flew out into space, then down into a deep pool below. He wonders now how he recovered his bike. He remembers wheeling it into the village, borrowing some tools from gangly Carl Brathwaite, the artist who painted him many times, slopping his bike with the oil Carl gave him, realigning the brake disks, and doing his shopping. He looks some fifty yards downstream to a dogleg in the Bearkill where Carl Brathwaite ended up celebrating one New Year's Eve by hanging himself from a willow after seeing his ex-lover dancing in the Pink Elephant with her new boyfriend. He has an impulse to find the boyfriend and strangle him.

To relieve this misery he looks up to the firmament. They're all there, the familiar navstars with their Arab names, the Greek constellations. The sky crackles with communiqués. But something's awry. The stars are where they ought to be. He checks that out with his peripheral vision. He blinks and finds they haven't moved. And yet this sky is untrustworthy. It's a doppelganger sky, a magnificent forgery. He won't bet his sea papers on it. It warrants a Cohiba. Lighting up, perhaps because he's so often done it out on a flying bridge after taking a star fix, calls to mind what sailors call a lume.

The lume is a seabag of phenomena. It's the exaggerated elevation of a thing—a spit of land or a vessel looming bigger than life in the trickster twilight or fog. It's a city's lights reflecting off cloud cover and blanking the heavens. It's the reflection in the sky of something below the horizon, perhaps a glow indicating an ice field. Its usual meaning is the cloud cover that belies the stars and makes it easy to spot big coastal cities at night, and it comes to Bo, puffing a cigar by the Bearkill after so many years seafaring, that Ulrike Theiss is his lume. She certainly has always appeared bigger than she is. But now he understands, too, that he's unable to see his navstars in her presence, and that's why this sky over Echo Tarn can't be trusted. I'll call it Ulrike's Lume, a painterly lume, he tells himself. Rembrandt and Turner understood them. He, Bo Cavalieri, understands them too, and he'll keep them very much in mind.

He senses the proximity of a lover dumped somewhere when, sitting briefly on the guard rail of the bridge, a young man and woman stop about one a.m. to sit with him and tell him that a friend has just blown them off because "some people just can't stand the truth," as the young man says. He's glad when they drift off like Dixie cups in the Bearkill. He feels a forlorn urge to go find the dumpee and console him.

Then a tall boy and a diminutive girl who seems exactly half his height scuffle over the gravel of the road's shoulder into a huge corrugated standpipe waiting to be installed in a feeder-creek bed and begin playing a plaintive high-pitched song, a protest song, the girl picking her guitar and nose-keening, the boy accompanying her by rolling the end of a stick against the ribs of the pipe, the improvised sound studio emitting a kind of perfunctory anger that alienates him. A poor imitation of heartland sorrow—Echo Tarn mocking its former genuine self like a hippie in her grandmother's dress. A blond head sticks out of a passing dyspeptic Impala—"Boogah, boogah!" Bo's expressionless face reflects his mind. Then he laughs. Boogah, boogah, Echo Tarn. It matters more to him whether katy did or katy didn't. More likely she didn't. But she should have. He wishes all the katies to have what they didn't.

He listens to the parliament of nags, the crickets and tree frogs. He thinks these young people to be members of such a parliament. He notices his hands trembling, signifying an ordeal to which his mind refuses to testify, signifying mute regression. A stray thought alights on him like a firefly: he needed recklessly to be liked when he was young. Maybe it had gotten him killed, and maybe he just didn't notice it.

10

He stands in the upstairs bedroom of Hart's cottage in Echo Tarn, clutching the rag doll Margaret Wadeleigh had found him mending in Cairnhall's attic. He's taken to consulting Kouf, a.k.a. Woofy-Poofy. Alien thoughts pelt him. Death's not an elective procedure. My fathers refer me to their wife.

The upstairs is a head tottering on a bloated body. Downstairs is freighted with Ulrike. He knows exactly where Hart is. Parked in a Castro convertible before the bay window of the parlor. But Ulrike is everywhere, while the cutthroat Bo Cavalieri shivers and clutches his rag doll. His thoughts turn to hail and bang his pate. He tells Kouf a story just to make sure he himself is getting it straight.

Woofy-Poofy listens, an oracle sitting in Bo's room in Echo Tarn a hundred and twenty-nine miles and a thousand years from Cairnhall, where she'd resigned to die.

"Ulrike always has a magic mystery peanut to dispense," he tells Woofy-Poofy. "One of her best paintings is a big vertical of a circus elephant. He's surrounded by acrobats, high-wire artists, a lion tamer, dancing horses, but you know where your eye goes?—it goes to a peanut in mid-air, not even to the elephant's trunk trying to catch it."

When he turns to face her his face is turned down in a clown's smile. Not a smile to be denied. Her work is cut out for her. She knows what he needs to know to be whole, things that happened to him at Cairnhall. She knows what was done to him in a brackish gut of Great South Bay, the abuses and their denial. Now that she's someone's confidante again she'll speak: Rest, Dacia, I'm going to tell him everything.

He lodges Kouf in the window seat upstairs and sets out on a walk.

Propped against a dank willow by the Bearkill as the noise of pestilent youngsters fades, he dreams.

★

To build a cathedral nowadays costs less than one B52 bomber, but the one he builds tonight, austere and soaring, very like the one he'd seen at Rheims, is bound to cost more.

He sees a tall man in privet-green cassock climb his cathedral's sunlit steps and enter. He hurries to inhabit him. He stops at the holy-water stoup in the narthex, dips two fingers and makes the sign of the cross. He proceeds to the nave, wholly one with the man and yet somehow observing him off to his right at a height of about eight feet. He bows toward the marble rood at the high altar and approaches. Suddenly he finds himself back in the narthex. Three seven-foot grotesques from nowhere approach abreast. They wear hooded green capes over vertically striped red and white tights. Each carries a hangman's noose before him like a sacerdotal element. Some deference apparently is due him as they pass, for they solemnly elevate their nooses. He lets them pass as a harried cardinal might a monastic procession, nodding but denying them eye contact. Where could he find eyes in these long manically sculpted faces? Now he stands in the stony narthex again. A slender brown-haired young woman in jeans and an unpressed man's dress shirt is forced to her knees by a brutish man he can only describe as a sheriff. About ten yards behind her Sandro Cavalieri, dressed characteristically in suit and buttoned-up shirt without tie, struggles with another sheriff, shouting in Italian, "God is outraged, you bastards!" The sheriff backhands him. His face and shirt are bloodied. "For the love of God, intercede!" Sandro shouts to him. This man exhibits far more religiosity, not to say literacy, than the Sandro he knew. The Sandro he knew thought priests leeches and child molesters. Aware that he's dreaming, he's torn. He struggles to hold the dream together as the air quivers and the scene melts. He enters the space between the young woman and Sandro, turning first to study her face. He knows that he knew her, but he can't dredge up her name. Are you Nefertiti, Akhenaton's consort? he hears himself ask. His voice is unfamiliar. The panic subsides from her face and she answers, Lord, I am who you say I am. He turns away from her to Sandro. And are you Alessandro Cavalieri, my stepfather? Tell these priests to go to hell, Sandro shouts. Yes, it's Sandro. Bo signs the cross in the air and the sheriffs whom Sandro called priests disappear, leaving the woman, Sandro and himself. This is a dream, he tells them, go in peace.

★

Bo schools himself to meditate on dreams. Sometimes he draws them. He draws this one under a phosphorous street lamp. Usually he gets a sketch right or throws it out. He gets this one right, but he doesn't like it. He tries charcoal, pencil, chalk, ink, all the goods of his baggy-pocketed camouflage jacket. Each time he gets it right it goes wrong.

As the days pass, talking to Hart Clement, bathing him, nursing him, feeding him, he comes to see the dream as a many-faceted emerald, catching the lights of his mind as he turns it. He comes to see himself as a star beast, tromping about the heavens, shaking off meteors like a bull twitches flies, dumbly nuzzling the emerald as if it were a planet. So familiar he becomes with it that he grieves the absence of Mary Mother of God from it and deplores that he didn't interrogate the woman and the sheriffs. He knows he can still do that, but he refrains lest he diminish the dream's grandeur. What would an alchemist do, he asks himself? Swallow it whole. So he does. He believes he's ingested an unknown substance whose properties will eventually transform him. In this way he embarks upon a vigil.

★

When he enters the house at dawn Hart is sleeping in the recliner. He fetches his searchlight from the car and checks out the basement, whistling the *Twilight Zone* theme. The basement is mud-hung and flaking, as if festooned with wasps' nests. The termites scuttle. If vampires have been cavorting here, they've gone prowling.

He showers, changes and sets out for a walk until the market opens at 7:30 and he can make breakfast. He pats his jacket down for draftsman's things the way men pat themselves down for cigarettes. Market Street is already filled with drifters, grifters, drummers and delivery men. Hippies make room, they're into accommodating. He likes that about them. One of the ways he adjusts to a new crew is to draw its body language. He's given a lot of thought to the way passersby behave. Here comes your classic navigation befuddler. He's bearing down on Bo about fifteen yards out and five points starboard. He's not a passive aggressive, he's an asshole aggressive, truculently slouching forward, giving his balls room to swing and losing way in the process. Damn bad sailing tactic. No matter what signal you send the asshole aggressive you find yourself on a collision course. This type is a collector targeting you. Sort of like spiders—if you see the web, look for the spinner. Sometimes he lightheartedly pins himself to an imaginary wall to let these body blockers by. Usually they're medium-height men, rarely women and rarely tall. The exception is the teen-aged girl who pretends not to see you so as to make you deal with her. This morning he simply defers and gives the wrathful man wide berth. In his lexicon are other kinds of befuddlers. A buoy generally tilts in the direction of current and tide and that's a helpful indicator when deciding how to skirt it. But occasionally, when a buoy's anchoring system is fouled, it tilts the wrong way, like an asshole aggressive, and that's how it is with people who seem to appear in your life for a good purpose but prove surprisingly contrary. Then there are the dreadnought chicken players, measuring how little seaway they can give you without having been said to violate the rules of the road. In true Navy fashion, Bo as a watch officer always orders the helm to hold a steady course in such instances. It no doubt altered his nature to have seen so many junk-flag merchantmen break their course lines when he bore down as the privileged vessel, the one, that is, with right of way. And, as the watch mate of a burdened vessel, the one lacking right of way, he always gave way smartly, leaving no doubt. Befuddlers interest him less than blinders. You can shine the full light of your being across a blinder's bridge and never get a signal of recognition. The blinder is locked in himself to the point of steaming into hectic Rotterdam on autopilot. The blinder gives you unblinkered, unfiltered stares that bypass ages of evolution. Beware the blinder in low bars and young women.

Then the whisperings of his navigational muse are dispersed by a jolting thought: what if hell is where everything is subject to unremitting interpretation? What if we're always denying the clarity we have here, and that's original sin? He tries to be appalled, remembering his own reassuring behavior in the dream. He's swallowed the emerald, dreamed the dream according to his own lights.

★

Hart Clement's four-story hotel dominates Echo Tarn. It's five doors up from the village green on Quarry Road, the second most important road. Its art deco furnishings squawk against its architecture. The strap-work of its immense, balconied dance hall testifies to all that art deco owed to the ancient world, particularly the Assyrians. Hedison Clement, Hart's grandfather, spent two-thirds of his wife Sarah's fortune on the place, and while he made and lost handsome sums on his own, Sarah had her final say by leaving what was left of her liquid assets to Hart, her only grandchild. She was therefore the enabler of his rustic indigence. Hart's father, Joseph, was practical. He ran The Granada for twenty-five years for tourists who wished to ogle the town's artists and writers but did not wish to reward them for their follies. Then one day in nineteen-forty-six Joseph and Edith, a renowned quilter who honored New York Indian tribes and clans by naming her patterns after them, packed up and moved to Sanibel, Florida, leaving Hart in charge.

The first thing Hart did was to wrest control from Schoharie One Corporation, a trust Joseph had set up. Hart argued that his parents demonstrated incompetence by abandoning The Granada to himself, an ill-prepared returning veteran. Judge Micah Brainerd's decision in favor of Hart may have been swayed by the Bronze Star that General Courtney Hodges, commander of V Corps, gave Hart for his parlous propaganda, but it flabbergasted the legal establishment and it undid Joseph Clement's immunization against local anti-Semitism. Joseph had set up Schoharie One, not as a tax or bankruptcy dodge, but to associate some of the most prestigious English and Huguenot and Palatine names in the county with an enterprise that otherwise might have borne the insults of race hatred. Hart, with his preposterous argument, now inherited the whirlwind. Next he shut the place down at the onset of the most promising tourist seasons since nineteen-twenty-eight. He'd be damned, he said, if he'd put up with those Jew-baiting officials and their anti-business regulations. In the ensuing years the regulations, which Joseph had amicably coped with, became ever more onerous, and Hart's squabbles with officialdom as he launched various eccentric projects to reopen the place became legendary. Neither he nor the goddamned anti-business, Jew-baiting Republicans who ran the town shared the least concern that it was in everybody's interest to have The Granada up and running and contributing to the economy. And now that the pinko-weirdo Democrats are in charge, the environmental and health codes are fanatically enforced, and so the biggest commercial property in the town remains a mote in the eyes of the politicos and a beam in the eyes of the perverse.

As Bo walks up Quarry Road with his bag of groceries he surveys the old mountebank's Moorish heap and remembers how it had been when Joseph and Edith ran it, filled with hard-eyed, tipsy New Yorkers on its terraces, festooned with banners announcing book and antique fairs, a Rudolph Steiner lecture . . . and he remembers Anders Ootwaert, the gaunt old Dutch farmer up on the Foundry Turnpike who had befriended him as a boy. He first saw Anders when he was biking home from the meat market in Starksville. Anders was sitting in his faded bib overalls among the headstones of his ancestors, eating his lunch. Bo made the grueling eight-mile run to Starksville because he'd decided that he and Ulrike needed more meat and the old German family who ran Schneller's in Starksville didn't cheat him out of his ration stamps as the Echo Tarn merchants did.

One day the old Dutchman motioned him over. He handed Bo a sandwich. They sat in silence. After a while Anders said, "I talk to them. They tell me what's what. You know what's what? I don't know how long they have to be in the ground before they get smart. Some of them were not so smart."

"How do you know they're still in there?"

"What you think then?"

"We put them there to get rid of the bodies, then they go away some place else."

"You like to think such things, boy?"

He nodded and Anders Ootwaert smiled like a jack-o-lantern just before it collapses. "Jah, my little friend, they see foolish old Anders sitting here and they come from somewhere else to talk to him."

"Will they talk to me?"

"That is a very serious question. If they do, my boy, you better listen, that's for sure."

Another day he stopped to watch the old farmer plow his fields.

"Hey, boy, you like my horses?"

Bo nodded.

"You a city boy?"

"I grew up on a farm."

"This is Lilibet. She's friendly. Here, give her a lump of sugar. That's old Herman. He's a stuffed shirt. You can't make him a friend with a carrot, but maybe for an apple he'll plow half a field. They're tired like me, but we have to save gasoline for the boys fighting over there." He pointed eastward to the wetlands of his forebears.

In time Bo began to work with Anders in the fields. He often ate lunch with the old widower. Then they'd drive down to Sandro's house in the woods, Anders' rickety truck loaded with vegetables and fruits for which he would take no money from Ulrike, or from Hettie when she was there. Bo would gladly have lived with the old farmer, much as he loved Sandro, and now, approaching Hart's folly, he realizes he'd deemed Sandro to be in Ulrike's thrall.

One day, as they walked Lilibet and Herman back to the barn, Bo asked the old man, "Why do they hate the Jews here?" He didn't know he loved the old man until the old man gave him the great honor of accepting his question.

"The shopkeepers, they're English. They used to have the Dutchman and the Frenchman and the Indian to hate—now they have the Jews. They hate the Jews because it's very hard to separate the Jew from his money without being nice to him, since money is the only thing the Jew was ever allowed to have. They would rather hate than be nice. The Indian they killed, the Dutchman they burned and cheated and stole his land. The Jews are a little more complex. Funny, yeah, very funny, boy, because lots of those artist and writer people are Jews and without them those English shopkeepers might as well give the town back to us Dutch."

Ulrike would have pretended she didn't know what he was talking about. But Anders Ootwaert talked straight. Characteristic of his race, he liked artists and for decades forfeited profits from his stony farm to feed them and rent cheap barn space to them. His huge white farmhouse was crammed with a fortune in work by Yasuo Kuniyoshi, Philip Guston, Milton Avery, Barnett Newman, Marion Greenwood, and now at this late date and far remove Bo remembers a Hans Hofmann as well.

The Kearneys from whom Sandro bought his house two miles east of town on Witch's Stool left some tools with which Bo tried to garden, as he had at Cairnhall, but the heads flew off or the hafts split when he struck rock. Sandro tried to fix them, but his repairs were good for about three strokes. The hafts were rotten and the heads needed sharpening. One day Anders brought Bo a dozen or more implements. They were old, oiled, sharpened and newly painted. Neither Ulrike nor Sandro thought to thank the old man. It was after all a deal struck between him and Bo. Remembering it now he sees that in their alcoholic fog they didn't think it necessary to thank the old man, but Bo knows that the demarcation between booze and bad behavior serves only dirtbags. Nostalgia guts him as he remembers Anders.

It doesn't seem so long ago, that year just before he came to think he was shamefully sexual, easily seen through by girls, repugnant to them. Ulrike hadn't yet conspired with Angelo, Sandro's lummox doctor-nephew, to counsel him that masturbating was destroying his mind and yellowing his face. One of the amusements of his adult life is to imagine kicking Angelo's balls up into his windpipe. Anders Ootwaert had been to him a safe harbor. Like the Old Dutch Reformed Church on the green, Anders was full of light and affirmation. Recalling now that Anders was one of those dear people from whom he'd been wrenched filled him with grief. He wondered what Anders would have said if he'd voiced his sexual fears, and this brought him to recollections of those shiny Dutch girls he'd watched at the Reformed Church Saturday fairs, round-faced girls fruity with pleasantness, stately hook-nosed girls freshly stepped out of Vermeer in their pure solemnity, filling him with longing.

At The Granada he sets down his bags and walks on by to gaze at Anders Ootwaert's church, to remember the girls whose smiles haunted him. How could he return those smiles, impure as he was? They were nothing but purity and light and he can't bring himself even now to think they were as scared of their own dry-lightning sexuality as he'd been of his own. Still, they had, some of them, been able to gaze on him forthrightly and smile. He remembers one tall, narrow-faced girl, sixteen or seventeen, hair like corn silk, eyes as deep as the glacial tarn brooding over the town. She'd cocked her head one Saturday at the fair and looked at him until he flushed and looked away, then was compelled to look back. She shrugged as if they'd shared a joke, then smiled so suddenly and brightly that he smiled back in spite of himself. He deemed himself later to have sullied her with his fantasies and never let himself wonder if she had sullied him with hers. I hope so, he thought. Where is she now? Here perhaps, gray and matriarchal, much loved and cherished? I hope so.

He resolves to find Anders Ootwaert's place, to lay blue chicory where the old man might rest. Anders used to make wreaths of blue chicory for Lilibet to wear.

★

While he ponders Hart Clement and the dream he reposed in an emerald it dawns on him that Hart is taking a girlish delight in his profane side. For example, after one of his nocturnal patrols Hart asks him, "What did you see?"

"The usual belligerent girls and a few eat-shit-and-die bars."

Hart's snicker in a man who can barely sip Ensure unnerves Bo.

At the hospital in Albany Hart began to end his chats with Bo saying, "I have many secrets." Back at Echo Tarn he says it in Ulrike's presence and she snorts, "You have secrets!"

"I'm sure hers really are bigger than yours, Hart."

The poor man laughs so hard Bo fears he's killed him.

He never says it again in front of Ulrike, but when she leaves he starts again. Bo decides to use this mantra to measure the breadth of Hart's reading. "I like your mantra better than Cato's."

"Cato?"

"Yeah, you know, *Carthago dilenda est?*"

Hart looks bleak but nods gamely. His worldliness is skin-deep. Bo takes a breath and tells Hart how the Nixonian Cato ended his every senate speech saying Carthage must be destroyed until the Roman patricians would have gladly torched their vineyards to shut his mouth. He finds Hart pathetically grateful for having been found out as a poseur. Perhaps, he thinks, he's accidentally uncovered one of the secrets.

"I'm really an illiterate man," Hart tells him, as if expecting to be rewarded with newfound health. The possibility that Hart is bragging about his secrets is at least as strong as the possibility he's burdened by them. Bo chooses the latter, asking him if he should bring a notepad to their bedside chats so that Hart might reveal what he chooses. Yes, says Hart, as if telling a boy how bright he is, that would be a good idea. He gets out a big yellow legal pad several times, but Hart merely continues to brag. Finally, when it occurs to the old rascal that he's trying to bait a fish of unknown species, he says, "Take that box behind the door and go through it one of these days when I'm dozing. Then you may not feel like keeping me company."

"Hart, when I take a test I like to know what the name of the game is."

"You're about to find out," Hart says.

Bo resents this game. The box stays put and Hart's study of Bo turns grave.

"Have you heard of the Bildeburgers?" Hart asks him one day. He pronounces it Bilduhboiguhs, although his speech is usually not Manhattan patois; it's more radio-ese. He once had an antiques show on WOR.

Bo shakes his head.

"Ah, well, you should ask your mother about them."

"In the meantime what can you tell me?"

"If Ulrike doesn't like the cut of your jib, as you sailors say, you're a Bilduhboiguh."

Bo passes his thumb and finger down his jaw and mugs for Hart, who cackles.

"You know the protocols written by the elders of Zion?"

"Actually I thought they were written by drunken Cossacks who'd jerked off till their brains went soft, as Ulrike might say."

"Now that's a bit of Ulrike lore you'll have to tell me about—if I live long enough. Compared to the Bilduhboiguhs the elders of Zion are schlemazels. The Bilduhboiguhs are members of a worldwide conspiracy to homogenize the human race, immunize it against its creative impulses and put it under the heel of pasty-faced aristocrats. The Rockefellers, Queen Elizabeth, the Agha Khan, the president are all Bilduhboiguhs. And all those froggies who go around whispering to each other, *Il ne pas mort,* they're Bilduhboiguhs too."

"Who's not dead?"

"The Big McMuffin." Hart inserts his palm between his pajama buttons and thrusts his chin. "C'est lui."

"Oh, *La Gloire.* It's worse for the French than absinthe."

"Us too, my friend," Hart whispers.

"To say nothing of the goose-stepping boiguhs, right?"

Hart nods solemnly, satisfied Bo has gotten it all. But Bo's not satisfied. Is Bilduhboiguh a reference to the Trilateral Commission, the one-worlders who arouse even more paranoia than the Jews? Are we talking about Napoleon and the Trilateral Commission? Bo's onto Hart's game: this stuff comes from him, the white Jew, and he's laying it on Ulrike.

"Where do you think she gets this stuff?" Hart asks.

He'd give anything right now to be out on the bridge wing of some freighter taking a star fix. But his face somehow miscues the old man. He misreads Bo. "Don't clean it up for me. It's definitely shit. Somebody's got a computer with the name of every conspiracy freak in the world in it and she's on the preferred short list. Her name has been sold back and forth by every neo-Nazi whacko in the world: the KKK, Aryan Nation, American Forever, Christians for National Salvation, you name it, she gets it, all the semi-literate trash."

Bo huffs tiredly and goes over to the window and watches two teenagers dribbling a basketball as they walk by.

"So how can a fairly intelligent Jew find this amusing, is that what you're thinking?"

"Amusing is not the word I had in mind," he says, not turning. Sandro didn't do much listening. And Hart's too busy thinking what to say next, and he shares with Ulrike the grandiose habit of insisting on what others think and feel.

"The Jews are a fatally amused people."

Bo turns and stares. "Twaddle."

"And you, I would say, are fatally bemused."

"I'm ninety-nine percent reconstituted." Well, you old fuck, let's both be flibbertigibbets then.

"You'll have your answer soon enough and then I wonder what you'll think. A few years back we were down in Florida and Ulrike wanted to go shopping. She stood at the door and looked straight at me. What're you doing? she says. I'm reading, but since it obviously doesn't matter to her, I tell her, I'm seeking truth. It's eleven in the morning. She's already spent her usual two hours in the mirror and she's snockered on vodka in her orange juice. But d'you think she misses a beat? You're a fool, she says, truth is any damned thing you want it to be.

"In that case, I say, forget the Holocaust. And, believe me, she has."

Hart is good for a certain amount of truth, no more. The man plays whatever game he perceives to be in play. It's a good thing I don't need truth from him, Bo thinks.

"What do they call you, your shipmates? I imagine they have a hard time with Bo?"

"Bo."

"As in *beau geste?*"

"As in bosun."

"But you're a navigator."

"Second mate, yeah, but I was a bosun and it stuck."

Hart measures his caretaker. His lips form the word Bo. It saddens Bo. "Bo, if a dying man may be permitted to be blunt, why are you here?"

Bo knows Hart appreciates not being conned about his condition and he finds the answer surprisingly available. "I guess I have a covenant with myself not to refuse help when it's asked. It's hard to ask. It takes a lot out of you."

"How'd you come by this covenant?"

"You know, Hart, you would've made a fair psychologist."

"A forensic psychologist perhaps. I don't care much about the living."

"Or care too much and do too little?"

The usual film of wariness clears off Hart's pale blue eyes. "Exactly. But what about my question?"

"I was buying time," Bo says, smiling. "I couldn't sober up. And one night as I was watching these big six-inch turds with tin wings clink across my ceiling—I had to go hassle with the Coast Guard over my papers—I puked all over myself. And after I half drowned myself in the shower I started to crawl around inspecting the grain in the wood floors.

Then I sat by the window until the sun came up and I heard inside my head, *I am going to open up a way.* I got up, dressed and took a long walk. The azaleas had stopped barking and I said to myself, The answer to everything is yes."

"But surely not to everyone?"

"Surely not."

"And then you stopped drinking?"

"I fell off the wagon a couple a dozen times, but that was pretty much the end of it."

"A religious experience," Hart muses. "The Jew has a peculiar problem, Bo. He can't be cynical about the goyim without poisoning himself."

"This is a Jewish problem? What an exclusive people."

This discursion entertains Bo. Hart is most amusing when he tries to be honest.

"Ever hear of the Nazca Lines in the Peruvian desert?" Bo says. "There's a German woman, Maria Reiche, studied them all her life. They go back to 350 BC. They point straight to Rigel in the constellation Orion. As Rigel shifted in relation to earth the Nazcan people drew new lines. They also built irrigation systems that made the conquering Spaniards look primitive. Hell, the Spaniards didn't even know how to keep up the irrigation systems the Moors left behind. What they really knew how to do was loot."

"You think religion has extraterrestrial origins, Bo?"

"You can't spend years looking at the stars and believe we're alone. I think whole civilizations have worshiped the stars out of a kind of homesickness. The Nazcans, for example—they ate this star-shaped cactus called the San Pedro because it gave them the sensation of flying, and their pottery shows a falcon on the wing with the San Pedro in its talons."

"Are you the ferryman at the River Styx?"

Death cuts out the crap. Bo knows that from experience. He's thought long and hard about the ferryman Charon and his Egyptian counterpart Anubis. If he's had any thoughts about Hart's recovering, he doesn't now. This is the unmistakable canniness of death.

"All I really know about myself is I tie good knots and plot a fair course."

"It doesn't become you to be disingenuous, Bo."

Fair comment, but Hart has taken in the core story of his survival cagily and now Bo has no heart to cast still more pearls. He sticks to entertainment.

Something you forget at your peril, Llewellyn told him, is that borderline psychotics have no remorse, no parameters.

Nothing is beyond the pale to them. They're unremitting. They don't care and, if you do, you're just crow's pickings.

Even when they're dying?

Perhaps especially then.

Here is the crux of a lifelong predicament: he finds his enemies engaging. He can't be like Sandro, mongoose to cobra. He has to taste the venom. That, Hart Clement, is what I'm doing here, and if I had mercy, I'd tell you, I'd affirm you in your cynicism, disabuse you of any notion of my goodness so that you might truly die in peace. "I laced some of this yogurt with cognac. Try some."

Hart nods like an eager child. Bo slides two mouthfuls between Hart's purple lips.

"I think you ought to call in your markers, Hart."

Hart feels somehow discovered even if he can't decode this cipher. "How so?"

"You and I have given Ulrike a lot of power. I think you ought to take yours with you. Ulrike's the sort of person who always acts as if she's got your number, even when neither of you have the faintest idea what your number is. You always feel like your number's up around her."

"Bo, for a man of action, you do a lot of living in your head."

"Admittedly that's bad for your love life. What's worse is pretense."

"How do I call my markers in?"

"Clever as you are, you'll figure out a way."

Hart feels so indebted to Bo that he begins slurping some yogurt in his honor. In the vise of death this adopted son of a crude mafioso keeps handing Hart new leverages on life. All my tricks amuse him, Hart thinks. My cordial disrespect becomes him. I'm getting lost in the crevasses of my brain. Is this dying? You fall down a crack in your brain? I've pissed on the notion of any blood tie between Ulrike and this man for more than twenty years only to find I like him more than I like her. Well, the two thoughts are not incompatible, are they? I don't like her. I can't imagine why I ever did. Did I? How could I like a person whose opinions are based on bad movies?

"I'm not what I seem to be," he tells Bo.
Bo smiles. "Who is?"

11

That night Bo rewires the big iron lanterns in front of The Granada. He installs motion detectors at the side doors. While he stands on the hotel's terrace, rubbing bits of wire, tape and rust from his face with a big red handkerchief, smoking a cigar and remembering the bicycle chain incident and the horror he'd felt being whipped with his own good intentions, a tall girl with a startling face that looks as if it has been sculpted by gifted thumbs comes by carrying a mandolin.

"Hello, strange man, can I have a puff?"

And what have you been smoking, strange girl?

He takes out a cigar.

"Nooo, I want yours." Unlike him, she inhales.

"You live here?"

"Ghosts live here."

"I like ghosts. Can I look inside?"

He studies her. She wears a leather band across her forehead. Her soft hair looks like cream soda and pulls back to an off-center ponytail. Wisps of it dance in the night air. Her eyes are so pale they seem to lack color. He searches for the dilated pupils that speckle Echo Tarn, but all he finds is an absence of earth hue. She's tall, only an inch shorter than he, and wholly comfortable with her height and angularity. Her mouth is wide, straight and guileless. He likes this face, these bones, and he steps back from his liking.

She takes the spot he vacates, smiling. "Can I?"

Lady, you can do anything. He thinks how Ulrike would say he's allowed village riffraff to case the place. "You play the mandolin?"

"You know it's a mandolin?"

"I'm Italian."

"I like Italians."

"I like Appalachians."

She shows him a mouthful of big teeth, his reward for perceptivity. "I play in a band at the Shady Nook." She strums. "Who do you like?"

"Janice Joplin."

"Oh Lord, won't you buy me a Mercedes Benz . . ."

Bo laughs. Her Joplin imitation is first-rate.

Encouraged, she goes on. "My friends all have Porsches, I must make amends," and she scratches her crotch zanily. He laughs harder, but perhaps she oughtn't to have done that because he's now aware she has a crotch. "I'm Tate."

"Tate, I'm Bo."

They laugh again.

"What's your last name?"

"That's my last name," she says.

"What's your first name?"

"You can't have it, it's sorta like my dildo. Private."

He smiles cautiously and then breaks into what-the-hell laughter no one before ever heard from him. "Well, you can't have my last name either," he says.

"Fine, what can I do with it anyway?"

Bo has never met—he sends his mind back into all the brothels and encounters of a lifetime—a woman so zanily, flat-out, up-front sexual.

They sit down on the steps, Tate strumming her mandolin.

"So what do you do, Bo?"

"Sit in front of empty hotels and wait for beautiful women to come by and ask."

"That's a good gig. What do you really do?"

"I'm a merchant seaman. Do I have to be what I do?"

"It's just a conversation. I could sit here and say nothing, but you might think I'm weird. Course I am weird, but you look kinda straight and I don't want you to blow me off."

"What man would blow you off, Tate?"

175

"Chicken shits. I scare some men. Especially the ones who like me."

"Yeah, I understand. I'm kinda the same way."

She catches her lower lip between her teeth and looks at him as if she has the biggest decision in the history of humankind to make. "I see you at sea, Bo. I do. You're there right now. But come back here, don't be scared of me. I'm not one of those girls who tosses her tits around and plays games. Fact is, I ain't hardly got tits."

Her West Virginia accent has returned. Tate doesn't really like too many men, but when she does her body sort of shoves her brain aside. This he sees.

"I'm not as young as you think I am, you know."

"You don't miss much, do you, Tate? I like you."

"I like you," she says, slipping her arm around his. "What's your real name?"

"Amir Cavalieri."

"A mirror on the wall?"

"You write songs too?"

"Yeah, Bo. Like I said, I'm not . . ."

"As young as I think. I didn't figure you were jail bait."

"I'm not trouble either."

He looks out across the road to the cemetery. "Neither am I, Tate. Neither am I."

She doesn't know what to do with this retort, so she perseveres. "You like my legs?" She stretches them, long, brown and moccasined. He studies them appreciatively.

"Let's take them for a walk, Tate."

"You blowin' me off or you comin' too?"

"I don't blow good people off. Let's go."

He gives Tate the grand tour of The Granada, but both of them are pumped and poised to sprint. They leave the hotel quickly and start walking toward the green. Tate, he notices, walks heroically, kicking her legs out in front of her. She takes his hand. Her hand is dry and cool and strong.

"Let's have one of your cigars."

As they walk east on Market Street towards Echo Tarn's

incongruous eighteen-hole golf course they begin to hear each other breathe, and their breath is exultant. Occasionally they look at each other and laugh.

"My heart is beating fast," he says.

She leans down to listen. Then he listens to hers.

"Sorry, not much there, Bo," she says, grabbing his hand and laying it on her breast.

He stops dead in his tracks and turns towards her. "You ever see any Egyptian art?"

"On wrapping paper maybe."

"All the women have small, high breasts. It was their ideal. Big is vulgar."

Tate's mouth opens with interest. "Little kumquats turn you on?"

He wants to say, You turn me on, but it would be incautious, unfair. "You are very beautiful, Tate."

They set out across the golf course to the copses of willows on its east side as the Bearkill abandons it. The willows carve the moonlight into rood screens and they sit. He takes both her hands to hold her gaze.

"Tate, I done broke my pick, you could say. If you get my meaning. Like, I don't always rise to the occasion."

"I could fix it maybe. Leastways, I could try real hard. I'm handy. Ol' mountain gal like me, hard-run and put-up-wet, don't necessarily insist on the big-bang theory of creation, you know."

He laughs in spite of himself. He gives her a look so grateful it embarrasses him, but not before she catches it by the strangest gesture he's ever seen: she passes the back of her hand down the side of his face and then tugs the V of her shirt as if she's taken something from him and dropped it fondly between her phantom breasts.

"Is it safe there?"

"Very. And whenever you want it, you can have it."

He feels he's seen what the priests do in the tabernacle, why they tie their feet so that they won't tumble into another dimension. He'll never know what this is about, and he doesn't want to know, but he marks it as something to die remembering.

When tears well to float this thought he has an even better one: he kisses her, slow and searching, their tongues consoling them for past loss and grief, their bodies childish, at play. When she kisses his eyes her nipples sear his chest, her breath is incitingly sweet. He's mad to dive and finds its source, to brush against angels' wings as divers do.

Big girl that she is, he lifts her up and, looking into her eyes, they fly over the greens and hover like dragonflies, and finally sink down where the Bearkill delights in leaving the town and laughs on its way to the Hudson. They sink down into each other and vanish for a long time, and when the moonlight finds them Tate is rocking, an enthralled girl-child on a white hobbyhorse, her eyes lit with pixie dust, her mouth transfixed. Beneath her, locked between long thighs, Bo thinks of dolphins playing, whales broaching, comets arching. Everything, he thinks, is worth this. Tate works on him with such patience and diligence you would have thought she was shaping her destiny.

★

Compared to Anders Ootwaert's, Hart Clement's taste runs to kitsch, as if he were thumbing his nose at Echo Tarn's white-walled passion for modern art. Bo is standing in the sun room. He's just managed to get some banana custard into Hart. He regards a gross cement casting of a Roman foot soldier on the lawn. The birds have already passed judgment on it.

"You know, Bo," Hart says, "our difficulties are not wholly unpleasant to our friends."

"What a cynic you are, Mr. Wilde!"

"Haven't you found it so?"

"I think you should eat more banana custard. It's obviously doing you some good."

"Oh, I don't think custard will improve on my cynicism. My mind is fine, Bo, it's just tired of its house."

Bo morosely considers this invitation to serious talk. Hart strikes him as a man in a British movie brushing drollery over into archness in his flight from serious engagement. He owes no gravity to the man, but nonetheless he's moved to make a pass in kind at this confession.

"I'm surprised you would share this view of the dark side of friendship with me, Hart, because I always suspected you regarded me as one who would find Ulrike's difficulties, and yours, not entirely unpleasant."

Hart looks at him as might a duellist who's just crossed foils. "Our friends, Bo, I said our friends."

Bo can take it to mean kin exempt, but he takes it exactly as it's meant. "I've noticed the phenomenon, Hart."

"Well, the reason you would is quite different from the reason I would."

Bo quizzes up his brow.

"You would notice because you wouldn't take pleasure in others' troubles and I would because I would."

Bo's organs slacken. He respects and abhors this admission.

Hart chuckles weakly. "It's very like you, I think, to make no protest. You know when not to speak. That's rare. I've studied it, but the knack eludes me."

"You don't know me, Hart. How could you?"

"You'd be surprised what we take in, all of us, and pretend we don't. We don't want to be caught dead knowing. Now I'm being caught dead knowing."

"Yeah, I think you're right, we do take in a lot more than we let on. I think it drives some of us around the bend."

"You?"

"Oh yeah, I've been around the bend so often I'm plotting it on a chart."

"Only the good go round the bend."

"And only the good die young? Nah, you don't believe that, do you, Hart?"

"No. See that shelf over there? There are twenty-two books I lifted from Nazi party headquarters in Munich in nineteen-forty-five. They were all around the bend, the Germans."

"Let's stick to Americans."

"Okay, let's. I had you all wrong."

Now Bo does something that would have earned him the

Dave Llewellyn Bronx cheer of the month. He changes the subject. "What you said about taking in more than we admit, artists fly in the face of that. They take it in and put it down. Take Ulrike, for example . . ."

"Bad example. She takes absolutely nothing in, she just paints whatever she wants to see. She doesn't give a damn if it's true or not."

"Well, I'm not talking about representational art only, I'm . . ."

"Let's not talk about art at all, let's talk about you before you changed the subject."

"Hart . . ."

But Hart is on a roll. He projects a response onto Bo. "Hart, you old son of a bitch, your change of heart about me and a dime won't get me a cup of coffee. Say it, Bo. Try."

"If you get out of my head and stay in yours, we can talk, otherwise it's rape, and I know a little about rape."

"I'm trying to tell you I received my view of you like the Torah from a rabbi."

"You didn't swallow the whole Torah, did you?"

"It was convenient. You'd be surprised how much of our relationship is built on Ulrike having this son who . . ."

"Yeah, I know. I know all about it, better than either of you."

"Listen, Bo, get a pad, a big yellow note pad. I have many things I must tell you."

But when he returns Hart says, "You know, your cleaning up my foot this morning reminds me of an incident outside Munich. I'm in this Third Army pysch warfare unit interrogating krauts, Ulrike should forgive the expression. I'm walking along the road with two other guys and we see this German sitting up against a tree with his helmet lying next to him. We walk over with our rifles at the ready and I say, Are you dead, you heinie fuck? In German I say it, and he opens an eye, just one—he's a hauptmann, by the way, a captain—and he says in perfect English, I'm trying.

"Lemme help you, one of the other guys says, and points his rifle, but I'm a hauptmann too, and I say no. SS? I say. The hauptmann chuckles and says, If I were SS I'd be wearing an

American uniform by now. I like this bastard's face, besides I'm addicted to irony. You're lucky I'm not a Jew, I tell him. He looks at me, a look of great intelligence, compassion even, and he says, Perhaps I'm lucky you are a Jew, Herr Hauptmann. I work on this hauptmann feverishly. My life depends on it. What do I know? His leg and shoulder are bleeding. I stop the bleeding. I give him a cigarette. I think he lived, I don't know why. When we leave he salutes me and says, *Auf Wiedersehen, Herr Hauptmann.*"

★

Snow dervishes infiltrate the town on the seventh of March, whirling into every cranny, sealing alleys and doorways, establishing a blinding whiteness of equality and immediacy. Hart fails. Bo calls in the county public health nurse, who declares an emergency. Next morning he bundles Hart in blankets and carries him out the kitchen door in a thick, slanting snowfall and drives him to Our Lady of Mercy Hospital eleven miles away.

Sitting on the examining table in the emergency room, Hart asks, "Is this the end?" Bo looks hard to see if Hart wants a respectful answer. He's constellating a response when Hart relieves him. "Do you believe in heaven? You're a Christian, aren't you, Bo?"

He puts his hand on the old man's shoulder. "Let's just take it all head-on." After a lifetime of exile and exclusion Hart feels he's been admitted to the circle of men. His breathing steadies and he looks at Bo as a gut-shot younger brother might.

Bo sits with Hart the better part of four days, holding his hand, smoothing his brow, and chatting between tests and the ministrations of the nurses. Hart tells him, among other things, that he and Ulrike never reported their Echo Tarn holdings to their tax accountant. "Is that good?" Bo asks. He knows nothing of such things. "What they don't know won't hurt the bastards," Hart replies. It's the first time since he stopped drinking that Bo takes aspirin.

The mother superior, Sister Anne-Marie Morrisette, bandies jollities with Hart. She too smooths his freckled, age-spotted brow when she speaks to him.

"Isn't it surprising," he asks Bo, "that they're so kind to a Christ-killer?"

"This is a serious question?"

Hart doesn't answer for some time, then he says, "It's always an issue for a Jew, even one who has tried so hard and so unsuccessfully not to be one. The Clements came from England. How they got there and acquired their silly name who knows? They became a blue-eyed, red-haired lot, thanks I suppose to so many raping Cossacks and other Jew-lovers, so they were encouraged to pass. You know what I mean by pass?"

Bo doesn't know what to say. He thinks of the picture back in Hart's study of a thin red-haired boy fishing the Bearkill.

"You didn't think I had anything serious to say, did you, Bo?"

Hart remains gabby until March twelfth when he slumps in his bed as if praying. He looks up only once. "Wake up, Bo, and smell the roses."

That's his last sentence. It is eleven in the morning on the thirteenth when Bo returns to Our Lady of Mercy. At four Hart sets up the cry he will keep up to the end: "Help, help, help!" He seems never to grow hoarse. Bo and the staff are unstrung. Hart is moved to a corner room and curtains are drawn around him to muffle his plea. A form authorizing heroic measures is handed to Bo.

"No," he says, "we'll let him be the hero." Bo calls Ulrike to say it would be a good idea to come.

"Is anything wrong?"

He winces at the mean theatricality of her question. "He could use the company."

On March fourteenth Hart is wheeled out of his room on a gurney for a test, still crying for help. He never returns. He suffers a devastating heart attack in the elevator. A young German resident doctor tells Bo, "Believe me when I say we did everything we could do." Bo wonders what to feel, but his emotions ambush him. He's surprised to weep. He finds Hart on the gurney under a west-facing window. Hart seems to be incinerating like a sacrifice in front of a sun plummeting into the snow. Bo kisses his forehead. It's all he can think to do.

When he gets back to Hart's cottage he doesn't feel he belongs. He has trouble going in. Burn the place down, it's full of plague, he thinks. He gets out some tools and opens the water supply to the hotel's laundry. He stuffs three thirty-gallon trash bags with bedding and towels and drags them across the driveway to the hotel. It takes him a while to recognize that something is pulling at his right arm. He'd gotten the same feeling in North Atlantic ice fields. Certain Navy watch officers would call him to the bridge to sense ice in a fog. They invented reasons for calling him, not wanting to traffic in extrasensory perception, but they knew from experience that he sensed the ice better than their best radar. It's always a certain part of his body. The hairs rise and lean toward the siren call.

In this instance the siren call is emitted from an old Jim Beam carton behind the front door. It's filled with file folders, doubtless some of Hart's precious secrets. Bo looks at the box as if it were filled with rat shit. He thinks of taking it out to the perforated oil drum in the backyard and burning it. But that doesn't seem like waking up and smelling the roses. What harm could it do to try to do what Hart admonished him to do? He starts leafing through the file labels—tax filings, hotel lien, bus. per., cert. oc., Siegel bills, Crane bills, fid. res., depreciation, etc.— nothing enticing, no roses. He straightens up and is walking away when "fid. res." rings a bell. Can it be fiduciary responsibility or is it the name of some savings and loan? He pulls out the file:

The last will and testament of Alessandro Giovanni Cavalieri.

He reads a page and a half before his eyes slow:

"Having bequeathed the aforementioned in recognition of my affections for the forenamed, I bequeath the remainder of my estate in its totality to my well-loved and admired son, Amir (Bo) Cavalieri, in the hope that he will pursue the career in art that Our Lord has clearly intended for him. (Remember Pierre-Henri de Valenciennes.)"

The document is twelve pages of mock-Edwardian legal jargon. In it Sandro leaves apartment buildings to his grandson, Salvatore, to his alienated daughters, Angelina and Theresa, and a sizable trust to Ulrike, to be administered by Stuyvesant Chemical and Trust. But the bulk of his estate, perhaps seventy percent, he leaves to Bo: two apartment buildings on Gramercy Park, what is now Ulrike's house in Echo Tarn, land on Long Island and in New Jersey, and liquid assets. Bo sees that it was executed about six months before Sandro's death. He studies the stilted language: well-loved and admired son and the obscure but fond reference to M. Valenciennes, neglected and admirable painter. His hands tremble. He sees that Ulrike is the executrix. She must have been infuriated. Sandro had had his way with this will, overriding the predictable objections of his lawyer to the eccentric language. He could hear Sandro say, Fuck you and your degree, this is what I want it to say. What moves him is that he knows Sandro must have greatly troubled himself to remember M. Valenciennes and Bo's youthful excitement at having discovered him. He remembers the day perfectly when he'd come from sea to see Sandro. He'd been to a museum in Nantes and there had found the teacher of Corot's teacher, Michallon. He breathlessly told Sandro, not Ulrike the artist, that he thought Valenciennes's work as good as Corot's, perhaps better, boldly prefiguring the Impressionists long before Corot. Now, over the years and from beyond the grave, Sandro is telling him to remember his discovery at Nantes. The more he contemplates this burgled message, the more he fathoms the real theft. The real crime was in depriving him of it. Only hours later do his thoughts turn to the mackerel-in-the-face Sandro's will must have been to Ulrike. What had he been thinking? What must he have told her? How did he make it palatable? Obviously he didn't. Perhaps he thought he had. Perhaps he'd convinced himself that she shared his wishes for their son. What did she say? He tried to give this matter the attention it deserved, but it came up undeserving. It's Sandro's admonition about Valenciennes that captures him. All Sandro had to go on was Bo's enthusiasm. Sandro himself knew little about art except it was more important than all the doctors and lawyers and politicians together, perhaps only one rung down from opera.

That night he awakes at three. He has dreamed that he

encountered Hart on a gray, featureless plain. Even Hart is gray. "Goddamn you to hell," Hart says. But he doesn't feel that Hart is angry, he doesn't feel the words are addressed to him. But if not to him, to whom? He dresses and goes over to the hotel to find something to fix.

★

When he returns from the medical examiner's office the next day Ulrike is holding court in the cottage. The tipsy banter stops when he enters by the kitchen. Those in her retinue, motley and fawning, study him from their chairs and sofas in the living room as the Nazi-loving Swiss bankers must have regarded the Soviet foreign minister Maxim Litvinov—baked rat under glass. He casts a baleful eye, like a broaching whale.

Ulrike, steeped in Rob Roys, gets in his face. "How is he?" The Rob Roy is a revolting drink. She rarely looks into his eyes and doesn't now. She watches his mouth. It's set, his teeth locked. "Is he worse?" He shakes his head. "He's dead?" Her banshee wail engages his humor. He stands waiting for the windows to shatter.

Her retainers engulf her, proposing drinks. Their circle closes north of him. Jillian Wurthen, a nursing supervisor from a Manhattan veterans hospital, trips on a fetid Oriental rug, her elephantine ass landing on the glass coffee table. In view of her size—she weighs two hundred fifty pounds if she weighs an ounce—it's going to be quite an operation getting her to her feet. The cargo officer offers no help. Marjorie Carmichael, a soap-opera actress of a certain age, studies him with casual hauteur. He might like to sketch her. Jerry O'Flaherty, an old queen preposterously driven to act like one of the boys, brings a beaker of something red, brown and dead to Ulrike.

No one offers Bo anything but attitude. He's wallpaper, which suits him. It offers a chance to see Hart up the hill and into the ground. He leaves, bent on this work, and isn't missed. Only later does he think it strange no one asked him how Hart died. He would have liked Hart to see this. Hart would have liked to see it.

Well, Anubis, he tells himself, let's do it. Doing it, he buys a mid-priced gray casket from F. Wilmot Brashears, the undertaker, then a six-foot slab of Vermont granite from G. Verplanck, stonecutter. Brashears tells him he'll have to freeze Hart for about six weeks and lay him in the receiving vault because the ground is too hard to open. These arrangements go well until Brashears asks for the name of the clergyman. He sees Bo draw a blank and recommends the Rev. Kidwell Gansevoort. Bo marvels at any name as improbable as his own. "Slip him three hundred, that should do it," Brashears says. "He's never at a loss for words." The next day at Brashears he finds a tall, heavy man, obsequious as he is booming. Kidwell Gansevoort. Bo has never met a booming obsequious man before—he deems it a carnival feat—and muses that sketching has its limitations. Do they call him Kid? Certainly he should be Guy Gansevoort. Yes, he's a guy. Brashears confides that Gansevoort joined Ulrike and Hart in matrimony, as he put it, only two years earlier. Had they had an undertaker for a witness? Had he really joined them? He's getting silly and enjoying it.

When Gansevoort asks him what he knows about Hart, Bo says, "He was a man totally unintimidated by the legal system."

"I'm not sure I understand," says Gansevoort, "is that a virtue?"

"Uh, well, as to virtues, you might speak with Ulrike."

"And she is?"

"His wife. You joined them in matrimony."

That's it, make the guy work for his paid intonations and bonhomie.

"I can tell you he was a man of extraordinary"—Bo runs out of chutzpah—"aplomb," he says brightly.

"Aplomb?" says Gansevoort, turning the word like a Martini olive and finding it somewhat less than elegiac.

"Humor?" Bo offers. Hart would enjoy this more than the last years of his life.

A hint of methane hangs over the solemnities on March twenty-ninth. His bosun's nose identifies sundry perfumes, cigarette smoke on clothing, booze, the detergent used on the funeral parlor's floors, the conditioner used on the leather chairs, breath mint, and methane, volatile methane, which no ship's officer ever ignores, especially on tankers. He notices Brashears watching him and he twitches his nose. Brashears smiles and coughs. Either Hart has been out of the freezer too long or the undertaker's apprentice forgot something or there are simply too many farts in Ulrike's entourage. Fearing the worst, he goes to Brashears and whispers, "Is it too late to close the casket?"

"Nobody will notice," Brashears says. Bo nods.

Gansevoort's rotundities and ululations are ripe. It's the first time that Ulrike's cast do their jobs well, nodding, weeping, moaning, affirming. Goya or Daumier would have sketched the casket shaking with the guffaws of its tenant. Jan Steen would have painted a twinkly-eyed Hart peering out from under the lid of his casket.

12

Hart's burial is fraught with expectation owing to the fact that the intervening weeks produce no fewer than five wills, all the while Ulrike smugly broadcasting that the cunning Hart died intestate so as to spare her having to pay inheritance taxes.

"That's the most cockeyed thing I've heard since Richard Nixon said, I am not a crook," says Judge Wiley T. Carolan, the head of the little law firm in the county seat Bo hires to settle Hart's estate. That's before five wills in five hands surface. "The woman is looking at taxes she wouldn't have had to pay if the man had had any sense at all," the purply Carolan tells Bo. But what really interests the old magistrate is why Bo is taking it all so equably.

The wills Hart did make, it turns out, are cunningly not witnessed by an attorney so as to convince the beneficiary—but not a New York State surrogate court—of his or her good fortune. Each beneficiary—four women, all younger than Ulrike, and one man—expect to inherit something of what Hart embezzled from Ulrike and which both of them lifted from Sandro's estate. Bo has six weeks to savor this flimflam, wondering what Hart extorted from these dupes, as he goes about settling Hart's estate. In the course of it he and the old judge become lunch chums. It seems the judge is proud of a son who is an officer in the merchant marine. The blue river and red road lines on his face-map attest to some hard drinking, but they affably drink too much coffee and smoke cigars as they savor Hart's curious blend of skullduggery and tomfoolery.

"D'you think he just didn't give a damn about your mother?" Carolan asks moodily one day.

"I believe that life was not particularly real to him."

"Hmmm." The judge exudes a ring of blue smoke.

"I wonder if you'd do me a favor, Judge." Bo pulls out Sandro's will. "This will be on my own account. I want you to study this document and tell me if it's valid. Not now, but when it was executed."

The judge takes the will, gets out his drugstore reading glasses, adjusts them low on his bluish nose and reads. When he's finished, he says, "Executed is the operative word. It seems to be properly executed. It seems to have been witnessed by two attorneys. That's what the state requires, what Clement's bamboozlements didn't have. Let me look into it. It would have been probated in Manhattan. I'll check the records."

"If there were records I'd have known."

Wiley Carolan stares over his glasses at Bo. "It's a felony crime to suppress a properly executed will. Even if it's improperly executed, as you well know, one must leave it up to the surrogate to decide."

"Yeah," Bo says.

"I like mysteries, my friend. This one is on the house."

★

At the burial Bo shakes hands amid the gravestones when a woman looking like a string of sausages appears before him. She wears a nineteen-forties beret. As he offers his hand she spits with Gypsy gusto. Och-toohey! He being two heads taller, her spittle splatters his heart. He snatches her beret off her head, wipes off her spittle with it and plops it back on her wiry head, wet side down. She's so astonished she farts. He nods appreciatively and walks off, knowing he's encountered one of Hart's swindled beneficiaries. He has little sympathy for them. They're fellow hornswogglers.

The five indecent and invalid wills turn out to be cheap tricks. All that's required is a desultory grapeshot of letters, taking no more than four billing hours at the small-town rate of a hundred and fifty dollars an hour. Dying intestate is another matter, particularly because the tax returns Ulrike and Hart filed separately before they wed and jointly later were perilously short of information. It turns out that the IRS had indeed caught up to them. A week after Hart's burial the IRS locks Ulrike down tighter than a rioting cellblock at Attica. She can't even use her Bloomingdales card.

Judge Carolan summons a tax lawyer who informs Hart's accountant in Manhattan of the hidden holdings. A week later the man, seeing he has been signatory to falsified returns for decades, is in Mount Sinai Hospital for a checkup. "We're going to have to amend everything," Carolan tells Bo. "I don't know what's going to be left."

The mess sorts out better than anyone could have predicted. In the end, the bulk of the estate, almost all of which had been siphoned from her own assets, passes to Ulrike. The IRS accepts amended returns, enriching Uncle Sam by some four hundred thousand dollars, and Judge Carolan & Company pocket thirty-seven thousand dollars, which Bo guesses is cheap. What's left of Hart's estate hardly represents an iota of what he and his co-conspirator wasted of Sandro's betrayed legacy.

Sitting in his office in the wake of this mishmash, surrounded by photo blow-ups of his son's ships—tankers, Bo notes with distaste—Wiley Carolan says of Hart Clement, "What a jackass." Bo stares out the window watching the oak trees clutch their tattered leaves. Carolan is a bit disconcerted to hear no amen. To fill the vacuum, he says, "Your mother, Bo, should we get her in to discuss her will? I presume she thought Hart had a good idea not making one out, but you're not a spouse. Her dying intestate would cost you. You are the only heir, is that right?"

Bo winks. He is now the keeper of his own betrayer's secrets and it gives him more power than a garrote and the will to use it.

A week later Carolan tells him what he's found out about Sandro's will. "Near as I can tell, this is a perfectly valid will which was never brought to light by the one person legally bound to bring it to light, namely your mother. It's not puzzling that Matthew F. Cuomo, one of the witnesses, made no inquiries. He must have assumed the will was executed. What is more than passing strange is that Francis X. Boettscher, who was your mother's attorney when she reported that Mr. Cavalieri died intestate, took no action, because he was the other witness. Boettscher is dead, but I spoke with his partner, who remembers the estate. He remembers your father and liked him enough to take a run over to Hackensack to dig out Boettscher's records. He found Mr. Cavalieri's will and I think he's as disturbed as I am, but, as he said, the statute of limitations has long since kicked in. So there you are, Bo. A very shabby piece of work."

Carolan takes a proper pass at righting things when Bo brings Ulrike in to sign off on the estate. He points out that a will provides a way to pass wealth decently from one generation to another without inciting government to lick its chops. A trust perhaps? As he speaks Ulrike rises and begins to pace from one window to another with her back turned to them. Finally she turns, draws up to Carolan's desk, fires a trapped-bubble paperweight over his shoulder and splutters, "What the hell do I care when I'm dead?"

Bo, uncomfortable with Carolan's effort to paint over the grotesque, turns her words over carefully. She might have said, Do you think I'll care when I'm gone? Then she could have said, What difference will it make when I'm gone? He does this sort of thing when he doesn't want to deal with the obvious, but Carolan won't let him. "I hope you heard what the lady said, sir."

Bo sits. He lowers his chin in a gesture of exhaustion and then looks up at Carolan with a wry smile.

"What the hell was he talking about, do you know?" she says when they're outside in the light of day. Bo says nothing. "Do you?" He helps her into the car. Then he turns in his seat and stares at her up close until she emits a genuine Dickensian harumph. He laughs. She stares at him and then she laughs in a moment of family togetherness.

Winter sets in.

*

Ulrike and Hart loved The Granada empty. It enabled them to play games. The town waited for developments. Entrepreneurs who coveted the place courted Ulrike and Hart. They enjoyed the scams grifters ran on them. It gave them something to talk about and it kept the police busy. They entertained themselves like this for twenty years. Their zeal for playing this game was equaled only by the zeal of those they manipulated. The codes and regulations and ordinances the town churned out bothered them not a whit. Again and again they said they were planning to reopen the place, and the local newspapers dutifully reported the grand plans. They spent more than half a million dollars on equipment, repairs and improvements that failed to meet town, county and state codes. They took in partners, fell out with them and swindled them out of years of dreams, sweat equity and even money.

The perversity of lavishing so much of Sandro's money on the place against all reasonable expectation of reopening it offends Bo so deeply that he begins to regard the local taverns, the Elephant Hole and the Buffalo Muffin, with longing. Even as an assassin his well-disguised passion has always been to do a thing right, and he corrects as many of The Granada's defects as he can without money.

Ulrike and Hart lived in Manhattan and Echo Tarn in monied filth. No wall has been painted in at least thirty years, no curtain washed, no bricks pointed. Hart's ties look like soup napkins. Ulrike responds to dry cleaners with paranoia. Laundries she regards as a breakdown in social order. She does not know how to use her toaster, her fans, the electric breakers, flashlights, door locks. The breadth of her mechanical ineptitude dismays him. A Volkswagen bug with two thousand miles on it sits on its rotten rubber in the driveway. It makes people think there's somebody here when we're away, she tells him. That equipment should fail, that a house should need painting insults her. It's an indignity to which some conspirator subjects her. Everywhere Bo finds evidence of food fights, encrustations, tumbleweeds of dust, rivulets of detritus. The hotel's fine, deep artesian wells were abandoned when the town foisted an expensive water and sewer system on eleven hundred leery villagers, picking shopkeepers' pockets. Suspecting that The Granada's basement might be flooding because ground water flows up from these unpumped wells in the spring, Bo cracks their iron caps with a chain wrench and finds them packed with beer cans and liquor bottles. He regards this discovery as his own past. Then he notices the wells have iron ladders in them, so he spends the next six sweat-blind days chucking cans and bottles up into the basement and hauling them to the dump where the attendant, who has been writing determinedly unappreciated poetry for fifty years, eyes him appreciatively.

Bo joins in the humor of the thing. "I have a powerful thirst."

"Hell, you had to take the fun out of it, didn't you?" the attendant tells him, "I preferred my own interpretations."

"Which were?"

"Take your pick."

"I'll do that."

Ulrike isn't drinking now, determined to outlive anybody who's ever gotten her number or even the remotest glimpse of it. That fools him. He didn't take them for drunks. Sandro, yes. But his view of drunks is still so alcoholically hospitable that he hasn't admitted them to the temple. This, he now sees, is a symptom of his own alcoholism. They were drunks. Drunks don't give a damn about anybody. But which comes first, the boozing or not giving a damn? He asks himself just that as he carts out the last cans and bottles, and his answer jolts him because it involves all that growing up that alcoholics have to do after they stop drinking.

"Who the fuck cares?" he says out loud. A balmy calm— amazing grace, he thinks it—settles down in him.

His discoveries pour into the hole in his head faster than he can absorb them. He starts to drown inside his skull. He resolves to spit more, which bosuns do at least as well as baseball pitchers, but it doesn't help.

★

Now Mercury does the boogaloo, as it does three times a year, transiting the May sky, propitiating the gods so that the crack between illusions can remain open long enough to restore the awe that keeps us from destroying ourselves. Mercury's boogaloo, which astronomers call retrograde, is itself an illusion. But when it happens cell phones trip heart pacers, computers crisp information, and storm light paints the quivering leaves a silver Papa Corot would have given his gypsies for.

Ulrike has painted in the storm light of this crack all her life. When she complained that Bo could only imitate the feelings of other children, it was a self-portrait. In herself she admired it inordinately. In him she detested it. Why should she play by the foolish rules of mortals? He's unwanted property, but that doesn't mean she's about to sell him.

She takes to ink-stick drawing. Her lines are as long as her ink holds out, intricate, erotic. In the manner of Asian calligraphers, she never goes back to improve. Her ink-stick figures dance like skeletons on strings. Their genitalia, lubricious little devices, splat the air. Bo admires these drawings, which he usually finds next to the telephone. She makes them while talking, looking away to the upper left and then quickly turning to draw with her right hand. At first he thinks these are sidelong glances meant to catch what the eye can't see, but in time he understands that her straight-on vision is failing. Only her peripheral vision remains. Yet she wears no glasses.

Mercury boogaloos in May of nineteen-ninety before we become an electronic body politic, before satellite navigation makes the sextant a back-up device, but Bo is steeped in the mythology of Mercury the Messenger's legendary ambivalence in the heavens and decides in the stillness after Hart's death to entertain himself with the notion that the Hudson River Luminists must have painted in the crack Mercury prised open, in the eerie light when the clouds race before a storm, and this entertainment brings him to the recognition that Valenciennes, Corot, the Luminists and Ulrike not only painted in the crack but required its light. Technically, Ulrike doesn't belong in that group because she has painted for the most part under fluorescent tubes. In fact, she pooh-poohs the vaunted quality of north light as romantic crap. But plein air painters could learn a few things from her because the light she uses is the stage lighting of her own mind. As always, she's unbeholden.

He's so excited by these contemplations that he stops merely feeding her and begins preparing feasts. Between his preparations he studies the Luminists in the Echo Tarn library, which is better than a thousand small-town libraries owing to all the poor artists and writers who left it their books in remembrance of its kerosene stove when they couldn't pay their fuel bills. There one day he finds a clipping charring in its own acid inside the cover of *The Hudson Luminists* by Angiel Slattery. It seems to be full of classified nostrums: Wystan's pruning shears, a revolutionary garden tool, Ostrander's cough elixir . . . but when he turns the clipping over he finds an Oxford-rule box containing calligraphy:

> *When the crack between this world and the world*
> *of lost powers opens, a certain kind of light is*
> *needed by each world's visitors. The air smells*
> *of gunmetal. The leaves turn ashen and daven.*
> *Buildings blanch; they renege on their promise to*
> *hold their shapes. We happen upon our true and*
> *eerie domain in this, which we call the storm*
> *light. Then the rain pelts and we return to our*
> *usual forgetfulness. We betray the storm light*
> *with our addictive expectancies. Great opportunities*
> *go begging. Compared to storm light the storm is*
> *an anticlimax.*

There's more, but the bottom of the box is cut off. There's no headline. Probably the author's name followed, perhaps with an invitation to attend a discussion of Madame Blavatsky's theosophical writings. Or perhaps the clipping was earlier than that, he has no way of knowing, but its coincidence with his musings thrills him. Mercury has handed it to him.

Bo quits the library, imagining the clouds are spritzing May wine and feeling he's entered the crack. On reflection, the clipping is even more disquieting. Its language, while theosophically opaque, isn't as antique as the clipping itself. He doubts a writer in the last century would have used the verb daven. He doesn't have a scientist's lust to explain. He wouldn't

195

be caught admitting it, but he thinks some science obscene. He's content, like most sailors, not to understand some things. But this is an adventure, a magic mystery tour. First came Sandro's will, then his recognitions about Ulrike, and now his contemplations objectifying themselves.

Bo knows storm light as well as he knows Saint Elmo's fire or green flash. At sea the petrels careen, the clouds reel and ships' helms wobble. Now, in the cemetery where he buried Hart, the dead caress the soles of his feet and the storm light irradiates the stones. Nothing in the town's jumble of clapboard contrivances, its Jesus wannabes and welfare saints with con-artists' hearts interests him as much as the dead. He can form no opinion about their state except it's urgent. They embrace him, a man who eluded every other embrace, in a quandary.

As he lopes down off Artists' Hill Cemetery he sees a misshapen old Volvo screech to a halt and back up into the lot across from Hart's house, firing gravel into the weeds.

"Hey, Ulrike, it's me, Eddie Breit."

Ulrike sits on the terrace. She shades her eyes against the setting sun. The man sits down as Bo draws up. He greets them and goes inside. They sit on the terrace for a while, but before long Ulrike is inside, pestering Bo: "Come out and meet my friend, Eddie. He was Hart's friend too. Please, Bo."

Experience of their choice of friends thwonks his shit detector.

Breit is a balding, sinewy man in his forties. He wears a fetid black tank top, cut-off shorts and sandals. His nails are dirty. He sports a rope-throw hairdo. His eyes are hard to find. Bo, the raptor, is bound to see him as road kill. Eddie Breit regales them with snapshots of Pueblo kivas and anecdotes of his recent life as an Aspen limo driver.

"My life's a spiritual search, Ulrike. There's power in those kivas. I'm not sure about the vortex down in Sedona. So . . . whudduyudo—Emir, is it? I heard a lot about you from Ulrike and Hart when I was up here working in the old hotel."

Bo waits with a faint smile for this louche feint to wane.

"Tell us about Aspen, Eddie," Ulrike says.

Mercifully he gets to the point. "I see you got a for-sale sign up. Tell me it's not so, Ulrike. You're not selling your dreams, are you? What would Hart say? All it needs is some knee pads and some honest sweat."

Here's the game again. She's loving it, flying in the face as it does of Bo's counseling to sell her properties and paint. She loves what Eddie says, not because it's good advice, but because it promises to aggravate her son.

This loud, self-congratulatory finagler, come out of the blue to reconstitute the family scene, amuses her son, not least because he knows she doesn't know it in her forlorn hope of goading him. Or rather, and this is more her style, getting someone else to goad him.

"Bo believes it would cost too much to open again. He says let some moneybag do it."

God, he's enjoying it. He hasn't been able to get her to spend a cent to keep the great ark from falling down. He looks at Eddie Breit's big yellow teeth and smiles. But Eddie doesn't get it.

"The codes 'n all that are shit, Ulrike. You slip 'em a few large when you shake their hands and you open the place up and laugh all the way to the bank, trust me. I know how to do it."

Bo chuckles in spite of himself. This guy doesn't have class enough to slip a bartender a tip. But he's made a mistake judging Breit. Correctly assuming he's not a serious person, he fails to take into account that Breit takes himself seriously.

"Lissen, Em-eer, I've got it right, it's Em-eer, right?"

He tilts his head to look at Breit from about 030 on the compass. He's had his alert.

"I wanna talk to you, mano a mano. C'mon over here." He motions to the driveway between the cottage and the hotel. It interests Bo that Breit knows how this gambit will titillate Ulrike.

"Ooh, I'm cold," Ulrike says. "I'm going inside to get a sweater."

Bo glances at the cheap oversized thermometer nailed to Hart's huge tulip poplar. Eighty-four Fahrenheit, the wind about one on the Beaufort Scale. Breit is already over on the macadam driveway beckoning, rippling his muscles like a boy in an itchy suit. Bo slumps in the filigreed white plastic chair and looks up at the cumulonimbus clouds as if he has a thought in his head. Then he looks at the man on a spiritual search and frogs his lips as he often does when something has to be done. He gets up like an old, tired man and approaches. When he's in reach Eddie Breit snatches his worn blue button-down Oxford collar and rams him against the clapboards of Hart's house.

"Look, fuckface, I dunno what your problem is, and I don't give a shit, but nobody laughs at Eddie Breit."

From his status as cowed old man Bo, seeming not to have reacted at all, drives Eddie Breit's balls up with his knee. The rope-throw lurches forward to reveal a mottled pate. Bo brings both hands together down on the back of Breit's neck. He debates a second or two within himself, then he kicks Breit off his kneepads with a work boot to the face. He watches Breit pinch snot and blood out of his nose and wipe it onto his tank top as if it was somebody else's. Then he pulls out a cheap White Owl Invincible and lights it, studying his assailant with a dispassion born of shipping under strange flags and expecting every damned thing in the world to happen. He knows that in some awful sense he's now fully himself.

"Are you done with your conversation? I'm coming out now," Ulrike calls. Yeah, Mom, I've been raped, hanged and every other way bent out of shape, but everything's okay, you can come out now. It isn't Cuban, but White Owl makes a pretty good cigar.

"I dunno, are we finished, what's-your-face?"

"I'll be back, you son of a bitch, and you ain't even gonna see me."

"Is that a nice thing to say about your friend Ulrike?"

Bo has reached a stage in life where the spoken word seems excessive. "You can come out now, Ulrike. We were just having a few laughs, mano a mano, so to speak."

Coughing coyly in the blue smoke trail of Eddie's jalopy, Ulrike stares at her son with what comes to him as dislike and admiration ladled out in Prussian blue. He in turn admires her for saying nothing. It's quite an act. He can't think of a single movie star who could handle it. Not even Ida Lupino.

"I'm gonna hike up the hill 'n see what Hart has to say, maybe say hello to some of the people who painted me in the good old days." Dislike spikes over into hatred. He likes it pretty well, reassuring and affirming as it is. It's not every day one's mom arranges a rumble with a hundred and eighty pound sack of shit.

13

As he rounds Vacco Mariano's frame shop and crosses over to Artists' Hill a camouflaged specter bearing a percussion drum materializes out of a spruce copse.

"You're a violent man," Wraithe says. In his mind her name has to be spelled with an e.

In respect for the awe in which her craziness is wrapped, he chucks his cigar butt, pulls out another el cheapo and lights it. He looks for her eyes, which she does not give up readily. "It's not worth contemplation."

She bangs her drum over his head.

"That's the stuff," he says.

He processes up the juniper-studded hill, his military specter in tow. Then he turns. The parting sun sets her orange hair on fire. He finds her eyes. Lion's eyes in an appropriate face. "Hey, listen, great soul, if violence turns you on, don't give it a second thought. It's vestigial."

Not once do the lion eyes blink. He leans in to see if the pupils are dilated. They're not. It's his gift to take the loonies of the world seriously, having never taken the big shots seriously.

"I need, I really need to think you're afraid of something," she says.

Her round daft face touches him. But in repose it does what goblins do. Her head is a hillock of ornery tussocks, her bones spring-hinged and unpredictable. Her eyes do not blink, slide or rest. They can no more turn inward than a lion's, and yet he rests in them. It's this quality he doesn't think can be captured by any artist. He knows that whenever artists try to arrest a changeling they make a caricature, at best a Pre-Raphaelite conceit. The fact that her name is Annelise Tenbroeck seems more inconsequential to him than any other name, even his own. He would stake his life that her personal history—parents, siblings, lovers—is little more indicative than that of a protected witness. She has no agenda and therefore she has power. The more he considers her the further he goes from seeing that they share the same blood, blood that is deaf to this world but electric and waiting. Indifference, beatings, rape, these make men strange, but for all his work with Dave Llewellyn, he can't let go the notion that they happened to him because he is strange and chose a stranger's profession. It suits the draftsman but not the artist. He admires Daumier and Goya because they have something to say. He doesn't understand that he respects what he sees too much to make it say anything except what it might impart to him if only he were respectful enough. This is the approach he takes to Wraithe.

She has watched him for weeks from doorways, from under trees, from Mill Run where she washes. He knows her name. She's from Bluestone, rich family, two kids who live with their father. She can't stand being indoors where every damned thing wants something, even in the dead of winter. The street people look on her as some kind of leader, but she never seems to say anything to them. She plods all day long in surplus Army boots, in summer in a khaki tank top, in winter in a field jacket with a filthy white scarf wrapped around her head. Sometimes, if you look at her, she looks away. Other times she bangs her drum and stares at you. She is liked and trusted, even by the cops. Her situation reminds him of beggars among the Arabs: God has cast her lot. He calls her a great soul and doesn't know why. It's unlike him, except that he likes street people. No one else in Echo Tarn or anywhere else ever called her that. And it seems to him no one else has ever said a more poignant or compassionate thing, not to him. *I really need to think you're afraid of something.* So does he.

"So do I," he says, listening to it echo.

★

By August Ulrike is dying, sitting in the sun on her terrace, furious with God for letting her age. She and Hart never had a good word to say about anyone and she misses the fun. She doesn't give a damn that nobody in Echo Tarn will miss her. She insisted Hart's eight-foot slab say, *Beloved by all who knew him,* and Bo doesn't tell her that somebody visits the grave and ritually shits on the beloved.

"When I die just stuff me with maraschino cherries and prop me up in a corner," she tells him. It's her last attempt to get any kind of rise out of him. She looks to see if he thinks it funny. Ulrike stuffed with cherries reminds him of dreaming as a child of her butchered and scattered on rooftops. He's spent a fair chunk of his life feeling guilty about it.

It's nice to take a hot bath in Ulrike's bathroom, to sit and drink her tea on the terrace in the fiery haze of fall, but Annelise Tenbroeck wouldn't have sat hour after hour listening to Ulrike if she didn't feel the moral obligation of the dead to the dying. Annelise lives with the dead, feels protected by them, and sees their yearning on Ulrike's face.

For her part Ulrike doesn't give a hot damn if Annelise understands her. She's forgotten all the manners of the elderly that she swore she'd never exhibit, except one: she can't talk to herself. Mutter, swear, sure, but she can't talk to herself. As an artist she's been spared introspection—or deprived herself of it, whichever view you like—because artists act out, as the psychologists say. She's never discovered her greatest flaw as an artist, perhaps even as a person: she needs a theater to perform. For artists and writers this is mortal. They must be able to create deep within the secret corridors and halls of their interior castles, and only then allow their publics to despoil them. If Ulrike fathomed this she would have sold her paintings instead of withholding them and complaining that the money-grubbing galleries were all too willing to sell for too little.

Annelise knows the living have nothing to say. She hasn't asked her friends on the hill about this, but they look down and see her listening hour after hour to Ulrike, as Bo goes about Ulrike's business, and they'll surely tell her one night if she's wasting her time. They value Annelise. She runs errands for them, keeps them informed—some of them. Others, the majority, don't want to hear anything about the town or the world, but occasionally they ask certain questions.

"Normal children don't do such things," Ulrike tells Annelise. "He was never what you'd call a normal child. Is it normal to stare? No matter what you'd be doing, you'd turn around and he'd be staring at you. He was like a maniac. It wasn't a stare at all, you know, it was a leer. I would try to play with him, amuse him, and he'd stare at my breasts. Is that normal?"

Annelise shakes her head.

"When I looked at him in *l'Hopital des Oranges* in Algiers it was the worst moment of my life. He wasn't mine. I knew it, but what could I do? That goddamn French bitch of a nurse said, I assure you, madame, zees bebee eez zee one. This was not Luc-Antoine's, or Soren's, or Ben Aissa's. It was not mine. A woman knows.

"What's wrong with him? I asked.

"What do you mean, madame?

"He doesn't cry. Babies cry. He's too small. Why is he so small? He doesn't look human at all. He looks like a monkey.

"He is weak, madame. He will cry and soon he will laugh, it eez certain.

"If this baby lives to laugh, he'll laugh at me, that's what I thought. The more he stared at my breasts the more I hoped he would not live. God singles me out for a hoax, and just so that I would get the message, he sees to it the boy is born with a blue veil, like a goddam Tuareg! And that's exactly what happened, he was like a Tuareg. You know what Tuaregs do? They steal babies. Too bad this was Algiers, not Touggourt, or I could give him to the Tuaregs.

"When Ben Aissa came—the French were not thrilled to see this *bash agha* walking around their hospital like Charlemagne in a burnoose—he picked up this little animal and said, Blue eyes, like you, Ulrike. He's a little Crusader.

"Please don't act like an ignorant wog, I told him. You can't tell the color of a baby's eyes. Whatever color his eyes were going to be, they weren't going to be human eyes. I knew that.

"He's not mine, Ben Aissa, I said.

"Then whose is he, Ulrike? The French are gross but not stupid, Ulrike.

"He played with the boy as if it was his, as if it were a normal child. Arabs are like that. They love children. They spoil them rotten. After a while he left. Then Rose MacQuarrie, a witch if ever there was one, came to see the baby. It should have been hers. One thing I did like about her, besides her looks, was she said what was on her mind. Has Soren seen him? she asked.

"What a question, Rose, I said. He's not Soren's. He's not even mine. Soren was this Swede she lived with.

"You'll get used to him, Ulrike, she says. Well, Rose, here I am in Echo Tarn all these years later, and you're as wrong now as you were then, you cow.

"For such an educated woman, she was stupid. I never did get used to him. Never. What's more, I doubt now that anybody ever got used to him.

"The next day a nurse brought him back. She handed him to me and said, What is his Christian name, madame?

"What makes you think he's Christian? I say.

"But of course, madame. However, *les indigenes* have names too, madame.

"*Les bicots*, you mean!

"Zut, zut, she says and takes it away, sucking air. Then her boss comes back. It's still sucking air. Madame, we must have zee bebee's name. I held this little purple prune by the cheeks and turned him this way and that way. *Incubus*, I said.

"An' zees, eet is an Arab name, madame?

"I laughed so hard my stitches burst. I curled my knees up I hurt so much, but I couldn't stop laughing. The nurse snatched the baby and as she was leaving, I said, Amir, his Christian name is Amir.

"As you say, Madame. How it is spelled, zees name?

"I spelled it. Amir was my paint boy. He carried my paints. He could paint. He had talent. He carried my paints because he wanted to go to Hollywood. That's all he wanted to do. He was handsome enough. I painted him so often I thought I owned him, which is exactly what the natives fear about artists and cameras.

"Never give a man your nipples."

Ulrike thinks the loopy grin she evokes in Annelise has to

do with the metaphysical marvels of her dictum. But Annelise is just remembering her two pregnancies, squirting her excessively fecund breasts at her brothers and masturbating fanatically while pumping herself dry. Ulrike thinks Annelise's circumstances are, like her old age, an aberration. Instead of living in the cemetery, slapping her hand drum around town, and occasionally boffing fellow misfits in the bushes, she'd soon rejoin her affluent family in Bluestone and resume the upbringing of her children. Therefore Ulrike feels a certain obligation to enlighten the girl.

"They want you to be their slave mommy. They only know how to desecrate women. Your nipples are for you. Wear them so boldly you make men cry—that's the closest they're ever going to get to the mystery of life. In every other way they're dipshits of the first order. Women understand sacred space. Men just want to stuff it because it scares them shitless."

The sun is poaching the town by the time Annelise decides Ulrike's story deserves an award. She pops open her camouflage jacket and shows Ulrike her considerable breasts. Ulrike has enough peripheral vision left to savor the event. "Wait here!" she shouts. She bungles her way to her studio in the rear of the cottage and returns with a big pad, ink and brushes. Her ink strokes are sure and incisive. Color would be a vulgarity. Annelise's coloring, sun droppings, is implied by lubricious teardrops of ink. In black and white autumn is unmistakable. She paints Annelise baring her breasts and staring straight at her portraitist with her loopiest grin. Her breasts see more than her eyes. When she's done she tears off the sketch and gives it to Annelise.

"There! You know what this says?" She can't remember the girl's name. Usually she doesn't care if she can't remember a name, but now she does. "Do you know? It says, Shit and go blind."

"Shit or go blind?"

"No—never give the bastards a choice—shit *and* go blind."

This old lady is crazier than I am, Annelise thinks. She thinks she ought to get in bed with Ulrike. Maybe if she went to bed with her this powerful old bat's perfect craziness will rub off on her. She gets up and patrols the perimeters to see if Bo's around. Then she takes Ulrike by the hand and they go inside.

Bo makes dinner for the three of them that night. But as he builds a fire in the fireplace the walls begin to lean in on Annelise. She slips into the night.

Next day Ulrike's ruminations continue, Annelise attending.

"When they brought the baby back to me I wouldn't feed him. One of the nurses grabbed my nipple and started milking me. She wasn't dressed like one, but I knew she was a nun, so I told her, Come back and do this when you've fed the baby. She blushed, put her finger to my lips to shush me and said in French, You are too naughty. I wouldn't feed him, but about four days after he was born I said to him, Everybody needs a mother. Maybe your mother was a frightened little girl like I was, maybe her father was not a normal person and did things to her, like mine. So I'll take care of you for a little while and we'll see.

"Rose MacQuarrie was full of useful information, which is often true of those who have no talent. Sea captains used to pay high prices for a blue veil to protect them, Ulrike, she says. Maybe this child will give you luck, she says.

"Don't count on it, Rose. When I said that I saw something in her face I can only call hope. She wanted this incubus. She's barren, I thought. Too bad. She had the right nipples for the work. I couldn't get her out of that room fast enough. Little did I know the child would stare at people just like Rose MacQuarrie. I didn't want her around. Her body, her face disturbed me. She was too bright. I had suffered too much to want what I hated. But it was very strange for me to know at that age because all my life I have suffered the terrible disease of not knowing what I felt. If you asked did I love you, I would say maybe. If you asked me did I hate you I would say of course not. Maybe the two major accomplishments of my life are that I know that and that I paint well. But neither has brought me happiness or peace. Peace is for women whose mothers didn't give them to their husbands. I've never needed that psychoanalytical crap to know that. If I had liked Rose MacQuarrie I'd have given her the boy and she would've taken him, but the thought of another person like her exceeded my generosity. So I suppose

206

I ought to say that I hated her, because I'm an honest person. I hated that she thought she knew me. I'm secretive. If I had to undress for a doctor to tell me what disease I had, I'd say, Let it kill me. All we have in this world is the face we put on, the movie we project on the screen. What gives anyone the right to undress us, to insist that anybody go naked in front of them? That's why I laughed to think when I got back to New York that my teacher Hans Hofmann thought I was so good. I never showed my good stuff because he believed in two-dimensionality—what you see is what you get—but I believed in other dimensions, like looking through a hole in a wall and seeing a secret garden with people from Deneb or Arcturus talking. I would have given the arm I don't paint with to have studied with de Chirico. But Hofmann was very good. Now he's even famous. He liked me. I spoke German to him. Most of his students didn't understand him, but it was okay because he made you understand one way or another. He'd show you something and he'd say, Neh? He'd keep on saying it until he saw that you understood. He liked that I never said ja, I just grabbed a brush and showed him that I understood. He did the same. He'd reach over your shoulder and draw these straight lines at a diagonal across your work. Force lines, he called them. They exist. Just watch people move. He liked the boy. This is Mister Hofmann, I said when I brought him to class, can you say, I'm pleased to meet you, Mister Hofmann? But he's staring somewhere, as usual, embarrassing me. Let him be, Hofmann laughed, can't you see he's painting? Great men are bigger fools than the rest of us. There is not one iota of talent in the boy.

"So here I am in Echo Tarn, and my story is back in Algeria. In five or six months, when it's clear the boy has those eyes like Rose's, Ben Aissa, who was not a talkative man unless Rose was pulling the strings, which he seemed to enjoy, made a wonderful little speech to me. It was so out of character it would have been surly of me to give anything but an out-of-character response. After two years of chasing my fair tuckus—as my old friend and enemy Hettie would say—he starts acting like I should do Rose's wash and keep my mouth shut. And he starts acting like maybe it was Rose's peachy ass he really wanted after all. Well, like the lady with the moustache says, a rose is a rose is a rose. I saw what she'd been doing.

"Ulrike, he says one day, pointing up at the sky like a marabout, Amir is not mine. That is written in the heavens. You say he's not yours. So whose child is he? I will answer. He is Allah's. That is true of every child, especially orphans. I want him because I see how he looks at me. You do not want him, and I see how he looks at you. Allah speaks as directly as the sun in your eyes. The child should stay with me. You should go home.

"You can't expect me to remember exactly how he said it, but it was like that. The Arabs are flowery even when they speak in French. I was going to say, 'And Rose?' but I am pleased with myself to this day I didn't give her the satisfaction. I said to myself, You bastard, you like blue eyes so much, remember these, and I stared at him until he covered his eyes with his eyelids, like a Tuareg hitching up his veil. I left with the boy and never looked back. The rest of their story is for somebody who cares. There is only one good thing I took with me: the Sahara's light in my mind, and that is what people who stand around my paintings are looking at while they ignore the paintings of other artists in the room. That light is my child; everything else is what foolish girls do in the heat of some damned fool's admiration. I thought maybe some day I would share this thought with Bo, but that was before he destroyed his mind masturbating.

"Words have never meant a damned thing to me. You can take all the words that have ever been written and you couldn't make a leaf out of them, but I can make a leaf. I can make people nobody's ever seen, but they will someday, people from stars we haven't named. I only know what I see, words barely reach my brain. I used to see a good-looking woman in the mirror, some even said beautiful, now I see an ape. How could God let us feel so much and let this happen? If there is a god I spit in his face. I care more about what I make than he does. Words are rats' asses to me.

"Huldah, my mother, used to say, Your father was such a dreamer. Dreamer? He was a . . . sometimes I think I'll call up

Hettie Warshaw just to ask her what the Yiddish word is for what he was. In Yiddish it sounds too true to question. Nobody lies in Yiddish. In German it sounds like gasbags made it up.

"He said we'd go to Australia. He talked about Australia until I thought I was there. He went to hell instead and I went to work. At fourteen. At fourteen I looked like twenty-one. At sixty-one I looked like forty-one. Now I look like a chimpanzee, a foot shorter than when I was a fashion model and those henpecked Steins who changed their names to Stone couldn't get their tongues back in their faces for looking at me. They got their idea of beauty from some little gland where the light doesn't shine. Men I hardly remember. A few maybe. Ullie, Ullie, Mr. Carlton used to say—if you think that was his name, you don't know New York—Ulrike, I said, my name is Ulrike. Ulrike, he said like he would choke. No wonder, it's a German name if ever there was one. Ulrike, he would say, I get no respect around here, why do I get no respect? You think rank has its privileges, you should consider what beauty gets away with. I say, Maybe it's because you don't deserve any. He says, Oi, vut a kraut. I didn't know kraut from weinerschnitzel. Kraut I left to Huldah. She was that rare thing, an angel men could get it up with. All I wanted to do was paint. To paint you have to draw, although you wouldn't think so to see what happened in the galleries. So I dressed and undressed all day and studied at Pratt at night. But the big money didn't come from what looked good on me. Everything looked good on me. The big money came from drawing. While the other artists are bitching because they're starving I'm going to the previews like a dumb blonde and going home and drawing what I see. Then Mr. Carlton and his hundred Russian Jew ladies burn up their Singers and flood the market with cheap knockoffs before the original ever sees the light of day. For this he forgets about a weekend at Grossman's with me and pays me what in those days is a fortune. So the dumb shikseh keeps his wife fat and his kids in college. For this he even remembers to call me Ulrike; it was like a penance. Hell, he even introduces me as Our Miss Theiss. What a funny word! I never belonged to anybody.

"So there we are on Van Nostrand Avenue where Huldah could impress the Loehmann's crowd with her Prussian German, her Preusse Deutsch. Huldah, Ericka, Dorothea, Ulrike, and Jurgen the banker. Papa Willi is already hung over in hell, which is too good for him. What he did to Erika, the oldest, I don't know, because she learned right away to talk like Freud and I would rather have gone to hell with Papa than listen to the reasons she had for everything. Dorothea, even an evil god would make you crazy if you touched her, she was so beautiful in her heart. Naturally she died in her thirties. Too much responsibility for God, I suppose. Jurgen is an educated moron, so naturally he became a banker. When I left for Europe Dorothea thought she was working to send him to medical school, but he was operating on an Irish chambermaid at the Ritz-Carlton with his sister's money. Jurgen is blind now. You know what Bo said when I told him? This is years ago when occasionally some ship he was on came to New York. It's the outward manifestation of Jurgen's permanent inner state, he said. What a terrible thing to say about your own uncle, you rotten bastard! I said and hung up. Then I laughed like a hyena.

"It's funny. I've been wondering how I think since I was a girl. No, that's not true. I was never a girl. But maybe once I was a child waiting until I could frighten men. What a pleasure! What is funny in my old age is to see after all I have something very important in common with my African souvenir. Bo said to me the other day, Life is a succession of freeze frames to an artist. I like movies very much, but they move too fast for me, I told him. Then he told me what a freeze frame is. Bo is also not a word man. He looks and he looks, just like he did before he could even focus his eyes, just like me, and this is what I always hated him for. I paint what I see. What does he do? Who knows? Who could ever know, unnatural as he is. It's unnatural for a mother not to love her son. Maybe I knew that, all those times I told him it's unnatural for a son not to love his mother. You know what? He never said, But I do love you, Ulrike. Never. Yes, he sent me letters, and cards and gifts, Love, Bo, Your Son, and I would shake my head and think, The hell you are! And I always thought of barren Rose at those times, how she would have liked to have him. But he's right. Freeze frames, yes, he's right. I still remember Gary Cooper's hand draped over a stair rail in some movie I forget. More erotic than a Dali nude. And Greta Garbo's hooded eyes. And Danielle Darrieux's elegant nose, like Bo's. I'm enraged to have to take these things to my grave up on that stinking hill with Hart and his lies, and what I can't understand is that I can't paint this anger. The calmer my paintings get—almost religious—it's like having Bo brought to me when I know he's not mine. The paintings are not mine, which frightens me because some evil mind has to be behind such a dirty trick.

"Bo was painting the hotel lobby last week and he had no shirt on. I saw this little cross around his neck, so I held it and asked him, You believe in Christ? He nodded. Then you're not your father's son, I said. I thought he would say something like, They believe in Jesus too, but he just stared at me and smiled. Exactly as I know that red-haired Highland bitch would have smiled.

"What a good son he is, they think, this town full of long-hair freaks and smart-ass creeps. What do they know about incubi? Don't say it, I know. I brought him here, something some stupid girl halfway across the world shit out from a squat, and now he's more American than I am. A hero, they tell me. An unnatural hero. A natural son would tell you such a thing, not keep it a secret so people would think he was modest. But the Navy has a big mouth, like Erika, like Hettie. They wrote to tell me, no, they wrote to tell Sandro, to tell you the truth, your son was wounded in action, we gave him a big medal for his trouble. Did he just stare at the admiral who gave him the medal? Who knows what that crazy Arab did, assuming he is an Arab? Who knows what he is? Not a mother's son, that's for sure.

"No, he's not here for the money. I don't think that, it's too normal. What I have to say in his favor—but who can make me like it?—is that he will take care of the paintings, of this I'm sure, because paintings he loves when me he can't even respect. Did any old lady ever have to croak on anything worse? It's a rhetorical question, I assure you. But maybe if you had a good answer it would help me die in peace. Then too it might make me so angry I'll live another fifty years. A thoroughly trustworthy bastard, my son, such is a mother's comfort. There's a game called snooker. I don't know what it is, but I know I lost. I hate games. Greedy guts play games. Jurgen loves games. I always waited till I was winning, then I kicked the table over. Now I have to play this game, because there is not one living soul I would trust my work to. Don't worry, I read your mind. Relax, he is not a living soul, exactly what I knew in my gut from the start.

"Ulrike is going to have the last laugh, you can bet your titties on it, in spite of Rose and Hettie—and Hart spending Sandro's money while I'm painting. Did I say Sandro's money? I earned every penny of it, I'm not sure he did. I slept with a hoodlum thirty-five years older than me for Bo. Did I get a medal from the Navy? Then I let Hettie sleep with him for me. That was smart. That conniving Jew girl had no taste. What she had was a big yap and, to be honest, a heinie that could break your heart. She will live a thousand years, like that maniac Hitler's Reich, because a German girl painted her. I have to thank Josef Mengele for that. What she has on her conscience would stoke the fires of hell. All that pretty piece of Cossack bait knew was how to betray. Even Mengele she betrayed. How else would the Allies know for sure what that monster did unless the person who kept his records told them? Because I know how she tasted I know how evil tastes. Cocaine is baby's milk compared to it. I wonder who Bo has tasted. Puerto Rican sluts in fuchsia panties? Hettie maybe? Thinking of a woman loving him is like thinking of Redon painting on black velour."

★

Ulrike's Medusa stare doesn't bind observant Annelise Tenbroeck. She knows from watching Ulrike that only out of the corners of her eyes can she see very much. Her central vision has been eaten away by macular degeneration. Everything she sees has a grid superimposed on it. Something in Ulrike's riff has torn off like a piece of cloth on a thornbush in Annelise's mind—Bo is not a living soul—Annelise can't wait for nightfall, for moonrise. She needs to confer with the others. Ulrike has handed her the reason she spies on Bo. She sits like a lioness, unblinking, hearing only her own plans. She knows just what to do.

"Some women sleep with men to break their asses, women like me, for example, to say nothing of the great majority of men who sleep with women to humiliate them. Which reminds me of something in Bo that I have to admit I like: I know, but I don't know how I know, that like me he can't imagine why a woman would choose to sleep with a man, women loving women being so exquisite. I admire it in him, but I hate that a man should know it. Men have no right to know it. They own too much already. I won't miss them. I do miss Soren von Melen, Count Soren von Melen. I think Soren belonged to a race that used to rule this world and we called them gods. Probably we were such barbarians, they got disgusted and went home. I never knew a kinder person. I used to see him walking around el-Kantara in white shirts and trousers, taller than everybody, poking his head into places like a bird. He seemed to know everybody and was fluent in French, Arabic, German and Swedish, which was his native tongue. Soren knew much more about the Arabs than they knew themselves and every few days I would see the boys and the men gather around him in a circle and listen to stories about battles and romances and voyages. Tell us about Hattim! they would shout. Tell us about Baybars! They would beat drums to announce that their friend was going to tell a story.

"I'm not a shy person, but Soren had such dignity that I felt shy about approaching him, so I started to sit in the outer circle and draw. He made the old men weep for the lost greatness of their race. One day, after he finished his story—my Arabic was too poor to follow it—he came over to me as I was packing my things. Fraulein, he said in German, I would speak English to you if I could, but I hear from the police, who are suspicious, that you speak German.

"I do, Count von Melen.

"I have the lifelong affliction of stuttering in the presence of beautiful women, Fraulein, but I am trying to muster the nerve to invite you to my home for dinner.

"I said, You came here to escape beautiful women?

"The poor man blushed, which, considering his complexion, was a considerable embarrassment.

"One does not escape beautiful women among the Arabs, Fraulein, as you know better than I, having painted the Ouled Nail, but one is relieved of the burden of entertaining them.

"In this way I understood I wouldn't have to deal with him as a woman, and I also knew that he was even more observant than me. He had seen I was content among the women—very content. Soren was in his sixties and had probably looked the way he looked a long time. He was gaunt. His pale blue eyes seemed lost in the white bramble of his eyebrows. I think he had been a white blond, so nobody ever noticed when his hair turned white. You felt you were the most interesting person in the world in his presence, and it had come to be important to the Arabs to bask in his attention. The French thought him cracked, maybe because he regarded them as beneath their subjects. We became great friends. He was a motorcyclist and he kept dismantling and reassembling three or four motorbikes to amuse himself. I have many sketches of him doing this.

"He used to take me out to places I wanted to paint, like El Golea with its mysterious barrel-vault roofs. We were quite a sight on his motorcycle, me in my blue burnoose and red Moroccan boots, my hair flying in the wind, Soren singing in his nasal German. The Arabs used to laugh like children because, in this way, we were like them. Soren was by training a horticulturist, and as I painted he would take notes about flora he found. He was in the habit of creating beautiful gardens around old abandoned mosques, and the Arabs considered this a gift of Allah, a devout and praiseworthy thing to do. He also did this at their cemeteries, which are rubble compared to ours.

"You are really a Muslim, Soren, I said one day.

"Oh no, Ulrike, he said, and it dawned on me that this sensitive man thought it would be offensive, ostentatious to affect a Muslim style of life. It belonged to the Arabs, you see, and he would be stealing it. That's how much he respected them. I think the Arabs understood this, because they considered him one of them. They'd seen many European converts, like Isabelle Eberhardt, but they knew that his heart was Muslim.

"I think I loved him, but I didn't know how I loved him. So when he asked me to live with him as his daughter—he was being circumspect—I went away with the Bedouins because I was confused and he was too polite to say he knew that men were not very interesting to me. I hurt him terribly, but at least I refrained from putting on my high dudgeon act. We enjoyed each other so much, you see. He had said the most correct thing he could think to say, and I owed it to him to explain, but I've never explained anything. It leaves you too naked. Never explain, dear, it gives the bastards too much power. I always got away with it because I never gave a damn if anybody understood. Being a woman is like bleeding in the sea, we attract sharks. The rescuers, they're worse. Ben Aissa was a rescuer. He wanted my life to pay for his nobility.

"The son of a bitch, I'll break his ass, Sandro used to say. It didn't matter which son of a bitch, it was just peacock strutting, although I'd have to say he probably did break a few asses. I've laughed at men all my life, and most women for that matter. Women are stronger. It's amazing how powerful a beautiful woman is if she can keep her trap shut, preferably both of them. Men's minds are easily knocked off their axis. I probably drove half a dozen men mad by not saying a damned thing. Hell, I didn't have a damned thing to say. Not Sandro, I have to admit. He thought he had my number. You got nothing to say because you're stupid, he said, sometimes I think you're right, the boy's not yours, he's too smart. Actually he wanted me to be right. He wanted nothing in the end except to outlive me, so he died a failure for all his wealth. If the boy had stayed and cared for his stepfather—oh, Sandro was his father to all intents and purposes—he would have kicked me out and laughed, except of course he knew the boy wouldn't stand for it. It's funny that Hart died in Bo's arms as Sandro would have liked to, and I'm supposed to repent because of this nobility? Let them drink vino together in some Sicilian heaven and admire each other, I'm no more impressed by cold-blooded decency now than I was when I encountered it in Ben Aissa. It's an affectation you put on when you've got no guts. I know what a poor damn excuse it is for ordinary human feelings. Did they ever make me laugh, did they ever once make me glad to be alive? Shit on their decency! Hart Clement, that little weasel, made me laugh till my guts hurt. Hettie, that little vixen, called Hart cynical. What a fool she was! How can you look at men and not be cynical? It was the very reason he made me laugh—he didn't believe a thing, and it's to my everlasting credit I respected that.

"I could spit in their eyes when men talk to me of strength, of courage. The lot of them choke on their secrets and blubber them all away to the first silent woman they fall for. But I can keep a secret. I killed my father. How's that for a secret, Annelise? They'll bury me with it. He ruined my life, so I killed him. Erika was beautiful, but her hands were as cold as her heart. I had a kid sister. If you knew her you would never doubt the existence of angels. She died of cancer in her thirties. Did Willi, my father, the criminal, crawl into their beds when Huldah slept? Did she sleep? No, she referred him to me, like a madame for my specialty, my innocence. So I had a filthy, drunken animal for my first man, Papa, my father, and no one to complain to. I was so frightened I didn't even ask the most important question until I'd killed him: why me? I'll tell you what freed me of that question. It was a vampire movie. The vampire says, I made you, so you have to do what I tell you, and I said to myself, You silly bastard, two can play that game. The creepy fag was playing by the rules, so I said to myself, Ulrike, do yourself a favor in this dreadful place—never play by the rules. And when you're beautiful, or even merely pretty, it's easy.

"I killed him with a look. Of course Houdini couldn't have staged it better. I waited for the full moon to light up the room. I pulled my nightgown just up to my golden mound, like any good daughter, no more, I made sure the moon would shine in my eyes and I stared at the dirty bastard without blinking until the thing that made me turned to putty. He was dead in two weeks. They said a heart attack, but I know better. He never looked at me again, and unlike Medusa I didn't even have to give up my looks. When they laid him out in the parlor—that's what they did in those days—I went in, like a dutiful daughter, and spit in his face. And, can you imagine, that stupid Huldah went in and screamed, My God, my God, my Willi is weeping! I laughed so hard I had to shut myself in a closet, and I kept on trying not to laugh till they buried him. They all had headaches from crying so much—and my sides were sore from laughing. Later I cried, not for him but because I didn't know why it had to be me. Her father never told her she was beautiful, that Hettie whined to me once. Lucky bitch! Willi told me I was beautiful, yes, he damned well did, stinking of whisky and cigars and his democratic poker.

"I kept his name for the very best of reasons: he saved me from running around the world a naked fool. He taught me that where men are concerned the tool of their trade is wholly unreliable. They are paper tigers, unfit to rule, hustlers and charlatans. Women are fit, so they're rightly feared, and the entire purpose of civilization after civilization is to oppress them. Yes, they're rightly feared, and God strike me dead now if I ever did a thing to alter that.

"God? I can't wait to see if God has breasts. Most of my life I've assumed so, because men are incapable of such humor. Grim and grunting unto death they are.

"I hate this dying. Of all life's dirty tricks, this is the worst. But I have a few tricks left. I keep faith with myself. I've never asked for recognition of the sacrifices I've made giving some Arab waif a life in America, educating him . . . oh, I see you smirking, Hart! Sleeping with an old mafioso was not entirely a sacrifice for Bo. It gave me time and comfort to paint, something that old man appreciated more than you with your posey ironies. Who the hell are you to smirk under your granite slab? You didn't have to moan and groan and ooh and ah with an orangutan. Christ, I was glad when that Hettie came along so I could let those two water buffalos grope each other! Smirking still, Hart? I know all about you too, you dirty old shyster! Yes, I liked Hettie, too. That way. I could draw her entirely in circles she was so round and lush, not a straight line about her. What a laugh when I kicked her out after Sandro's funeral! Take your stinking money and get out, you traitor! It still makes me laugh. Two hundred thousand he gave her, can you beat that? Only an old man would pay that much for a few pokes, but what kind of man would make his widow pay her? He was tricky, that bastard, but I fixed his wagon in hell. Of course you know about that, don't you, Hart? I fooled both you stinkers, Hart, you and Sandro. You know why? Because while you were strutting around like Mexican generals with high-priced Anglo whores I was creating a world in my own image, like God himself. All this drivel about imitating Christ. Who was he anyway but a crazy Jew carpenter who pissed off the Romans and the rabbis and got himself killed for it? I had aunts in Pittsfield who went to communion every day—it was Christ this and Christ that—and what good did it do them? They died. But I'm not going to because I could paint. Smirk about that, you old kike. Don't worry, I give you credit for helping me when Sandro was taking his time dying. Eleven strokes—you'd think he was Atlas holding up the world. He was holding me up. And Hettie still making love to him."

Ulrike blows out a lungful of disgust, across the road and up the hill to Hart. "Filthier than you and your diseased tsatskes who I notice are rapidly joining you. Yes, you helped me. Did you know, I wonder, that he called you Mother Hubbard? I never told you because you helped me when Bo, my so-called son, was whoring around the world as crazy and cold as he was born. But you were paid, weren't you? You never had the money you pretended. It's a wonder, now I think of it, Sandro didn't climb up out of his hole and chop off your cojones. God knows Hettie would have helped him. You both got what you paid for. You, you fool, were content, but Sandro lost the boy who meant more to him than Hettie and me put together, me to wear and Hettie to wear out. I could have told him, but he wouldn't listen. Where's the boy? he kept asking. When I got fed up I said, He doesn't need an invitation to do the wrong thing, you know. And he sits up in his bed with blood in his mouth and says, Get out of my sight, slut.

"Do sluts tell the truth? Truth, dear, isn't worth a sack of shit. Could you run in and heat up the water for some more tea?"

Annelise is as much at home here, in this house, as she had been growing up in Bluestone, which is to say alert. The familiar impenetrability of motherhood warms her in an old and horrifying way. Her own bones, which she knows she owns more than Ulrike owns hers, make no complaint about men's urgencies, but she wonders with a familiar and maddening sense of retardation how women like Ulrike and Cala, her mother, admit enough of anybody's urgency to create a child. God must hold children cheaply to allow them to venture out from such mean holes. When she brings out the kettle Ulrike is still talking.

"Hettie was some piece of work. Thank you, dear. Her blood was near the surface of her skin, which made her radiate . . . sex, energy, nerve. She was like Madame Renoir, impossibly fruity. I said she appeared to me all circles, loops and ovals, except for one thing: the lids of her eyes formed a sharp gable, a roof over two blazing sapphires seeded with diamond dust. Her fingers glowed and were so perfect that your hairs rose up in search of their touch. Her teeth were spaced, which Mengele said betrayed her Jewishness. I found them sensual in a loony way. They made her mouth a kind of madcap playground in which I wanted to play hide and seek. Her mouth was something of a long bow, elegant. I loved it, but not what came out of it, filth and absurdity. For example, I told her as a compliment that her eyes reminded me of Garbo's, and she says, That cow couldn't keep them open, life bored her so much. Mine are open, she says, believe me, Ulrike.

"Did it occur to you, Ulrike, men bored Garbo? she asks me. The most beautiful woman in the world she's talking about. Garbo was unearthly. That you would never say about Hettie, but Hettie Warshaw had a thousand faces and I spent ten years of my life painting them. I pleaded with her to show me pictures of herself before they took her off to Auschwitz, but later I realized she lost everything, including her soul. I wanted to see what those years did to her. She wanted Sandro for herself, but with me came the boy.

"There's a certain kind of girl I've been desperate to smell all my life. Men say of her she thinks her shit don't stink. She's not haughty. Haughty is flirtatious—she's remote. But that's not what's going on, I know it. She looks all sun-struck, so naturally I want to hold my nose up in her shadows. I had a friend, Blev Abernathy, who told me shamefacedly he used to sniff girls' bicycle seats. I knew he told me to excite me. But when he saw how much it did I didn't have to fend him off anymore. Ulrike, he said, why d'you waste your time on men?'

"Blev, there are some men I take pity on. They have their uses.
"He said, Me?
"God no, you're too inquisitive, I couldn't trust you with my necessaries when you're in my bathroom. So of course he spent the rest of his life thinking about me.

"I need to taste these girls. I just do. Not the ones who wrap it up and jiggle it for men, but the ones who act like it's beneath them to care. All my life I've known just how to get these girls. It's a favor only I can give them. They know they're not going to meet anyone else ever who can give it to them, so they better not lose their chance. And they almost never do. I make them blush. I make them flush. I make them run wet down their legs. I make them wonder till they tingle. I make them guess that maybe, just maybe I've been wondering about them. I make them think about the state of their underwear.

"I have to laugh at what men think of as dirty girls. They're thinking about sluts, trashy girls. Stupid girls, really. Nothing in their heads, so naturally they don't mind what you stick in their other places. Why should they? They're empty. But my dirty girls, men just naturally short out if they catch a glimpse of what goes on in their heads, not as to say their other parts.

"The truth is I can't remember very well how I felt about Bo before that certain moment when I knew that he knew all about this. He knew all about me. He just caught on. So naturally I'd have to hate him—from then on anyway. How could you make nicey-nice with a dirty little boy just growing hair on his lip, jerking off every chance he got and knowing such a thing about you? Some mommies can, you say? Bullshit.

"All this crap about madonna and child! I tried to make myself come when he sucked my nipples, I heard it feels good. It didn't. It felt like control. He was controlling me. Little Dracula drinking my blood. Yeah, there was some milk there, but I didn't see why I had to give him any. I knew he'd suck it until he drew blood. But I did think of all those dirty girls, choir girls, drinking it. It didn't matter. I dried up fast. He looked like a goldfish, sucking, sucking. I used to pinch his cheeks in my hand and splatter him with milk. He'd just suck air and I'd keep on splattering him till we both got so mad the room turned red. I guess I never stopped seeing him that way.

"There's not much pentimento in my life, damn little in my paintings for that matter. It's not the formula for a happy life. You know what happy is? Silly maybe. What I mean is you can't fix people, you can't cure them of being what they are or where they want to be. If some bald kid in a saffron robe said so they'd write checks and kiss his feet, but everybody's doing all they can do as well as they can do it. Once you've got that, you sweat less, sleep better and move on to the next best thing.

"But there's a catch—isn't there always?—the catch is we always, almost always, get stuck on a lesser person, people who can't do as well by us as we can do by them. We get stuck because we can't leave them back there on the road where they belong. We start thinking our whole life depends on them, whether they like us, whether they'll sleep with us. I don't give a rat's ass. Never have.

"Take Mr. Generosity over there, I looked down between my legs and there he was, a little raisin. He might as well have been some lesser thing playing down there in my garden while I figured out what to do.

"Artists really don't have to get stuck fixing on anybody. They make their own beauty. I never met a collector I liked. They're freaks. Paintings, people, what difference does it make? I don't collect. If they want to suck up, fine, that's where they are on their own journey, sucking up. Not me. I'm closer to God. I want to find that sonofabitch and see if he can look me in the eye. He knows I'm looking for him. That's what I'm doing now. I want to see if he can look Ulrike Theiss in the eye, because I already know the damned three-legged other half of the species can't. I have to give Bo credit there, he can look anybody in the eye, because his eyes aren't connected to his brain."

★

The stone terrace bakes them in the late afternoon sun, but Annelise shivers. Ulrike stares into the sun like a blind eagle. Annelise goes inside for a blanket. Cala Tenbroeck too had spoken to her with icy contempt about masturbating, about it destroying her mind. You will always have a masturbator's face, she said. People will recognize it. I'm weird, Annelise thinks. Like Bo. But that hasn't been her perception of him. Why would a woman be embittered by his very existence? He seems to Annelise the least intrusive man. She can't dance or shake or shiver or sing the answer away. She can't wash it away in a stream. She can't walk it away, and she can't bear being indoors for fear of hearing it. Cala is embittered by her existence, and Annelise shares with Bo the knowledge that the reason why is worthless.

If there are any secrets in Echo Tarn that Annelise doesn't know, they belong to sirloin-faced men in suits who consider them capital. She knows all the kinds that emit animal noises in the night, all the bad behavior craving witness, all the obsessive rituals in windows and their attendant prayers that someone might be watching, caring. Annelise watches and cares. Her business in Echo Tarn is to witness and thereby to cleanse. She repeats nothing to the dead, for if she did they would no longer trust her. They are in any case uninterested. What interests them is rite, ceremony. She is the officiant of their liturgies and she has never initiated a single soul.

Listening to Ulrike's monologue is not the price of tea, a hot bath and fleeting respectability. It's a signal event, and she does not miss the signal. She knows any number of women in

Echo Tarn who would benefit from Ulrike's example, and she has no intention of sharing it with them, because they would treat it as they allowed themselves to be treated, with contempt.

From her hundred stations in bushes outside houses she sees the contempt with which we treat each other and the terrible little ways in which we try to heal ourselves. There is indeed, although no cop would ever say it, no reporter ever write it, a compact between Annelise Tenbroeck and the people of Echo Tarn. Every town has such a compact, but Echo Tarn's is overt.

Nothing as hifalutin as being seduced happens to Annelise, and this is not how she looks at her encounter with Ulrike now, but nonetheless she feels mugged. Annelise Tenbroeck drums and dances her anger away. Rain and snow wash it away. Acid rain eats it away. Hunger and cold and the contempt of passing society shake it out of her bones. But she stands withal in Ulrike's kitchen and shakes with cold and anger, and the cold is from within.

Their tea party is interrupted by a howl. Annelise knows all the howls, groans, moans, cries, screams and screeches of the Catskills—tortured men and women gone feral in the night—and she has heard a howl like this only once, a bobcat up on Kettle Mountain bitten by a timber rattler. She had been camped nearby. She tore herself to shreds thrashing through bullbriar to find that cat and when she did she hauled her to her campfire, cut her leg from fang to fang, drew the poison, and cauterized the bite with a white-hot knife. Not once had the cat resisted, clawed or bitten her. The ranger who lives atop Kettle Mountain wouldn't believe her and his disbelief tipped her off: to live as the cat lived.

"Go see what's wrong with Bo, dear."

Doubletakes in Annelise's condition are out of the question. Ulrike's sangfroid doesn't belong to the living. Annelise is comfortable with that. She walks across the driveway to The Granada and takes up a position at the head of rough-hewn stairs to a sub-basement in the back of the building. This is what any number of animals would do. Annelise chooses the comportment of a barn owl.

Sloshes and curses are what she hears first, then debris being heaved around. As her eyes adapt to the dark she sees a fat beam of light splashing at intervals on the walls. She rows her behind down the steps until she sees Bo. He's wearing Hart's boots and his usual snap-shackle belt and dungarees. His searchlight is the biggest she's ever seen, its face as wide as a dinner plate.

Once Annelise encounters someone she likes she has to spend a lot of time restabilizing her relationship with everyone, an impossible task in the press of four walls. That's why the dead are such good company. For this reason she's careful not to like too many people, although she acts as if she likes everybody. Bo she doesn't like or dislike. He's inevitable, and you don't meet many of those, and when you do the odds are you'll blow them off or fuck them over and spend the rest of your life wishing you hadn't, glad that you did, and knowing damned well you'd do it again.

She knows all about people who take up more space than is allotted anyone, smearing you on the wall, shoving you in front of cars. Such people are crowds of one. Annelise doesn't even bother to spy on them. Bo's passage through life is surgical in contrast.

He takes up a short two-by-four and props a kind of hatch open. It's another sub-basement. He slips through and disappears. Annelise knows the building better than he does. There are winter nights in the Catskills when it's a life-or-death matter to get in out of the cold. She knows there's another hatch to this vault and she slides around in the shadows to reach it.

Bo has found during his rummages dozens of colored renderings of Hudson Valley scenes—the steamboat Mary Powell ice-bound, the brick kilns of Bluestone, Ichabod Crane a-horse, Hudson's crew bowling with the Indians, Saugerties when it was a port, Rondout in its heyday. He has found antique Oliver typewriters, china from the Prince of Wales Hotel in Manhattan, nickel-plated cookware by the carload, silver flatware engraved with The Granada, block and tackle for repointing the brick exterior, pipes to build scaffolding, glass window sashes enough to build a greenhouse, iron grilles, a cache of geometric quilts, the wine cellar of a Pullman magnate, a huge brick oven for bread or pizza, enough Adirondack furniture to pay a Third Avenue antique dealer's rent for years, a head by William Zorach, a painting by Anton Refregier, a bad original drawing by Georges Braque whom Bo has always suspected of having been red-green color-blind, and a blessed absence of the kitsch cluttering Hart's cottage. He's found work by Andre Breton, mouth-in-chief of Surrealism, but no traces of the metaphysical art, *pittura metafisica,* to whom Ulrike's languid Amazons owe their domain. Nothing to dismay, little to excite.

This is different. This turns him inside out. He charges up from the sub-basement, up from the basement through the kitchen into the great hall girdled by a balcony. And then, as he stands in the middle of the hall under the three-story timbered ceiling he imagines the crush of water tinkling in his ears. He imagines looking up and seeing the surface like a broaching diver. The Granada seems submarine and foundered, something wrongly ballasted, sunk by human error. And yet, thinking of Hart Clement dying alongside this beached, chagrined behemoth, he crawls with the silliness of it.

In this foundered hulk, when he was a boy on a bike and had not dreamed a single moment of the life he's lived, Dutch and Jewish and Yankee brides danced here before anyone imagined heavy metal or acid rock. He stares at the long mahogany bar and remembers Sandro. Sandro's goombahs would have liked to play cards and smack their lips over Corvo in the upstairs rooms. They would have liked to store their mysterious packages in these cellars. He remembers being here with Sandro, at that bar, one night when he was fifteen.

"C'mon, we're gonna go for a walk," Sandro said. "Show me what you like about this town." Sandro hardly knew the town. He came up weekends and sat among the wild roses drinking wine and singing arias from Italian operas. When they saw The Granada, Sandro asked, "You thirsty?" The bartender, a bearish lunkhead, ignored Sandro deliberately—karma, racial memory, whatever—so Sandro grabbed his arm and said, "Hey, my friend, my uncle here is thirsty."

"Who told ya I'm yer friend?" The bartender shoved Sandro. That is, he tried to shove him, but Sandro was made like a tank. In a split second he grabbed a fistful of greasy hair and crashed the bartender's face on the bar. He must have broken the guy's nose, but he said, "So yer not my friend. Wipe yer unfriendly face and get us two Ruperts." They sat on stools and Bo told Sandro about Echo Tarn as if nothing had happened. That's what Sandro was like before his eleven strokes.

Bo weeps.

At sixty-five Sandro had the reflexes of a welterweight. He used to fence with Stanford White at the Silk Stocking Regiment's armory on Park Avenue.

Bo fears that the only thing that may have ever fazed Sandro was Bo leaving him.

He walks in widening circles. He's splashed by moonlight pouring through the balcony's Palladian windows. Annelise hides behind the cash register by the kitchen door. He switches off his searchlight.

Why had Hart done such fool things with his money? Bought equipment and made improvements that could not pass code? Hung on and refused to sell, paid taxes and spent Sandro's money without a goal?

Suddenly he stops in his tracks. Then he walks straight past Annelise's crouching figure and goes back down to the basement. She takes up her former station to watch. He begins clearing away scrap lumber. He finds a bare overhead bulb and pulls its cord. Annelise's head is upside down between her knees so she can see. He's clasping his heart like a Victorian maiden. She can't see what he's found.

Bo is staring at something that is to him worse than finding the carcasses of a vampire's victims. Dozens of Ulrike's paintings from Algeria, and later, rock almost imperceptibly in some three feet of fetid water, grimed, their stretchers splintered and rotting, frames dilapidated. He rubs his chest incredulously. He throws a few sashes aside and wades into the marsh to examine the carnage. He sees that many of the gem-like Algerian works, done on burlap because it was cheap, have been amateurishly transferred to linen. He holds one up to the bulb. Glue, not hot wax, as is proper, has been used, reeving blossoms of the painted surface through the fibers as the glue contracted, destroying the painting. The stretchers were the cheapest, too flimsy for the size of the canvases. He's dizzy. His stomach lurches. His eyes burn and water. His mind loses hope of words. He struggles to put down a compulsion to beat his head on the wall. All his life he's wished to paint and hasn't dared—and Ulrike, with all the money she needed, singled out her own gift for her worst contempt. It doesn't occur to him he's following suit.

This time he wails. The sight of it all makes him feel suicidal. Slowly he turns around. Then he turns again and again until he's whirling like a dervish.

"You crazy, stinking bitch." He listens to the grand acoustics bringing his cry back to him: " . . . itch, itch, itch."

He throws himself against the crudely parged wall, clawing its extrusions. "Don't you respect anything?" He kneels, sobbing. "Any damn thing, you crazy fucks." Ux, ux, ux, The Granada answers, moving him to grin in the teeth of anguish. His sobs rise like diver's bubbles to a place of less despair.

Upstairs he walks to the bar, opens a dusty bottle of Saratoga water, wipes its neck and drinks it down. Then he goes out front, sits down on the steps and smokes a cigar.

Cars slow to scan The Granada. Soon a craggy blond in his 30s—a rock impresario, Bo tells himself—strolls up from the village green with a proprietary woman in tow. He stops to examine the facade professionally.

"Howya doin', man? You own this place?"

The woman looks prepared to show interest till Bo shakes his head.

"What's it called?"

Bo eyes them through smoke-squinted eyes until they rearrange their bones. It looks like hell itself.

"Gehenna," he answers.

14

Shapely pooplets plop on his name. Somebody shits on the *beloved by all who knew him*. Day after day, amused and annoyed and most of all glad for a respite from Ulrike, Bo climbs the hill with pail and brush to scrub Hart's flat gravestone. G.Verplanck, the stonecutter who is often on Artists' Hill, comes over to him one day and says, "You know, when your mother passes on, I can blast it off." Bo pats the inscription.

"You think it'll stop this shit?"

That day he spots clothes and blankets lodged in the crook of a tree at the northwest corner of the cemetery—and dozens of shiny trinkets such as crows collect. Wraithe's aerie. She bathes in the brook behind Carl Brathwaite's della Robbia. Her nest is as tidy as a finch's.

The Indians chose certain meadows, ledges, knolls, glades, cracks between worlds, for dreaming and sacred rites. The rockers who now outnumber Echo Tarn's artists and writers, if not the native ghosts, respect these places. Here the new and the pre-Columbian ages marry.

Bo is unaware he's shared his discovery of the ravaged paintings with Wraithe. Nor does he know that, following her own radar, Wraithe has been doing her own rummaging, until one night as he takes up his usual station on the steps in front of the hotel, half hoping to see Tate, Wraithe comes around from a side door of the hotel toting one of the paintings. She sets it on its bottom on top of a planter so that it's eye-level with him.

"You fish that out of the cellar?"

"It's one you missed. It was under something."

A young man, a boy really, his chest sunk in The Granada's

muck, stares over the viewer's left shoulder. His turbaned head is in the clouds. The twenty-by-thirty-inch canvas is punctured in the upper left-hand corner. The boy is handsome and because he's so young he may be taken at first glance as serene, but as Bo studies him he sees that his muscles and tendons clench. Then he notices the boy's eyes. A green eye gazes into the distance, but the other is red and in that red Bo sees an anger that has burned off its impurities and become a glowing coal. This eye is fixed on the artist. It has a mote in it, or rather a dark spike pointing up at the pupil. Some would call this eye wicked, but Bo is not just any viewer and he calls it wronged.

Bo replaces Wraithe's hand on the painting with his own. He holds the painting up to the lantern and turns it around. On the back, in charcoal, he sees, *Amir, Djelfa*. No date.

When he turns Wraithe is gone. "So it's you," he says. He sits under the lantern watching, as it comes to him, his own murder. He has uncovered his own corpse—and the means to do a thing he didn't know he had to do: forgive Ulrike. Only profound self-hatred could have led her slowly to destroy her own paintings and he now finds it difficult to hate someone who is doing the job for him so well. These are the paintings—the Algerian, surrealist, abstract—she vowed so ostentatiously she would never sell cheaply. She never sold any of them. There are none in museums, and none have ever been auctioned, which would establish their value. But these considerations no longer anger him, as her other lies have.

This red-eyed boy is not angry at a parent or a sibling or a boss, he's angry at the artist, his maker, the one who will have the last say. Perhaps he's angry because he knows already that she will have the last say. That the boy Amir might be his own father occurs to him but fails to interest him. What interests him is that implacable red eye. How like Ulrike to paint her own handiwork. Artists often capture emotions they engender, but this is different. This is a farewell, but not a salute. This is a meanness so talented that the chill of it comes off the night Sahara after all these years. This is the boy who, according to Rose MacQuarrie, tracked down Ben Aissa and killed him.

And no one will ever know if Ulrike made this painting before or after the killing.

"Thanks, Amir. Can't take you back to Djelfa—you still belong to her, poor bastard."

He walks down Quarry Road to the village to buy some el cheapos when the thought that he's just kissed off his father ambushes him.

★

It's unseasonably hot the next evening. Artists' Hill flashes with fireflies. He takes a bottle of water and heads up the hill to stand a watch at Brathwaite's della Robbia. He notes the stones as he passes. They're tended eccentrically. Some endure plastic flowers, some elegant arrangements freshly removed from some church's altar, some tattered flags. An old rose engulfs the four-foot Vermont granite block of Willem Ruttenber. Chrysanthemums and geraniums cheer Peter Eltinge. Shiny poison ivy guards Carlos Hoyt. Lichen blurs the north side of the old and pitted stones. Condoms, pebbled flower beds, the occasional whiskey bottle or beer can, a boy's plastic boat, Jews and Christians, agnostics and atheists, communists and fascists, sleep side by side, some remembered, some forgotten. A massive granite slab totters over two thin slabs, the wives. Were they his duckpins? The plight of dead women moves him. Part of him hopes they played hell, loved where they could find love and be loved. Part of him fears for their sons. Slowly the place consumes him. He sees that he's not so much tending Hart's grave as he's begging to be told that here lie at least a few ordinary beloved sons of someone. The moonlight scrubs the stones. Hart's has not yet received its nightly deposit. To his left, following the tree line about a hundred and twenty yards, is Wraithe's nest.

He notices that the VFW has finally installed the bronze holder with its tiny national flag that he requested for Hart's grave. He had to get in the local commander's face to get it.

A tambourine tinkles over his head. He grabs Wraithe's ankles behind him, yanks forward and plops her on her behind.

"I'll never sneak up on you again."

"That'd be a good idea. You okay?"

He gets up and walks slowly over to Hart's slab. When he turns to Wraithe he says, "I have a sheet of metal over at the hotel that sounds like rolling thunder when you shake it."

"Can I have it?"

"I'll leave it by your tree tomorrow."

"Promise?"

Then, like swamp gas by the brook, she winks out and is gone.

Six days later on a night so hot the cats sit in front of the fan she comes to him at Hart's stone again. He still hasn't caught the phantom poopster. He's seen a light in Wraithe's tree and feels her approach. The moon finds the new gravestones and swarms her eyes. He gropes for words but settles for a nod. She has snapped off a spray of Queen Anne's lace and puts it in the V of his polo shirt where his little silver and turquoise cross dangles. She smells her wild carrot sprig and leaves. It's his favorite flower.

★

The mothering sea, cognac, Cuban cigars and cat houses, they awaited him all the ballsy roar of years, but when, as he ages and needs his head to hold open the floodgate of his blood, the disingenuous ghosts reappear, and he feels like a short-changed boy again with his nose pressed up against candy store cases. Promises of unfulfillment whisper to him from the crannies of the town, as they had so many years before.

"What's your opinion of sex," he asks Wraithe when she reappears one evening.

"No decent woman'd ever want to soil you with it."

"Are you crazy?" He jumps up angry and jangled.

"What would possibly make you think otherwise? What does that have to do with it?"

"I mean, dammit, what am I, Jesus Christ? And you didn't answer my question."

"I answered it better than you asked. I've learned to masturbate without thinking of anybody."

"Is that possible?"

"Well, I'm not a man, but if you're crazy enough it is."

"What do you mean, soil me?"

She shakes her tambourine in his face. "You have a pure and serious heart. It gets in the way of everything. It screws people around. You know, like John the Baptist—women either leave you alone or go for your head. But I'm going to introduce you to someone who won't do either, because she knows better."

★

Weybrandt Gundersen once came out of the wheelhouse with a nip of sake and a question: "Why is it every nutcase on every ship we've ever sailed thinks he's gotta tell you his life story?"

"You gotta a sharp eye, Gundy."

"Not me, mate, I don't shoot stars and I don't shoot bull."

"Hey, chiefie baby, if we weren't crazy we wouldn't be out here. Ain't none of us fit to be anywhere else."

"Gotcha."

"Say what?"

"Ducking a question. First time I ever seen you duck a question."

Bo put down his sextant, scribbled down his fix, and said, "You ever lose your wallet in a shit trough on a Navy ship?"

"This is gonna be good, right, Bo?"

"I'm keepin' the nutcases cool so's they don't lose it and stick you with a marlin spike."

"You're doin' it for me?"

"Right."

"Geez, I didn't know I owed ya so much. Here, have another pull, you been workin' so hard. Know what I think? I think it's because you're one of the blessed few sumbitches I know isn't always thinking of the next thing to say."

"Shit, Brandt, that makes two of us."

Gundy punched his arm and went in, leaving Bo to the wild weather he liked and concluding one of those rationed moments that makes the loneliness of seafaring bearable.

★

He smiles at Wraithe, remembering this incident. She's far more at home with craziness than she knows. "I'm thinking where craziness drives us, to the sea that doesn't give a damn, up a tree, to prison, to . . . I don't know."

"Battle stations."

"Yeah, how'd you know that?"

"My father was a gunny."

"Gunner's mate or a Marine?"

"Gunnery officer. Now hear this. Man your battle stations. This is not a drill."

"You're a Navy brat?"

"Manning my battle station."

"Darken ship!"

"You got that right, Bo."

They sit in the moonlight grinning like polecats.

"So tell me about the gunnery officer."

"Steam launch blew up, killed him."

"Leyte, CVA-Thirty-Two, Boston, nineteen-fifty-three. I know."

The lion's eyes widen. "Boom, boom, boom, that's all he knew. I'm one of his booms."

"You loved him?"

"Kids have bad taste."

"Undeveloped."

"Bad."

"Okay."

"You liked the Navy, Bo?"

"Only mother I ever had."

"So how come you joined the merchant marine?"

"Boom, boom, boom, cracked head. Thirty percent disability."

"I believe you."

"What's not to believe?"

"I believe you're cracked. You a father?"

"Not that I know of."

"You remember everybody you sewed your seed in?"

"You better shake your tambourine a little, Wraithe, you're getting hostile."

But when he looks up he sees tears. "I think I do. Remember," he says.

★

Wraithe floods his days. He thinks of her carnally when she's gone. When she's there he doesn't. She distracts him from Tate. He's resting from the treacherous demands of—what? He knows what should come will come. Whatever we want, he knows, is the wrong thing. The right thing is unbidden.

Everything David Llewellyn told him sinks in one way or another sooner or later, except one thing. Stop pimping for your mother, Llewellyn said. He'd let it slime off him with a dishonest smile. Later he asked Llewellyn what he meant. But Llewellyn wouldn't answer. Why not? Because I don't like your question.

"You crazy fucker," he shouted, "where do you get off screwing me around on my dime?"

"I like your anger," Llewellyn said.

"You smarmy fuck." He walked out and stayed away for two weeks, although he was still in the claws of drink and refused to go to AA. When the bars started seeming more attractive than the museums and galleries, he called Llewellyn and said he needed help. When he got to Llewellyn's office and sat down, Llewellyn repeated, "Stop pimping for your mother."

He sat glaring at the other man. He felt neither rage nor vexation. They sat for four or five minutes staring at each other. The clock took over the room. Then Bo said, "Sandro found me. You could say I introduced them. She made me take responsibility for the marriage when I was eleven. She said Sandro's asked me to marry him, should I? That'd be great, I said. Is that what you mean, Dave?"

What would Dave Llewellyn say now? Now that Ulrike has referred her useless husband to him, assigned his last moments to a person she allowed to consider himself her son. What would you say, Dave? He resolves to call and ask. But he might say what he said before. Nothing. This is clearly a stinger he wants to leave buried under Bo's skin to swell and fester.

He doesn't see things in black and white, although that's

how he draws them. The color of everything daunts him. His circuitry is occasionally tricked by pheromones or by the constructs of his imagination, but his hand remains as averse to color as his penis is to signal.

Only after years of trudging in the snake-shot swamps of his depression can he remotely begin to fathom Llewellyn's words: someone who has renounced responsibility for you must also renounce all claims to your duty to them—that's as much as he can make of it.

"Well, one thing you've got to admit, Dave," he says to himself, "depressed men don't call their shrinks crazy fuckers."

Dugan's deathward, darling, wrote Alan Dugan, a poet he liked too much in his depression. But no, goddammit, he'd bury Hart and Ulrike, but he wouldn't get down with them, not yet, not by drink or dearth of feeling or denial.

He goes down to the city to see Llewellyn. "Dave, you helped me cross the abyss, for which I'm forced to be grateful, but you're a fucking illiterate," he told Llewellyn. To which Dave answers, "By the way, Bo, I have to raise my fee to eighty-five."

He writes the check and goes to the door without saying a word. Then he turns and embraces his relentless hired friend.

15

If there is anything of Salome in a girl or woman, Bo believes something hapless in him will call it out. He's the ideal witness to a woman's bad behavior. And that's why chagrin rises like vomit to his mouth when he stands on the ridge overlooking the south plat of the cemetery one September dawn and sees Wraithe, her bronze hair on fire, dancing naked among the stones. He kneels in a triad of arbor vitae. Too fast to be a pavane, too romantic to be modern, her choreography is perfect. She has done it often. When she's done she sits cross-legged before the lichened stone cross of Flossie Wattrous de Graaf, eighteen-ninety-nine to nineteen-twenty-eight, pours something from a homely decanter into a glass, sips and enters upon a conversation, speaking animatedly, nodding when addressed, gesticulating. Then she rises, picks up a towel, drapes it over her right shoulder and knots it loosely above her opposite hip, and departs, talking to her companion.

A priest elevating the sacred host at mass might as well be a porter compared to the sacred and feral scene he has witnessed. His left leg feels reinforced by a rod when he tries to rise. He shivers and is unamused. Wraithe has the kind of body Ulrike paints. Capable like a dolphin's, not lithe. He can't even begin to address the companionability of what he saw, not until his unwitting blood sets. Then he gets up and draws closer, taking cover behind more arbor vitae. If the girl were beautiful, would it be trite? If she were not, would it be compelling? Wraithe doesn't wish to be beautiful, but she can't banish her looks.

He has studied the gravestones here. He's noticed the cross marking where Flossie Wattrous de Graaf lies. He goes to it now and is unable to shake the odd sense that Flossie isn't there, has left with Wraithe. The two Dutch women have gone hand-in-hand for a walk in the dripping wood. A sense of emptiness envelops him. He walks over to Peter Hammer's stone next to Flossie. Here there's no emptiness. Peter Hammer lies there at his feet. He walks back to Flossie's stone and once again he feels bereft.

In subsequent days he makes inquiries about Wraithe. She appeared six years ago. The town board discussed her. The county human services department was consulted. The police declared her harmless, but pressure for her removal built until Police Chief Evan Sanders stood up before the town board and said, If you're going to get rid of Annelise Tenbroeck, why not the junkies? She at least was sober, if mad. But she continues to have her detractors—cluckers, Sanders calls them—because she's indigent. So are the longhairs on the village green, and near to indigence most of the artists, writers and musicians. The young cops are offended by her enemies. Why pick on her in a town of authorized loonies? These pony-tailed cops are a far cry from the high school bullies he remembers. He takes to leaving food in the crook of her oak. He wraps it in plastic bags stowed in a big nickel-plated kettle from the hotel. He leaves her some silverware in deference to her obvious education. He watches from his evergreen blind as she sits at various stones, eating ceremoniously, chatting, feeding cats, squirrels and birds. This gives him more pleasure than anything since he filched food from Cairnhall's pantry and took it to eat in his bullbriar retreat, talking earnestly with his companion and advisor, Amir. This girl reminds him of that nameless bullbriar boy and his friend Amir. God knows he needed a friend in that genteel hell. Yes, and God gave him Sandro, and now Sandro is like everyone else on this hill, except for Wraithe and maybe himself—and Flossie.

The autistic need to control their environment, to touch the world only on their terms, these matters he understands. There's little difference between him and Annelise Tenbroeck. They have broken down on their own terms and must mend in the same way. He touches the jagged scars in his head. The only touch he ever trusted was that of Navy doctors and nurses. How can you yearn for touch and yet not wish to be touched? Bo knows.

★

So compulsive is his doodling, as he calls it, he'd hardly miss a notebook and he doesn't miss one of the sketchbooks he leaves in his blind on the hill. When he was young his doodling consisted of catenary curves resembling scimitars, sea routes, power lines. Not surprising in a navigator familiar with great circles, but he'd probably agree if it were pointed out to him that these early doodads were redolent of the Russian constructivists. He might even have agreed they derived of his autistic need to stand clear of people. But his many visits to the Netherlands— he knows every buoy and bell and light in the Nieuwe Maas— drew him inevitably to traditional draftsmanship. He spent many hours sketching in the Stedelijk Museum in Amsterdam. He has no idea to this day his work has been admired by talented peers looking over his shoulder in museums around the world. He's devoid of aspiration. He merely wishes he could draw. He can't think of a more enviable skill. He wonders from time to time if he'd have nerve enough to enroll in art classes, but these reveries are always burgled by remembering the day he showed Ulrike some drawings when he was fourteen. "Oh dear, I'm afraid you're a klutz. But it's all right, maybe God has given you other skills."

★

With no particular thought in his head, except perhaps for a New Jersey lawyer who seems to be diddling Ulrike out of some of Hart's stock, he carries egg salad up the hill one morning to find Wraithe bejeweled with six or seven rectangular plaques that catch the sun as they turn in a light breeze. They're clear plastic sandwiches with holes drilled at one end so they can be worn as pendants. He's seen art on paper sandwiched this way. Wraithe turns slowly like a dervish in a trance. Then a piece of paper falls from one of the plaques. She doesn't see it. Her eyes are closed.

238

He picks it up. Others have seen his drawings—Peter, Moira, Uthman, Lakhdar, Ute-Britt, many others, but no one honored him with an exhibition, especially not on a crystalline morning in a cemetery. Wraithe moves away, down a gentle slope towards the della Robbia, wearing the contents of his lost notebook. He sets his plastic bowl of egg salad and rolls in the crook of her tree and grins broadly with an inspiration. He takes out a little note pad and writes:

I'm quite enamored of your drawings. Please call me.
Clement Greenberg.

He adds Ulrike's number. Not that he can imagine the famous critic being enamored of anything that doesn't affirm his presuppositions. He puts his note and the fallen sketch under the bowl and leaves.

That night, as he sets out on his patrol, Wraithe breaks off her conversation with some shamanic drummers to shake her tambourine at him from across the street. He's already passed her when he realizes she's given him a smile certain artists would foreshorten their lives to paint—a girl he's never seen smile.

They intrude on each other's privacy, spy each other out, and yet hardly speak.

Two days later she introduces him to Theodora Wattrous de Graaf, eighteen-eighty-four to nineteen-twenty-six. Will-o'-the-wisps wink around Brathwaite's shrine as they sit at Theodora's stone.

"She killed her husband because he was molesting Flossie, their daughter. Then they killed her. She would like you to draw her and Flossie."

"How did Flossie die?"

"You'll see."

"You talk to the others, Wraithe?"

"Some of them. You can too. Kurt Meissner over there—he was famous, you know—says you're wonderful. He'll help you if you let him."

Wonderful? He shivers in the critical acclaim. He knows the sculptor Meissner's work and admires it.

239

"I have very strong feelings about bending children out of shape. My feelings might get in the way."

"Flossie knows that. She told me she'd like to be your lover. She's very pretty. She made a bad marriage. She was very unhappy. She died of sorrow."

"Any marriage would've been tough, don't you think."

Wraithe looks solemnly at him until he sees she apprehended before he did that they are, all of them, children of abuse. Then she turns towards Flossie and says, "She says that's true."

He follows her gaze, hoping to see Flossie. "Flossie can't be my lover now, can she?"

"I'll show you how."

"That would be a *ménage a trois*," he says and smiles.

Wraithe's eyes, not her mouth, smiles. "Oh no, I'm like a concierge."

If your life has been in the hands of an unwilling parent, you probably either babble to fill the void, which you fear is disapproval, or you emulate the parent. Early on he babbled, but when Sandro, appreciating that Ulrike had nothing to say, and pursuing his own mythology about the demeanor appropriate to a Saracen, began to muffle his mouth with a huge hand and a wry expression, Bo launched upon his lifelong compulsion towards silence. More than any other gesture, he remembers Sandro's and even now feels the love in it.

He sits and waits.

"Flossie never wanted any man to touch her. That's why she wants you to draw her naked."

Does this make sense? He shakes off the question. What does make sense? It's not his ignorance of how to draw Flossie—perhaps like a forensic artist he can draw her from Wraithe's mind—it's her use of the word naked that possesses him. Or is it Flossie's?

"I've never sketched a nude."

"Just sit and wait. You'll see her."

He fetches chalk, charcoals and pencils and sets them out on the grass. He opens a sketchbook and shuts his eyes. He feels the sun climb his back, breathe on his neck and overflow onto

Flossie's cross. At first he's conscious of Wraithe's presence, but by the time his hand moves he's unaware of her. Within the hour he has drawn a tall, angular woman in her early thirties. Her long face is unutterably sad. She wears a transparent calf-length dress. Her neck rises like a lily stem from ruffled lace. He has used chalk and charcoal, not opening his eyes to tell their colors. Like Tate, she reminds him of someone, but he can't remember. He finds he's drawn her with blue chalk and charcoal. The line delineating her lips from adjacent flesh is as sensual as a Mongol bow. He knows from experience this delineation is telling, one of those details on which a drawing, but not necessarily a painting, depends. Her eyes stare straight at him, an effect he doesn't believe he could have gotten if his own had been open. They disturb him. They belong to someone else he knows, but who? She is blonde. He can tell that as clearly as you can in some old black and white movies, and wisps of her hair stand in the air. She has the prominent nose of that memorable Dutch girl at the church fair, and he imagines her skating on the Rondout, hands in a beaver muff, easily taken for haughty if you did not see the honesty of her face.

He's drowning in nostalgia for this face. He must come home to this face; he has been at home with it. He tries to lift the page, but his hand trembles too much. Flossie Wattrous de Graaf looks straight at him. He shifts the sketchbook one way and then another. Impossibly she keeps on looking at him. Hungry. Wisps of her hair curl at her temples. Her pubic hair is long and silvery. He knows. Her exquisite fingers cover her right nipple, and her other arm extends downward in an elegant curve. But this isn't what he's drawn—it's what he'll go on drawing. He's barely breathing.

I'd give anything to have her. He must say this to Wraithe. But he knows her answer. You have. Have her? Given anything? He turns and finds Wraithe sitting cross-legged behind about five yards off, her eyes closed and nodding. He's concerned for her: isn't this like finding your sister in bed with your lover? He gets up and shows her the drawing.

"Flossie is my dearest friend. I would do anything for her."

He nods gratefully. He can't think of a thing for which he's been more grateful.

"Now you're not entirely among the dead," she says.

He furrows his brow.

"This is death—what you think is life." He thinks of the gray, featureless plain. Hasn't he lived on that plain? "They've gone on to live, to reflect, to be everything they couldn't be here. If you draw them, the ones Flossie tells you to draw, they will be your real friends for the rest of your life. Your death, I mean."

"Will Flossie speak to me?"

"When she's ready."

"Do you want this, Wraithe, for Flossie, I mean?"

"Oh no, she's your lover."

★

A collector of clutter who discards people profligately, Ulrike is unnerved by the stowed and battened ways of her stranger son. She lurches from room to room pursued by death, seizing the humblest item he leaves about, and one morning it's Flossie Wattrous de Graaf. He comes upon her in his room. She trembles violently as she holds Flossie's sketch to the sunlight. He's seen men do that when they've picked up hot wires. He turns and leaves.

All that day, under pretense of errand, he searches the pictorial archives of the Quarry County Historical Society. In two hours he's found de Graafs and Wattrouses. Indeed their patronymic connections look like a road map of the county. He leaves off to amuse himself by leafing through the foxed pages of the defunct *Quarry Telegraph*. Please, he says aloud when he spots Flossie de Graaf, her left arm above her head, holding the frame of an arbor:

Miss Flossie Wattrous de Graaf, valedictorian of the class of nineteen-twenty, Clearwater Women's College.

He'll always wonder why he said that word. Please stop this? Please let me wake up?

It's the young woman he's drawn, beyond any possible doubt. Younger, fragrant: the scent of lilac rises from the browning page. His breath comes hard. He feels sweat quit his temples and run down the back of his jaw. Her pose is wrong for its time. It's not demure—it's bravura. What is she looking forward to? She has already suffered grievous wrong. Is this a pose? Her thin, hooked nose is so poignant to him that tears start from his eyes. He drifts in a night sea of intimacy and loss. He's swamped by his urgent need to give everything that has ever caused him to wonder to this girl. His desire for that and for her chokes him.

It takes all the charm he can muster to persuade the tidy archivist to let him copy the crumbling page.

His bones hurt when he compares the newsprint image to his sketch: the suppleness, the fey disorder of her hair, the ghostliness of her eyes all match impeccably. Eyes are often shadowed in old photographs, especially in newsprint reproductions, but Flossie's are just as he drew them. Few men would be themselves in that gaze. Right on, Flossie, he thinks. She was—is—a towhead. The hair of her forearms and thighs—and her buttocks—must have to the eyes of a lover looked like winter wheat in Canadian light. He imagines himself the sun drowning in her navel. If she weren't so alive to him, he'd give up to desperate mourning.

"I don't answer why questions and someday when you grow up you'll stop asking them," Llewellyn said.

This is a good time to grow up, he thinks.

Dream by dream, Flossie comes to him. By day he pits his confusion against a growing sense of fulfillment. He has three sketchbooks filled with her images. The first book is conventional. He's studying her face and torso. The next two books are different. They startle him when he's finished. He's pictured her riding her bike, parking it, undressing at the brook, sleeping, preparing vegetables, gardening in front of a big stone house. That's it, the house. He goes into Bluestone and digs out old real estate books, the kind in which they used to put drawings of famous properties in bound editions. After two days searching in the basement of the county library, he finds it: De Graaf House, Holly Hill, overlooking the Hudson. It shocks him to touch his own hair, he's so electrified by this find.

On his way to the library to find a picture of a bike of her period a compulsion to speak seizes him.

"I want to tell you the meaning of the twenty-six parts of my bicycle brake, Flossie. It's taken me twenty-eight years to figure it out. I had them all laid out on the floor of the garage so I'd remember how to reassemble them. I was oiling them, trying to see how they worked together. It was a wonderful game. I was lost in it. I was eleven years old. Ulrike came in and got hysterical. She was so mad she started to throw tools around. I had a pretty logical mind, so I started to worry that if she mixed up the way I laid out the brake disks and other parts I wouldn't know how to put the bike back together. Then she started hitting me with a grass whip. I had the kind of mind that wondered why the grass whip, why not a broom or the bike's fender. So while I fended her off I chuckled inside me because I knew how blunt the damn thing was. But do you know why she was pissed? No, not pissed. Panicked. It was because she saw her whole summer going down the tube. Jesus, it's taken me all these years to figure it out. It wasn't a metaphysical problem. It wasn't psychological. It was practical. It wouldn't've occurred to me that gods worry about logistics. Only little jerk-offs like me did. See, everything depended on me, this eleven-year-old kid. I did all the shopping, everything. On that goddamned used bike. The whole operation depended on me all summer long, and I didn't get it. The only exception was the booze. Sandro brought that on the bus every Saturday morning, because it was so important. She kept hitting me with that grass whip until she realized it wasn't doing much good. Then she snatched the bike chain and lashed it around my head and pulled. It was like a chain wrench. It nearly tore my face off. I had to kick her. She hurt me so bad I could hardly think straight to put the bike together again. Blood kept getting in my eyes and I was shivering. When I finally got the bike together and working I had three brake disks left. I still don't know why, but I put them in Ulrike's jewelry box. They're probably still there. She keeps everything she buys, even food."

Snot and bitterness explode from him. He weeps until he retches and has to stop and hide under some willows near the library. He throws up and is so startled by it that he starts to run. When he stops he looks at Flossie's picture again and says, "Nothing's as lonely as vomiting and eyes are never bluer than when rendered in black and white."

Flossie's look heals him.

"If I ever had a boy I'd tell him what depended on him."

He sees agreement take shape in Flossie's eyes and he begins to grope for the shape of a thought—it's more like trying to shape water. Every time he urges his bone-aching desire for Flossie toward regret, contentment settles in his bones. To wish her alive, he begins to think, would be less than this, whatever this is. To suffer, to be battered and betrayed by those you love, those who should have loved you, and then, by mainstrength, to break the cycle, to refuse to repeat the crime, is not to free yourself of ghosts but to be one, to live among them, and then at last to see that many whom you'd supposed to live are neither dead nor alive. The dead are not lost. Can the lost die?

"Is this true, Flossie?"

His hand skips and races until Flossie's eyes light and she smiles.

"Do only the discontented haunt, Flossie? No, I think not."

The most difficult thing he's ever learned to do is wait until the truth of something catches up with his gut. No truth given or earned is of any use until then. So now his childhood knowledge of the cemetery as a resting place mends the broken circuit of his life: he can be, he is what that observant boy was, and this he owes to a mad girl who lives in a tree.

"No, this I owe to me, dear, dearest Flossie Wattrous de Graaf."

★

Contrary in the parsimony of her soul, it takes Ulrike two weeks to say, "Bo, I happened to notice a sketch of the most beautiful woman in your room."

"I saw it in a gallery and I bought it."

"I didn't know you collect art."

"You like it?"

"Only a very fine artist could do it, but so many die unknown. It's not worth much, you know—it's unsigned. How much did you pay for it?"

"I don't know."

"That's a strange answer."

"She's beautiful, you think?"

"Very."

Ulrike too feels longing, and for her longing he feels compassion, knowing she's always preferred the sanctuary of women to the invasion of men. It escapes him that Ulrike, who despised making him, has praised a thing of his making.

"She asked me how much I paid for it."

"What did you say?" Wraithe asks.

"In the light of the hunter's moon you look like a tiger."

"I'm anything I want to be. What did you tell her?"

"That I didn't know. Do you know?"

"How old're you?"

"Fifty-two."

"That's what you paid."

"Is it enough?"

"Flossie thinks so."

★

His desires clamor. He can't stop drawing her. He can't see, it's veiled to him, that he's used color, not much, blue at first, then a few others. He wants to desecrate this place with his doubts, like the Seljuk horsemen letting their horses poop on the altars of Santa Sophia, but deference prevails. It's a done deal. He must go on drawing her until something happens. This man who has never been afflicted by the impendingness of things waits breathlessly.

★

"I'll tell you a little secret," Llewellyn told him, "there are very few mental illnesses I care to cure. Most are too creative. The fact is I'm not sure who the nuts are. The people we call nuts don't have filters. They let everything in and it undoes them. They feel truth. We browse through catalogues."

Keep this in mind, he tells himself. At fifty two, what've you got to lose?

246

The word deprecation arrives in his head. Some artists, when they sketch, have an idea and let it evolve; others draw until they see the idea. He has this idea of deprecation. He lets his mind draw, and it draws upon the past:

Am I supposed to do something with this squash Mr. Russell left for you?
Where do you meet all these weird people?
What kind of boy hangs around cemeteries?
Are you sick in the head?

Dave Llewellyn would say the questions belong to her, Ulrike, and the answers belong to you. That little boy has to contend with those questions. Bo travels back into the boy's mind. Is he frightened and putting a good face on it? No, he's putting a good face on Ulrike. He knows, deep down, these are not motherly questions, but this is the only mother he has. Pimping for Ulrike, that's it, that's what Llewellyn meant. He feels like a sonar man who suddenly recognizes the signature of an enemy submarine.

Flossie Wattrous de Graaf sleeps beside Theodora, her protecting mother. Where will he sleep? Not at Woodlawn. No, he wouldn't rest well there. He and Sandro did not come to a good parting. Artists' Hill? With Hart? With Ulrike? That Flossie is there too troubles him, and he walks faster to get away from his thought.

No sooner does he leave the boy and those deprecations behind than he comes up behind two little fellows walking arm in arm like Genoans, chatting amiably about the progress of their fathers' psychotherapy. They can be no more than six. He can't imagine them in another town.

"He means well, but he's pretty hard to live with."

"Mine throws things. He breaks everything. My mother says just stay out of his way."

"Does she?"

"No. He broke her nose last week."

"Gentlemen," Bo interrupts, "just to set the record straight, the world is full of crazy mothers too. About the only thing to do is have an ice cream cone. I know your parents said don't talk to strangers, so we won't talk, we'll just have ice cream, okay?"

One of the boys replies, "My mom provokes my dad."

Bo smiles, tousles the boy's head, keeps his promise of silence, and waves them into the Rum Raisin.

"Don't close up yet, Miss, you've got three ice cream freaks here."

He walks away feeling sheepish to have patronized the boys. Few of the artists did that to him, and he was considerably less articulate than these boys. God knows what it will cost them to see that their childish parents unerringly found each other.

★

The Granada is chock-a-block with bad paintings of women who had trifled with him when he was a boy, women ruined by their choices, drawn as much to him as Ulrike. These paintings are trite. The artists could not even catch the lasciviousness. Ulrike's women, the women of her paintings, are, by contrast, enigmatic, iconic. Their clothes are tattooed to them. Their enormous hips belie their cuntlessness. Their breasts are prepubescent, one invariably larger than the other in the style of Amazon archers. He recognizes some of these women, his mother's and the others. Some of them lie up on the hill, but he doesn't know if they rest. Pitiless teases. He would like to remove Theodora and Flossie from them.

He encountered one of them just the other day, at the post office. She walks with a cane now. They looked hauntedly at each other. Amir, she said. Rheumy tears rose in her eyes and she hurried away. She hadn't changed.

How has he become a man who delivers the goods, he wonders, having grown up among women who didn't?

The lovely appliance man's wife who blushed gorgeously and kissed and held him in the stockroom, the mountainous blonde checkout clerk at Eldredge's Market who'd opened her blouse to him in the meat locker—they imbued his longings with illusoriness and the hard conviction that deprivation was his lot. All these women left it to others to reward him for whatever it was in him that prompted their lovely naughtiness, and he too believed the promise until it cooled within him.

"As I get older," Llewellyn said, "it seems to me there's not a dime's worth of difference between seducer and seduced." Bo thinks of the beautiful artist who stripped and arranged herself on the floor and when her suddenness iced his ardor she dressed and touched his face and said, You're such a good man.

"I don't suppose it occurred to you to say, Kiss off, you angry bitch!" Llewellyn said.

"She wasn't angry."

The therapist smiled a huge, shit-eating grin. "Stop pimping for your mother. I want you to say, Kiss off, you angry bitch!"

He couldn't. "I failed her," he said.

"You think your dick's stupid? Listen to it, it's smarter than you are. Chokes you to say it, doesn't it?"

"Feels like heartburn."

"Well, that's progress."

★

He now knows that Evert de Graaf, Flossie's father, was a highly respected judge. Theodora Wattrous graduated from Vassar with a degree in biology. Flossie, for some reason, was considered a formidable expert on Hudson River watercraft. Why were they buried on Artists' Hill in Echo Tarn and not in Bluestone overlooking the Hudson? He'd found the Honorable Evert de Graaf's resting place. It was a family mausoleum in Bluestone.

The microfilmed records of *The Bluestone Patriot* reveal little. Flossie is married to Jonathan Ross Waverley when Theodora shoots Evert. Had she just discovered the molestations? Could they possibly have continued after the marriage? Flossie has no children, and she's buried eight miles away under her maiden name. She died only two years after her mother was executed for a murder the reporter calls cold-blooded.

He searches the records of the Dutch Reformed Church. Evert is accorded the usual enrollment. Theodora and Flossie are banished.

"Go see Marley Faircloth at the Baptist home," an old

typesetter at the *Patriot* tells him. "Marley's an odd kind of historian, never gave a damn about the usual stuff, just liked all the stuff people try to bury. That's what we do here, y'know, bury the news. Good stuff never gets in the paper. I ought to know, been setting these lies for nigh unto fifty-three years. Course Marley might be dead now, for all I know. Ask the Baptists. They keep 'em alive a long time. Us Episcopalians, we like to bury 'em first chance."

Marley Faircloth is barely alive, hooked up to an oxygen tank and palsied, but she remembers the story. She can't talk, but she manages to scribble something:

Library, Larned Meany's *Goethalskill Tales*.

He runs out and comes back with flowers. Marley Faircloth smiles with ancient eyes.

Goethalskill Tales is a thatch of plain, sturdy stories, fiction with the usual disclaimer. He sighs wearily. Perhaps Marley's memory has failed or she misunderstood him. But leafing disappointedly through the frail pages of the old book, a freighted Victorian drawing arrests him. It's overwrought in the Aubrey Beardsley style, and like Beardsley, full of detail. A neurasthenic young woman sits propped against a tree, her head fallen to one side, her legs straight out. She's handsomely dressed. A fur hat has tumbled to the ground. One hand rests in her lap, turned up, the other lies on the ground. She's enveloped in ice. The Victorians liked this scene. It frequents their literature. He begins to read the story next to the illustration. *Winterkill* purports to be the lay of a well-born young woman, Sophie Vernooy, who persists in an illicit relationship with a cousin after marrying a young man from one of Rhinebeck's finest families. The husband discovers the affair and shoots the lover. While he's being tried, Sophie skates out to Ancrop's Island in the Goethalskill and sips brandy laced with laudanum until she freezes to death. The story croaks on its deceit.

"Y'know who Larned Meany was? Can't find him in the microfilm," he tells Stosh Obrycki, the old typesetter.

Stosh rocks his head up and down, trying to shake the right memory loose. "No, but there's a Mrs. Layton Meany works over to the courthouse. Mess around the courthouse long enough, you pretty know much all the dirt, and she's been there forever."

Mrs. Meany is a spectacled silo who appears to live up to her name. But she proves to be a sucker for proving how much more valuable she is than the nail-buffing chickies who make the judges' coffee. "Larned Meany? Yes, he was my husband Layton's uncle. He worked all his life for Judge Evert de Graaf, sort of a cook, chauffeur, gardener, what have you. He was at sixes and sevens when poor Judge de Graaf's crazy wife shot and killed him. The judge didn't expect to die, so he didn't write a will leaving Larned anything. After that Larned was just a kind of handyman. But he was a grand storyteller. Oh yes, I remember that."

He leaves it at that. *Winterkill* is the cover story, the feel-good story. The victim is made the culprit and everybody is happy. If he dug deeper he'd probably find de Graaf connections to the *Patriot*. He's so angry he can hardly bear to bring the tawdry book back to the library. He'd like to chuck it in the Goethalskill. When he does bring it back the librarian asks if he enjoyed it. "It's full of lies," he says.

"Well, really, it's only fiction," she says.

"You got that right."

★

"Why do you spend so much time up there? He's dead," Ulrike tells him. "He didn't like you anyway."

"Would you like to drive up there with some flowers? The veterans have put a little flag up."

When they get to the crest of cemetery hill he parks the car. They walk past Theodora and Flossie and down the slope towards Hart's grand slab. He has handed Ulrike a bouquet from the Grand Union, but when they reach the site she hands it back to him and stares down. He sets down the flowers and walks away towards the della Robbia to leave her alone. When he returns she's still staring.

"Do you see a pattern like a chain fence on the stone?" she asks. "I thought it's still summer, but everything seems gray and brown."

Days later an ophthamologist in Bluestone tells them about macular degeneration. Ulrike has lost her central vision, but her sidelong vision enables her to grope about.

She now takes to moaning in her sleep, and one night he's awoken by a piercing scream. He jumps out of bed, races to her room and finds her staring out the window into the dark.

"What's wrong?"

"Do you think I'm a good person?"

"I'll make us some hot cocoa."

"Do you?"

"Well, you're really up against it now, aren't you?" he tells his old pal Bo. He can't nod. She wouldn't see it. He must speak.

"Yes, Ulrike." Still pimping for mom.

"You're not a very good liar."

"Is that a compliment?"

"Take it any way you like. I'll have my cocoa now."

He goes downstairs to the stoves of hell. There's no way in hell he could have done better by her question, but an honest man would have done better—one way or another. He catches his reflection in the black face of the microwave. "You son of a bitch."

He has cocoa with her in silence. At some point he rubs her spiny back. Then he turns up some all-night talk show on the television and leaves. He's wide awake and angry. Between Larned Meany and his own lying he can't find a way back to decency or any kind of contentment. He stuffs a small sketchbook into his jacket pocket and takes up his usual midnight watch in front of the hotel. The moon unrolls a silver carpet across Quarry Road to Artists' Hill. He gets up and follows it like a dowser, not knowing where it will lead. It leads him to the half buried bluestone memorial to Kurt Meissner. Wraithe says you think I have work to do up here, he tells Meissner. Lead the way. He takes out his sketchbook and a pencil.

Captain Martin Shellenbarger, killed in the Ardennes in The Great War, materializes as he draws. He's a thin-faced young man, not unlike the poet Arthur Rimbaud when he arrived in Paris to ruin Paul Verlaine. Like the red-eyed boy, Martin Shellenbarger is somewhat walleyed, but his one steady eye is clear and penetrating.

He turns a page and begins to draw Elaine Witte, who died while he was a boy hereabouts. She's oval-faced, eyes long and wary, buxom and lovely.

The moon offers enough light to sketch seven more faces.

He can't find photographs of all of them in the Echo Tarn library or in Bluestone, but when he finds Martin Shellenbarger and Elaine Witte his fingers tremble so violently that he can't turn pages. Martin stands beside a racing scull with three other young men at Yale. They've just won a race. His hair falls down over his bad eye and he looks straight into the lens just as Bo drew him. Elaine is running after a badminton shuttlecock. The camera has caught the sunlight in her eyes. She is the woman she becomes in Bo's sketch. Four other photographs match his graveside drawings. His mouth is parched.

To what purpose am I able to draw the dead? What kind of gift is it? Who owns it? Me, Wraithe, Kurt Meissner, Flossie?

He draws for several days but makes no further effort to authenticate his drawings. Then considerations of Ulrike intervene.

No sooner does the giantess of his fears begin to shrink than he notices that in stores and restaurants she's being handled by the eternal gum-snapping girls as if the raptor angel of death were about to nip them. Their leeriness reminds him of his own. He knows that other men have watched dismayed as chickie dim-bulbs treat their mothers like lepers. Given Ulrike's tipping habits, Ulrike deserves it. But he doubts that many men have shared that same revulsion all their lives. And when a young woman is kind to the diminished Ulrike, who has suddenly become a decrepit chimpanzee, he envies the girl her largeness of soul.

Ulrike now spends most of her time muttering under the sun on the terrace, continuing her lifelong practice of attracting an extraordinary number of grifters, bullshitters and skells. Wraithe comes and goes, depending on whether she's hungry or wants a bath. There are times when he looks up that Bo sees a toothy cheshire grin capping Artists' Hill. Occasionally he flips Hart a British salute, which has always struck him as both disturbing and comical.

The interminable ooze of sleaze stopping to pay court to the chimp merely reminds him that at the last hour her paranoia usually spares her a fleecing. More often than not she fleeces her shady pals. How much cause, Bo wonders, has Hart to grin? She buried him, didn't she? Correction, he muses, I buried him, and I think he will, unlike Ulrike, stay put.

He keeps sane not by remembering Sultan Taimur's fabulous gifts or Uthman's caravel or Rose MacQuarrie or Moira and Peter or Llewellyn and Gundy or Dacia or Tate, who is doing gigs along the Mohawk, but by remembering what he shared with a young barmaid in Hamburg. The guest boy rests in peace in Oued Zem, but this guest boy knows no peace and has no Oued Zem or anybody to ferry him to it. He has dropped Tate into a crevasse attended by his ceremonial rationalizing about their difference in age, about not wanting to make a fool of himself. He feels relieved and righteous and ill.

This is his country. He has bled for it. Algeria is the red-eyed boy's, Ulrike's even, but not his. But this country does not feel like home. Sindbad had Basra to revel in when he was old, but Manhattan's merely a place where Bo drowned an answering machine. He wishes he could reflect on this with the old sultan. His life has been a verb. Only when he meets Llewellyn does it become a noun. Adjectives, treacherous and haywire, elude him or he'd fathom the old sultan's fondness for him.

He walks every which way and winds up always in the cemetery. He's filled five sketchpads with the residents of Artists' Hill. The October sun stands bolt red, threatening the damp sleep of the Catskills until the darkness opens. He rises because he hears the sun thundering like sheet metal. He sits in the back of Hart's cottage watching the sun lift out of the Hudson, sore and demanding. He draws the tree line, a doe nibbling elderberry, the gravel pile. Then one day he walks down to Gaia's Art Supply and buys dry colors, at first chalks, then crayons. Finally he buys that most unruly of media, watercolor.

"She'll probably leave that street person Annelise everything she owns," G. Verplanck warns him. "But perhaps you know better."

"I know Annelise better," Bo says.

He's painting Flossie on the hill when Ulrike Theiss dies in Annelise's arms of a massive stroke.

Alton Brainerd III, having summoned him, reads Ulrike's will to him. Unlike Sandro's sabotaged will and Hart's hokey wills, it's straightforward. She leaves her estate to Estelle Cavalieri, her granddaughter. Everything but the paintings. These she leaves to Bo—without funds to care for them.

"May I ask, where is your daughter, Mr. Cavalieri?"

Bo rises, turns his back on Brainerd and looks out onto King's Street.

"Is there another son, a daughter perhaps? Help me here, I'm at a loss. She said she'd tell me how to find this Estelle Cavalieri, but . . ."

Bo turns. "She'll show up. They always do."

"They?"

He's leaving when Brainerd catches up with him from around his desk.

"Look, you should take this will to your own attorney. That's all I can say."

Wiley Carolan's offices are in the same Old Fort neighborhood.

"This is not a valid will, Bo. It's not properly executed. You really don't know who this Estelle is?"

"I really don't."

"Well, my friend, I advise you to ignore the bloody thing. It's a bad piece of work, as you well know. She doesn't even make Brainerd the executor. There's no executor. That means you're it. Do what you will. This isn't worth the paper it's written on. Oh, it could make some trouble, sure, but you know all about that. Come to me right away if this mystery girl shows up."

★

He smells Schneider's amazing assortment of weiners down Orange Street when he leaves Carolan's offices. The white November sun is beating everyone's brains out. He strolls into Schneider's garden and buys a knockwurst drowned in sauerkraut. He thinks of Anders Ootwaert's tools. Would they still be in the little shed in the woods beside Ulrike's old cottage? If so, he wants them.

In the shed, pulling the old farmer's tools out from behind broken mirrors, sashes and bedsteads, he thinks of Rudyard Kipling's poem, *If.* Lottie Donovan at Cairnhall had made him memorize it after Johnny McKewn gave him a shiner. He memorized it and then trudged down to the McKewn's Kozy Korner tavern and asked Mr. McKewn if he could see Johnny. Johnny, yer friend from the school is here, Mr. McKewn called to his son. Johnny appeared smirking and Bo decked him. Just like that. Then he stood there waiting for the boy to get up. That'll be enough, Mr. McKewn said, and it was. Except for *If.* Two lines scull in from the mist:

> . . . *If you can bear to hear the truth you've spoken*
> *Twisted by knaves to make a trap for fools,*
> *Or watch the things you gave your life to, broken,*
> *And stoop and build 'em up with worn-out tools . . .*

What had he given his heart to? Nothing—no one but Dacia. And yet now he can see that he gave his heart to be loved by Ulrike. He stoops and picks up Ootwaert's tools. He notices some words scorched into the haft of the hoe: *Whatever you set your heart on becomes a mirage.*

The wind rattles the poplars. Chipmunks scamper in and out of their stone-fence dens. The huge oak he climbed as a boy to see the town two miles away complains arthritically in the wind. What has become a mirage? A red-shouldered hawk stoops. He set his heart on Ulrike liking him, if not when he was young, then in their old age. Not love, complicated and unreliable, but liking. He takes the measure and weight of Anders Ootwaert's hoe as if it were a weapon and nods.

16

Angle of vision is everything to landsman and seaman and especially to artist and navigator. Bo never acquired more than one angle of vision when it came to Ulrike. An ant in the Parthenon has the liberty to crawl around, to tour Athena's behind, Hermes's balls, but a worshipper must remain seemly and so forfeits angle of vision to painted gods. He sees as he stands in the driveway listening to the oak creak and watching the buzzards wheel that he's shouldered time's job of blanching object and beholder, not because color is ephemeral and therefore deceptive, but because it's unbearable. He sees why he drew but didn't paint when so many paint who can't draw.

To paint or draw well means knowing when to leave a thing alone. That means Ulrike's will. He could do nothing about her will while she lived, he will do nothing about it now.

He looks up past the house's octagonal cupola, its empty, improbable cupola. The sky shakes and furls an inch to the left, south to north, confirming his suspicion it's a stage prop. He hears shook metal, the sound old-time radio studios made for thunder. Lights out, darken stage. Winterkill.

★

"Gundy, bear a hand, mate."

"You got it."

"I need a motor vessel with a little range to her. I'll charter her. I need a sixteen-foot sailboat, something in that range. I don't want a sailing dinghy, I want a little class, like a Lightning maybe. I'll buy her. I gotta buy her."

"What's up, pardon me for asking?"

"Bear with me. I'll tell you later."

"Lissen t'me. Down in Edgewater there's a forty-foot Ocean Pirate, British, twin 300-horse diesels—you like diesels, right?—carries three hundred gallons. I can add maybe two hundred more if you look for a good hole in the weather. I run it for charters for this guy in Hoboken. Whuddya think?"

"Do it, pal. Get her ready for me. Three days water and food, tops."

"Go to City Island for the sailboat. Some yard's always got a lien on something. I'll give you some names."

★

Will Brashears obtains Ulrike's death certificate from the county coroner and prepares her for burial. The earth being still warm, she won't have to wait for spring thaw. He alerts G. Verplanck, but he's not sure Bo will want The Reverend Gansevoort again. G. Verplanck calls Bo immediately.

"Execute Plan A?"

"Yeah, maybe that'll satisfy the shitter. Then cut an identical stone. It'll say Ulrike Theiss. Next line will say artist. Next line will give her dates. Gotta get back to you on that. Next lines will say wife of Alessandro Cavalieri and Hart Clement."

Then he drives into Bluestone and buys six yards of the finest white silk he can find.

"I'd like you to bear with me on this, Will," he tells the undertaker when he gets back. "I don't want to handle this like Hart. I have to be gone tomorrow. Could we meet Thursday morning?"

Wilmot Brashears likes Bo and is prepared to cut as much slack as he can. "Sure, nine-thirty, Bo."

He drives down Route Nine-W and the Palisades Parkway to Edgewater to inspect the Ocean Pirate, which is named *Windhover*, an inept name for a stinkpot but admirable in itself. The extra diesel drums have no hoses leading to the main tanks, no valves and no gauges. He calls Gundy to ask if this can be remedied. "Whatever you want, my friend, you get," his old mate says.

Back at Brashears he tells Will, "This catalogue has her authorized biography in it. I crossed out her birthdate and put another one in. I want to straighten a few things out for the art historians. Don't use anything I've crossed out. She lied a lot."

"Will the historians care?"

"Someday, yeah. She's a very fine artist. Call obits in to *The New York Times, The Washington Post, L.A. Times*, and of course the local papers. They'll want to note her death. She's had reviews in them."

"Survivors?"

"Jurgen Theiss, a brother, lives in Cologne. Estelle Cavalieri, a granddaughter, dunno where she lives. I wrote a couple of sentences about my stepfather. I'd like him mentioned along with Hart."

"And your father?"

"I'm a bastard, Will."

"I would never say that, Bo. Can I help in any way?"

"Just bear with me. I'll get back to you. Verplanck's cutting the stone. Don't worry about a service just now."

"I didn't think you'd want Gansevoort."

"Yeah, there was quite a methane problem."

★

City Island lies just west of the Intracoastal Waterway that dissects Long Island Sound. Sailors from New Jersey, New York and Connecticut keep boats there because it gives them access to the sound and some of the East Coast's best sailing. Ohlstrom's Boat Yard looks like a hurricane has been playing jackstraws. Everywhere he looks he sees boats in distress.

A stocky old codger with a one-inch white flattop is pickling an engine block in a bathtub next to a shack.

"You the boss?"

"Depends who's asking."

"Name's Bo Cavalieri. I'm a merchant seaman. I need some help."

"*You* need help!"

Bo smiles appreciatively while Ohlstrom sizes him up.

"Okay," the old man says, "what can I do ya?"

"I need a sailboat, somewhere between sixteen and twenty-one feet. Nothing tubby. I don't much care about her condition as long as her hull is sound."

"Take a look around."

"All I see is fiber glass. I want wood."

"Nobody wants wood. Nobody knows how to take care of wood anymore, nobody has the time."

"Wood."

"Got this nineteen-foot Cape Dory Typhoon. Looks sorry as hell, but her hull's okay."

They walk over to a slip near the rail lift. "Name's *Shadow Dancer*, not so you can tell. But that's what the owner called her—some Wall Street smartass. Probably rooked a bunch of old ladies out of their money and went to jail, assuming God's still in his heaven."

"Slap some white paint on her. Put her name back on the transom—I like her."

"Well, sir, when you say slap some paint on her . . ."

"Look, Mister Ohlstrom, I don't expect you to understand. I don't want her caulked and sanded and finished. Like I said, just slap some paint on her and I'll pick her up next week and haul her out of here. But I want that name on her."

"You got twelve hundred bucks on ya? That'll pay for the whole nine yards. 'Course ya gotta register her with the state or the Coast Guard."

"Who's she registered with now?"

"Just the state. She ain't documented."

"Make up the papers and . . . let me give you an address."

He'd figured on paying between two and three thousand dollars, so he peels off the twelve well satisfied.

Will Brashears, unlike his father-in-law and predecessor, has a sense of decorum. His father-in-law, who'd been vice chairman of the local Republicans, used to joke that nobody but "idiots and aliens" dared to vote Democratic because "they know I'll bury them upside down." Will regards this behavior as unsuitable. He remembers the scars of the dead, their poignant deformities. He thinks of them as wounds incurred in heroic battles. He remembers those bidden farewell lovingly and those sent off perfunctorily. He knows the kind of strata underlying almost every cemetery and family in the county. He knows the clergy, even some Buddhist priests. He keeps secrets and intimate friendships with the dead. For this reason—he's seen Bo sketching on Artists' Hill and recognizes a fellow reverent—he bears with Bo, even though he's never seen the like. Bo swathes Ulrike's body in white silk and takes it.

He and Ulrike arrive at Edgewater on a Saturday night. He takes her into *Windhover* and sets her down in the salon. Then he makes up a towline for *Shadow Dancer* from a nylon anchor rode, turns over the engines and makes a final check. He realizes he hasn't checked the inflatable dinghy. He inflates it and leaves it to see if it holds its air. Then he secures it upside down to the foredeck. At 10:30 he casts off his lines and heads slowly down the Hudson to New York Bay. He rounds the tip of Manhattan and heads up the ruffian East River. Midtown he salutes Ulrike's apartment at Beekman Place. He plays Erik Satie on the *Windhover* sound system. Entering Long Island Sound, he heads toward City Island, ties up, and takes a nap. At dawn he picks up *Shadow Dancer*, fastens the towline to her bow's samson post, then heads eastward through Long Island Sound towards the Atlantic.

Eight hours later, at latitude forty-one, longitude seventy-one west, due south of Dartmouth, Massachusetts, well off Long Island and Block Island, he hauls *Shadow Dancer* alongside *Windhover*, secures her to the larger vessel, removes the towline, and arranges Ulrike's body in the cockpit of the smaller vessel. He surrounds her with a hundred white roses and twenty sprays of baby's-breath. Then he soaks the old wooden hull with gasoline, lashes her tiller, raises her mainsail and jib, gets back aboard *Windhover*, and begins to pay out the line. When *Shadow Dancer* stands twenty yards downwind he turns up Debussy's *Pavane for a Dead Princess*, aims a flare gun at her and fires, deeming high-tech detonation indecorous. He lets go the line and watches *Shadow Dancer* heel and head flaming out into the Atlantic on a ten-knot northwest wind. He stands at attention for the first time since he left the Navy and salutes, not with the heart as required by etiquette, but hand to head like a sailor.

When Ulrike Theiss is nothing more than an oil slick the color of peacock feathers, he thinks of hoisting the yellow Q signal asking license to enter port: *my vessel is healthy and I request free pratique.* But instead he reaches into his old flag bag, pulls out a yard-long royal blue burgee with its gold cross streaming and hoists it to the starboard spreader. Then he looks up and takes a breath deeper than any before. He keeps his head up, like a wolf alerted to something new. Something is different. The wheel groans at its lashing, the burgee cracks in a northwest breeze. No sob cinches his lungs for the first time since he arrived at Cairnhall. He breathes clear. He has free pratique.

★

"We'll have a graveside service, Will. Use the same kind of casket we buried Hart in. I like the Burial of the Dead in the *Book of Common Prayer.*"

"Father Culbertson at Holy Redeemer in Bluestone, Bo. I'll get him, okay? I can do it Thursday the sixteenth at one. Will there be many there?"

"I don't know, Will. I'll just go through her address book and see what happens."

★

When snow comes, democratizing the town's eccentricities and misshapenness, Bo, having shipped Ulrike's paintings to a conservator, re-keys her properties' locks and leaves. He says goodbye to none but the dead, not even their Wraithe.

In a year's time, the calls from Echo Tarn remain unanswered. Tate's letters, fanciful, offering dried leaves and petals, by turns plaintive and plucky—they too go unanswered. On a hot Indian summer day he stands in Pennsylvania Station waiting for the Washington train. He understands for the first time that he has become one of those self-possessed, dignified men at whom he used to marvel when he was a frantic boy, and, to signal this realization, his gaze falls upon a boy who studies him. He smiles the most reassuring smile he can summon.

17

Entering The National Museum of Contemporary Art in a tuxedo feels like dropping into a drowned cathedral in a wet suit. Maybe I became a diver so finally I could get to the bottom of something, he thinks. He hears Angelus bells and a thrumming behind them. The angels are echolocating, he thinks.

The great hall, filled with flashing silver and crystal, thriving with angels and socialites rushing acquaintances, strikes him as a wreck site undesecrated for thousands of years. He struggles with his desire to run.

Brandt Gunderson is already here.

Bo hardly has time to be grateful for being unnoticed before someone notices him.

"When I bought this I wondered if this'd be the suit I'd be buried in."

Bo surveys the speaker like a Hong Kong tailor, as the remark invites him to do.

"It's the goddamnedest thing to say to a stranger, I know, but you look like a man who'd enjoy it."

"I do, I do," says Bo.

"Allow me to introduce myself. Inigo Darnley-Hines." Pause. "You fancy it?"

"Yes, it's a bravura name."

"To whom do you think it might belong?"

"An art historian, I would hope."

"And you are a man of modest hopes? uh . . ."

"Amir Cavalieri, and yes, I am."

Inigo Darnley-Hines' globular eyes fondle something over Amir's shoulder. His precipitous forehead forces one to search out his eel eyes. He's a man who stares away to collect his thoughts. His listener's gaze distracts him.

"The artist, however, was not," the man said.

"I don't know. I never wondered."

"Of course you know. Consider the furnishings, Mr. Cavalieri. She obviously furnished a world she hoped to occupy. Yes, yes, altogether a very Egyptian show. She's shipping her hoarded belongings to her new home, taking it all with her, you see. You are her Anubis. Notice the shabtis. See how animated they are, not like the royal deceased. That is because the shabtis serve the royal deceased, fetch water, clip toenails, massage, perhaps even make love."

"Shabtis?"

"Yes, the little figurines. They're slaves. The aristocrats always sit there with their hands on their knees, looking as if someone has just shot them up with high-grade heroin. It's not dignified to look animated, you see. That's the essential eroticism of Egyptian art—the aristocrats are so remote, with their adolescent breasts and mere hints of pubes, that you're free to ravage them in your imagination."

Amir swabs his hairline with a handkerchief and asks, "And does this artist succeed, d'you think?"

"Poor woman. My idea of hell'd be whatever heaven the hoi polloi choose. Would you wish to inhabit her world eternally?"

Amir Cavalieri gives Inigo Darnley-Hines the baleful look of the gray whale. "It's not inhabitable by men."

★

"Oh Amir, you must . . ." He wards off Ida Kaplan-Bouscaren, the museum's twentieth century curator.

"Let me catch up with you in a few minutes, Ida."

She still suspects him of knowing Arshile Gorky's birth name because when she'd baited him on the phone, saying, "Darling, I'm sorry I have to run, I'm hanging Vosdanig Manoog Adoian today," he'd refused the bait.

When his gaze swings back to Inigo Darnley-Hines he finds a changed visage.

"Faces are what I care about. We're kindred spirits, are we not? You are not a man to be turned lightly."

"Not recently," Bo says.

"Ida discounts me because I'm not a critic. I'm an historian. Criticism is trash, narcissistic trash, don't you think?"

"Kitsch, yes."

★

There are young women whose repressions blast the looks they give men. There are men who misread them and are ruined. You could write a book describing what they mistake them for. You could conjure and palaver. And when you'd done all that you'd be about where Bo is, champagne flute in hand in the great hall of the museum, contemplating the daunting stare of a serpentine girl some ten yards away, her head cocked five points off its axis, her right elbow pivoted on the palm of her left hand, hip-slung like a model, unsmiling, waiting and getting unstrung by his cool consideration of her. Her free hand is prinked, fingers spread like a cobra's hood. He likes her stance, exorbitantly stylized. He finds it poignant, vulnerable in its bravado. Sensual, not beautiful or even pretty, and dressed to accentuate it—the sort of girl who acts pissed when you acknowledge it.

The pressure on a diver's lungs at one hundred feet is . . . forget it. He needs the word for her body language. He's about to give up when the words arrive from Passaic: I'm a girl, hon, so get the fuck outta my way.

Expressionless, he salutes her with his glass, then pours its contents into an urn. Brandt catches him in the act and salutes him.

★

A man capable of imagining and enjoying a world ruled by women would probably be easier to find than a man capable of imagining indolent women ruling. And a world ruled by women with unimaginably big tattooed hips and worrisomely small heads may well be beyond the scope of even our hallucinations, or was, that is, until Bo persuaded a Manhattan gallery and then a Washington museum to take notice of Ulrike's paintings.

266

Now Bo understands a great deal about Ulrike and a great deal less about her work. That they're good, a dozen or more better than that, he has no doubt. His love of painting is so great that he would not have labored for their recognition were it not so. There are enough schlockmeisters around already. It hasn't been a labor of love, far from it, but rather of conviction.

Tonight he's oppressed by his formal attire, even further distracted by a determination to say goodbye to her paintings. He's come down to this reception with Brandt Gundersen, who in spite of Jolene's and Bo's misgivings looks like a Nobel laureate in black tie. Gundy is having a grand time chatting up the swells. Every once in a while he picks up a flute of champagne, catches Bo's eye and ostentatiously dumps the drink into the punch. Even though they have in the past year shipped together three times as captain and chief mate, they still need to make something of not hitting the sauce.

Newly restored and framed at steep cost, Ulrike's paintings glitter in the bounce-light of strobes, their Titian greens tinting the assemblage. Bo regards her greens as better than Titian's, struck as they are with luminous washes of white.

Were these women in her paintings rulers, changelings, androgynes, aliens, slaves of unseen owners?

They're not sexual objects. They're only faintly sexual. Each has a sinistral breast like a moon in near-full eclipse. Their hairless pubes are vestigial, their faces gray and saturnine, their eyes perfunctory.

It's the behemoth hips and thighs that command focus. Tattooed with unknowable hieroglyphs from waist to toe, the women hold strings of balloons and long limp leashes of mythic placid beasts.

They stand on beaches or in Egyptianate palaces whose floors are tidal. In some, felucca-like boats ply gemmy waters between immense arches radiating every color of which a palette is capable.

In every painting the corona of the moon illuminates a darkening sky before total eclipse. But unlike the mute copper eclipses familiar to Bo, Ulrike's are lunar caustic. This amuses him, affirming as it does the artist's conceded right to see things as they might be and the right upon which Ulrike had always insisted that things are what she said they were.

A few critics—only now would historians contemplate them—trace them to the magus of surrealism, André Breton, but Ulrike herself often said there was nothing new about surrealism except its French literary baggage, and Bo had persuaded the catalogue raisonné essayist, I. Borden Cameron, that the paintings more properly belong in the pittura metafisica school, whose exemplar, Giorgio de Chirico, Ulrike adored.

The sense of absence and antisepsis in pittura metafisica gives way here to whimsicality, perversity and ultimately decadence. You might, out of curiosity, trust yourself in a de Chirico, not casually of course but cautiously, glancing off-center frequently to see that the frame would hold. You would not, unless you intended to abandon your former self, enter a Theiss because you would instinctively know—you had been warned—that the rules are personal and perverse. Hers are subversive paintings, for all their gonfalons, acrobats, carousels and wolves pawing mandolins, and it's the particular distinction of this show that Darnley-Hines apprehended the paintings' menace. These women, whatever their status, inhabit an order abandoned by others—and they're not going to tell you a damned thing about it.

Bo feels foolishly grateful to the effete Darnley-Hines and three times in the course of the evening favors this nettlesome and predatory man with a smile, trusting it won't be misinterpreted.

Hines knows a fellow predator when he sees one, and he's clearly seen one in Ulrike.

Each painting of Ulrike's early maturity bears some exquisite cache of pain for Bo. He regards them as a patient does his gallstones. These elegant grandees and attendant poseurs might celebrate Ulrike Theiss, but her son celebrates something else entirely.

When he salutes the hip-slung girl with the daunting stare his mind travels for a second into the signal shuttling between her own thoughts and her stare and he shudders in the desolation of her being. It has taken him thirty-eight years to attain his state of grace. As he braces for another round of polite conversation he wonders if the girl will ever know that such grace might be worth attaining. She is, he sees, a fellow child of abuse whose outrage at the theft of her innocence looks out mute and mad behind barred eyes. He recognizes her as vampires and homosexuals recognize each other and therefore has not flung her challenge back but holds it until she has to consider it. He knows what she'll have to suffer to soften such a look at the hands of all the men who'll rise to it and disappoint her and be dashed in turn. In his cold eye the girl loses her nerve, shrugs and fakes interest elsewhere.

This hurt, hurtful, hurting girl is here because Ulrike Theiss cannot be celebrated without her.

He finds his way to the guest register and finds her name, Estelle Cavalieri. The sinkhole opens before him. To fall from grace all he has to do is lean into the maw of questions: who, how, when? There have been so many imponderables. Please, Bo, he hears himself say, leave this one alone.

Gundy comes up behind him and clamps his shoulder. He turns, pats his friend's arm, and scans the huge hall. Estelle is circulating. She seems unaccompanied. But her body signals her awareness of him, bats the signal to him, and he, but not she, can decipher it: Come offend me, come suffer my disapproval, come atone for your importunate existence. Their eyes meet across the room and he nods gravely.

As he stands outside the museum in the fecund autumn night he pulls out a telegram he'd received in care of Ida Kaplan-Bouscaren. He can't imagine a soul who would know how to reach him in this way. It's from Margaret Wadeleigh.

> *Cosmic justice is yours. I garden, I teach, but most of all I miss you. Come live with me, as it was always meant to be. Dacia.*

The words cosmic justice slop at his consciousness like medical debris on the Jersey shore. That an elegant mathematician should sum up their encounter in penny-dreadful language spares him all remorse.

Improbably, lilac is in the air. Carefully he folds Margaret's yellow telegram into a paper airplane and launches it into the museum's manicured gardens. He's never made a good paper airplane in his life, but this one soars over the care of man into the darkness. A street lamp across the street becomes a dandelion rosette. It splits and Flossie's eyes regard him calmly. He closes his eyes, breathes deeply, and the night swells with the sweetness of Tate's breath.